RUN WITH THE HARE,

HUNT WITH THE HOUND

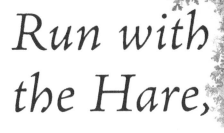

Run with the Hare, Hunt with the Hound

PAUL M. DUFFY

cennan

chester county,
pennsylvania

Published by Cennan Books of Cynren Press
5 Great Valley Parkway, Suite 322
Malvern, PA 19355 USA
http://www.cynren.com/

First published 2022

Printed in the United States of America on acid-free paper

ISBN-13: 978-1-947976-34-4 (hbk)
ISBN-13: 978-1-947976-35-1 (ebk)

Library of Congress Control Number: 2021949110

Cover design by Kevin Kane

Cover art by Matthew Ryan, Historical Illustrator

Do Shíle, mo laoch agus mo chroí,
agus do Fhéilim, mo chomrádaí ar na bealaí fiáine

History has rhythms, tunes and even harmonies; but the sound of the past is an agonistic multiplicity. Sometimes, rarely, a scrap of a voice can be caught from the universal damage, but it may only be an artefact of the imagination, a confection of rumours.

—Tim Robinson, *Connemara: Listening to the Wind*

Ireland *c.* 1171

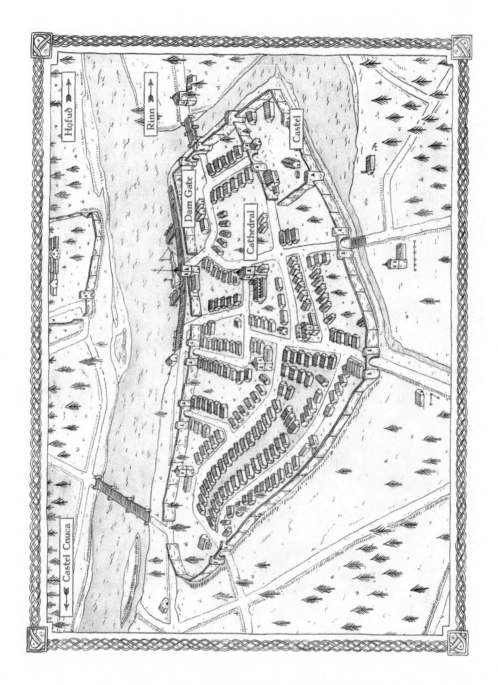

View of Dublin *c.* 1172

Contents

Dramatis Personae

Áed Buidhe	'yellow/blond Hugh', a fictional member of the historical Ua Cearbhaill family who ruled the land to the north of Meath
Alberic FitzJohan	son of an Anglo-Norman slave in Gaelic Meath
Angret	household servant to Hugo de Lacy
Aodán	a warrior of Áed Buidhe Ua Cearbhal's household in east Bréfine
Caoimhín	a wealthy *bóaire* in Míde, client of Mánus Máel Sechlainn
Cearbhaill	monk of the abbey of St Féichín
Cathal Crobhdearg Ua Conor	'Cathal of the redhand', brother to the High King Ruairí Ua Conor
Conn	son of Mánus Máel Sechlainn
Donchad	chief warrior of the household of Mánus Máel Sechlainn
Erc	warrior of the household of Mánus Máel Sechlainn
Étain	woman of the household of Mánus Máel Sechlainn
Fiacra	boy of the household of Mánus Máel Sechlainn
Folzebarbe	jester to Hugo de Lacy

Gormflaith	wife of Mánus Máel Sechlainn
Gunnar	Ostman of Dublin
Gryffyn de Carew	household knight of Hugo de Lacy
Hamund	Ostman/boy of Dublin and servant to Hugo de Lacy
Johan the Sasanach	John de Crécy, Alberic's father
Lochru	man of the farmstead of Mánus Máel Sechlainn
Milesius	(Malachy) Ua Ruairc, *coarb* of the abbey of St Féichín
Mór	woman of the household of Mánus Máel Sechlainn
Ness	woman of the household of Áed Buidhe Ua Cearbhall
Ruadán	warrior of Luigne
Saer	steward to Hugo de Lacy
Thorkil	Ostman of Dublin
Tuar	*ollamh* to Mánus Máel Sechlainn

Historic and Mythological Personages

Áed Mac Bricc	saint of the seventh century
Anluán	character in the mythological tale 'Mac Dá Thó's Pig' from the Ulster Cycle
Basilia de Clare	sister to the Earl Richard de Clare (Strongbow) and wife of Robert de Quincy
Brian Borumhne	Brian Boru, High King of Ireland, AD 978–1014
Conall Cearnach	mythological hero of the Ulster Cycle
Conn Cétchathach	legendary High King of Ireland and ancestor to the Connachta
Crom Cruach	pre-Christian deity
Crom Dubh	later name for Crom Cruach: 'the black stooped one'
Cumhal	mythological hero and father of Finn of the Fianna, killed by Goll Mac Morna

Cyhyraeth	Welsh spectre similar to the Irish banshee whose cry presages death; said to sound for Welsh natives dying far from home
Cynan	Grufyd ap Cynan, Welsh prince who grew up in North Dublin
de Angulo	Joyceln d'Angulo, possibly of Pembrokeshire, knight of Hugo de Lacy in Ireland, later Baron of Navan
de Feypo	Adam de Feypo, a knight of Hugo de Lacy in Herefordshire who followed Hugo to Ireland
de Tuite	Richard de Tuite, Anglo-Norman knight serving first Strongbow, then de Lacy
Diarmaid	mythological warrior of the Fianna, Gráinne's lover
Finn MacCumhal	legendary warrior from Gaelic Irish literature
Flann Sinna	ninth-century King of Meath and cofounder of Clonmacnoise
Gautier de Lacy	Walter de Lacy
Gráinne	mythological wife of Finn MacCumhal and Diarmaid's lover
Henri Plantagenet	Henri Cortmantle/Henri Fitzempress, King of England, Count of Anjou and of Normandy, regent of Aquitaine
Hugo de Lacy	Lord of Ewyas Lacy, Weobley and Ludlow in Herefordshire, England; later Lord of Meath and occasional Justiciar of Ireland; husband to Rohese de Monmouth and father of Hugo and Walter
Hugo Tŷrel	knight of Hampshire, in Hugo de Lacy's retinue in Ireland, and Baron of Castleknock

Hugo	Hugo de Lacy the younger, later Earl of Ulster
Iosa Críost	Jesus Christ
Launcelot	mythological knight from the court of King Arthur and featuring in epic poetry of the medieval period
le Petit	William le Petit, knight of Hugo de Lacy
Lorcán Ua Tuathail	Abbot of Glendalough and later Archbishop of Dublin
Mac Morna	legendary warrior from Gaelic Irish literature
Mac Murchada	Diarmait Mac Murchada, exiled King of Leinster
Mánus	Máel Sechlainn, claimant to the kingship of Meath in the later twelfth century
Meyler FitzHenry	son of Henry FitzHenry, an illegitimate son of King Henry I, by Nest, daughter of Rhys ap Tewdwr; cousin to Raymond le Gros
Midir	member of the mythological Túatha de Dannan, a son of the Dagda and judge to his people
Mog Ruith	mythical druid, father of Tlachta
Muircetach Ua Bríain	King of Munster, descendant of Brian Boru
Patricius	fifth-century St Patrick, a British slave taken to Ireland; after escaping, Patrick returned to convert the Gaelic Irish to Christianity
Raymond	Raymond FitzWilliam de Carew, known as Raymond le Gros
Rohese de Monmouth	wife of Hugo de Lacy and mother to Hugo the younger and Walter
Ruairí Ua Conor	High King of Ireland
Simon Magus	biblical figure known as a sorceror
St Agatha	third-century virgin martyr of Sicily

St Brigid	fifth/sixth-century saint, abbess and founder of the great monastery of Kildare
St Kevin	seventh-century saint, founder of Glendalough, co. Wicklow
St Féichín	seventh-century saint and founder of Fore Abbey, co. Westmeath
St Lasair	Gaelic saint associated with sites in cos Monaghan, Fermanagh and Roscommon
St Michan	eighth-century saint, patron of St Michan's Church, Dublin
St Samson	ninth-century Welsh saint who had a connection to north Dublin
Tigernán Ua Ruairc	King of Bréifne
Tlachta	mythical mother of three heroes, daughter of the druid Mog Ruith
Ua Bríain	Kings of Munster
Ua Néil	Kings of Ulster
Ua Ragallaig	a lord in east Bréifne
Yonec	romantic hero of a twelfth-century poem attributed to Marie of France

Historic Place Names

Airgialla	'Uriel', ancient kingdom equating to south Ulster
Alba	Scotland
an Rinn	Ringsend, Dublin
Ard Mhaca	Armagh, co. Armagh, centre of the cult of St Patrick and one of the pre-eminent Christian centres in Ireland
Áth Cliath	Dublin: 'ford of the hurdles'
Baile Átha Troim	Trim, co. Meath
Baile Griffin	Balgriffin, co. Dublin: 'Griffin's homestead'

Beal na bPéiste	place of pilgrimage in 'the mouth of the serpent'
Ben of Étair	Howth, co. Dublin: 'hill of Étair'
Bóinne	river Boyne, co. Meath
Bradogue	river Bradogue, co. Dublin
Bréfine	ancient kingdom equating roughly to cos Leitrim and Cavan
Brega	ancient kingdom equating roughly to north Dublin and southeast Meath
Bridge of the Ford	Drogheda, straddling cos Meath and Louth: 'droichead átha'
Brú na Bóinne	Newgrange, co. Meath
Ceannais	Kells, co. Meath, an important ecclesiastical centre
Cluain fada	Clonfad, co. Westmeath: 'long meadow'
Cluain Tarbh	Clontarf, north Dublin: 'meadow of the bull'
Cluan mhic Noise	Clonmacnoise, co. Offaly, an important ecclesiastical centre: 'meadow of the sons of Naoise'
Cluin Ioraird	Clonard, co. Westmeath
Cnucha	Castleknock, co. Dublin
Croagh Padraig	Croagh Patrick, co. Mayo, holy mountain associated with pilgrimage
Cullenswood	modern Ranelagh, to the south of Dublin
Dubh Lough	the Black Lake at Tailten, co. Meath
Duiblinn	Dublin: 'black pool'
Éirinn	Ireland
Ferns	Ferns, co. Wexford, Mac Murchada's capital
Fore	Fore, co. Westmeath
Gleann da Locha	Glendalough: 'valley of the two lakes', an important ecclesiastical centre
High Street	a street in the heart of medieval Dublin running between Christchurch Cathedral (priory of the Holy Trinity) and Dublin Castle

Hǫfuð	Howth, co. Dublin
Island of Manannán	Isle of Man
Laighin	roughly equating to the modern province of Leinster
Leith Moga	'Mugh's half': the southern half of Ireland, south of a line between Dublin and Galway
Leth Conn	'Conn's half': an ancient name for the northern half of Ireland, north of a line between Dublin and Galway
Lífe	river Liffey, co. Dublin
Lothlind	Norway
Merswy	river Mersey, cos Lancashire and Cheshire, England
Míde	co. Meath
Mumán	roughly equating to the modern province of Munster
Osraige	ancient kingdom equating roughly to modern co. Kilkenny
Sionainn	river Shannon
Sláine	Slane, hill in co. Meath, visible from Tara
Sord Columbcille	Swords, co. Dublin
Steyne	river Steine, Dublin
Teamhair	Tara, co. Meath, royal centre
Tethba	ancient kingdom including parts of modern cos Meath and Longford
Thule	Iceland
Tuamhain	Thomond: 'north Munster', relating in this period to the kingdom around Limerick
Ulaid	historical kingdom in east Ulster
Vadrafjord	Waterford
Veixfjord	Wexford

PROLOGUE

1166

It began before my story. Some short years before, while I, Alberic, laboured still in Yrlande. I heard it from a poet who came to Milesius' monastery. He claimed to have seen it all. Their approach to a town above low, vine-covered hillsides of fragrant black soil, studded with white pebbles and wind-fallen grapes. Stumping like pilgrims, walking their horses and mules with Mac Murchada at their head, driving on. A cloak shading over his brow. Through an unending country they had travelled, from landfall at Honfleur, through Roeun, Chartres, Chinon and the uncertain wooded expanses between. *Routiers* and mercenaries in the desolate places gauging the prey and, at each new town, the welcome uncertain, the castellan high-handed or the burghers wary.

Mac Murchada driving always onwards, silent, lips cracked and gaze beaming ahead. And everywhere they went, the king's tracks in the street, the piles of bone from feasting. The favoured still fingering their furs and gilded surcoats and other gifts richly given. The transgressors black-faced and purple-tongued, hanged from the appointed places.

At Samnur, finally, they caught sight of his pennant flying on the slighted castle, lithe, lions on a field of red. Henri Plantagenet, Henri Cortmantle, Henri Fitzempress—King of England, Count of Anjou and of Normandy, regent of Aquitaine.

They stopped below the town, leaving the road to pass between rows of tortured vines. Mac Murchada pushing into a cave strung with bushels of lavender, garlic and the wooden tools of the vendange. The broad farmer and his sons falling away meekly before the dark determination of that crook-backed, bear-shouldered foreigner.

Wordlessly, his small retinue went to work, pulling cinched leather packs from the mules' flanks, unfurling the cotton wrapping and flattening out the saffron-dyed shirt, the woven trews, and beating out Mac Murchada's mantle. Rich gifts for the King clanging from hand to hand.

The warm rain streaming along the rutted streets, carrying straw and ordure down the hill. The old bear, stepping like a maid across the plank pavement with his cloak caught up over his arm. The water dividing around his ankles. Peasant boys paid a *denier* to run ahead and announce his coming.

Quick words between the steward and *latimer* at the hall doorway. Across the threshold, steady as a Roman consul, Mac Murchada strode forward, his step devouring the length of the long room with courtiers shuffling indignantly around the verge. He paid them no heed, pacing on, and, reaching the foot of the king's dais, he bent his knee in a continuation of his forward momentum, sweeping his cloth before him in a wide, luxuriant bow. And at once—in that same impulse of trajectory that had driven him across the seas, gripping the side rail impatiently in the dense heaving of contrary waves, beating horses' flanks illiberally, grinding down the French hillsides with the irresistible passage of his boots—words shot from his mouth. A quarrel from a crossbow. A wrecked voice, hoarse, yet sibilant. The *latimer* rushing up alongside, launching desperately into his fervid translation.

'May God who dwells on high save and protect you, King Henri of the Engleis, the Normans, the Poitevins, Angevins, Gascons, Bretons, Welsh and Scots and of many more living and more again yet to be born, and may he grant you also the courage and the desire and the will to avenge my shame and my sorrow which my own people have brought upon me. Noble King Henri, hear where I was born and in what country: I was born a lord in Yrlande, and in that country I was acknowledged king before the devil Ua Ruairc wrongfully cast me out from the kingdom, so that I come here to a distant land where I know not the paths, over waters wide and through dark valleys and high hills, to appeal to you fair sire before the barons of your empire and to swear, powerful king, vested emperor, that I will become your liegeman for as long as I live, provided that you will help me, and so that I do not lose everything, I will submit to call you lord in the presence of your barons and earls'.

Mac Murchada finished, his head lowering almost to the ground as his breath expended, fell quiet, and it was to all as if a powerful wave had come crashing through the doors and in one fluid, elegant and unstoppable motion had broken at the feet of the dais, flinging bouquets of bright foam against the stones. And even as the *latimer's* meagre tone stuttered on, delivering the ending, it was plain for all to see that the King was affected by this man, so lofty and fine, yet bent so low, but with a vehemence and a determination that yet radiated from his person.

The king's hand rose slowly to his beard, and, pinching together the long hairs at the corner of his lip, his fingers twisted them delicately into a curled taper. His eyes lustrous beneath the dark ridge of his brow—an idea forming rapidly in his far-reaching, prophesying mind.

He opened his mouth. A word emerged. And everything that followed sprouted from that seed: Mac Murchada's flight back to Honfleur on brutalised horses, the crossing of the channel that lay down flat for him, the shouldering into flint-hard castles up and down the Welsh March with the king's writ in his fist and loud words of rich reward and fertile field for any who would follow him across the sea to Yrlande and help win back his province. The Earl Pembroke stepping forward finally, his cloak tawdry, his fortunes straitened, saying, 'I will come, I will serve', licking his lips, 'and in payment—your daughter'.

Without pause, Mac Murchada gripping the Earl by hand and by elbow, seizing him with steel-edged joy, tasting on his tongue iron scale, grit, the dirt of the fields, hearing in his ear the roar of the trees, the song of the Gael, and deep in his gut—blooming out like a drop of milk in a pail of water, chiming like the silversmith's craft—the grim fire of anticipation. For vengeance. Gripping the Earl's arm, drawing him in, pressing him into that warm, embracing fury, he kissed the Earl's cheeks. And in that same action, he opened the gate. Yrlande a sow on her back. And the knife pressed into an Engleis palm. And that was the beginning. Of the sack of Yrlande and the conquest of the Gael. That was the beginning of what would come to be my story.

PART I

The Stone
in the Mud

CHAPTER I

Kelt, 1171

UNLIKE MY FATHER, I was born in Ériu. Hibernia. Yrlande. I grew up far from the sea, in a world contained within the bend of a river and the slope of a wooded hill. We belonged to Mánus, a lord of local importance—a *tiarna* who ran a herd of ten score cattle and boasted that even his slaves wore shoes. This was an exaggeration. We were occasionally shod with old scraps of leather, and then only on fair days.

Mánus ruled over many farmsteads and had a claim to the province of Míde, a wide kingdom of green, dripping herbage, broad, slow-looping, clear-watered rivers and deep woods alive with grouse, capercaillie, deer and wolf. A land soft underfoot and to everything a name of ancient descent and to everyone a place in the order and a value on his head. *Rí, taoiseach, tricha cét, ocaire, boaire,* lawman, cleric, freeman, bondsman and slave. Everyone with a strict honour price encoded within ancient laws. A nobleman's worth measured in heads of cattle. My worth, by contrast, was a portion of a sheep. This meant simply that if a churl, unstable with drink, jostled me in a market crowd, took offence and struck me dead, he would owe the Tiarna a sheep's hind quarter in restitution.

7

This was something Conn never let me forget, often leaning his tall frame against me, forcing me into the low thatch of the corn kiln or the wattle of the bakehouse. He would tap the side of my skull with the butt of his axe, uttering his warning—'Don't test me, Sméar, I'll carve you up and gladly pay the shank of mutton you're worth'. And depending on the severity of his mood, I would often counter by asking him, who would he practice ball with then? For I was fast and had a firm shoulder, and I helped give him and the other well-born lads the run-out they needed to keep form. And this would often make him laugh; my temerity in the face of absolute powerlessness. 'Alberic, you stupid Sasanach', he would say then—their word for Saxon. A word they flung at Father and I. Not understanding that we were Engleis, that we spoke the tongue of the great King Henri of Anjou. That our fathers had crossed the seas from Normandy and had ground the Saxon under their boots. I pointed this out often, and earned many clouts for it. Despite my station, it is true that at times, I found it hard to say nothing.

Conn was Mánus' eldest son. Low nobility and a boy of my age. My friend and tormentor. *Sméar*—he called me that because of the broad purple stroke of a birthmark that swept back from my eye across the side of my forehead and fingered in beneath my hairline. It was a twisted sentiment. *Sméar* is their name for the blackberry. He did not mean it kindly—not the firm, noble berry of clustered rounds. He meant the pulpy leavings in the basket after all had been eaten. There lay my place, at the bottom. The son of a bondsman owned by a failing lord. A fleck in the eye of a fly. A seed in the storm.

Fitting, then, perhaps, that I was there at the parley on the hill when this old world was shattered. I witnessed the violence of kings, coming face to misshapen face. Both unshakably convinced of the iron-wrought firmness of their destinies; of their favour with God; of the terrible power of their own will. The earth shook. A trembling sod. This the nexus on which the world was to pivot, the two poles of my existence shifting. Engleis and Gaelic. Britannia and Hibernia. De Lacy and Ua Ruairc.

I will not recount the endless days that came before. The fevered dreaming on the hillsides. The long conversations with the night. I will not list the tedious and body-ruining labours. Nor speak of the brotherhood of the oppressed and its snatched, tender moments in shaded places. I will begin rather with the breaking of things. With the beginning of the storm. With the first steps on the path that took me far from Míde and through the turmoil of the wider world.

I was still young when the fulcrum began its pitch. Fortune's wheel clanking around in its inscrutable way. It was the year that the sky ships were seen in Ard Macha. A silver host, spectral and gold illuminated the heavens, emerging from the cloud with their glistening sails and their ghostly hosts peering down, blazing with light on the men below, who shrank from them in terror. And in that year also, the crozier of the bishop of Cluian Ioraird spoke to its owner, words of radiance and doom setting the kingdom alight.

Though we saw no such miracles to presage coming things, the Tiarna had a dream. He saw a great light rise from the mound on Cnuc Bán. A *sídhe* mound guarding the high pass over the valley and below—a stag belling, a wild dog of two colours devouring a heron's nest and, above, a sun rising in the west, spreading brightness over a darkened east. A weapon shining at the heart of the mound. A weapon of immense power.

The Tiarna ignored the words of his wife and councillors, he disregarded his *ollamh,* he closed his house to the monk and chewed his thumb long into the night. Night after night ruminating beside ashen fires, forging his resolve. Until, one darkening day, he sat on his horse commanding the unthinkable. Watching us scrabble and shift moss-thick stones from the ancient cairn.

We worked in silence, frantic in our task, working to quieten the dread that rang out in each of our heads. To stave off the flesh-creep as, hour after hour, we watched the sun pass its peak and begin to drop away westwards over the shoulder of the cairn. The mound's passive bulk thrumming with threat, and the *geis*-breaking sound of stones rolling free, rising to swallow everything else. Swallowing the champ of the standing horses, the rare lilts of the wind through the woodland below, the keening of buzzards circling. We cast the stones out beyond the kerbing into the heather, hoping they would land soft. Flinching at each cracking strike as they collided with hidden rock among the furze. Dread and skeletal hands clenching slowly within our skulls as the darkness thickened in the east.

'Ho', Lochru cried out—the first human sound in hours—and he came around the curve of the mound, his palsied face white, his hands trembling. He motioned to the Tiarna, who urged his horse onwards. Tuar, his *ollamh,* and the monk, Milesius, cantering on also. We all followed to where the youth Fiacra stood, unnaturally still, his eyes fixed upon something in the scree. With great reluctance, he raised his hand and pointed at an opening which showed amongst the loose stone. Two rough pillars leaning towards each other, forming a narrow doorway as wide as the span between fist and elbow.

We stood steaming in the cold. Shudders passed among us, and Milesius, hand on the psalter hanging in a satchel at his side, mumbled Latin incantations. The Tiarna gazed coldly. He looked to where his son Conn stood by, leaning on a spear. I saw the subtle question in the Tiarna's eye. I saw Conn's face lowering to the ground, refusing the wordless request, and, to disguise Conn's refusal, the Tiarna's voice came sudden and barking.

'Send in the Sasanach', he said without looking in my direction, and my bowels dropped within me. I stared ahead at the terrible and absolute blackness, a blackness that inhaled the failing light, and did not move. Lochru came towards me, grabbing my arm and pulling me past him with a blow that cupped the back of my skull. I staggered forward, feet twisting among the stones, and fell to my knees before the doorway, backing instantly, as if from a wild beast. I looked to the Tiarna on his horse and Milesius at his side. Their faces as hard as the stone of the hill. I breathed through my nose, a forceful breath. Another. And another. I made the sign of the cross, rose, commending myself to God and the Saints Patricius, Féichín, Lasair, and stepped forward.

I moved towards the dragging blackness. Towards the mouth of the underworld. Towards the realm of the *sídhe.* I approached as if it were cold water, step by step, clenching something deep within. My hand reached out to touch a pillar, and its frigid surface drew the warmth from me. I turned side-on, a welling panic, though I did not stop. I slid my shoulder into the gap and pushed my chest through, feeling the pillars scrape at once along my spine and breastbone. I dipped my head, without looking back, and entered the dark.

The space within forced me to crawl and I advanced blindly, my bulk blocking the light from the opening. The stones pressed in all around so that I could neither stand nor turn. Pools of water splashed beneath me, a dead air, stale in my lungs. My eyes moved wildly around, though nothing changed in the depthless dark. Hands slipped and scraped, and I struck my head frequently on the uneven roof. Yet I moved, and in moving, there was hope.

After a time, the space around me opened out, and the taste of the air changed slightly. I stood, and the roof of the chamber rose above me. I felt all around with great fear looming over me, though I could stay ahead of it by moving on. Around the chamber, I felt along the walls and found that there were alcoves or passages leading off in four places with low lintels, and in some of these places, objects were placed. I felt around large stone crucibles filled with grit. And among these crucibles, I touched something smooth, hard and cold. My hand closed upon it, and my skin formed around its smoothness. I stood, lifting it from its resting place. Sightless, I felt its shape—almost like an axe-head, though made of stone. A thing they call a *kelt*. A thing of the otherworld that turns up in ploughed earth or on dried-out riverbeds. A thing of magic.

I tied it up in the fringe of my garment, and the world pitched beneath me. I fell, striking a slab, and blood welled slick on my forearm. Cradling the *kelt*, I moved towards the passageway, seeking escape, and, stumbling again, I reached and touched solid rock. Fear flared up, breaking over me—a heavy mantle cast over my shoulders. A drowning cat within my chest. I moved around the chamber, feeling into each alcove and following short passages that ended in cold stone. I moved as one pursued, not heeding the knocks and the gouges, feeling hands all around me, feeling mouths opening in hideous forms and shapes, and they greeted me and looked at me and said to me as if in flattery and scorn, 'The other men in the world who are wise do not come here until they are dead'.

And a howling began in the crevices of the chamber, rising up from below with a creeping force. I pawed at the walls, clawed at shapes until my fingers were raw. The howling grew louder, circling and circling the chamber and pressing down upon me with such force that I could no longer raise myself from the stones. I do not know how long I lay there beneath the awful force of that deadening sound, diseased with fear. No thought in my mind, the tether of my soul to my body stretched to breaking and all sense of myself lost in that howling weight of terror.

And then came a tremendous cracking, a thunderclap of unknown immensity. Light pouring down upon me, so that I saw myself, my bloodied arms before me on the flagstones, and the howling now reduced to a ragged scream emanating from my own throat.

Above, the capstone of the chamber had been dragged aside, and Lochru's reluctant face appeared in the opening.

'He is here', he cried out over his shoulder, and to me he called out, 'Up, lad, quick now, up out of that place'.

I stood uncertainly, and Milesius appeared in the breach, his voice raised, intoning powerfully as he cast down drops of water from a metal vial.

'*Credo in Trinitatem sub unitate numinis elementorum*'.

I reached out a bloodied hand and he lay on his stomach, reaching down to clasp it, drawing me up, feet scrabbling until I was out, blinking in the weak twilight. I fell to the slab and saw the work that had been done clearing the stone from the top of the chamber. Staves and pry bars and ropes scattered around.

Milesius took my face in both of his hands, staring into me with a careworn intensity as Lochru stood by, dumb as a post.

'What is your father's name', he said sternly.

'Johan', I said, and beyond understanding, the words brought tears flooding over my cheeks. Milesius thumbed the red birthmark that enfolded my eye, rubbing forcefully as if to be sure of it. And I perceived what they feared. That I was changed.

'And where was he born and how did he come here?'

'He was born over the sea in England and sold as a slave to this land'.

'Who is Tiarna of this place?'

'Mánus Máel Sechlainn'.

'Whose church stands in the valley?'

'St Féichín'.

'Who is the redeemer and saviour of man?'

'Iosa Críost'.

Milesius' regard softened. He leaned in to kiss my forehead.

'Well done, boy', he said, and I heard Lochru release a long-held breath. The Tiarna's booming voice cut through the moment.

'Well?' he roared from below.

I undid the garment tied at my chest, allowing the smooth, weighty *kelt* to roll into my palm. A blue-black stone, ingrained with flecks of white. I marvelled at its surface, lustrous and speckled as the night sky. I fought the urge to hold it to my breast, to curl myself around it, to descend back into black oblivion. With my last reserve of will, I passed the seamless object into Lochru's waiting hand. Milesius drew me to my feet and impelled me gently towards the edge of the cairn.

'Away from this place', he said as he scratched the sign of the cross onto the underside of the slab with the bronze-shod butt of his staff, and to the others standing around the opening, 'Seal this up quickly'.

At a distance from the cairn, the Tiarna on his horse cupped the *kelt* in both hands, and Tuar and his other household men gathered close, straining to see. Conn did not approach them, hanging back, his jaw set. He looked up as I appeared over the edge of the mound and held my eye a moment, black shame boiling beneath his brow. He made no other sign before turning and working down the broken trail, alone and unnoticed.

I picked my way down the side of the cairn on uncertain legs. Reaching the bottom, I slumped to my knees in the heather, shaking from all that had gone before. None of the workmen reached out to steady or help me. Uneasy faces. And already, the word passing fearfully between them. The word for one who has been spirited away by the *sídhe*, taken to the underworld. And the word for the broken thing that has been left in their place.

Síofra—changeling.

The Tiarna made no acknowledgement as he turned his horse towards the trail, though as I watched, Milesius cantered his horse alongside, a hand reaching out to rest upon the Tiarna's wrist, low, urgent words in the Tiarna's ear, and then they were both looking at me. The Tiarna considering, a reluctance dissolving under the monk's patient silence. He nodded finally, his hand waving as if warding off a biting fly, and Milesius turned back to me, extending his arm. I jogged forward, climbing up onto his horse and passing my arms around his waist. Without speaking, he spurred the horse down the hillside, separating from the Tiarna's party and striking out for the monastery in the valley.

CHAPTER 2

Milesius

WE TOOK THE HARD ROAD, and I clung to Milesius with bloodied arms as he steered the horse with his thighs and a fistful of mane, mumbling incessant prayer. I fought the urge to look behind for fear of what I might see following through the night. We gathered speed on the lower slopes, cantering over the soft turf, and in the cushioned drum of hooves on earth, I heard the voices from before, intoning into my ear.

'Dead, are you dead? Not of this land. No blood in this soil'.

I burrowed my face into Milesius' back, squeezing my eyes shut, and, in this way, we came to the great monastery on the plain, its walls of earth and timber hulking in the darkness, ringing the spaces within, and we passed through the stone gatehouse into the outer precinct. I slipped from the horse and touched the sanctuary cross with great relief. Milesius left the lathered beast with the gatekeeper, leading me onwards. The massed houses and workshops silent. And along the paved way, I followed, through the next gate into the middle precinct where the cells of the monks flanked the scriptorium, the schoolhouse, the food hall. Milesius cried out with some urgency, calling names into the sleeping space, his voice deep and carrying over the muffled night. I followed his labouring back across the open *platea*, pausing fearfully at the next gate, guarded by a looming cross of painted stone. The dark opening, a pool I shuddered from, leading into the saint's sanctum. I hesitated at that threshold, the sacred space within housing Féichín's bones, the great church and the chapels. The relics and gold-bound books. A space I had only ever been to on the saint's day, when the Abbot walked in procession through bunched throngs who battled to catch sight of the golden reliquary, reaching out forlorn hands, at once supplicatory and violent.

Milesius turned impatiently, yet when he saw me, a boy fearful of his next step, the chiding faded from lips that tightened into a smile.

'Simple Sasanach', he said, his voice warm with fondness. 'You throw yourself headlong into the underworld and contend bodily with the *sídhe* yet falter at the threshold of sanctuary and saint-hood. You baulk at the Godhead'. I shook my head, desperate to defend myself, yet I could form no words. He laughed then, saying, 'Come, you soft fool, there is work yet to do', as two clerics came up beside us, their heavy tread speaking of broken sleep. 'Coltsfoot, and hawksbeard', he said, and they passed on ahead, moving confi-dently as those used to waking in darkness to trudge to prayer. I followed Milesius through the gate, the great churches, tombs and shrines, indistinct shadows passing on each hand.

He led me into a stone chapel, its walls dimly lit by crackling rushlights, the smell of tallow rising, masked by the heavy odour of gorse flower. At the altar, he bent his head and kissed the stone slab, his voice low and incanting still.

He approached me then, putting his hands on my shoulders and pushing down with sudden strength. I folded to my knees on the cold flags of the floor. Standing over me, he produced a short sickle from within his robe. He pressed it into my hand, saying, 'Hold this tightly', and I perceived in some cleft of my memory that the *sídhe* cannot bear the touch of iron. I clenched the sickle to my chest. Then he drew forth the silvered vial I had seen earlier. He shook the thing once, and I felt a misting vapour settle over me. The two clerics entered, bowing towards the altar and coming on with herbs and a cask of water. As they prepared the draught,

Milesius approached them with a small book of psalms and dipped its edge into the cask. He then passed a candle in a circle around my head, reciting prayers. I waited patiently throughout the rite, the cold stone warming beneath me, drawing my heat down into its hungry lifelessness. My muscles began to tremble once again—deep, uncontrollable shudders born of cold and fear and exhaustion. My head fell back, and I became lost in the dimness above, the vaulted arch of the roof swimming with painted shapes, knots and spirals with faces—both animal and human—emerging from the tangle as if peering from the chaos of a forest in storm. I stared upwards until it felt like I was falling, falling towards the faces that waited with placid eyes and bared teeth.

'Drink', Milesius said, standing over me with a wooden cup, and I did as I was told, the cold, acrid draught curling like a serpent, stabbing down into my body and filling the empty bag of my stomach. The sweat gone cold on my back and a sudden violent hunger coming over me.

'Might I have a crust of bread?' I asked, ashamed suddenly at these profane words emptying out into that sacred space.

'In the morning, lad', he said. 'It is best that we cleanse the spirit before feeding the body. Tomorrow you will break your fast with us. But now we will pray', he said. 'Pray through the night, and I will pray with you'.

'What is it', I asked, 'the *kelt*?'

'It is an object of the otherworld', he said, watching me, considering what my wrung mind could handle. 'Some say they are thunderbolts, thrown down when lightning meets the earth. Others that they are fashioned by the artificers of the *sídhe*. A weapon perhaps, a repository of their power'. He saw the fear on my face, and he spoke again. 'Peace, Alberic, they will not come for you in this place. And with the first touch of the sun, you will be safe'.

I nodded and spoke. 'Let us gird ourselves with the power of God'. He smiled faintly and began to pray. I followed his Latin words as best I could, adding my meek voice to his, and the sound resonated around the sacred space, bringing me strength.

'*Sancti Patricii Hymnus ad Temoriam*'.

'I am a refugee, a sinner, a simple country person, near sixteen when I was taken prisoner from Britannia. At that time, I did not know the true God. It was among foreigners that it was seen how little I was. I tended sheep on the mountainside every day, and it was there that I turned with all of my heart to God. Faith grew, and my spirit was moved. I was like a stone lying deep in the mud. Then he who is powerful came and, in his mercy, pulled me out and lifted me up and placed me on the very top of his wall. My name is Patricius'.

Milesius recited these ancient words to me the following morning. He read them from an immense book of cowhide in the empty, sun-warmed scriptorium, where his voice lapped against the walls. I sat, as I often had, among the frames of pinned parchment and the venerated books, watching through the narrow window, the brothers below at their tasks in the herb garden. My belly full of honeyed oatmeal and my head drowsing pleasantly.

Milesius read these words in sympathy, to soothe my young anger, my devouring frustration—to show me that at the dawn of time, the greatest of all saints was once in bondage like me. That through his belief he was elevated in life and became a leader of kings, beloved throughout Yrlande. And though Milesius had his own ends in sight, his words gave me power. A power which settled deep within the bole of my being and allowed me to draw upon a pool of strength when the kicks and lashes became too much, when the burden cracked my young joints and twisted my sinews. Over the previous years, he had furnished me with a spirit that became difficult to dim. A spirit fed by belief. A belief that there would be more for me on this earth and that I would be raised up by the grip of a firm hand. Though 'he who is powerful', when he made himself known, proved not to be the Christian God, nor was his beneficence eternal. De Lacy. That morning, I would hear the name spoken for the first time.

'The world is changed, Alberic', Milesius said, placing down the book, and I waited to hear more as he bent his face to the studded cover, his lips kissing silently. 'Mac Murchada is dead and the foreign lords he brought home with him have taken more than was their due. The Engleis King, Henri, has crossed the sea with an army to lay claim to Laighin. Not only that, the King has promised Míde to one of his captains. The Baron de Lacy. An outrage. Unspeakable in its wrongness'.

'Henri here? In Yrlande?' I spoke to quieten the tumult of feeling this news had caused within me. And to disguise the hope I felt deep within, I said, 'Mac Murchada never had true claim over this land'.

'Indeed', Milesius said, watching me closely, 'this is why the Tiarna takes such rash decisions. Looking for answers in ancient mounds and placing his faith in heathen objects. The gaze of one of the most powerful kings of Christendom is upon us'.

'Will Ua Conor meet his gaze?' I asked.

'Surely', he said, 'and my cousin Ua Ruairc in the vanguard no doubt. And, as ever, the innocent will be trampled in the clash'.

'The purpose of all war is peace *a mháistir*'.

'Perhaps', he said, shrewd eyeing me, a thick, ink-stained finger pushing his lower lip into the gentle chew of his teeth. 'What is certain—your worth has risen, lad. The Tiarna will look to use you and your father to his advantage'.

Milesius—Máel Ísu in the tongue of the Gael—of the family of Ua Ruairc, was a great scholar, and he enjoyed his role, bending me this way and that with the current of his thought. I could not discern at first why I warranted special interest, why I was so often granted access to the workings of the monastery. Many of the clerics presumed sodomy, though, despite long hours in the close dimness of the scriptorium, he never laid a hand on me in that way. The only time his touch lingered was in tilting my head to show the Abbot or some visiting deacon my birthmark, saying, '*Leag Dia lamh air*'—God has laid his hand on him.

This earned me much scorn from the community of monks and lay brothers—one as low as I within their sanctum. Though their scorn was a paltry thing, and I learned to walk tall, uninjured by the bramble of their looks on the back of my neck. In time, they, too, forgot the outrage of it, and I sank into the background, becoming part of the life of the foundation, coming from the Tiarna's farmstead on my due days to render service—invisible against the high banks of the enclosure, the painted crosses, the stone shrine.

Milesius had been to the realm of the Holy Father in Rome. An unspeakable journey across oceans and burning wastes and forests deeper than the blackest cavern and through heathen lands and mountains so high that snow lay ever on their peaks. Along this route, he passed the vastness of territories controlled by that Imperator of the west—King Henri of Anjou—and read in the stern faces and high-walled fortresses of those Engleis and Normans of what was to come. Forearmed with this knowledge, Milesius fostered me in a way. He saw the value in a half-Engleis lad of reasonable wit. He crafted me, perhaps, as a worker of alder crafts a shield to hold out against future blows.

He knew the law also. A man of great learning, esteemed, it was said, by the bishops at Ceannais and Ard Mhaca. He spoke to me often in the ancient triads that encode the lawman's wisdom. And I came to know the responses:

Three sons that do not share inheritance?

A son begotten in a thicket, the son of a slave, the son of a girl still wearing tresses.

Like many churchmen, he abhorred slavery and worked to redress it through representations at councils and through his wild-eyed sermons, which he gave at farmyards and market crosses and fording places and anywhere that men congregated within the territory. Whenever he could, he invoked Cain Adomnán—the Law of the Innocents—to protect women, children and bondsmen.

On another level, I believe he enjoyed my company, as I formed a link of sorts to the world beyond the *túath*, beyond the bounds of Yrlande. For my father had been an Engleis man of rank, before his abduction. He was sold into slavery in Míde before I was born, at some seaport he did not know the name of. That I and Father spoke the tongue of the Normans to each other—a kind of Frankish speech—made me receptive to Latin. I found I could parse its workings quite easily, a fact which Milesius was quick to learn. Each time he read the words of Patricius to me, with every clandestine lesson, he was sending me on another step towards a life in the church, preparing me for the time when he would challenge the Tiarna publicly. When he would draw upon his energies and skills of *oratio* to shame the master into freeing his slave. Like Patricius lighting the great fire of Sláine in opposition to heathen kings. This was the hope that kept me strong in those early years. I was about fifteen.

CHAPTER 3

File

WE SAW SIGNS OF THE FALL. Of the havoc wrought far from our lands by the Engleis. Dishevelled bands of exiles travelling north on the *slighe*. Fires beyond our borders and reports of silhouetted horsemen furtive on the hills. The Tiarna kept vigil, the *kelt* ever in his fist. Then the poet came, and his approach heralded destruction. That itinerant wizard. That unholy satirist. He signalled the reckoning, whether he knew it or not. He signalled the intrusion of the outside world. The small fruit of my existence bursting open, its rind splitting and wasps spilling from galls to crowd the opening and feed on the juice.

Lochru saw him first, late that next day. He came to fetch me from the monastery and bring me back to the Tiarna's farmstead, the lad Fiachra with him leading a donkey, his eyes full of suspicion. On our return past the low meadow, we stopped to try our hand with the winter geese and saw the poet wandering at the edge of the bog that ran away eastwards from our borders.

'There's a crane yonder in the meadowland', Lochru said in that archaic way he had of speaking, his dropsied face muffling his words and his snout pointing over the sedge. We lay on our bellies behind a crisping brace of fern. On the flat before us, a riot of geese clamoured and fouled the ground with their black excrement. Slings in our fists, we lay still, watching the birds rooting at the damp earth for whatever it is that gives them sustenance.

'Crane?' I whispered, and Lochru snorted, letting me know that my youth had betrayed me. That there was no crane. That there was something strange somewhere. Something out of place in the sloping scene before us. I said no more but studied the foreground where the great tumult of geese jostled. My eyes ranged farther, beyond the limits of the river, marked by a line of bulrush rising from the grass. And beyond that, a glistening wet ground, full of the swollen river overspill with willow and elder un-coppiced and growing wild. I saw nothing to remark upon. Lochru waited still, his satisfaction that his old eyes had seen what I could not competing with his mounting impatience.

Then I saw him, stooping as he moved slowly around the tree roots, navigating the edge of the wide bog. His head covered with a bolt of cloth which fell around his shoulders and, beneath, a green cloak skirting his knees. The colour of his cloak announced him as a man of status. A man that should be on the *slíghe* with a retinue and a horse, not travelling alone, slopping through the turf.

'Exile?' I whispered, remembering the Tiarna's cousin, hounded into the wastes, fleeing from dispute before his eyes were cut from his head.

'*File*', said Lochru. Poet. A man to traverse boundaries. A man of twelve years' learning who would know by heart the endless genealogies, the forms of praise and of redress. A man respected and feared who, if the words were with him, could raise up a *tiarna* in noble verse or destroy him with satire, break his power, throw doubt upon his legitimacy. If the skill was with him, his words could raise a blemish or even slander a man to the doors of death.

'Stay low and watch', Lochru said, 'and tell me all that he does. Do not move or follow until the stranger has gone'.

Lochru surged forward in a swift but awkward movement, letting loose a stone from his sling before landing heavily on his knees, crying out with the effort. The geese erupted, taking flight in competing panic, brewing upwards in such a cacophony that my eyes rose with them, watching their combined bulk empty into the grey sky. When my gaze returned to scan the edge of the bog, I could no longer see the poet. At length, I picked out his stooped form behind a hummock. As the geese cleared, his distant, shaded face searched in our direction, looking for the source of the fright. Lochru stood up then with great effort, groaning and pressing on his knee to rise in the manner of a rheumatic man. He walked down the slope, towards the river, mumbling expressively to himself. Bending, he came up with a gander shivering in his hand. He made a great show of inspecting the bird before pulling its neck and hooking it under his belt, lustily clapping dirt from his hands. He turned, making his way back uphill towards the eaves of the Tiarna's wood where Fiachra waited, cutting withies by the donkey.

The poet watched all of this from his hiding place. He watched as Lochru, with his uneven gait, made his way upslope through the furze bushes. Lochru played his part well, and from where I lay, I watched him re-join Fiachra, holding up the bird in triumph. The poet waited for a time, crouched low, waiting until he was satisfied there was no danger. He stood out from behind the heather and took up his labouring tread to the south. I watched until his slow progress took him from view.

When I reached the treeline, the withies were cut and piled up in great stacks beside where the donkey was tethered, waiting dourly. A fire smouldered under cover of the dark wood, and the goose was roasting on a sharpened ash rod with sprigs of smoking plumage sticking from the carelessly plucked skin. The light waned as I settled in beside the fire, and the time when our absence would be noted was approaching. Lochru took the bird from the spit, pulling it apart with his broad fingers, and he shared it out in three ways according to our status. We sat back from the fire swallowing hot gobbets of the flesh and gazing up at the small parcels of the dying day through the canopy above, savouring the moment as a breath of freedom.

'And Mac Murchada dead', said Lochru, repeating the news that was on all lips.

Fiachra did not speak, and I filled the silence.

'A tyrant, they say, though the Tiarna liked him well enough'.

'True', Lochru said. 'Raided with him into Osraige in the

days of Toirdelach. And Mac Murchada never came here seeking vengeance with his foreign mercenaries'. Fiacra spoke up hotly.

'They say his body rotted around him while he still drew breath. A great putrescence coming out of him'. He looked to me, his dark eyes glinting. 'A curse, surely, for bringing the foreigner'.

'But will his foreigner soldiers leave now that the old bear is dead?' Lochru said, his fingers thick within the gnarl of his beard.

'Ask this one', Fiacra said, his regard sly and lips glazed with grease as he tossed a bone in my direction, 'the worst foreigner of them all'.

'They say at the monastery that King Henri is come to Yrlande to lay his hand on Mac Murchada's land'. I said this to stop Fiacra's windpipe. 'And that there is a man with him—de Lacy—to whom Míde has been promised'. Lochru erupted in a high, brash laugh.

'Haah—now Christendom's most powerful king comes to claim our lands. Well, lads, will I live to see such wrongness?'

'He will sweep this way surely, and who is there to stop him?' I said.

'And you and your father will be there to welcome them with arms wide, having buried knives in all of our backs', Fiacra said with vehemence. 'But the foreigners have not heard of our own king—Ua Conor, and his war-dog Ua Ruairc. They will be sent back over the sea with spears in their backs'.

'So that is our choice—Ua Ruairc of Breifni or the Engleis?' Lochru said loudly, casting his eyes upwards. Fiacra spat into the leaf litter as Lochru laughed. And that settled the matter. Not a word was spoken of the poet.

We struck our small camp, burying the embers and hiding the plumage. Lochru loaded the donkey, stacking the withies high, and Fiacra and I tied bushels to our backs, carrying yet more on our heads. We walked on, joining the small *bóthar* beyond the meadow, and Lochru came alongside me as I took a turn leading the donkey. He spoke in a low tone.

'What did you see of the *file*?'

'I saw him stay low while you retrieved the goose. He watched you return to the wood, and then he continued on his way, looking back now and then to see that none had paid him heed'. Lochru nodded and said no more.

'Why do you say he is a poet?' I asked after a time, and Lochru, tiring under his load, replied sharply.

'Because I am old and have seen many things'.

'Will you tell the Tiarna?' I asked.

'Was there welcome at the hostel of the quicken-tree?' he countered.

I fell quiet, and we walked farther in silence, each feeling the weight of his load as the donkey tired, with his hooves catching at times on the rough stones of the *bóthar*. I worked over Lochru's words as we went. There was indeed welcome at the hostel of the quicken-tree for Finn and his Fianna. A welcome which proved false and treacherous.

We arrived at the Tiarna's farmstead before sunset, clattering across the wide boards of the *tóchar* in the high field. The manor looked well, laid out below in the setting sun. Deep shadows from the palisade around the Tiarna's house striping the fields, smoke rising from the thatch of the mead hall and, further downslope, from the kiln, which was working hard to dry out the harvest. Mangach leading cattle up from the crooked meadow, Mór and her women bringing water from the river to prepare the evening meal.

We descended, grateful of the sloping ground, and brought our load to the shack beside the gate into the Tiarna's compound. Erc stood guarding the gate.

'Bring the withies in and leave them by the rampart', he said roughly, ushering us into the space beyond the gate.

It was rare to be so close to the Tiarna's house, and I took the opportunity to steal glances here and there to see what we might observe. For most, the Tiarna was a figure beyond comprehension. A man of learning and of power who inhabited a realm as different to ours as the realm of the clouds to the earth.

When the Tiarna appeared at his door, wrapped in a *brat* of fine red weave, Tuar his *ollamh* at his elbow and both speaking easily, with their hands describing some distant plans over the river land, Lochru and Fiacra sought to dissolve into the shadows, bending in upon themselves with a kind of fearful deference.

I watched the Tiarna, however, with those darting glances which are the currency of the bondsman. In the same language, with glances and the faint constriction of my eyes, I told Lochru that now was his time to approach the Tiarna and tell him of the poet on the margins. Lochru's eyes refused sternly, urging me to walk on. I looked back at the Tiarna and Tuar, sharing, as they spoke, something steaming from a wooden cup.

When your life is not your own, you learn to move with apology. Low head, the lightest of steps. Not meeting another's eye. That is how to blend in to the skyline. That is how to live with the least resistance and allow those larger than you to determine your course. I was satisfied with this no longer, and, though I had not yet recognised it, I longed to provoke change. To make something happen.

When Erc turned his back, I dropped the bushel of withies I had been carrying, broke from the others and walked towards the Tiarna in an arcing line which skirted the darker places alongside outbuildings and thatched awnings. I was as invisible to them as the children playing with straw figures by the pig house.

'*A thiarna uasal*', I said, which is their respectful address, used from one man of quality to another. They both looked down at me as if I had materialised from the empty evening. The Tiarna's voice trailed into silence, and Tuar's mouth fell some way open, the deep revolutions of their converse broken.

Anger blazed across Tuar's face, though the Tiarna seemed on the verge of laughter.

'Forgive me, Tiarna, I have seen something that might be of consequence to you'.

Before I could say more, a blow brought me to my knees as Erc clapped his open hand onto the back of my neck, forcing me to the ground. I tried to raise my head, but Erc held me so that my gaze could not rise above the Tiarna's knee.

'You are not at your monastery now, Sasanach', Erc said. 'Show some humility'.

'Let him be, Erc', the Tiarna said. 'The boy has travelled far with word. He comes to us all the way from the distant willow coppice'.

All three men laughed at the Tiarna's wit, and, seeing the wisdom in this, I laughed too. Erc's fingers squeezed discreetly at my neck.

'Please do share with me your tidings, Alberagh', he said, for that is how they say my name. This was the first utterance of it, however, that I had heard from one of such importance. It spurred me on at precisely the moment that I flagged. It gave me a substance I had not previously felt.

'A poet, beyond the river'.

'A poet beyond the river', he repeated slowly, and I heard the cryptic sound of these words carried back to me. 'Are these the tidings we have so anticipated from one that has been to the underworld and back?' he said, still jovial, though sharing a glance with Tuar. 'And what manner of poet would you say, and why is this of interest to me?'

The mocking had stopped, and the Tiarna motioned for Erc to step off and let me stand.

Three glories of speech: steadiness, wisdom, brevity.

'By his attire and his aspect was he a poet. By the twist in his hair and the feathers on his mantle. By the fork in his beard was he a poet'.

'Even so. What is that to me? He is not of my retinue'.

'Perhaps he is not. Though perhaps he means to be', I said significantly. He was silent at this and stood back against the low doorway. He looked again to Tuar and spoke to him in Latin, saying, 'What of this?'

Tuar replied in the same language, saying, 'The speech of Rome is no foil to this lad. He can follow us quite well no doubt'.

'Is this so, boy?' the Tiarna said in Latin, yet maintaining his aspect, facing towards Tuar and not letting it be seen that he addressed me.

'*Ita vero*', I said—it is true.

'Of course', he said, 'you have been receiving Milesius' favours'. This was said with a hint of scorn. I replied carefully.

'I speak with the monk and heed what he would teach'.

'Heed what he would teach', the Tiarna repeated slowly, the amusement draining from his face. 'I can see perhaps that you have been spared the rod, boy. There is humility lacking'.

He let the silence stretch out after this. Full of the spectre of violence, looming in the space between us like smoke, flecked with ember, rising upwards in front of moonlit skies. Then he lowered his hand to his neckline, bringing forth the *kelt* from where it hung, bound by its end to a cord, and by this act, the menace was dispelled.

'Come in *kelt*-bringer', he said, inviting me across his sill as if it were as natural a command as 'clean out the ashes' or 'bring me in water'. I did not look to Tuar for his expression but kept my eyes down. So it was that I crossed the threshold into the house of Mánus Óg Mac Murchad Máel Sechlainn. Though I did not look behind, I knew that there would be bushels of withies cast down to the earth with ferocity, with incredulity, with amazement, as Fiacra, Lochru and Erc watched me dip and disappear through the low door frame, extinguished like a taper touched to water.

CHAPTER 4

Tiarna

I ENTERED THE TIARNA'S HOUSE, and at first, my eyes refused to see through the dimness. The warmth washed over me, the smell of broth, thick on the air. When my eyes adjusted to the firelight, I could see that the walls were high and decorated with hanging shields and axes, an adze, an auger, a saw, all suggesting a lustre in the low, red light. Around the edges of the room were benches draped with skins and rich cloths. On the women's side of the house, a kneading trough, iron vessels, a washing bucket. Naked children raced and shrieked around the wooden bath while Gormflaith, the Tiarna's wife, nursed a baby as her ladies spun wool together. The Tiarna's favoured hounds lounged on the rushes by the fire in the centre of the room, ears twitching and nostrils flaring as the smell of meat rose from the hanging cauldron.

And from the shadows, amongst the women, Conn's eyes suddenly staring from where he had been playing with the younger children. His face hot with embarrassment and outrage, compromised by my presence. His veneer of strength and manhood not yet fixed within the safe confines of this place.

'Here, *giolla*', the Tiarna called from beyond the fire. I approached, and the Tiarna's household guard Donchad stepped out from inside the door, a warding presence by my side. 'Do you play, *giolla*?' he said mockingly, as *giolla* is what they call a kind of squire to the high born. He motioned to a board marked with squares set in a bench and, beside the board, a broken cup containing two bone dice. His mocking was twofold, as only the nobility were permitted to play such games. I chose not to respond.

'This is a game that trains the mind for politics, for battle, for the reading of other men and their wants, their workings, their weakness'.

'My father speaks of such things', I said to push back gently.

'Of course, as he would', the Tiarna said, thinking on this briefly, rolling the dice and moving the whittled gaming pieces on the board. And then he looked at me with some intensity, preparing to read my reaction. 'Tell me, why would a poet come to me when it is known that I maintain my own *file*', he said, gesturing to Tuar, 'when my family has been served and lauded for generations by the masters of the Ua Dalaigh? Why would a *file*, hungry for his livelihood or seeking a new horse in payment, come to me and my house, where there is surely a surfeit of poetry? And then, seeking to win acclaim by the verse he must so fully believe to be superior in all ways to that of the poets of this land, why then steal away and not announce himself?'

The Tiarna stared as he spoke, seeking to unsettle me, and I wondered, under that gaze, what oracles he had read in my face.

I replied carefully so that my meaning would be understood but not explicitly stated. 'Perhaps he is waiting for a praiseworthy event to occur. An act of bravery and daring worthy of commemorating in verse. Perhaps he intends to arrive once this act has been carried out so as to disguise foreknowledge'.

I could feel Conn's stare on the back of my neck, willing me dead for speaking so freely. The Tiarna's eyes finally released me as he looked to Tuar significantly. In Latin, he said, 'Does the slave speak to me of our *táin*? Of our coming raid to the north? How could that be, as only my captains know of this'. Tuar played the game.

'Surely not, Tiarna'.

Of course I had heard of it, such secrets unable to be kept by the straining youths of the household, bent on winning honour, dreaming aloud of great deeds to come and their own place within them.

'A secret told to more than one is difficult to keep', I replied in Latin.

'Your thinking is sound, but it must go deeper', the Tiarna said. At that moment, he looked up at me again, his bright eyes amused and dangerous. 'Why, for example, would I allow you and your kind to eat my fowl without sanction?' Sharp, icy veins of fear travelled my spine as he watched his words worm into me. I faltered in that warm, smoke-filled place, intoxicated by sudden guilt. By my sudden and inescapable visibility. By my nakedness in front of such inquisition. Sights of the room came to me as powerful visions, amplified by fear and the overpowering sense of the momentous. The surety that, regardless of what I was to answer, the past would be burned by it. Would be no more. And I was dazzled, as my eyes sought escape from his insistence, in glimpses of the beautiful looped chains on his hounds. The painted shields on his walls. I answered.

'I would suggest that the Tiarna knew the value of such secret pursuits in expelling the energies of youth with no more than the loss of a winter fowl to himself'.

His gaze remained on me, and I could not say in those moments what else was passing in the room, in the compound, in the world, as he channelled something into me through those impassive brown eyes. Finally, as all sound subsided and even the hounds seemed to hang on his word, he made his pronouncement.

'There may be some truth in what they say of you. You are changed'. He laughed lightly then, seeing the fear on my face. 'You may stand where you are, *giolla*. If there is no poet found, know with certainty that I will teach you humility by beating you from here to the river until your ribs show through your skin'.

His eyes returned to the gaming board and the pieces there arrayed like fallen rondels at the foot of a lathe.

'If you are proved true, you will ride with us on our *táin* to the north, and you will share in the dangers and the rewards'. He spoke to Donchad. 'Take a horse and ride out to see if you can spy this mover on the fringes. Do not alert him to your presence if it may be helped, and return to us with news'.

The tall warrior was gone without the hint of a question, though he cannot have thanked me for being sent into the night as the smells of the evening meal were filling the house. The Tiarna was silent then a long time, and he and Tuar resumed their play, leaving me to stand by and watch, trying to order the moves, to understand the rules. Trying to allay my fears of what tidings would return with Donchad and whether he would search with purpose or wait in the woods for a time before coming back to the warmth and food to watch me flogged.

After the passage of some play, the Tiarna spoke. 'So Mac Murchada is dead and the Sasanach King thinks to keep what was promised him'.

'Ua Conor will set them running', Tuar replied grimly, his hand hovering uncertainly over the game board.

'You speak the language of the Sasanach?' he asked me.

'Yes', I replied.

The Tiarna looked down to his board and rolled the dice out of the cup.

To Tuar he said, 'Stammering with foreign lips and strange tongues will God speak to his people'.

And to me, 'Ask your father what he knows of this King Henri and also of the Earl of Pembroke, FitzGerald and FitzStephen. Remember these names. There is also a man come with the King, an older man of some reputation. De Lacy. Ask your father above all of de Lacy'.

I nodded assent, and once again they fell silent. As I stood, alone and on trial, I was visited by my mother. Her spirit shuffling around the fringe of the house where the sloping roof swept towards the floor. She inhabited, as she often did, the form of a bird. This time, the strange figure of the Tiarna's crane standing on one leg, its clipped wings folded sadly, drawing no interest from man or child. She tilted her head in sympathy and showed me the glassy depth of a black eye. I stood my vigil in her company, waiting into the interminable night. Greenwood hissing on the fire. A last and lonely wasp butting the thatch. A ball of sackcloth plugging a hole. The unfamiliar heat and smoke of a wealthy household lulling me into a comfortable haze. Low talk and the clack of gaming pieces moving from one square to another.

It was late when Donchad returned.

'You found him, then?' the Tiarna said, and the warrior nodded. My legs almost buckled with relief.

'I followed him to the hurdle ford at the edge of the *túath,* and there I watched him move down out of the treeline to meet with a man and his retainer on the *slíghe*'.

'A Gael?' the Tiarna asked.

'A foreigner on a horse. And his retainer was a Gael. If I were forced to it, I would say that it was a son of your enemy Ua Ragallaig of Bréifne'.

The moon had fallen low over the treeline when I was given my leave of the great house. My breath clouded around me, and I stumbled in the dark downslope towards the mill-race, passing Donchad's steaming horse in its paddock. I followed along the watercourse until it brought me to the mill-house, where I joined Father's drowsing form on the rushes and flour dust in the small space around the grindstone. I told him of the long day's events, and those of the day before, speaking to his broad back. He listened to it all silently. The cairn, the *kelt,* the monastery, the rite, the poet and the interview with the Tiarna. I awaited no reply. Like the Tiarna's, Father's thoughts moved slowly, cycling through the significance of each small element, attempting to trace future events and predict their effect on us. The following day we would labour at the mill, stooped over the juddering wheel, feeding the grain into the funnel, hearing the heads pop, the white marrow spreading across the rough face of the stone. I would hear what he had to say then. And it would bring me no warmth.

CHAPTER 5

Athair

THE MORNINGS ALWAYS BEGAN the same. And I can see him now. Up before the tumult of the hens. Before the sky blues up from the east. Before the morning chaos of rooks, like endless dark darts, flocking across the farmyard, wheeling to a hundred conflicting impulses. *Mo athair*—Father rises from the damp boards of the mill-house, leaving me slumbering, and passes down for the mess of willows standing in the long pools of silvery water spreading out from the river which has over-reached its course, heaving its bulk smoothly, without violence, like a sow onto the bank, spilling over the low grazing in this saturated land where the air itself is like a hanging gauze. The brown earth engorged beneath the deep sheen of the grass accepts the shape of his foot as he pads along the narrow, sharp cutting of the mill-race which is full to the very brim with a body of water sliding along at speed.

In the fields beyond, he rises with the ground, long, loping steps upwards towards the outer pastures, where he goes to mend a hedge or find a stray goat, or some other excuse to get him beyond sight so that he may make his way into the wood to a mossy stone where he stops and kneels and says his prayer in a tongue not of that land. A language that intrudes into the cadence of the morning. He speaks to Mother through the spongy black earth of leaf rot and fruit fall. He speaks of me I am sure, and of the news he has heard of his countrymen—of the Engleis away south. Every single morning, he maps out his own solitary way.

His name was Johan. A man who maintained a firm countenance, yet a tender engagement with the physical world around him and the problems encountered in its organisation. In the absence of a mother he would not discuss, he sheltered me, taught me and claimed me.

He had been the reeve of the manor of a place called Frodsham in the shire of Chester, which meant that he ran the farmstead and oversaw the *villeins* and collected taxes for the Earl. He had a wife and children, two oxgangs of his own and two servants in a fine wooden house with low, sweeping thatch. That was before raiders had happened upon him alone on the banks of the Merswy.

It had not taken the Tiarna long to recognise his worth. Father had an aptitude for every craft and action required on the farmstead, and while his counsel was often sought in matters of sowing and grazing and managing the mill-races and fishing weirs, this did not free him from menial work. We broke our backs with the rest, bending with the sickle, the rhythm of the rip and tear of the barley stalk, the building of the rick and the twist of the harvest knot. We worked the kiln also, stoking the fire to dry out the grain after the harvest had been winnowed. We fed coppiced branches of a certain size into the flame, the fire kept even, making certain not to set the roof ablaze nor to scorch the grain. His value to the master gave me some measure of protection, and I was, at times, happy, having not known any other life.

The Tiarna entrusted the running of the big mill to my father, grinding the kiln-dried grain between two heavy millstones powered by the waterwheel—an ingenious arrangement of paddles and flues that Father had helped to improve upon.

A lifetime it seemed that we spent within both kiln and mill telling tales we had heard, singing rhymes, mostly in Father's tongue. It was within that space that I demanded the story of his abduction again and again, watching his face go sombre and grave, until it became as real to me as if I had been there myself, accosted in the shallows of that wide estuary.

Later, as Father and I worked our way along the millstream clearing clotting wads of dead leaves and windfall, I asked him of these Engleis—if they would bring us freedom. Father quelled my excitement.

'They are only mercenaries. Just another war between cowherds who would be kings'.

I recited the names as I remembered them—Pembroke, FitzGerald, FitzStephen.

'Striplings', he said. 'Hungry youths is all. Half-Welsh brigands'.

I asked then about de Lacy and what his coming meant, and a change came over Father, his eyes growing cold upon the sounding of those words.

'There will be no freedom under a yoke of that name', he said.

It was the reckoning then. The vengeance I had poured so much of my soul into praying for, willing, clenching with every fibre of self, pledging with broken-toothed conviction in the fevered hours before dawn as I slept in the byre, or among the Tiarna's hounds, or sat watch by night over herds on the verge of some rough mountainside. I prayed to a God I did not fully understand. On behalf of Father. For freedom. For justice. Justice for a life stolen.

We sat together that night and ate our oats. Something was different. Something had changed. I felt more substantial. I felt, heady with the fever of youth's vanity, that I had earned a place at the high table, leaving my father behind. That I had acquired a new sight. A power of perception recognised by the Tiarna.

'Tell me again', I said.

'Tell you what?' he said, churlish.

'Tell me of how you came to this land'. And in the telling, as always, my ear trained to the inflection, to the tremor, to the missed rhythm, to any word that could, by its shape, or the shadow of its shape, tell me even the most miniscule thing about my mother.

I do not recall a particular realisation but rather a slow dawning. Over time, noticing slight changes in his story. An accumulation of evidence. Marking small contradictions over the seasons as my probing, my hunger for a glimpse of a different world, of a far-off life, grubbed up inconsistencies. I came to know, as my mind matured, the ways of deceit, and after being in the presence of the Tiarna, after studying with Milesius, I was more alive than ever to how language could be used. To say one thing and conceal another. I listened for the jarring word, the shading of the eyes, the discord of a phrase. It became clear by slow revelations that he had not been, as he maintained, at the riverbank on that fate-filled day inspecting fish traps for his lord. He was there in some way profiting from an exchange. Inveigling gullible peasants onto a waiting galley? A shameful commerce he no doubt had a decade to rue. To consider the workings of God's justice, which had steered the hand of the pirate to take him on-board also and keep the fee promised him. I felt some small victory that night, accepting this truth, and it gave me a secret power over him. A power which emboldened me to say what I had wanted to say for so long.

'And where was Mother in all of this?'

He looked up from the rough, wooden bowl, and his hollow eyes shone dark with a lustre of anger. The intensity of that stare stripped me of any illusion of power.

'She was already on the boat', he said. His eyes filling along the brim as he stared at me, his face betrayed and furious. It had been so long since I had seen him react with passion to anything that a tremor ran across my shoulders. But those slim words, illuminating in their scarce brevity a hundred things I had yearned to know, brought warmth also. She had been there all along. In that scene I had visited a hundred times. Her face shaded, sitting on the boat. She was not a Gael, then, but a Saxon, or Norman—Engleis. She had crossed the sea with him. And this revelation forced me onwards, recklessly pushing for more.

'She was a stranger to you then?' I pressed, and I saw everything move slowly, unreal in its ferocity. The bowl flew from his hand, spilling porridge, before clattering against a roof post, his eyes and face growing suddenly bigger as his unfurling legs propelled him towards me. His fist closed on my temple, and the first blow sent my head backwards to crack against the boards. He was on me then, with two more punches falling before a blackness descended.

When I came to, the sharp iron scale taste of blood in my throat, the small space vibrating with his cries. He howled and howled with his face shoved deep into a mound of straw bedding so that the sound came out like the fury of a storm invading the thatch above us as his fist landed shuddering blows onto the damp plank floor.

I sat up with ringing in my head and a sick feeling in my stomach. I crawled over to his bowl and saved what oats I could. Lifting his small wooden spoon from the floor, I set this across the bowl and placed them both on the edge of the millstone. I curled into my own bedding to think about Mother, knowing that the worst was over.

CHAPTER 6

Immána

CONN SOUGHT ME OUT the next morning, his gaming stick in hand and a determination in his regard which spoke danger. He smiled coldly when he saw my face, inset with a blackened eye. Father watched me go with his mouth a grim line on his silent face. We went to the long meadow by the river, Conn stalking ahead, the roll of his shoulders communicating his displeasure. Fiacra was there when we arrived, and the kennel master's sons and some noble youths of the household—Conn's cousins and younger brothers. All had their sticks for *immána*.

Fiacra drove the tightly woven ball of horsehair out long across the grass, and we contested it between us, taking a line, slamming shoulder to shoulder. The blows were hard and Conn's strikes went wild, cracking off my thighs and ankles. Fiacra read this as permission and scourged me with his stick at every opportunity, hissing out curses beneath his breath.

'Unholy lump. Wicked leavings. Devil stool'.

I had more strength in my frame and could take the hardest knocks—the pain entering into a different part of me, a straw-filled part where agonies are absorbed, a part unique to the slave. Conn

43

was fastest and had the finest flourish with the ball at the end of his stick, sending it this way and that with complex turns of his wrist and clenching of fingers on the haft. More than once, I was sent tumbling into the tussocks of grass.

'Up *ollamh*', he said striking the ground hard by my head, his stick biting deep into the black soil. 'Up, Sméar, and show your worth'.

As the sun rose, a warmth crept into the day despite the lateness of the month, shining through brittle leaves. We stripped to our waists and played on until our faces were flushed, bodies slick and the strength gone out of our arms.

Fiacra came up with the donkey then, and they had some sport on it. I held back, unwilling to give him more opportunity to bait me. I watched from beneath a blackthorn tree as they climbed on in turn, gripping the coarse hair in fistfuls as others lashed the poor beast along the flanks with briars as it kicked and bucked, sending bodies careening into the grass. They went on at it until hoarse from laughing and too bruised to do more. The donkey forgot its troubles just as soon, nosing in the dock leaves nearby.

After this we stripped and swam in the river, dipping our heads into its cool waters, its placid bulk seeking to carry us away downstream. Away towards the great river Bóinne and on to the sea, and as ever, I felt compelled to let it take me, to ferry me past the Tiarna's house, onwards over territories increasingly distant. Beyond our *túath* towards the monastery at Baile Átha Troim, along the way to Sláine of the Gaelienga and then to enter that strange land of Aengus Óg and the Brú na Bóinne, where the great mounds of the *sídhe* stand guard on the banks, and beyond again past the Bridge of the Ford to the sea. The sea that neither I nor Conn had set our eyes upon. Father described it as an immense heaving body of deep green which no man could fathom the bottom of. A body of water so large that it took four full days to cross if the wind was onside. We spoke often of sailing on it, over the depths hiding untold serpents, leviathans and strange fish with the faces of men. Back to Chester Shire, to a free life and the land he owned there.

I lay back in the water, feeling the river's pull, lost in these dreams with my toe hooked into a willow root. I lay still so that sprat swam beneath me, breaking the water at times, safe in my shadow from stalking herons. Conn stood among the reeds in the nearby shallows. He cupped water in his hands and liberated it over his face and shoulders, and I watched it rilling down his long body. And if it were another day, I may have judged it right to shout out with a taunt, to call him in to the deeper water and name him coward with a smile on my lips. But today was not a day for levity with him. I had intruded into his world. I had seen him on the floor at children's games as I stood in the sphere of the Tiarna, trading words of weight and provocation as he watched in bitter awe from the shadows. My shins and shoulders bore the swelling welts of his displeasure, and it was for me now to play contrite.

I unhooked my toe and swam in to the edge, setting my back to the land, looking over the water. He came close and sat on the bank, his legs sliding into the water beside me. His thigh rested against my shoulder in an act of familiarity.

'*A thiarna*', I said, unable to banish the sullenness from my voice as I kneaded my bruised knuckles. He ignored my formality and came finally to the point he had been making all morning with his stick.

'You should have come to me with word of that poet. I would have brought it to Father and we both would have benefitted'. I remained silent, and he spoke some more.

'You believe yourself to be intelligent. But your thoughts are there to be read in your every move. Every veiled look, every feeble scheme and sleight of hand. It is tolerated because of your father and his favour with the Tiarna. Not, as you may imagine, because you have earned some respect here, or because the monk is protecting you. That monk will do nothing, Alberagh, no finger will he lift to better your station, and if you run away to a life in a monastery, your lot will change little from what it is now—less ball, perhaps, and more prayer'.

He draped his arm over my bare shoulder. I had begun to shiver, the cold settling in.

'I am your route to a better standing in this life, not my father. He will treat you as a curiosity and he will laugh about his pet Sasanach who speaks tongues and shovels shit'.

His hand searched out my chin and directed my head up to his. He spoke softly, 'I and I alone am your way forward'. He let my face drop, and I climbed out onto the grass, pulling my ragged *brat* over my body.

'I am to be fostered', he said to my back, and that news fell like a stone into a pool. We had both begun to believe that he would not be sent away. It is their most ancient custom that a lord will foster his son to another to promote peace and alliance. Though not always, it was usual for the fosterling to be six or seven. Conn had grown old.

'I am to go to Tigernán Ua Ruairc', and even as he spoke the name, I began to seek out the route of the Tiarna's thinking—the grain of his strategy. Where would alliance with Ua Ruairc bring advantage, and against whom?

'When do you go?' I asked, and he rolled into the grass beside me, pulling part of my *brat* over his chest so that we both lay there gazing at the white sky, naked beneath the thin weave of my garment.

'Soon', he said. 'I will need you to represent my interests here and keep watch over my young brothers and those cousins who would make a place for themselves in the nest that I must leave'.

He spoke to me as confidant, as lieutenant, and I weighed the moment.

'And you would offer me what exactly, Conn, for my loyalty?'

He laughed to the sky and reached his arm and slid it beneath me so that my head settled on the crook of his elbow. He drew me across to him, his arm clenching so that I was pinned to his breast, his muscles tightening on my neck.

'Have you had dreams, Alberagh? Dreams of women? Dreams of being a bull in a field of cows? Have you woken in the night with a pain and a hunger that is like a fire all over?'

'I have not', I said, although I knew well of what he was speaking. He squeezed tighter, until I could barely breathe, and he whispered into my ear.

'Liar'. I felt blood pounding in my head, and white points of light appeared around the edge of my vision. And then he laughed and relaxed his grip.

'Always asking for more, Sméar', he said. 'Not enough that I show you this favour'.

'One who is unfree must be bold. Or be broken', I said to him, my head on his breast.

'Be my man here', he said, 'and when I return and take up my father's house, you will be a free man, a man of my household. We will keep counsel and expand our power and capture cattle and take hostages from north, east and west. We will spend evenings at *fidchell* and other games of the mind, surrounded by food and drink and good hounds and a fire stacked high'.

As he spoke, his free arm came down along my side, down my thigh, and he turned his body to me completely, still gripping my neck so that my face was buried in the cold and firm flesh of his chest. We lay that way for a time, hidden in the riverside grass as Fiacra hunted for frogs beneath the undercut banks in the slow backwaters of the river and the others, farther upstream, competed, pitching stones as far as they could into the water.

We must have dozed for a time, for we were roused suddenly with Fiacra shouting from the top of the field.

'Lochru is coming'.

When we saw him arrive, riding hard on an old *gearrán*, we knew that the moment had come. We stood up and threw on our shirts, jumping and whooping as we ran through the meadow towards him, the others following close behind. He was breathless when we reached him, his face lit with vigour.

'Now crows will drink a cruel milk', he proclaimed, the mad smile raging on one side of his face only. 'The cattle calm upon the plain. Áed Buidhe has brought his cows down from the summer pastures and they are gathered in his meadows'. Fiacra and the others crowded around with their hands on our shoulders, jumping and shouting out wordless exclamations of excitement. It was the first raid any of us had been old enough to participate in.

'The master has called the *táin*', Lochru said to them, bubbling with the news. 'We leave within the hour and will travel across friendly territory for the remainder of the daylight, passing into the lands of our enemies by dusk. We will cross their lands in darkness and lay our ambush for the first light of the morning. Speed now on your young legs, back to his house, and help with the preparations. *A thiarna*, you go ahead'.

He slid off the horse, cupping its chin in his hand, as I bent to make a cradle for Conn's foot. He jumped up, grabbing the beast's mane, and pointed him towards the household, the tired run of the horse somewhat comical as he strained forward on its back, full of visions of glory.

When we reached the compound, all of the Tiarna's household men and fosterlings were there in great tumult, singing scraps of songs and shouting emboldening words from heroic verses and calling out things like 'Where is mighty Finn?' to which others would call out 'He is ready to lead', pointing all at once to the Tiarna on his horse, where he sat in his quilted jacket, and 'Where is mighty Coillte, whose speed is without peer?' and they would point to another warrior similarly arrayed. And so, the mood was set.

We ran in to help where we could, loading the packhorses and feeding the mounts horse bread for the journey as the pageant continued.

'And where is Oisín, the son, strong gifted warrior out to prove his arm?' They all roared 'Here he is' as Conn emerged from the house, an outsized quilted coat bolted to him with a leather vest, his shoulders thrown back and an axe in his grip. They went on like this as the warriors tied their gear to the woven matting that served them for saddles. And the roaring and shouting continued with a crowd coming in through the open gates. The labourers and the women and small children running around like hares with excitement. Donchad shouted above the noise, 'And this the axe to give Áed Buidhe a shave!'

Erc, not to be outdone, roared louder, 'Here the spear to give him a new navel', and other voices took up the boasting.

'Look on the *scian* that will bring back a head'.

'And here is the horse that will drive the herd'.

It was difficult for me to know if this was a spontaneous outcry or if some ancient rite was being observed. I watched to see if their calls followed an order of rank or position, but after a time I was caught up with the tasks at hand, helping charge the horses and lash javelins into braces. And suddenly it was over and the Tiarna was leading his men out the gate, the *kelt* hanging at his neck, Tuar by his right side, followed by the cheering crowd.

I walked along at first with the rest of the children and the straggling crowd, afraid that the Tiarna would forget his promise. And then Donchad grabbed me up by the *brat* and I climbed up onto the rear of his horse, pressing myself against his back and gripping his garment.

'Take a seat, lad, there will be time for walking yet', he said, and I could see that Fiacra and a number of the other youths were being similarly caught up, riding with Erc and other men of the household, looking around in awe. I suddenly felt ill prepared, with no spear or weapon of my own and nothing between me and the blades of an enemy except a threadbare cloak.

The songs and shouting continued as we passed the nearby farmsteads of the Tiarna's brother and cousins and brother's widow and men filed out slowly on their best horses, shouting greetings and boasts until we were a host of three dozen horse, though many rode double. These were the freemen and lower nobles, the pride of the *túath*, with the Tiarna at the head, his eyes steel grey and hungry.

Before the crossing of the deep ditches that marked the northern limit of the *túath*, we descended into a dell fringed with venerable overhanging oak and ash, the floor a carpet of spent husks. In the centre of the dell, a solitary hawthorn bush stood fluttering with scraps of fabric tied to its branches, and beneath, a spring of cool water pooled in a deep well before trickling away through a narrow cleft. The Tiarna dismounted and, muttering a prayer, tore a strip from the hem of his garment and tied it to the bush. He dipped his palm into the well and drank. He stooped to a large flat stone that had two deep depressions within it. These marked the spot where St Lasair had knelt when she had first come to this land to teach the heathens of God. With the weight of His message, her knees had sunk into the solid rock. The Tiarna dipped his fingers into the depression and blessed himself. He raised his voice so that all could hear.

'Bless us, Lasair of the ewe. Lasair, daughter of ready Ronin, bless us, holy woman, great and noble, and bless our purpose'. The men crowded the bush, tying strips and repeating the Tiarna's actions until the dell hummed with half-uttered prayer. I came forward among the last and bent, pressing low into the bush to find a place to tie my scrap of *brat*. From a projecting thorn, a narrow slip of embroidered cuff fluttered in front of me, its weave so tiny and precise, its design so lavish, that, God forgive me, I reached out and snapped the twig upon which it hung, palming it as I emerged from the tangle of thorn. I secured the piece of fabric behind my belt. I drank from the well, dipped my fingers in the pool and prayed my own prayer.

'Do not be displeased, Lasair, I beg. But rather guide my steps so that I may honour you in my actions. I take this prayer from your tree to ward against the hand of the *sídhe*'.

When all had done, we mounted the horses and continued through the gap in the ditches, onwards to the fording place, leaving our *túath* behind. The calls and singing had stopped, replaced with a restrained anticipation, and as we passed from a place of safety into the world beyond, the bright clatter of hooves off the river cobbles sounded on the air like the music of a many-stringed harp.

CHAPTER 7
Táin

THE GROUND CHANGED as we travelled northwards, sudden ridges rising up like ripples on a pond. We followed a small *bóthar*—no more than a cow trail—around the base of the hills, some wooded and some crowned with small forts from where the people watched, withdrawing when they saw us. We passed quicker and quieter and they knew by our faces, black with intent, that we were fixed on something farther on. Donchad knew the way, though even with his knowledge, the hills closed in around us, and it was difficult to tell one vale from the next with the woodland and hawthorn scratching close.

We stopped before dusk, setting our tents in the lee of a hill beside a small lake. As the camp settled, Donchad climbed to the summit. I followed with Conn and we looked across this strange land. Hills everywhere and bogs in between and small, clear lakes collected in the hollows like dew caught in upturned leaves. Thin spindles of smoke rising here and there from unseen houses. The hills low and shaded, the breeze agitating the grass and scrub away into the distance, giving the whole the impression of movement, like a massive herd of long-backed swine all rooting along together towards the northwest.

We lay on our bellies in the grass, and darkness fell as we watched Donchad holding up his opened hand, sighting through his fingers, counting off fading features on the landscape, finding his bearing. Such a wide land. So many *túatha* and so many shadows to hide unfriendly hosts.

'We will scour this place of our enemies, leave them ruined', said Conn.

Donchad laughed lightly at this febrile energy, Conn's raw fear showing through. He turned over in the grass, looking at us both.

'You sound like your father', he said to Conn, settling into the turf, hands behind his head. 'Many years ago, when we were not much older than you, we joined a great hosting and raided deep down into Leith Moga, as far south as Osraige, thousands fleeing before us. Mac Murchada rode with us at the head of the men of Laighin. The men of Mumán came against us and the Tiarna led us on. All about, men on the battlefield fought and heroes came out to challenge each other. The Tiarna clashed with the son of Muircetach Ua Bríain, fighting with swords on horseback, until they fell to the sod. They fought on, and not a man came between them. Not a javelin cast from either side. And in the end, when they could barely lift their arms, our Tiarna slid his blade in behind Ua Bríain's knee, cutting the tendons. Mac Murchada came on then, lauding our Tiarna, and went to move past him, to claim Ua Bríain as prize. He was a towering figure in the fullness of his manhood, yet your father stood against him, breast to breast, until the Rí of the Laighin relented. Your father blinded Ua Bríain and sent him back to Mumán in ruins. Such was the power of Míde in those days. "Wellspring of generosity", it was said, "and great hospitality, abounding with enlivening food and repose with music and ale feasting by every hearth"'.

Donchad fell silent, carried off in the flow of his memory, chewing on a stalk and gazing at the sky. Then, remembering himself, he sat up, looking to us both with smiling eyes. 'Yes, those were times—and us not much bigger than you two *ciaróga*'.

We stood and walked down the hill, Conn ahead, moving with purpose, his shoulders back, breaths of the darkening sky in his lungs and his head full of the glory to come. I walked behind with Donchad.

'What will I fight with?' I asked.

'Don't worry, lad', Donchad said gently. 'You keep the javelins coming to the hands of the warriors. Keep the horses settled if the men close on foot. Keep an eye on the treeline and the hilltop for surprises and you'll have an equal share in whatever renown we win'. He nudged me with his powerful shoulder. 'There may even be women', he said, laughing.

We moved before sunrise, silently and swiftly breaking camp. We pushed on beneath uncertain moonlight, the *bóthar* widening out to a more substantial roadway—becoming a *slíghe*. The lightly armed scouts they call *kern* padded the hills on each side, calling down softly at times. I rode behind Donchad at the head, and at some invisible sign or landmark, he held up his hand, stopping the host, and led us off the *slíghe* and into the treeline. I could not imagine what he could read in the darkened surroundings that prompted him to move with such confidence. I began to feel fear. What if he had missed his path? What if he had sold the party over to ambush for the grant of a *ráth* and a woman somewhere in these hills? The darkness began to take shape around us. Donchad's broad back ahead of me. Shadows in my eyes. Shades coming across the greyness. We pushed through branches which trailed us like the fleshless fingers of crones. We came to a wide, untended ditch and crossed over where the bank had collapsed into the bottom, green grown with bramble and nettle. *Kern* ranged out, making sure none guarded the border of the *túath*. Through the thinning trees, a blue-grey sky appeared, and as we approached the eaves of the wood, we saw a sloping meadow running down to a stream and, beyond, emerging from the mist, the *ráth* of Áed Buidhe.

The Tiarna rode up and Donchad dismounted. Shielding themselves behind a large stump, they spoke in low tones, pointing down over the scene below, towards the outer stockade around the *ráth*. This was where the herd could be seen, shifting and lowing, brought in for the night against the depredations of wolves or raiders. My eyes strayed back to the stump to find the Tiarna and Donchad both looking towards me. The Tiarna called me over with a motion of his hand. I slid from the warm back of the horse, handing its tether to the man beside me, and approached. The Tiarna sat back into the bole of the tree where the heartwood had been eaten away by louse and fungus and took both my hands in his. He spoke softly, his voice full of assurance.

'Now, young *kelt*-bringer', he said, smiling, 'I have another thing to ask of you, and this, to one who has challenged the *sídhe* in their own house, will be a thing of no consequence'.

'We need you to open the gate', Donchad said, bringing me around to the edge of the stump and pointing to the wooden doors set between thick posts with a watch-house rising above—a dark square space beneath its awning of thatch, impenetrable in the pre-dawn. He pressed something into my hand, and looking down, I saw it was a long-bladed knife, the length of a forearm, the type they call the *scian mór*. 'Go now, do not think on it. Move before the light strips the shadows from the valley. Run low and straight, and do not fear. If the alarm is raised, run to the river. We will be thick around you before the household can drag their fat bellies from their beds'.

He laid his large hands on my shoulders and guided me out into the open and, before I could protest, pushed me gently forward. The hillside took me then, momentum dragging me forward until I was running, clear of the trees, through the meadow grass and onwards towards the *tóchar*. I ran faster, and faster still, until I was running simply to keep upright, the stream approaching fast. The pounding of my feet, the pounding of my heart, echoing like an army of tree fellers in a valley, and I watched the blackness beneath the awning of the guard turret, watched for movement, for a shout, for an arm rising to strike a bell.

As the slope bottomed out, I missed a step and fell, tumbling violently. I lay still for a moment, amidst the stalks of meadow grass, brushed with their moisture, smelling their greenness and listening. A waking dove cooed in the trees, the imperative sound carrying far. No hint of movement in the treeline, though I knew they all watched, too tense to speak. I crawled forward, staying low, and, reaching the stream, I slid down the side of the bank and moved upstream towards the *tóchar*, the water fast and lively beneath me, masking the sound of my passing. Beneath the *tóchar*, I climbed across the underside, grabbing the beam with my hands and hooking my ankles over. I dropped into the moss and leaf litter on the far side and pushed up the bank on my front, peering through the sparse branches of a blackthorn.

The palisade stood not fifty paces from me, its circuit built of roughly split beams set into the earth of a bank raised up over a ditch. I studied, in the waxing light, the set of each beam on the stretch closest to me. I looked for the uneven line of one against the other that might afford a handhold in their imperfect join. A cock crowed from within, and this spurred me onwards. I stood out from the bush, hunched over, ready to run for the palisade. And to my left, not four paces away, a girl stood. A woman. Lithe, pale, beautiful beyond propriety. I had not seen her, shaded by the rail of the *tóchar*, and at once, I realised that the dove cooing with strange insistence had been Donchad from the trees, warning me of the danger.

She did not move, standing tall with her garment hanging, brushing the ground. Her bare feet planted in the grass. Her hair, the blue-black of a raven in sunlight and a basket on her hip. She did not move, and I raised my hand slowly, as if to a skittish colt.

'Áil a n-uír', she said with an unnerving clam—a stone from the earth. Her words unmasking me. Her curling lip and dark eyes stripping me. I shrank back into the thorn bush, feeling naked and exposed. The blackness beneath the awning of the guard tower glared from over her shoulder, sharing her disdain.

'Please', I said, bringing my hand to my mouth, gesturing silence.

Her eyes scanned the valley then, probing the margins, looking for more like me. Considering whether to raise her voice. My life in the balance. And then she took a step forward, onto the board of the *tóchar*. And as she went, she spoke over her shoulder in a low voice, as if recounting something of little consequence.

'The gate is unbarred. The spears sleeping'. She walked on, and I watched her crossing the stream and turning to follow its margins, looking through the growing shrubs, sorting their lolling heads as a kennel master sorts the hounds.

To trust her word and run to the gate? Into a javelin hurled at my breast? The cock crowing once again, the rooks in the trees beyond waking, the crake of their voices tearing the soft fabric of the moment. Lifting Lasair's embroidered strip from its place beneath my belt, I put it to my lips, invoking her protection.

I looked back to the darkened treeline, beckoning Donchad forward with my arms, and ran on, hunched low, towards the gate and whatever might come. No shouts rose up, no javelins rained down, and I pressed myself flat to the heavy oak doors, invisible from the tower above. I put my shoulder against one to find that the bar had indeed been raised. I eased the gate inwards, taking the *scian* from its sheath, slipping into the space between. The yard was open, a broad space with few buildings. A second gate beyond, it, too, with a watchtower. I slammed myself back into the palisade, out of view. Hens scratched around in the dusty light, and behind a rough stockade of lengths of roundwood, the herd jostled and steamed in the morning chill.

Looking back through the gap in the gate, I saw movement in the woods, riders nosing out onto the slope. Looking to the watchtower on the inner gate, I caught some movement, heard distant voices and saw a guard with a turned back, speaking down to someone in the inner yard beyond. I slipped out and put my back to the gate, pushing the door slowly inward, my feet scrabbling for purchase on the dew-slick ground. Dogs began barking from somewhere within, and nervous grunts rose from amongst the cattle. I moved to the second door and, setting my back once more, began to push it inwards. And the alarm went up. Looking back to the inner watchtower, I saw the guard perched over the rail, shouting to me in challenge. I waved up to him casually and shouted back vaguely, words of pasture and fodder, pointing to the cows.

'Wake yourself, Aodán', the guard roared out, and from above in the tower over my head, a face looked down, eyes puffed with sleep. I heard the distant drum of hooves and looked to the slope behind me and saw the Tiarna's host descending, racing towards the *tóchar*. The vision of their approach filled me with a wild energy, an empowering flush of blood beating through me. I crouched low behind the door at the sound of feet descending the steps from above. Voices and shouting from the inner gate, which opened now, men and dogs spilling through. I judged the sound of Aodán's approach and sprang from behind the door, launching myself forward with the *scian* out before me. Aodán rounded the open gate a moment too late, my blow missing his chest, rising instead and shearing through his cheek as I rammed into him, barrelling him over onto the stony muck of the yard. I rolled and came up as he howled, clutching his face, giving me the instant I needed to fall on him, digging my blade into his exposed breast. An inexpert strike, and the knife turned awkwardly on his breastbone, sinking into him in a direction I had not intended. Aodán stopped moving instantly, though I could not liberate the blade easily from his body, the others bearing down on me, the red-mouthed dogs at their head. Stooping, I grabbed Aodán's spear and ran towards the open gate, seeing Donchad charging up the slope from the stream, Erc close behind and the rest of the host strung out beyond. A javelin bit into the ground by my heel; I could hear the dogs closing. I feinted, then turned, bringing the spear level as the lead dog leapt, catching it in the breast, piercing its lungs as the others swarmed over me. I thrashed and flailed as their jaws sought purchase, gripping and shaking my *léine*, tearing and snapping.

'Help, help', I shouted as Donchad's horse drew level, spurring on past me into the compound to close with Áed Buidhe's men. I kicked away one of the hounds just as the other bit, sinking its teeth into my shielding forearm and shaking its muscular head. I roared in pain, punching with my free hand and rolling backwards down into the ditch, separating from the hound in the fall. It leapt up, unsettled in the narrow, slop-filled channel, out of view of its master. I stove its head in with a log as it scrabbled at the loose sides, and when I climbed out, the day was won, Áed Buidhe's men having fled back to the inner enclosure, flung javelins from the ramparts to little effect. Our men were already driving the cattle from the stockade.

I stood by the gate, pressing a wad of torn wool into the puckered holes in my arm, dutifully hooshing the cattle on as they came out of the opening, their eyes frantic, nostrils flaring. Conn came out with a spear raised high, riding past me tapping at the beasts' flanks, a wild light on his face. It was Tuar who pulled up his horse and reached his hand down to me.

We overtook the girl in the meadow and carried her off with the oxen. She was standing mute by the stream, wavering, perhaps, between running and standing still. Her form, slim and bright, against the streaming nets of dewed spider webs on the furze. She did not fight. Or call out as Donchad lifted her from the spot. She accepted the happening and offered no rigidity to the wave as it broke around her. No overwrought keening or tearing her face in front of Donchad on his horse. She went into the unknown, towards possible violence and hardship. And I have to conclude that she was not leaving anything better.

They caught us at a fording place some miles distant as we tried to keep the herd together, urging the cattle across the knee-deep water. Áed Buidhe himself came at the head of his household, emboldened by rage. They pulled up before reaching us, probing our numbers. We kept them off with javelins, and Conn at the head of five men sprang from the woods uphill where they had been hiding, anticipating pursuit. Conn struck a warrior with an overhead blow of his axe, and the man slumped on his horse. Two others fell to javelins. They pulled back in commotion, and we drove the herd on through the waters. We lost a good many strays who fled up the riverbank, but we were hurried in our work, knowing that Áed Buidhe's messengers would be raising the *túath* against us. None knew of the insult Áed had born the Tiarna, but the raid had wounded deep. Winter would be hungry. Winter would be hard. Not even his beasts of burden would be spared the pot, and that would bring its own terrible hardship in the warming spring.

Once across the ford, we worked hard to herd the beasts together and drove them through the morning. Every time we passed a farmstead, the local youths came at us, dancing their horses around our flanks, yelping and whooping and shouting distracting words— praise and insult—looking for an easy prize, sensing a temporary breakdown in the order of things. They worried the odd beast free, driving one off into the woods or one into the bog. A great spoil for a young man. Erc wanted to chase them down. To burn their homes. But we had not the time to leave the herd, Donchad calling us ever on from the front, reminding us of the dangers.

When finally we saw the great ditch that signalled the edge of our *túath* worming across a nearby hill, we all cried out in joy, laughing, intoxicated in the midst of the hot herding work. And when we crossed that boundary, all of our voices were raised with triumphant shouts, with thanks to God and Lasair and a host of the saints, with wordless howls of victory, and in this flush, I cried out in exaltation, the Latin words Aeneas spoke leaping unbidden from my mouth.

'Fire rages in my heart with the impulse to avenge my land, and to inflict a toll upon her enemies'.

Tuar at my back and the Tiarna who rode close broke into immense laughter that could not be stopped.

'The vagabond Virgil', Tuar cried, the Tiarna riding close and tousling my head as Conn looked on darkly, not knowing the Latin nor of Virgil or Aeneas at all, lacking the imagination to see beyond the oak wood and river, the long pasture and the gaming field. Lacking the sight to imagine the sea, let alone what might lie beyond. And after some careful searching in his memory, Tuar called out to the Tiarna, more words from Virgil in jest, though I took great pride in what he said.

'From foreign shores a son should come, who, mingling race with ours, shall lift our name to starry heights'.

They laughed uncontrollably as we rode steadily through friendly lands, each man calling out and praising the others, the cattle running before us along good tracks, growing less flighty.

Through all of this, the girl was silent. We drove the cattle to an empty paddock on the edge of the Tiarna's manor and closed them in with cut brushwood, and all waited on the masters' judgement and benefice. He called for his *récire* and harper. He sent ahead to his house, calling for a cask of wine and for the women to come down. He sat up on an old cart with Tuar on his right side while Tuar stood and shouted congratulations, singing praise to the Tiarna and to his men. The *récire* stood then and began to recite verses whispered to him by Tuar, annunciating in their dramatic way. These were words that had been formed in the quick pulse of the *ollamh*'s mind on the journey from the ford, words poured into the strict shape of their verse like running lead filling a mould. Beneath the rhythm of the words, the harp wended in gentle, unexpected ways.

During all this, Donchad began the tally and confirmed what we knew—three score seven beasts. The Tiarna rose then and began to call upon each man in turn, the *récire* repeating a word of praise for each, and bestowed gifts of cattle. Once all of this was done, and Lochru and some of the horse-boys had arrived from the farmstead with wine in a donkey cart, Erc approached the Tiarna, leading the girl forward.

'And for you, *a thiarna*', he said, bowing and edging her forward, his hands on her hips, 'for your household'.

Mánus Máel Sechlainn drained a horn of wine, looking down upon the girl, his expression difficult to read.

'I am no advocate of slavery, girl', he said, looking around at the men who had fallen silent, 'though a gift given must be received'. He drained another horn of wine, slid from his perch on the cart and extended his hand to the girl. 'First, a conference to learn what she knows of our enemies', he announced loudly with a performative flourish and led the girl towards a broken byre at the back of the enclosure. The men erupted in laughter, and I felt a sudden flood of hatred for his eager, foolish face, hurrying towards the tumble-down shed lacking even the nobility to walk slowly. He emerged soon after stretching upwards and regarding the open blue of the sky. Wiping sour wine from his mouth, he cried out like a brute and the men cheered, and, in that moment, taken with a sudden intoxication, he made a pronouncement that was to cause me much lasting pain.

'And what of our poet Virgil? Our *kelt*-bringer? Our stained *síofra*? The one who opened the gate for us and was chewed on by Áed Buidhe's hounds? Does he not deserve to bathe in the spoils?'

They all cheered, laughing, those that were close, pounding down on my shoulders. They knew there were women coming. That there would be more wine. They were happy with this magnanimous jest. All but Conn, who saw through the heady vapours to the right of the matter. The insult to him that a slave should sow seed in place of a lord.

I was caught up and pushed through the warm, jostling bodies of the cattle with a rising clamour from the men that peaked in a shatter of vulgar laughter. They shoved me into the byre, crowding the opening, coarse laughter and lewd sayings filling up the dim space inside.

She lay sideways on the heaped fodder, her hair in strands falling over her cheek, shielding her eye. The rough soles of her feet on display. Her robe settled within the deep curve of her hip. I will not say that my first thoughts were noble.

Erc shouted from behind, 'He doesn't know what to do, lads!'
He pushed forward and caught the back of my neck in his wide
hand, pushing me to my knees and burying my face in the vague
location of her pubis. 'What you want is in there, Virgir', he cried,
showing his ignorance, and he left, closing the door violently, and
I could hear his mockery continuing outside.

I moved towards her with a warm blush in my groin. She rolled
on her back and looked up at me standing there, spurred on by
shame and held back by fear. Her face was blank. High colour in
her cheeks. Some years older than me. She motioned for me to sit.

'What is your name?' I asked her after a time.

'Ness', she said, and did not ask for mine.

'Why did you not shout when you saw me at the *tóchar*?' I asked.
When at last she did speak, it was with the contorted vowels of a
northerner, akin to the tongue of Alba.

'You appeared from the ground, sprang up before me, your face
stained, and I could see that you had been touched'. She reached
out and traced around the shape, her fingers following the dappled
line from the hollow of my nose across the ridge of my cheek, in
and out before she held her fingers flat to my skin, trying to mirror
the shape.

'Like a hand, or a wing. A grey deer before spring. A shroud of
sorrows. Howling on every face'. I drew back, confused, frightened
by her words, which struck, sending a low vibration through me,
touching some memory. 'I saw that you might strike at that place,
that blade-bristling fort. A spear upon a shield'.

'And why did you not flee', I asked, 'instead of trailing in the
meadow?'

'Did you never yearn for change, Sasanach?' she said, her cool
palm still pressed against my face. 'Great *kelt*-bringer, shape-shifter?'
She laughed then, laughed at my confusion, and I strove to know
her, to cut through the mist she wound about herself.

'Are you hurt? Was the Tiarna rough with you?'

Her hand fell away from my cheek.

'He did not touch me', she said, her eye falling to the ground.
Rather, he asked me about Áed Buidhe and his household. He
said that the men's passions were stirred outside and that to save
me from any misdeed, he would send a boy in. A lamb. One who

would do me no harm until the women arrived and I would be safe'. My face burned with shame.

Sitting up straight, she leaned towards me.

'Sometimes', she said, 'the lamb is more noble than the wolf'. She spat on her palm and, reaching beneath my *léine,* took my *gléas* in her hand, her touch almost unbearable. Her hand moved gently then, fingers clenching, her eyes searching my face. And I could not bear it. My seed leapt free, like a salmon breaching, spilling up her wrist and across the backs of her fingers. I fell forward into the fodder, and she wiped her hand in the straw, her fingers coming up studded with chaff. She lay beside me and kept herself secret beneath the strands of her hair.

'Stay a while more', she said, 'and then go out and say you did what they told you. Tell them that I cried'. We lay there, still, breathing. The byre sanctuary, and us momentarily oblivious to the wild sounds beyond the door. In the silence, my heart said no, I will not go. I will stay forever and there will be no tears. I will stand over you here forever and take raining blows and weapon strikes to protect you and keep you safe. I will free you. I will free you. And in the end, I stood, with no word to say, and went out and did as she had told me.

That evening we rode across the Tiarna's lands, driving the spoil of cattle in great procession. At the head, the Tiarna and his men clung to their mounts, falling drunk and gesturing like returning Caesars while the people of the farmsteads came out to applaud and hail and sing their joy. The praise amplified as the Tiarna bestowed each household with a plundered beast. I came at the rear, walking behind, forgotten trying to keep sight of Ness where she walked with Mór and the other women around her. Trying to gauge her welcome.

The cattle were tired now, plodding and offering little resistance as we striped their flanks with long rods of hazel. At Lasair's well, we turned uphill along the ditch and my heart sank, seeing that we were bound for the monastery. Riders spurred on ahead to give the Abbot warning. The fields were quiet as we approached, the Tiarna driving his cattle across the sown winter fields, the passage of hooves and feet churning the dark soil, crushing the rills, picking out and turning up the bright seed.

The old Abbot was at the gate, his welcome as thin as the smile on his face. Milesius fumed in the background as the Tiarna rode up to the gate, and I held back for fear of the venom in my mentor's eye. I could not hear the words, though I could read well enough the movements of the men. The Tiarna in his cups, loquacious and overbearing with his generosity. The Abbot thanking him as seven heads of cattle were corralled aside and taken in hand by a group of lay brothers appearing from the shadow of the gateway.

A bounty worth bearing. Worth the loss of saved grain. Worth the wasted hours of broad casting seed into the receiving earth, broken and turned by the sweat of the men. I knew exactly what Milesius would say—that it was a thing to shame the saints, to see plunder taken in violence valued more than the honest labour of a man's back.

We turned towards home, and the fierceness of the low sun blinded us from above the woods, adding a final touch of the unreal to the day. Following the long wakeful hours of the *táin*, tiredness threatened to overwhelm me on that last push across the outer meadows, shapes suggesting themselves in the corners of my vision.

Word had been sent ahead to the Tiarna's house, and billows of smoke and steam rose into the massive arch of the evening sky. The entire farmstead was arrayed there, waiting dutifully, crying out and singing victory.

When we arrived at the compound, we could see that a huge feast had been prepared, and a steam laden with the smell of broth and meat and bread escaped through the doorway. The Tiarna entered first, and Tuar ushered all inside. The house was scarcely able to accommodate us all, and yet the women and the servants poured in, pushing through the crowd trying to carry in food and ale. A large board had been set out and the Tiarna's benches arrayed around the edges of the house draped with furs and linens. Feasting began immediately with the Tiarna and the warriors still in their quilted coats. Regardless of the boisterous mood and the drunken state of many of the men, etiquette was observed without deviation as to who sits at the Tiarna's right hand, who at his left, who beyond that and who can eat a morsel before who and drink from which vessel. A fire burned high in the hearth, and those standing by were singed by its flame. The merriment and celebration were widespread as the tales of the *táin* were recounted through mouths full of meat. I stood by the door, ravenous and waiting for something to pass my way.

The storytelling became increasingly loud as Erc proved to have the strongest voice, which carried over all and commanded attention. He was recounting how we had gathered the cattle, and I heard my name spoken. Suddenly the Tiarna cried out, 'Where is my Virgil of the North? Where is that purple Saxon?' and it was clear from his voice that he was very inebriated.

Donchad and even Conn cheered in an irresistible upsurge of mirth. They gripped me and propelled me forward along the benches, and among the blur I caught sight of Father's face in the crowd as he laboured to keep the tapers lit and the firewood in and the ale flowing. His expression a pale gulf within the feverous celebration. A kind of sad pride hung on his face. It seared me, this look, and I can see it still through the veil of years, haunting me with its foreknowledge. He saw the danger that I could not, the danger in the novelty of a lord's regard.

I was passed up by the fire, crowded hounds nipping in the chaos and the blaze of the fire illuminating a red press of faces.

'A verse from you, boy! A verse!'

And the hall erupted in the unquenchable turmoil of the drunkard, and they chanted loudly 'a verse, a verse', and nothing would do, as I stood there terrified, sickened. Ness sitting by the door with Erc, his lecherous face bent to her ear.

And I began to shout out in Latin the first words that came to mind. A thick hand from the fireside cuffed me roughly, and a cry went up.

'Speak words we can understand, you cur, none of your Sasanach drawl here', and the laughter and turmoil rose beyond what I had ever heard, overtaking my senses, and in the heat and shame my face boiled red.

'Dawn', I shouted with as much force as I had, and the crowd was quelled into a quieter kind of tumult,

> Over Ua Ragallaig's country,
> Herself knew not,
> Of the warriors dark within her wood,
> Untouched by her light
> Like Trojans in their horses

Cheers went up with claps and hearty derision. I pressed on, grabbing words from the air, from I knew not where.

> Until they sprang into battle
> And slew all who stood
> Between them and glory
> Back over foreign hills driving
> Spoil and fame before them

'Enough, enough!' shouted the Tiarna with tears in his eyes as he laughed and coughed and drank and laughed more at my butchery of the metrical precision of their poetry.

Tuar baulked at the sacrilege, the mockery of his craft. His lips pursed, and he raised a warning hand as if he would cast a curse. And, unchained, I could not hold back. Standing high on the bench, emboldened and drenched and permeated with everything that had happened, I shouted with the fullness of my throat, from the bag of my belly, pointing.

> The poet's look was black
> As I, the lowest boy
> Profaned his age-old cant

In the uproar a bench tilted over and laughter split the roof beams and dimmed the fire and filled the dark, and even the *ollamh* himself smiled in that brief moment when the fool was king, and I was almost transported on it. Carried away. To a place where I was not the meanest, the least, the unfree. To a place where I was someone of worth, someone of note. No longer the least speckle on the meanest egg in the smallest wren's nest on the measliest branch of the most beggarly tree. Until I saw her again, by the door, her eyes dark. Her mouth silent. Her body hard.

CHAPTER 8
Oígidecht

I SAW HER AGAIN some days later on the feast day of Áed Mac Bricc as we prepared for the *óenach*. I came to the Tiarna's compound early, carrying word from the stables. Donchad met me at the door of the house.

'Come in, red Sasanach', the Tiarna said, calling me happily across the threshold. I bowed low through the doorway and came up into the warm, dim interior, my eyes adjusting slowly.

'The horses are ready, *a thiarna*'. I spoke with an outdoor voice, which boomed into the quiet space within. I fell silent, embarrassed.

A low murmur of talk came from the women's side of the house—the only sound and, looking that way, I caught sight of the Tiarna's wife, Gormflaith, consulting with Mór and picking out jewellery and clothes from a carved timber box. Mór passed these back to Ness, who folded the items into a leather bag, her eyes low, her head bent.

I could feel the warmth of embarrassment spread over my cheeks.

'Redder still, Alberagh', the Tiarna said, seeing the direction of my gaze and smiling, though he did not push further. 'Are you prepared for the *óenach*?'

'I am, *a thiarna,* though I am not sure what to expect'.

'Expect a great gathering; games, markets, song and drink, and at the centre of it all expect Tigernán Ua Ruairc sitting like a hen on the egg—consolidating his power over Míde and dispensing his laws and judgements'.

I nodded slowly, appreciating the meaning of his words. Understanding now that he had not struck a blow wildly against Áed Buidhe.

'An air of understanding descends upon him', the Tiarna said with detached amusement, as if speaking to an absent adviser. He turned his back and led me towards the *fidchell* table.

'Yes', I said, and I am ashamed that it has taken so long to fall.

'And what is it that you comprehend?' he asked, lifting a box to the table. I looked around to be sure that neither Conn nor Tuar lurked in the shadows, before remembering that they had been sent ahead to the *óenach* the day before.

'Not difficult to tell', I said. 'I see that in attacking Áed Buidhe, you have attacked Ua Ragallaig. And that in attacking Ua Ragallaig, you have struck a blow for Ua Ruairc, positioning yourself on his side'.

'Indeed', he said. Opening the hinged box and reaching inside, he took out an object wrapped within a scrap of wool. Opening it, he extracted a palm-sized cross, filigreed gold wrought in tiny, intricate detail and inset with shining red and black carbuncles—garnet, jet perhaps. 'You perceive much. But not all. Much will depend upon this meeting. And much will be needed to mend the breach that lies between my house and Ua Ruairc'.

As he spoke, he took two more wrapped objects from the box, uncovering each and setting them on the table. A silver brooch, lustrous in the low light, its value apparent in its heft; a simpler, more ancient ornament with the large terminals coming together to face each other fashioned into the shape of thistle heads; the third object, another brooch, this one gold, the ornament as complex as the thin massed roots of the dandelion, inlaid with amber and glass *millefiori.*

'What gift for a king?' he asked, and I considered carefully, feeling the Tiarna's scrutiny. Feeling that my answer would have an effect on some farsighted plan he was forming for me. My eyes played over the three objects, considering all. Their artistry, their material, the significance of their shapes. He watched me placidly, not hurrying or pressing for an answer.

'Give him the *kelt*', I said finally, and his demeanour changed. He stood up straight, his hand straying to his chest where the smooth teardrop-shaped stone hung. The thunderbolt. The *sídhe* stone, plucked from the otherworld. 'Press it into his hand and tell him of your dream, and of the labour involved in its getting. Of the risks taken in awakening the *sídhe* host, in crossing that threshold'. A shudder ran across my shoulders as I spoke these words. 'He will be honoured'.

The Tiarna stood, motionless for the span of several heartbeats. His hand fell from the *kelt* then, and he wrapped the items and put them back in the box, all except the cross. This he placed in a pouch at his waist.

'The King will not want some heathen stone. He will see a compliment in the cross. Piety, beauty and strength'.

'Of course, *a thiarna*', I said dutifully.

'Of course', he replied with a sternness that was not there before. 'Now run ahead to the stables and tell them we ride'.

We set out in the mid-morning with a good company of men and the women of the household riding or following on in a number of rumbling carts, Ness among them, and I found myself searching out her gaze, finding pretext to ride by. I rode one of Áed Buidhe's horses, wheeling ahead with Erc and Fiacra, driving the remaining herd of the captured cows along the *bóthar* ahead of us. We rode, as is their style, astride mats slung over the horses' backs, steering with thighs clamped firm to the beasts' flanks. We drove towards the appointed place, and, passing through the Tiarna's *túath*, we gathered people from the smaller holdings as we went—men of all degrees, *aire, boaire, betagh*, men, women and children joining our march. And as our path led on to the royal *slíghe*, we met and mingled with people of other *túatha* leading carts full of wool and grain and salted fish and all manner of things to be traded or sold.

As we got nearer to the *óenach*, the traffic on the road became more frequent, and soon we had difficulty keeping the cattle together. It was a sight to behold, the *slighe* full of moving bodies far ahead and behind, all travelling in one direction towards the great meeting.

Despite a cold wind and squalls of rain, there was an excitement among people that was difficult to contain. We spoke to those coming from away east, from Brega and Airgialla. The talk on every lip was of Mac Murchada's Engleis mercenaries and their doings to the south. We heard that following Mac Murchada's death in the summer, the foreigners had pushed west into Tuamhain and even north as far as the territory of the Ulaid, burning and killing and upsetting the natural order. Erc was maddened by this, as we had heard no talk of our own *táin*. He pronounced loudly that the foreigners had not dared set foot within our borders and boasted of our raid within earshot of all who would listen. In fact, our actions were widely known, and some people on the road congratulated us. An old woman spoke to me of it as we stopped by a stream, letting the herd drink.

'A fine deed', she said, 'made even finer given there was no damage to the farmsteads you passed'.

Others, men associated with the Ua Ragallaig, hissed or jeered at our passing, but nothing more was done. It is one of their most rigidly applied laws, that all must approach the *óenach* under truce, regardless of the myriad different grievances and feuds. No blood to be shed at or on the journey to and from the *óenach,* no feuds to be prosecuted, no politics to be progressed or raids avenged. No women molested and no forced elopements. We were safe from Áed Buidhe's vengeance, even if he had had the strength to challenge us.

The day was long on the road, and despite the high spirits, we were worn down by the constant herding, keeping the bullocks especially from veering off into pastures or upsetting donkeys and their loads. Though the location of the *óenach* was barely a day's journey from our *túath*, we had made little over half the distance by the time the sun began to dip in the west. The Tiarna led us off the *slighe* into the surrounding country, where he brought us to a farmstead of one of his clients, a *bóaire* who came out expectantly with his household arrayed behind, full of the laws of hospitality.

'*A thiarna*', he declared, his arms opening wide, 'you are expected. Come forward and leave your horses and your servants with my people. Come and take the first bath and you will be the first to be seated in our mead hall'.

As the Tiarna, his family and his warriors were feasted that night, we spoke to his servants and his stable master around a fire in the open yard. They spoke fearfully of foreigners on the *slíghe*, passing up and down and seeking out information on who was king here and who claimed lordship there. Erc, emerging from the hall to drain his bag, laughed over his shoulder, saying, 'There is no fear of foreigners in our *túath* while this arm holds a spear'.

'Though now it holds a twig', I said, low enough not to be heard by him, and those close to me smiled. He approached our fire then, suspicious of the silence, looking around to the young bondswomen of the household. His eyes settled finally on Ness. His neck thick and his eyes small. He went back to the feasting, and I moved around the fireside to where she sat, lowering myself down beside her. I spoke gently into her ear.

'It may be best not to sleep in the stables with the others tonight. I fear that Erc will come looking for you when the fires burn down and ale has deadened his fear of the Tiarna'.

She looked to me, her eyes black in the flickering light. She placed a finger on my chest, and I shivered like a horse in a cloud of midges.

'Your foresight is indeed transcendent', she said with her lips twisting. 'Did the *sídhe* leave you with any other gifts beyond that of divination?' I smiled in the low light, surprised when her slim hand slipped into mine. We walked from the fire, our eyes adjusting to the darkness and looking into the shadows for a place to stay. We struggled with the door of the small stone house where they kept the malted grain until it opened, and we crawled inside. Making a bed for ourselves as best we could, we lay side by side, invisible to each other in the dark.

'I have thought of you every night since I saw you first at the *tóchar*, a bloom on the meadow', I said, and I heard the air exhale from her nostrils in disdain.

'Since I rubbed your *gléas* for you', she said. 'Speak true. Speak of your red lust. Not of meadow blooms'. I shrank back from the vehemence of her words. 'At night', she continued, 'I pray to Scáthach. I plead to her every night that I might find her power—the power to murder all who have harmed me'.

'You will need more than prayers', I said lightly, spurned, and she responded with softening tones.

'I will need more than you—a dumb beast in the field'.

'I am what you have', I said, smiling unseen, 'and the world is changing. The Sasanaigh are coming, the Engleis, those who speak my language'.

She reached out, her hand gliding beneath my *léine*. She touched me as before in the byre. Rougher. And in the darkness, blinding light sparked. I could hear the strangled sounds coming from my own throat. As if from a distance. She wiped my seed on the dead slabs of stone and brought my hand to her cleft, moving against my fingers and pressing this way and that. She made no sound. When she had finished, I kissed her unmoving mouth and made all of the mooning promises that young men make. That I would free her. That I would take her away. That I would kill all who had harmed her.

'It would be different if women ruled', she said.

'Because there would be peace?' I asked.

'Because our blades would be sharper', she said with venom, 'blacker. And men would never hear them coming'.

Voices cut us short and we fell silent, listening. The Tiarna and his client, pissing against the wall.

'I receive you of course with pleasure, *a thiarna*. With the full regalia and bounty available to me. I keep your border, I clear your roads, I send men to work your cornfields, to dig the ramparts around your house. I am bound to assist you in blood feud and I escort you to the *óenach*. In return, our covenant demands that you keep us safe from the depredations of outsiders. I need to know that you will come to our aid, that you will keep the foreigner away. They have come as far as our ditches, and while they have not attacked us, the people they have dislodged arrive before them like a wave before the bow of a boat'.

We listened quietly, waiting for the Tiarna's answer. We heard them fixing their garments and the sounds of them moving off, the Tiarna's voice drifting back to us.

'All will be well, Caoimhín; after the *óenach*, all will be well'.

CHAPTER 9

Óenach

IN THE MORNING we pushed on, rejoining the *slíghe* to find it lined with tents and campfires. We passed an ancient hostel by the roadside which was surrounded with makeshift camps and wagons. A monk was giving Mass beneath a huge oak tree, dotted with sparse, clinging leaves, and we stopped on the outskirts of the congregation. A way was made for the Tiarna and Gormflaith, who went forward to receive the blessed bread, passing through the dun-coloured crowd in their aristocratic red cloaks. The priest's voice raised in sermon.

'Forget not the ills visited upon the Ostmen of Duiblinn for their sins—chief among them, their blind and stubborn insistence on perpetuating that ungodly practice of slavery'. My face glowed red with shame and anger as I burrowed into the crowd, not wanting to meet Erc's eye or feel his elbow dig into my ribs with amusement.

'God's vengeance', the monk went on, 'has taken the form of the Sasanaigh, the grim-faced soldiers from over the sea, clad in iron rings and riding powerful horses. None shall be safe while the sinful walk tall in the guise of the righteous'. The Tiarna pulled his cloak over his head, walking away from these words, and I could see that his restless mind was seeking ways to turn these fears and grim-faced soldiers to his favour.

The crowds on the *slíghe* thickened as we approached the appointed place, and going was slow. The road closed in on either side, rising through a narrow pass, and even the cows had nowhere to go and were constrained to amble along with the current. The *slíghe* rose up then and ran between the top of two grassy hills, and as we crested, we caught our first glimpse of the land beyond, sloping away gently downwards towards the Dubh Lough before rising again on the far side up to the eaves of a dense oak wood.

Everywhere that we looked, there were crowds of people, spilling down the slopes towards a flat central disc of green beside the shore of the *lough*. As we descended, I saw people setting up camps and stalls where they could, uniting in their *túatha* and kin groups. Temporary corrals held cattle herds, sheep, pigs and horses around the outskirts of the camps. Tents covered the slopes, set as close as the teeth of a comb, and in the still air, smoke rose upwards in trailing columns from a hundred fires, and it was as if the low sky rested upon these spindles. The large oval sward of level ground at the edge of the lake was bare of people, and this was the heart of the *óenach*, the space where the horse racing and the ball games and the contests of strength and skill would take place, and at the edge of this greensward on a low outcrop of rock, the dais of Ua Ruairc had been erected with wooden poles constructed above, carrying a roof of fabric bowed like a full udder. It was from this platform that Tigernán Ua Ruairc would address the gathering, read out his laws and decrees, bestow gifts upon his supporters and officiate ceremonies invested with such strange antiquity that their meaning was obscured to all but the highest *ollamh*. And this, ultimately, was the purpose of the *óenach*—to dispense the king's rule and to renew vows of fidelity with the multitudes drawn by the goods to be had and to compete in the contests of strength and speed, of horsemanship and *immána*.

Looking out over the massed field of people—lords, ladies, lawmen, artisans, hostages and slaves—I perceived every one of them caught up in the net of the politics of that part of the world. Obsessed, one and all, by their place within that mesh and how it might be bettered by the swing of an axe or the wedding of a daughter or the taking of a hostage or the blinding of a brother.

In the press of people, we approached a row of large stones and, beyond, the boundary post draped with bushels of barley and hung with harvest knots of all different shapes. A young *file* stood on a boulder, his arm crooked around the post, and as we struggled along in the vast crowd crossing into *óenach* land, we passed slowly, receiving all of his gesturing cant.

'Well travelled and well met to the *óenach* of Ua Ruairc, where one hundred thousand welcomes are laid at your feet. Come and find your place among the three busiest markets in the land—the market of food, the market of livestock, the great market of the Greek foreigners filled with gold and fine raiment. Find your place on the slope of the horses, the slope of the cooking pots or the slope of the women, met for embroidery where no man of the host of the noisy Gaedil may harass them. Come hear the trumpets, the harps, the hollow-throated horns, hear the pipers, timpanists, the unwearied poets and meek musicians. Come hear the tales of Finn and the Fianna, a matter inexhaustible, of sacks, forays, wooings and keen riddles. Disport yourselves, noble men, in the truthful teachings of Fithal, in the dark lays of the Dindsenchas. And you of the lower sort, fear not. For you, pipes, fiddles, gleemen, bone players and bagpipers await. A crowd hideous, noisy, profane full of shriekers and shouters waits for thee'.

The crowd laughed and called out in passing or threw sods and scraw plucked from the earth as the *file* cavorted across the boulders.

'And here arrives a great lord', he cried, seeing our company, 'whose fine raiment, noble bearing and radiant wife announce his name to us all, who have heard of his great deeds—surely from the house of Máel Sechlainn he comes, Mánus of the bright cheek and quick mind'. All looked towards the Tiarna, who smiled thinly, and I could read uncertainty behind his eyes. A foreboding crept into the air as we passed, entering the *óenach* land. I felt it too. The *file*'s heaped praise tinged with something barely perceived, yet there all the same like the faint taste of shit in a clear running stream. Scorn. We pushed onwards with the *file*'s fading words following us doggedly.

'The King, noble and honoured, pays for each art its proper fee. Tales of death and slaughter, strains of music; his royal pedigree, a blessing throughout Míde. His battle stark, his valour terrible'.

The horse-boys had been looking out for us from the grassy slopes, watching our approach and running to tell Tuar. He met us close to the boundary and led us through the crowds to a place, close to the eaves of the wood beside a small stream where several tents had been set up and a stockade made for the beasts. Already a fire shimmered before the tents with a tripod of irons carrying a cauldron of broth over the coals. The Tiarna's men had gotten a barrel of Frankish wine and two barrels of honeyed ale from the markets, and the servants came forward with horns brimming with drink.

Conn came forward, too, taller seeming, a light on his face. He embraced his parents, and all three sat on the sun-warmed grass by the entrance to the tent and drank wine as we drove the cattle into the stockade and unloaded the carts. He called Tuar to his side then and asked for information. What lords were here and where camped. What news and what conflicts and what were the odds and favourites in the contests to come. Had Ua Ruairc arrived and had any addresses been made. He spoke quietly then in Tuar's ear, and the *ollamh* called Conn to his side and they stalked away downslope, disappearing between the tents. The Tiarna lay back in the grass, stretching the full length of his body, as we all waited nervously for what would follow. He called for food and was brought a steaming bowl from the cauldron. We all sought food then, whatever we could find. I looked for Ness, finding her eye as she stood by with the lady's bag. I brought her an apple from the cart and we shared an oat biscuit, sitting in silence, eating, surreptitiously watching the Tiarna, fingering the *kelt* at his neck, his lips mumbling unspoken words as the weight of the moment hung heavier with each beat of the heart. Conn came back eventually, standing gravely before his father, communicating his message with a single nod. The Tiarna stood and, looking to the sky, breathed in deeply before calling Donchad and Erc forward.

'Ready the cows. We will make our submission to Ua Ruairc', he said—the heaviness in his voice clear to all who heard.

Donchad, Erc and the other household men went ahead, clearing the way for the Tiarna. We came behind, harried with keeping the cows together along the tight tracks between camps. All of the household was needed for this, and even Mór and Ness paced along with switches, keeping the beasts calm with coos and touches of their palms on broad, knobbed backs. And as we descended, the slope drew the beasts onwards, some trotting on, unnerved by the smoke and noise. Women scolded our trespass as bullocks went astray, and it felt before long that the whole camp was against us. The sense of foreboding grew with each step downhill, and the greensward came into view, empty and waiting and ringed with masses of people, eating, trading and drinking around its fringes.

We stopped at the edge, looking across the grassy expanse. At the far end, figures moved on the dais, and we could clearly see the shapes of people, though their faces were too far off to discern. Two came forward, stepping from the dais and walking towards us. Their gait announced them before their faces resolved themselves with certainty. Tuar and, by his side, Milesius came on with his sturdy staff. I smiled at this, taking some comfort from the monk's presence. Tuar came in full dignity holding the slender white rod of his office.

They stopped before us, officious and distant, the *ollamh* and the cleric. Milesius did not meet my eye, nor did he show any sign of affection or kinship with the Tiarna. Tuar raised the white rod several hands' breadths from the ground and spoke in precise tones.

'*A thiarna*, you will approach the dais with your company, state your name, declare loudly that you come with peaceful intent and make your presentation to the Rí. In your address you will acknowledge him as King of Bréifne, Conmaicne and lord over Míde. He, in turn, will acknowledge your submission, and the monk will bring forward the great relic Domnach Airgid, upon which you will swear your vow'.

The Tiarna nodded and Tuar turned, leading the party onwards. The Tiarna walked ahead, Gormflaith and Conn at his right hand and his men fanned out to each side. We closed the distance slowly, the shapes on the dais becoming clearer. As we progressed, I became aware of a silence descending, spreading outwards from the sward. Even the cows quietened, comforted by the open space and the lush grass underfoot. Ahead of us, Ua Ruairc sat in majesty on a wooden chair surrounded by *ollaimh*, lawmen and warriors, his sons, grandsons, foster sons all. Ua Ruairc among them as if within a spear-bristling fort, and as we drew closer, the king's aged, ruined aspect resolved itself, its horror becoming clearer with each step forward. His face carried deep ravines, the scarred flesh puckered and dulled with time, his left eye long since gored from its socket. And all who beheld him dwelt upon the stories of the men who, on a moonless night, had slid from the shadows to end Ua Ruairc's reign, who had stabbed again and again at the old king's head until, standing back from the fallen hump breathing wetly at their feet, they had watched him rise, implacable from the bloodied ground, axe in hand.

He sat forward now in the chair, immobile, the mass of his shoulders looming, giving the impression of an eternal crag facing the sea. His good eye alone roved, restless and bright within that terrible face with its bulged, badly knitted lips, its cheeks and chin crazed with torn, white furrows upon which no beard grew.

We approached, and it was as if we neared an abyss. The mounting silence like a weight on my shoulders. Though I burned to look back and find Ness, I dared not draw attention. Milesius climbed the dais, bending to speak into his kinsman's ear before taking his place behind the chair, and Tuar stepped forward to announce the Tiarna.

A small commotion from the crowd stalled the words on his lips. A figure pushed forward violently through the congregation gathered at the edge of the sward and wheeled clumsily into the space between our party and the dais. A staff in his hand, black feathers in his hair, and I recognised, in the flash of his face before he turned towards Ua Ruairc, the *file* I had watched with Lochru, skulking along our borders. The *file* Donchad had followed. The *file* in the pay of Ua Ragallaig.

Several of the warriors jumped down from the dais, coming around him, and he cried out in an awful voice, like the croaking of a hundred startled herons. He threw his satchel over his shoulder, his *brat* flinging back as his arm came up, lifting one leg and closing one eye in the sign of a curse. The warriors faltered and he began, speaking the most terrible words with a throaty welling of invective.

'Is it Ua Ruairc the cuckold I see before me? Playing king over a land that will not bear him?'

The shock of his speech ran through the assembly, a shuddering horror, and though the expression on the King's face did not change, his whole body tensed into a rictus of anger.

'Is it Ua Ruairc, the stingy, grudging lord? The stinking gummed, half-blind oaf? The withered leper? The shameless, misshapen monster? See what befalls when a king is blemished!'

A stupefied silence reigned among those surrounding the sward, while farther off, beyond the massed crowd, sounds of oblivious commerce, music, shouting and laughter travelled lightly on a breeze.

'Is it Ua Ruairc whose deformity brings blight and hardship to his people? The wicked, incompetent, feeble boor? A man divested of his wife by the Mac Murchada pretender? Is it Ua Ruairc, lapdog to Connacht, an old, infirm, impotent lecher who calls this assembly? Woe to he who would follow this worm. Death to he who would call him king'.

The *file*, his satire delivered, slumped forward on his staff, the outpouring of bile dragging with it all of his force. All eyes turned to Ua Ruairc, who sat still, absorbing the poison of the *file*'s words, his chewing mouth eating the malicious spellwork with a power of his own. Hatred. Spite. Eternal things burning at his core. Sustaining his old body with unholy light.

He stood slowly, revealing his height, his gnarled strength evident in his grip as it reached behind for the long haft of his axe.

'And who', he roared, 'has sponsored this outrage? What villainous, pus-addled scab has sent this pitiful cretin before me, gasping malformed words into the gale?'

'One who sees you for what you are—*rí* of ordure, doom to his people'. Ua Ruairc's men closed in on each side, axes and swords ringing clear and pressing into the meagre frame of the *file*. 'Will you now go further in your transgressions', the *file* said, 'and break the *géis*, drawing blood at an *óenach*?'

Ua Ruairc turned from the *file*, addressing the crowd.

'Behold. A starving beggar of little skill sent against me with feeble words. Sent on the promise of reward. Is this the depth of my enemies' desperation?' And, turning with a savage swiftness, he spat a full gobbet of phlegm at the *file*, who raised his hand against it. 'Flee. Flee now, you stunted crook. I will break no *géis* for the likes of you'.

The *file* said no more but pitched on a bad leg and tramped from the sward, his face twisted, fearful, with drops of sweat clear on his brow. The crowd fell back before him, and he passed—a sickle through the corn.

The silence extended out, engulfing all, as Ua Ruairc sat, resuming his posture, his eye fixed now, frozen and unseeing, his jaw set, his brow thunderous. Finally, with a motion of his hand, he called Milesius forward, and they exchanged low words. Looking back to our party, the Rí raised his hand slowly and beckoned Tuar onwards. The *ollamh*, with faltering voice, lifted the white rod and intoned.

'Mánus Mac Murchad Ua Máel Sechlainn'.

The Tiarna stepped forward, his chin resolutely high, as Ua Ruairc lowered darkly. He bowed his head, inclining his body forward, and those of us behind him perceived the slightest of trembles along his calves. The Tiarna raised his voice then as much as he dared into the charged air, enumerating Ua Ruairc's many titles.

'Rí, I come before you to make pledges—to come under the protection of your house. I pledge the service of my lands and subjects, of my grain-fields and my herds, of my milking parlours and butter churns, of my mills and kilns. I bring you these cows, taken from Áed Buidhe, a man loyal to your enemies. I also bring you this cross which has been in my family from the time of Flann Sinna and with which I part with very sombrely'.

'Bring it forward', Ua Ruairc said, his voice as ragged as his face, though with an imperative force, his words tempered with hot iron. As the Tiarna approached the dais with the cross cupped in his joined hands, Ua Ruairc reached down and, bypassing the cross, reached for the *kelt* hanging at the Tiarna's throat. Ua Ruairc's hands like the exposed roots of an ancient tree closed upon the stone, lifting it silently from the Tiarna's neck. He sat looking into its black, burnished depths as the Tiarna stood, his proffered hands outstretched, the cross spurned. 'You are very generous, Mánus. This I will gladly have. I can feel the magic within its grain'.

The Tiarna's hands closed, coming slowly downwards. His head lowering in shame. 'Very generous', Ua Ruairc continued. 'You are very generous with *my own* cows, Mánus. For you know I claim lordship over Áed Buidhe and all that he owns. Áed himself came before me this morning carrying a suit against you. Looking for distraint and seizure of your herds. Looking for a payment of fine'.

Behind Ua Ruairc's chair, Milesius' eyes flashed, first to the Tiarna, then to Tuar. The Tiarna spoke low and quick, hissing his words to Ua Ruairc alone, though we were close enough to hear.

'But, Áed is an agent of your enemies, he holds Ua Ragallaig in his heart. In moving against him, I sought to show you friendship'. Tigernán Ua Ruairc sat back slowly, his hands running over the smoothness of the *kelt*. He spoke loudly for all to hear.

'I am not sure if you are friend to me or foe. What is more, I do not think that you yourself know yet. What is clear to me is that you arrive here offering me my own cows, driving them over the playing ground, and at your head, a pox-ridden *file* who slanders me with illegal satire'.

A low, tentative murmur of laughter passed through the crowd. 'How can I be sure that the ancient renown of your household's name—those once great Máel Sechlainn kings of Míde—does not weigh heavily around your poor neck?'

'Not so. That *file*, you must know, has come straight from Ua Ragallaig, who intrigues with the foreigners'.

Ua Ruairc reared up, half standing in his seat, and the suddenness and violence of his movements sent the Tiarna stumbling backwards.

'Do not speak to me of foreigners', he shouted. And then, quieter, but with no less menace, he said, 'It seems, poor Mánus, that you are very well informed on Ua Ragallaig, that bitch's runt, that exile of no repute, and on those that he conspires with. How should I read that?' He sat forward again, his eye burning, the Tiarna shaking his head in denial, mute under the weight of that stare.

The moment was broken by a fit of deep, shaking coughs which reverberated through the old king's chest, and he sat back, his face pinched with pain. When the coughing subsided, Ua Ruairc spoke in tones approaching tenderness.

'I have decided to trust you, poor Mánus. And to seal the bond between our houses, I will take your son into my house'. Gormflaith stiffened by her son's side, her hand reaching out instinctively to grip at his *léine*. 'Is this the boy?' Ua Ruairc continued, gesturing to Conn. Mánus turned from the dais, looking back to his son.

His face stricken and helpless, his head still shaking. Gormflaith tensed, her other hand rising now, the fingers clenching a fistful of Conn's *brat*. Tuar, seeing the shape of disaster looming, sensing things that would be said and never undone, moved quickly to her side, speaking low words as his hands subtly worried her fingers free. Tuar laid his hand on Conn's shoulder as the boy looked to his mother, childish fear in his eyes, and led him forward towards the dais. I heard the mangled sound of a scream, swallowed, confined to Gormflaith's throat, her mouth clamped mercilessly shut.

'Bring forward the book', Ua Ruairc said, and Milesius went to an elaborate wooden box shaped like a small church. He opened a clasp, the side of the box falling open, and he lifted out that most venerated of things, the Domnach Airgid that all have heard its name. The book that once belonged to St Patricius, encased within a silver reliquary of unsurpassed beauty. Milesius raised the thing high, the lively flash of light from its surface cutting the dullness of the day. He stepped from the dais and held the book flat before the Tiarna, who lifted his hand slowly and placed it on the silvered surface. As he recited the long oaths and pledges with the air of one waking from a nightmare to find himself in a burning bed, Tuar led Conn to Ua Ruairc's side.

When all was done, Ua Ruairc stood, his hand closed around Conn's arm, and he proclaimed, 'A fine lad. A sturdy warrior'. He lifted his axe from where it leaned beside his chair. He pressed its haft into Conn's hand. 'You will be welcome in my household, boy, and we will foster you to such manhood that you will be an immovable pillar within the rich plain of Míde upon which we will build our palace'. Conn trembled, unsure whether to respond. 'And your first service to me, boy, will be to follow that false satirist from this place, burst his skull and bring me the tongue that has offended. You, and you alone, boy, to do this deed'.

Conn looked to the Tiarna, the terror of breaking a *géis* curdling his features. 'Do not look to him, boy', Ua Ruairc roared in sudden fury. 'I am your father now, your *athair altrama*. Hear me and obey'. Conn, startled by the Rí's sudden fury, jumped from the dais and loped away in pursuit of the *file*, the giant axe awkwardly over his shoulder. I looked instantly to the Tiarna. Mánus Máel Sechlainn looked to his retinue from before the dais, quickly scanning the faces, and when he found mine, his eyes slid sidewards meaning-fully. I slipped back between the cows and, passing through them, bent low, entering the crowd and following in Conn's wake.

I was not alone. As I followed, others came also, young men and women coming behind as Conn stalked on ahead, the long axe over his shoulders making him appear boyish. A tremor of excite-ment ran through them as they jostled each other, speaking Conn's name, some reciting his lineage—placing him within the order of things. Though none dared to call out, to jeer, to whoop. The shock of the *file*'s satire, the wrongness of it, a sick pall in the air. I kept ahead of them, some distance from Conn as he stalked past the boundary marker, his heel striking determination. His hand clenching and unclenching on the haft of the axe, the roll of his shoulders, all gestures to fight the fear.

Steps came smoothly up behind me. Fingers, quick and cool, pressed my neck, splaying upwards into my hair, and I turned in anger, ready to strike the waif who would sport with me and the sharp words died on my lips when I saw her, smiling, her hair, gath-ered behind, making her face seem longer. I shrank from the hungry light in her eyes as she ran forward, her trailing hand, catching mine, pulling me onwards, and as the *slíghe* rose towards the pass between the hills, the *file*'s labouring back appeared in the distance.

Conn crouched and, leaving the road, jogged lightly into the wild grass of the esker ridge, and we saw that he thought to cut across a bend in the *slíghe* and take the *file* by surprise. Ness pulled me forward, and we ran to catch up.

'He must not talk', she said to me, and I caught her meaning, hissing low. Conn turned and we pointed towards the *file*, covering our mouths with a hand. Conn nodded and padded on. He dropped to his belly and crawled forward in the high grass to the edge of the *slíghe* and waited for the *file* to make his slow way around the bend. The crowd approached nearer to us, and we warded them off with gestures. The *file* came into view, the top of his head visible over the swaying grass, forehead glistening with exertion. When he drew level, Conn jumped down without a word, his arms grappling around the *file*'s shoulders as his hands tried to clamp the churl's mouth closed. He was unsuccessful, and an excrement of malediction burst from the *file*'s lips.

Conn shrank back from the words, falling against the bank of the road.

'I am protected here by the laws of this land. Who would break the *géis* that is upon my coming and going?' The *file*'s voice was raw, commanding, and for a moment, Conn did not move. The *file* closed one eye and raised a hand tensed into a long claw. At this, Conn sprang forward and knocked the *file* to his knees. He brought the butt of the axe down with tremendous strength onto the crown of the *file*'s head. The old man's eyes rolled back, and he fell forward, making no attempt to raise his hands, to soften his fall. He hit the ground like a pitched log, scraping on the stony slope, and his eyes disappeared to their whites, his body shaking like a sick lamb. Conn hammered him again, this time on the temple, and a big purple bulge came up through his hair, the way a pig's tripe spills out under the butcher's knife. He stopped moving then. Conn looked to us as a dread quiet descended—the small crowd coming up around us.

'Dig a hole', Ness said.

'Dig a hole for this villain?' I said, looking at the thin soils of the hillside.

'Dig now, dig fast', she barked, 'before his soul escapes his body, or you will never again have peace'.

These words awoke Conn, who had been standing, staring down at the body. He walked a short way from the *slíghe*, and I joined him. With axe and knife, we started to scrape into the slope, through the wild grass and through the stony yellow clay. We threw the weapons aside then and found slabs of shale to gouge out the hole deeper, and behind us Ness busied herself with the corpse, doing we knew not what, but her *scian* was unsheathed and bloodied when we finally looked up from our travails—the hole sloping and as deep only as our knees. We heaved the body towards the pit and the crowd backed away, not wanting to come too near.

We threw him down on the lip of the hole, the bulge on his scalp bursting and thick sloe-black liquid oozing lazily from it—no beating heart to drive it outward. And we were calmed somewhat by that. Ness came up with a stone then, a fist-sized river cobble. She opened the mouth and put her hand in—four fingers gripping the lower teeth—and she wrenched down and jammed the cobble inside, the jaw springing back shut fast to the stone.

'Lay him on his face', she said, 'and should he wake, he will dig, thinking he digs towards the light, all the while clawing deeper into the hill'.

We rolled him in, and all three of us began dragging the scattered earth back in over the body, quicker and quicker in a frenzy, in fear of the corpse rising, of heaping dread curses on us, despite all we had done to break his power.

We pushed through the gabbling crowd, which opened to let us pass. Among them I caught sight of Fiacra, who shrank away from us, fear etched on his face. On the way back down the hill, Ness produced a dripping hank of flesh from her pouch, ragged at one end. The *file*'s tongue.

'He will craft no further ills with this muscle', she said, passing it to Conn. And we had a light inside us, though we had broken a *géis*, the worst kind of taboo.

When we returned to the *óenach*, the evening fires had been lit, and there was much drinking and feasting beginning. Conn presented Ua Ruairc with the tongue and was lauded loudly by the Rí's party. Ua Ruairc cast the tongue on the fire, enfolding Conn in an embrace, leading him away towards the ale barrel, pressing a horn into his hand. Ness went with the women to the slope where men were not permitted. I watched her go, a tugging feeling in my chest, and stood awkwardly on the fringe of the firelight, no place within or without. I watched Conn then, caught up in the frothy tumult on the dais, danger all around him, before my eyes strayed back to watch the tongue curl and spit in the flames.

'The bad cess leaving it', a voice at my shoulder said. I turned to see the Tiarna, his fine red *brat* tight about his shoulders and drawn low over his forehead. Sombre amidst the revelry.

We continued to stare at the tongue, no more now than a blackened gall. 'Take a drink', he said after a long time, and I took his proffered horn, my fingers playing absently over the silver hound's head decorating its tip. I went to the barrel and dipped the vessel into the sharp wine, and I drank it in one from brim to bottom.

'Come', he said, and we made our way up the slope towards our camp. We sat down on a stone beside the fire and listened to the sounds of the place, distant songs rising up, shouts and laughter and harp music from the camps all around. The rip and tear of a dog fight. Large fires dotting the hillside below. The trickle of the stream chanting close by. The hum of the treetops in the wind. We sat through it all, in silence, the Tiarna's mind quietly working, until his retinue slept, full of wine and sated with fair-day women.

No revellers came up the hill, and I busied myself with gathering firewood and feeding the flames. For a long time the Tiarna was silent, staring at the burning sticks or humming gently to himself. He finally called me to him when the breeze had died down and his musings had reached an end.

'Most men', he said, 'accept the order of things. They accept the wisdom of God's will that I be lord and you be slave. They do not consider that tomorrow may bring a change that reverses our roles'.

My throat restricted and a kind of fearful shudder passed over the span of my shoulder. His eye had stared into my soul. Had seen the yearning. The prayers and incantations I had offered, cast widely like seeds in a field. Offerings to God, to Patricius, to Lasair, to Féichín, to *sídhe,* to idol and to devil. I feared he had perceived it all. A vision in the flames. His way of sucking his thumb for wisdom. Father and I riding tall horses among the host of the Engleis. But as he continued, I understood it was himself he spoke of.

'I have meditated on that since you and your father came to me', he said, his eyes still anchored to the flame. His voice low with that truthful weariness of the deep night.

'For despite his imperfect speech, he had the bearing of one with a touch of nobility. It forced me to consider how I would fare in his position. If I would be possessed of the strength to remain noble even though flung down in the mud'.

I did not know what to say, so I stayed quiet, and he spoke no more, feeling perhaps that change was inevitable now. Terrible change—a violent wave. And I prayed to Lasair and Féichín, I prayed that after the wave had crashed upon us, that after it had passed into a seething murmur, I might rise in its wake. I might find her on the other side. She might come to me, her heart open. Her eyes warm.

CHAPTER 10

Saoirse

KILLING THE FILE was like crushing the wasp after it had stung. Though Ua Ruairc had boasted and swaggered for the remaining days of the *óenach* and held feasts each more lavish than the next, his legitimacy had been damaged. And all who rode home in the deepening winter felt the cold more keenly, and several days after the last warming draft and enlivening meat had been consumed, the only thing that anyone could remember of the great assembly was the *file* and his words. The *file* and his death. The *file*'s tongue burning and spilling its tallow onto the logs.

Faith in Ua Ruairc was shaken to its foundation, particularly in the fringes of land he laid claim to. The Tiarna's clients came from all around to seek his counsel. Smoke lifted from their fires deep into the night, creeping through the thatch and rising slowly like a sleeping breath. Father was called again and again to the Tiarna's house to answer their questions, never returning until the blue morning. Entering the mill in silence, he would eat, wash his face and apply himself directly to his work.

Fearful of what was coming, of the eroding of the edges of my world, I tended flocks of sheep on desolate hillsides, waiting for the voice of God to speak to me. For a bush to burn without being consumed. For a star to shake loose its mooring in the sky and lead me to somewhere of significance.

We heard more of foreigners upon the *slíghe*. Of a hostel sacked in Luigne. A mill burned in Fore and violence against the people there. As the days grew short, we received the first exiles coming across meadow and through wood following no known path, tearing themselves on the *scéach* and bramble as they approached. I helped Lochru bring them skins of water and buttermilk as they congregated at the bottom of the hill below our farmstead.

'See a deer in open country, running wild, the wolf is sure to follow', Lochru muttered from the side of his mouth as we came close to them. Wretches all, their eyes shifting, their faces haunted, waiting for a blow.

The Tiarna bade us take them in. A sod house was thrown up outside the palisade, and he fed them oats and put them to work on his borders, clearing out the ditches and rebuilding the banks. In the woodland he set them to plashing—that ingenious weaving of live saplings and bramble, turning the green things in towards themselves so that they coiled together, growing in tightening knots into a kind of living, choking basketry that none could breach. The Tiarna prepared. And through his preparation, the danger became real to us all.

One day while tending the flock, I saw four riders on a distant hillock, surveying and pointing and talking with their hands. In strange raiment, they made broad arcing gestures over the land, sitting high and proud on leather seats clasped to their horses' backs. Before, I would have run to the Tiarna with this, tripping over myself to fall at his feet, offering the news for a moment of conspiracy, a moment within the circle of light thrown out by his hearth. Now it was different. It fell to me to decipher the signs.

Conn was gone, the Máel Sechlainn claim to Míde gone with him. One of Ua Ruairc's sons killed at Ceannas, murdered by an Ua Ragallaig. Weak claimants attacking forts and killing hostages all across the kingdom. It was not difficult to see the hand of the foreigner behind all of this, bolstering some, weakening all.

The great feast of *nollaig* came and went—Christmastide, a muted celebration. The winter bit hard and food was not plentiful.

One bitter morning, to shake free the gloom that hung over the *baile,* the Tiarna took the household to the hill of the hunt, to watch his hounds chase the hare. I went ahead with Lochru and Fiacra with the timber and cloth to make up a tent. We pitched it three sided with a sloping awning and set a fire at its mouth. We walked the course then, looking over the boundaries and making sure that the *scéach* and gorse were sown tight and in good order. When we came back to the hill, the Tiarna was there with several of his clients speaking earnestly into his ear. The household guards loitered around the bottom of the hill, long spears in hand—Erc and Donchad amongst them. Gormflaith stood to the Tiarna's side, and behind her, holding the lady's mantle in the place of Mór, stood Ness. The sight of her, as ever, like a hand pressing on my chest. Lochru cuffed me gently.

'Stop staring, you mooncalf', he said. Fiacra followed my gaze but said nothing.

We joined them on the hill as the harpist began playing and the hounds were brought forward, their gilded chains making a delicate music of their own as the kennel master led them amongst the Tiarna and his guests. The Tiarna named each one proudly, his hands rubbing their jaws with playful roughness. The kennel master led the dogs down to the flat, and Lochru followed, carrying a wicker cage. The kennel master held the chains tight as Lochru reached in and brought out a hare, one hand gripping its ears, the other curled beneath its rump. He introduced the stricken animal to the dogs, walking up and down before them as they quivered, mouths open, eyes straining. Then he paced out into the course, setting the hare on the ground, and looked back over his shoulder at the hill, waiting for the signal. The Tiarna raised his arm and then let it fall. Lochru released the hare and stood still as it sprinted away down the narrow course and the hounds, released, sped past him on each side. Shouts rose from the hill, and all eyes followed the chase. The hare tried her turn before the end of the course, and the lead dog barrelled into her flank, bringing her down as the pack descended it in a frenzy of rending and tearing. Cheers went up from the hill as wagers were tallied.

Fiacra served them wine, and the rest of us stood on the slope, the cold slowly invading our bodies, watching the hounds streaking down the long, narrow course again and again as Lochru's baskets emptied.

When the wine had done its work and the party on the hill had fallen to laughing discussions, Gormflaith put her mantle on against the cold, and Ness stepped back from the tent to the edge of the hill, kneeling in the grass to rest her legs. I saw Erc sidestep slowly towards her, stopping at her shoulder, his mouth forming words I could not hear, his body leaning into her. Ness edged backwards from the brow of the hill until she was out of sight of the Tiarna. Erc, in full view, could not follow. I came up behind her, hooking my finger around hers, and drew her down the hill. She threw a glance back at Gormflaith, who sat deep in conversation with one of the visiting men and his wife, and followed. We slipped in through a breach in the hawthorn at the bottom of the hill, pushing onwards to a small stream grown over with willow. We hid beneath the falling branches, and she kissed me, excited by our transgression.

'Come away with me', I spoke breathlessly, holding her hands in mine.

Her eyes narrowed.

'Where would we go?'

'To the camp of the foreigners. My father is a man of some standing among them. We will present ourselves as husband and wife. I could translate for them and guide them through the land. Share in their takings'.

She looked away for a time, climbing lightly over the tree trunks that grew at all angles across the stream. After a long pause, she said, 'Mór will help us', and my heart bucked in my chest. 'It is clear what is coming', she said finally. 'Neither Brega nor Laigin could stand against them, nor Osraige nor Airgialla. The Tiarna could barely stand against a northerly breeze and must trust Ua Ruairc, who will hold him out as a shield against the army of the foreigners'. I laughed at her astuteness.

'You perceive much', I said.

'I will not become one of those wandering wretches clawing the land for roots and grubs'.

A strange lightness came upon me, settling in my limbs as a quickness, an energy I had not known.

'Husband and wife?' I asked, not blinking from her dark regard.

'Wife and husband', she said, a half-smile lighting her face.

We emerged from the trees, and though the wan sun had not changed, I felt warm against the wind. Until Erc stepped out from where he had been waiting, Fiacra behind him, and a chill descended.

'Look at his stained face', Erc said. 'It must be her time of the month'. The stupid, ulcerous churl laughed then at his own coarseness, looking back to Fiacra. The younger man did not smile, his face indignant. He pointed and spoke in a voice quivering with anger.

'An síofra ocus an cailleach'—the changeling and the witch. Erc came at us without warning, knocking me to the ground, and ploughing onwards, he enfolded Ness with his arm, forcing her backwards into the bushes. Fiacra, standing over me, stamped down on my back, and I stifled a cry. Rolling, I kicked his legs from under him. I moved to follow Erc, casting around for a stick or stone, his broad back disappearing into the undergrowth, and Ness swallowed by his frame. I ran after him, clawing at his shoulders. His elbow jerked back powerfully and sent me sprawling. I lay still a moment in the damp grass, willing my mind calm until I came to wits. Jumping up, I darted past Fiacra's lunge and ran to the bottom of the hill, shouting.

'A boar, a boar in the bush'. The cry was taken up, and I heard the Tiarna's voice trilling out in excitement, calling for a hound to be brought over. He came skittering down the hill, in his cups, howling like a boy, his guests full of mirth behind him.

Erc, hearing their approach, came slinking back from the hazel, his slow eyes casting around, reading the situation.

'Yes, a thiarna', he said, 'I believe we saw it. I gave chase, a black beast, but it may just have been a wild dog'.

'The hunt, the hunt', the Tiarna cried, plunging ahead into the bush, half of his retinue blundering behind him, boys running after with the dogs. In the commotion, none noticed Ness emerge, skirting the small crowd. She smiled when she saw me, her teeth white and etched around with fine threads of blood as if a scribe had traced the gum line with his finest quill. She walked back to the hilltop without letting a tremor show, taking up her place next to Gormflaith, and I stood close to her, seething and plotting escape.

We did not delay, and it was not difficult to go. Knowing Erc's violence only too well, Mór helped us to gather things discreetly. She found us a shapeless leather bag, cracking in places but fit for our purpose. Over the course of several days, we stole oaten cakes, rushes and tallow, a strike-a-light. I took a fleece of wool from the shed and made a small bag of flour from the leavings in the mill. She took an old linen cloak and folded it into a bundle she stuffed beneath her garment. We left late on a moonless night, through the open palisade and across the meadows to the *tóchar*. We went slowly, unsure of our way in the dark. I led her past the hazel coppice, skirting the monastery lands to the summer pastures on the high ground to the south. A land of deep heather and mountain bog. We walked well into the following day, until we came to an old *buaile* hut and crept inside to eat something and sleep beneath the clothes we had stolen.

The next day we walked on, southwards, farther than I had ever been. I knew not the landmarks, nor the placelore, nor the inhabitants of the distant *ráths* we saw with meek smoke rising. The weather came in from the east quicker than we feared. Before we knew, the darkness had set in, the fields dying and the leaves blown all from the trees. We skulked like the bands of *fianna*, banished to live in between lands in the company of wolves and foxes. Watched by the spirits living in animals of the woodland, in the birds speaking loudly to each other. A hoard of old gods banished to the underworld. Denizens of heaven cast out at the Fall.

'Live your life like you are always in company', Father would say, 'be it that you are the only soul on a hillside watching sheep. There are eyes and ears all around. Some belonging to God the Almighty. Some to the saints, some to mother Mary and some to the devils and stray spirits that fill the dark'.

Fear and confusion, our steps seeming to turn us backwards, the sucking bog pulling the strength from us, until, without acknowledging it, we knew we were on our way back to the *buaile*. A second day and night of the same trudging, and we ended up back at our *buaile* once more, cold, drained, and we sank down, clinging to each other beneath the damp cloak and fleece, too exhausted to build a fire. Our fingers too numb to root in our bag for the last of the food.

We did not try a third day, the weather worsening, the gusts of wind raking the hillside, given body by the drifts of dead leaves raised and flung down like flocks of mad starlings. And it grew colder. We burned more to stay warm. On the mountainside owned by no one. A wattle-built hut, like a basket upturned, and we made what repairs we could, the withies woven into themselves so thoroughly that neither hail fall nor winter wind troubled us. The fibres wound so tight that no spark from the fire, no crackle-shot ember, could find tinder to corrupt. We heaped bushels of heather on the roof, lapped over and over and fed into the coiling lattice, tying them tight with sedge-grass rope. Our hut, low and impervious and invisible from within anything but a few paces. Hidden on the flank of the hill. Just another tuft on the rib of the giant, sleeping beast. Unseen between the peat hags and heather expanses and rilling mountain streams.

And we settled in, without ever speaking of it. We ate the birds that landed in my traps and the beasts, large and small, that could be hunted or dug out from their setts. Snails from the stony places, worms from the streams. Root of the reed and the sap of the birch. Leaves of cress and *praiseach* and *neantóg*. Honey from the wood, and the last nuts of the hazel bush. Set in stores for the winter. Pits dug in our floor. Lined with charcoal and packed tight with acorns. Every night we left the fire and the rush bedding and walked to the crest of the hill and looked for lights below. We held each other's hardening bodies beneath the grand canopy of the night. We closed out the world. Corralled ourselves in and let the shades fall down around us.

And she laughed deeply when, out of nothing but custom, without thinking on it, I built the bed on the man's side of the house and gave myself the chief place.

'Lord of your *lios*, is it?' she said, pushing me against the wattle and her eyes watching, searching into me for any sign of a birthing tyranny. Looking for the hubris that a dwelling and a woman can wake in a man.

She found nothing of it. Not that she saw all. I kept guarded my fearfulness tempered with an awe and a hunger. My need for her to yield to me. To share herself somewhat. And always I was enflamed by her closeness. That formative first touch. The memory of her wrist, the shaded eye under fine stranding of hair in the byre never far from my thoughts. The smell from her skin of musk and milk as she pressed me there, making me hard as a whetstone.

She would say she found no pleasure in it when we finally coupled. Comfort, yes, in the warmth and closeness, and she could sometimes even be tender, melting afterwards on the heather, moving me out of her warmth. Though in the end her ferocity spilled over.

A clear night and a *sídhe* wind blowing. She brought a dangerous forage back, leaves and sprouts I did not recognise. I chewed what she gave me and we lay in the house with the doorway unblocked— the trickle of fire smoke easing out of the low frame.

And after we had, in silence, spun with currents of silent under-standing for what seemed like days, watching the stars flicker and form signs and rags of cloud progress across our vision carrying symbols, she rolled on to me, that driving gaze replacing the immense canopy of night. She reached beneath my *brat* and found me ready and sat back holding me in her fist and forcing down in one long draw, taking all that I had. The explosion of pain and energy. She began moving in sharp arcs of her back, driving down onto me with her eyes smothering mine. Her breath humming outwards with each push. And her hands moved from the earth astride my head, over my shoulders fixing at my neck, her sinew-strong grip clamping onto the blood flow as she thrust herself with more violence and her breath breaking the threshold of voicelessness into sound. My vision faltering and a roaring noise, as of distant surf filling my ears as she pinched off the vessels in my neck, her thumbs coming together over my windpipe, pressing. Her vocal cords resonating and she fought on, squeezing with every muscle, soughing out deep exhalations of sound and rutting, rutting as if rutting away every evil that had ever entered her through that way. As I fell from consciousness into a dense black forgetfulness, I saw her as if from afar as she finished, ferocious, like a woman coming up for air.

In the morning, I looked for her far and wide. In the forest and in the valley. In the bog and over the hillsides until the buds came on the blackthorn, never knowing if she simply moved on to something new, in the way she had given herself up to us on the day of the *táin*, or if in despair she had thrown herself to her death from a ravine, or whether a wolf or the host of the *sídhe* had carried her off or a man took her at the river. At first I was frantic and full of fear, stumbling and calling out and creeping to the edges of nearby homesteads to see if she was there. And then I grew despondent and thin, and lightheaded. Looking everywhere to the point where I almost forgot the object of my search. And I began to see the deer. Ever as I searched, a doe strayed near. Or stood watching from a rise behind trees. And finally, I began to believe it was her and that, as in the old tales, one day she might come to me in a clearing and bear a fawn and that fawn would become a son. I waited a long time in the woods, lost in a strange fog of sorrow and loss. I waited until the doe came no more.

> I hear the stag's belling
> Over the valley's steepness
> No music on earth
> Can move me like its sweetness

In the end I had to accept that she was gone. That by then she could be as far away as Magog at the edge of the world, or in the Asian kingdom of Prester John, or a concubine in the land of the Mongol or on the island of Hy Brasil in the far ocean. I followed my feet back across the wild and dangerous bogs until I came to our *túath*. I took the punishments, which were swift and savage, though no one had the spirit to bear enmity overlong. It soon became clear to me that the Tiarna was glad I had returned and that my absence had been due to the foolish moonings of a boy in heat and that I had not gone across to Ua Ruairc or the foreigners, selling secrets for freedom. Father said little, though not one single blow did he land on me. I believe he was happy I had come home.

CHAPTER II

Tlachta

THE FIRST WE KNEW of the parley was Milesius hammering on the plank door of the mill, a burning rushlight in his fist. He cried out in Latin so that we might know his purpose.

Father and I were sleeping on a nest of sacking over the wide boards of the floor with the wheel disengaged and the bronze bog waters running freely down the timber chute beneath us and clamouring into the mill-race beyond. Father rose, and I could just make out his shape in the dense blue dark. I stayed prone, paralysed with a child's fear on sudden waking. Men flooded into the small space, crowding around and stooping beside the millstone. Milesius led them, looking wild in the lamplight with embers rising, settling in his hair, in his beard.

'Watch the thatch', Father said as sternly as he dared. In the ruddy light, the scene was unreal, men of high degree entering our humble room like magi from afar, bursting in upon us with tidings of great consequence. Milesius bustling at their head with Tuar close behind him, anger thrumming in the space between them as the Tiarna himself pressed forward and the space closed in around us, the signs of conflict knitting his brows. Fiacra was there too, pushing his face in as close as he dared. Eyes swollen with the happening, darting around like fish in a shoal. His lips moving already—waiting for the first chance to shout out in condemnation. And beyond, I could sense a body of men crowding the darkening door frame.

Milesius spoke in Latin, out of respect to Father.

'Seáhan', he said—for that is how they say 'Johan'—'I need you to accompany me tonight'. The Tiarna's arm shot out, thumped into the axle of the millwheel, breaking the space between Father and the monk.

'No', he roared in the language of the Gael, 'I have said no, he may not go. He is needed here to tend the mill, to thatch the forge, to lead the milking. He will not go'.

'The Rí has need of him, Mánus', Milesius said.

'The Rí! Your Rí. Ua Ruairc the war-dog. Ua Ruairc the pretender. Ua Ruairc the cuckold who set this madness in motion. Your mother's cousin, Milesius. I am Rí in Míde, not Uí Ruairc'.

Milesius continued in Latin, undeterred.

'Your claim to Míde is dead, and already the factions feud over the leavings, even as the foreigners chew at our hindquarters. The King of the Engleis has granted Míde to Hugo de Lacy. Support Ua Ruairc or suffer the hand of the foreigner'.

'This is my *túath*', roared the Tiarna, and I was frightened by his rage. Unsettled by his lost composure—to see this negotiator, this silver tongue, this Odysseus of the west, so uncontrolled.

'Well have your say now, Mánus', Milesius continued firmly, 'Gael or Engleis, for that is the only choice before us. De Lacy is coming to claim what has been promised to him'.

The Tiarna did not move. His hand, planted on the axle, barred the monk's way. Milesius pressed on, speaking to the shadows beyond the door as much as to the Tiarna himself.

'There are many who say the Engleis are sent by God to punish us for the un-Christian act of slavery that persists in the dark corners of this land'.

Voices fell silent. Those who could understand Latin felt the barb keenly, the others cowed by the change in the atmosphere. Night-sound re-entered the mill. The tumbling waters below. The snapping of the rushlight slowly consumed. I felt my father's hand reach behind for me and guide me up.

After a span of silence, the Tiarna spoke.

'Seáhan will not go, he is needed. Take Alberagh. He speaks the tongue'.

At this, Father's hand ushered me behind him, and he backed up, pushing me against the wattle of the wall, my face buried in his shoulder. I both heard and felt his voice, resonating through the cavities in his strong body, treading that familiar shadow ground between deference and defiance.

'*A thiarna*, no, not my son', he said in the tongue of the Gael, and the faltering words and heavy accent of his speech, as ever, caused me shame. The Tiarna came forward and took Father by the shoulders. The grip was measured but firm. I felt Father's bulk resist for the space of two breaths before he moved aside. The Tiarna spoke words of assurance into his ear as Milesius came forward.

'Mánus, please', Father said—the Tiarna's name, shocking from his lips, provoked exclamation from the shadowed door frame. But the Tiarna spoke gently to him.

'All will be well, friend. He goes with the monk and will be protected by Ua Ruairc's people'. Milesius had slid around them both, landing a hand on me, spiriting me outside.

'Come, lad', he said, 'the Rí needs you'.

He hurried me away from the mill with vivid movements, and I perceived then that this had been his desire all along. Alberic and not Johan. He cast the dying rushlight into the mud, and we followed the run of the millstream that Father and I had dug out two seasons previous. I inspected it, as ever, mindlessly in the half-light for signs of silting or fouling as Milesius dragged me onwards by a numb hand.

We passed downslope past the farmstead alive with the commotion of events, to the head of the valley where a company awaited us at the crossroads beneath the wide bulk and greening canopy of an oak tree. There were some important-looking men on horses and a group of their household soldiers on foot. One of the horsemen cantered out to meet us, and I recognised, even in the poor light, the face of Conn Máel Sechlainn, his hooded eyes silent and questing, probing Milesius, seeking some word or sign of his father. The monk pushed me towards the rear of the caravan as he walked towards the head, Conn beside him, stooped in hungry conversation. Foster son of Ua Ruairc, blood son of the Tiarna. A shadow between two houses.

Milesius spoke to the horsemen and set off ahead on foot, his stride urgent. I walked behind with the servants. As we passed down the *gleann,* five of the Tiarna's men came out to us, from the smaller farms, to honour the hosting and keep safe the hostages. Milesius stalked ahead of us all, his gnarled, bronze-shod gorse stave striking the earth, a *brat* over his head and his bare feet finding the way along gravel ridges between the bogs, leading us along low hills threading between woodlands and dark meadow. We walked into the sunrise, and I caught whispers between the others that we were bound for Tlachta—a place of consequence, a hill of mist and sorcery where the ancestors were close, watching all from behind a thin veil. We moved towards a meeting of kings. My mind swam, trying to catch up with the pace of events. I wondered as we walked whether the Engleis would have slaves, and whether I would understand when they spoke, and whether my ancestors would be watching, given I was not of that land. But mostly as we walked, and the mild breeze took on body, stirring Milesius' *brat* from his shoulders, I wondered if I was to see Father again, and who was to fetch him his buttermilk now and help him in the early light to weigh the wefts of thatch onto the roof of the forge in the bottom field.

We came at the hill from the west, finding a large force of men assembled in a clearing at the bottom of the wooded slope. They had ordered themselves into a field camp with the provisions and nobility in the centre of a palisade of men bearing spears and axes and the entire circle crowned by a wheeling chaos of rooks, doing their dawn dance, falling in from the surrounding trees. Ua Ruairc was there in the middle of the gathering, surrounded by his household men, and Milesius led us through the circlet of warriors. He bade Conn organise the men who had arrived with us, and he called me with him, hurrying towards the side of the Rí. Ua Ruairc sat on a wooden stool with his *ollamh* and lawmen gathered around on woven matting. His household soldiers stood outside these, and all others were made up of soldiers and bonds-men sent from his client kings and vassals.

Milesius pushed through the guards, holding fast to my wrist. We passed without challenge. He brought me forward and pushed me towards a group of men standing beyond the seated advisers but within the circle of guards. The talk fell silent as Milesius took his seat, beginning to speak as he lowered himself onto his heels, and I was surprised by the sudden silence he commanded. I stood with the others. There were a dozen of us, poorly attired, and all with the gaunt look of the labourer. Servants, slaves, all, I learned from Milesius' speech. All foreigners gathered together from Ua Ruairc's allies in the hope that we might understand the tongue of the foreigner. Ua Ruairc sat immobile, the storm of his face arranged at its most baleful. Thunder clouds on the horizon over passive purple bogs. His one eye, roving, found me as Milesius spoke, and I could not bear its gaze; I withered under its power as I remembered him at a distance absorbing the *file*'s satire, his body a battered shield. And then Milesius was speaking my name, as if from a great distance.

'Boy', Ua Ruairc addressed me directly, 'these men around you, speak to them in turn and choose the five who understand your tongue the best. Bring these five men to Eochadh here and we will speak with you afterwards of a place for you in my household'.

And then the roving eye was gone, passed on to the next matter as scouts and *kern* came into the circle from all sides in a steady stream with updates on the Engleis position. On movements on the *slíghe*, of the watchmen farther out on the approaches, on the advance negotiations on the hill between Ua Ruairc's and de Lacy's stewards.

Eochadh came towards me, a broad-faced, tall man, wiry though exuding an impressive air of strength. He gestured towards the group of foreigners, and I approached them. As a test, I spoke quickly and tersely from the *Chanson de Roland*, those verses almost sacred to my father, words he had recited again and again at my demand on stormy nights in the byre, his tongue tripping along his native words like a swift stream over rounded stones:

Carles li reis, nostre emperere magnes,
Set anz tuz pleins ad estet en Espaigne:
Tresqu'en la mer cunquist la tere altaigne.
N'i ad castel ki devant lui remaigne;

There were some looks of confusion—Bretons and Saxons who had no knowledge of our language. Though there were those who caught my meaning and took up immediately with the following verses. I picked out those who recited clearest and spoke to them quickly, to be sure they could parse my words. There were two Engleis, a Frank and a merchant—a Gael who had sojourned long in the realm of Burgundia, this last one an older man, the best part of his nose consumed by a black canker. He spoke with strange inflection on the words, though he was as quick as the rest to understand. I indicated to Eochadh, and he led us out from the circle, took our rags and dressed us as soldiers. He put a leather *ionar* over my shoulders and a pair of thick *osian* over my legs.

'What is to happen?' I asked as Eochadh added some touches to my disguise, tugging at a cross belt and hanging the long blade of a *scian mór* at my waist. He addressed us all.

'You will go to the summit with the Rí, each of you mounted with one of our men. Listen to what is being said—not by the negotiating party but by the soldiers, the guards, the servants that may be up there. Keep your eyes and ears keen for signs or words of betrayal or ambush, all the while feigning incomprehension. If there is anything said that suggests attack or treachery, you will grip the handle of your *scian* in its sheath like this, so that your companion may see. You will be rewarded for loyalty. Any move to deceive us or to aid our enemies will be met with a long blade driven slowly home'.

Then he called out to several of Ua Ruairc's household men, placing us each with one of them. I was to go with Eochadh himself, who laid his large hand on my shoulder.

'Our emissaries are up there now, negotiating since dawn. They will agree on the parties with the Engleis—how many men, what weapons are allowed, how the parties will approach one another, how the parties will address one another'.

'We will be with the Rí?' I asked.

'We will be abreast of him. And we will watch, still, like stags in the woodland, ready to rush to the protection of the old wolf'. Eochadh laughed, 'Though it is likely to be this de Lacy who needs protecting', and he looked back at the Rí—a spider in his web, assessing the tremblings coming to him from his network of men arriving still from south and north. Runners padded constantly into the clearing with words passed on and then gone. The rhythm of the camp, quick but regular, showing up the slowness of our waiting. A restrained feeling all around us. Some of the men singing in low voices or throwing javelins into the earth to dispel the tension.

Eochadh hung a worn quilted jacket on my shoulders—the kind that absorbs blows—and pushed me out in front of him, turning me around, saying loudly, 'A warrior of legend or I am much mistaken'. Some of the men within earshot laughed, looking at me in the oversized coat and the loose trews. Despite their mockery, I had never been so richly attired, and I noticed my bearing had changed, shoulders pushed back, muscles stretched tight across my breastbone.

'No hope of winning the hero's portion with this one around', someone said, and there was more laughter, heads turning to see, hungry for something to break the tense waiting.

'Were Anluán here, he would best this *bodach*', said another, and I took up the game swiftly, dropping to the ground and gathering up a clod of muck. 'But he is here—his head at least', and I threw the clod at the warrior who had spoken so that it struck his chest, breaking apart in a shower of crumbs. This move echoing the part of Conall Cearnach in one of their favourite stories. All laughed and praised my swiftness, and Eochadh clapped a big hand on my shoulder.

'All right, lad, well played. That will do us now'. Eochadh could sense the laughter bringing on a flightiness, and some of Ua Ruairc's party were taking notice.

'What do you know of this place, Sasanach?' he asked, addressing me loudly for the benefit of all those within earshot.

'This is Tlachta, the place where the fires of Samhain are lit', I said, 'the place where Ruairí Ua Conor convened his synod'.

'Yes, this is the place', he paused, looking around at his men. 'The monk says you have a sharp mind. So tell me, why do you

think we are meeting here, at this hill?' This was something I had
been turning over on our journey.

'Because this hill is clearly within the territory of the Rí and
holds meaning for the Gael. The Engleis should be vulnerable here,
not knowing the land or the ruling families. The Rí is more likely
to agree to a meeting here'.

'And what benefit to the foreigner?'

I spat in the dirt and decided to speak plainly. 'Either to show
a desire to reach accord by submitting to the legitimacy of place—'
I said, pausing.

'Or', Eochadh prompted.

'Or to craft a lure to draw the Rí into danger in his own territory'.

Eochadh nodded, the rough palms of his hands running loudly
over his cheeks. 'I can see why they call you the hay-barn *ollamh*
behind your back', he said, watching to see the effect his words
would have on me.

'Many fine things began in a manger', I said swiftly, and some of
the men laughed, Eochadh himself smiling beneath a raised hand.

'Tell us then, *ollamh*, who was Tlachta?'

I could not answer, and Eochadh continued. 'Tlachta was the
daughter of the great druid Mog Ruith, who learned the profane
secrets and forbidden magic in the Holy Land. She accompanied
her father on his travels and learned the dark secrets. She was
raped by the three sons of Simon Magus before she fled to this
place, where she gave birth to three sons. She then died of grief'.

The men fell silent contemplating this, and I could see the mark
of leadership clearly in Eochadh's actions. Breaking the tension
with humour and then focusing minds with a reminder of the
hilltop and its grave past. I noted such things, as ever, and learned
by them where I could.

Into the silence, a voice rose in the clear metrical run of their
poetry. I looked up to find it was the old Gael with the canker on
his face, the back of one hand tapping softly into the palm of the
other, marking time.

> A wage was given to Mog Ruith for beheading Johan the Baptist;
> this then was the wage of Mog Ruith—his choice of the maidens.
> Then Mog Ruith the splendid went to kill Johan, though

it was shameful. So he took to Herod the head of
Johan on a dish of white silver.
For this sin, it is contended, the feast of Johan
will come upon the Gael, so that there shall not survive of the
race of noble Gaels save one-third unslain.
The single third which will be left on that day
of the host of the Gael and the foreigners, oh Son of Mary,
it is a sad thing that they should all be visited by a black pestilence.

The words dropped into the congregation like a black boulder, sinking into a clear pool, dislodging gouts of black silt and scum from the bottom—muddying the waters. We waited the rest of the time in silence under the hanging threat of that curse.

The emissaries returned down the hill, the morning still young and the sun with several spans to rise. Ua Ruairc, though he had not shifted in hours, stood up in one movement, like a dog who has heard his master at the gate. He showed no sign of complaint or stiffness in his joints bar a slight stoop to his back. The palisade of warriors opened to admit the men coming down the hill, closing again quickly, and I lost sight of Ua Ruairc and Milesius in the close, conferring huddle at the centre of the ring.

Eochadh stood and readied his men, calling for the Rí's horse. We arranged ourselves at the base of the slope, the circle of warriors behind us. Ua Ruairc's *ollamh* came out from the circle and shouted the words 'fifteen and five', and Eochadh responded immediately with a brusque and swift ordering of his men, sheering off several of them until we numbered fifteen, all mounted except the five of us sent out to spy, sitting in front of the household men of Ua Ruairc. Another set of *giollaí* came forward to give Ua Ruairc's horse a final brush and to lay it with a woven mat of fine purple linen. The garland of warriors opened and Ua Ruairc came forward with five of his councillors, and I was heartened to see Milesius by his side. Conn was there too, surrounding the councillors as part of Ua Ruairc's guard. Two *giollaí* followed carrying a basket which contained gifts. Ua Ruairc walked as straight as his old body would allow. His face like a graven idol, his one eye trained at the hillside ahead, entirely engaged in trying to see the future—as if it were a distant bird on the breeze. The *giollaí* helped him to mount, and he moved on instantly, steering the horse by squeezing its flanks with his thighs and tapping its head with a length of crooked stick.

I mounted in front of Eochadh, and he set his mount to the slope, climbing towards the summit. The horse progressed slowly up the hill, and as we went, we passed individual *kern* perched in trees or within stands of broom watching the approaches, alive to treachery.

We crested the hill, facing into the morning, and Ua Ruairc and his advisers shouted out angrily when they saw that the Engleis were there waiting. They had placed themselves at natural advantage on the bones of what must have once been a kingly *ráth* with the broken banks still piled high. Their backs were to the rising sun so that their outlines were all that we could see as we faced into the lensing light.

Eochadh cantered us out wide. His eyes roved across the hilltop, and the anxiety of the situation was writ large in the set of his jaw. He guided the horse then to Ua Ruairc's flank, his fist deep in the horse's mane, his other hand crooked in his belt, knuckles knocking the smooth wood of the axe handle that dwelt there. The household guard fanned out to reflect the arc made by the waiting Engleis.

Milesius and the *ollamh* led the Rí forward, his black mount's coat sheening beneath him. They halted midway to the Engleis. Ua Ruairc's regalia, dun and flat coloured in the sun. My courage faltered when I saw Milesius strike out alone across the empty ground, twenty paces to the waiting foreigners on the *ráth*. We all watched Milesius' progress, tracked his movements, until he was but an outline against the rising sun, which peeled away the true colour of the world, leaving patterns burned into our eyes. A figure came forward to meet him, and they exchanged words. Milesius turned and raised his hand. Ua Ruairc dismounted stiffly, his belly sliding down the horse's flank. He stood straight, pulling his *léine* down tight to his frame, took his axe from a waiting *giolla* and strode forward towards the conclave of foreigners standing in the sun like blackened, immovable posts. Ua Ruairc's retinue surged forward together, keeping pace with their Rí and fanning out in the shape of a gull with wings outstretched, we on the inner flank to ward off encircling. His *ollamh*, hurrying to keep pace, began to announce 'Tigernán Ua Ruairc, Rí of Bréifne, Tiarna of—' until Ua Ruairc slapped at the man's chest with the back of his hand, silencing him as his own voice came tunnelling up out of his chest as he stalked forward. The sound came gargling up into the light and broke like a colony of gannets on a cliff, hoarse and phlegm riddled, the deep lung rot sounding, the determined power of his voice carrying over all the signs of his age.

'King of Bréifne, Prince of the Ua Ruaircs, ruler of Tethba, despoiler of Laigin, receiver of the cattle tribute of Airgialla, hammer of the *gall*, and ruler of Míde by the hand of Ua Conor, Ard Rí and highest authority in Éirinn'.

The party of Engleis came forward to meet him, five in total, walking towards where Ua Ruairc had stopped, the butt of his axe planted in the earth. Then came their fifteen men over the curving bank to match our number. But these men came riding large, fearsome horses that clattered as they walked, such was the weight of gear hanging from them. The riders, too, clinked in mail cloaks, and Eochadh drew breath sharply when he saw them. And it seemed in that moment that our ruse was in vain, that their aspect as they approached in such force was the answer we had sought to obtain through cunning. The riders fanned out to mirror our formation, coming close as a javelin cast while the delegation from each side met in the middle.

Eochadh became agitated, looking down the line of horsemen to the small gathering of men around his lord, reading the military strikes that could be made, the counter-strikes. The danger was clear. He made to move towards the middle, and the Engleis horseman marking us sent up a shout. A single word.

'*Arestare!*'—stop. And without warning, my heart trilled in my chest like a wren caught in the fist. These foreign horsemen becoming, with the sound of that one word, the heroes of my father's verses. Ua Ruairc's men looked to Eochadh, uncertain. Milesius shouted up the line.

'Hold firm!'

I looked to the delegation and found that I could now make out the Engleis party. Five men, their shaved faces gleaming like boys, one whose head was in the shadow of a long cloak, whom I took to be a priest. Another was announcing de Lacy and his titles in Latin as the lord stood by. I strained for a look at this de Lacy. He was shorter than the rest, his mail shirt coming to his knees, cinched by a narrow belt at the waist from which hung a long sword. A red glaze covered one side of his face, which I took, at a distance, to be a birthmark, and I was overcome by a sudden feeling of fraternity.

De Lacy stepped forward, and there was a fierceness in his aspect, a baleful confidence that carried him, eye to eye, with Ua Ruairc, who met the challenge, immobile. What I had taken to be a birthmark revealed itself as a ruinous scarring—fearsome and red, spreading down from his right eye in lumpen ridges, like molten candlewax. For the span of twenty heartbeats, these two stood face-to-face, immobile without word or acknowledgement. It was frightening to behold as the sun climbed slowly above them, exaggerating their terrible features with the intensity of light and shade.

De Lacy spoke then in Latin, and the low tremor of his voice fell below hearing. He indicated to his councillor, who produced a roll of vellum, inked edge to edge with writing, trailing a heavy lead seal.

A shudder passed through Ua Ruairc, and he shouted ancient Gaelic words in a deep phlegmy rumble, sounding like the final crack of a stump in the earth that has borne hours of axe blows and shovel prying. He spoke the ancient words of the poet—

'Thou shalt seek no other charter except thy own reliance on thy courage to charge against the spears that pierce thee—that is thy charter to the land'.

Ua Ruairc looked from face to face, seeking challenge.

'And you will be pierced before long, Tigernán', said the hooded shape from the group of Engleis, speaking words of the Gael, coming forward and pulling back a cloak of foreign cloth to reveal a bearded face.

'Ua Ragallaig', Eochadh hissed, and, spurring his horse onwards, he roared up the line, 'We are betrayed!'

The effect upon Ua Ruairc was immediate, and in a swift movement, he leaned his weight backward, pitching his weapon up before lunging forward as the axe's swing reached its apex, driving the blade down towards Ua Ragallaig's face. Ua Ragallaig raised his forearm, the iron blade striking hard and shearing clean through the bone. At the same instant, de Lacy drew his sword and struck at Ua Ruairc's exposed nape, driving the blade downwards with force. Conn and the other guards had surged forward, grabbing Ua Ruairc back, axes crowding into the space, spoiling de Lacy's blow.

Arrows flew from over the brow of the hill, striking Ua Ruairc's men, and the Engleis horsemen charged forward with long spears levelled, causing Eochadh and the other warriors to dive from their mounts. Screams of treachery on all sides, and I could hear the cries repeated down the hill behind us. Eochadh loosed a spear that gouged the breast of an oncoming charger, the horse bucking and throwing its rider. Eochadh ignored the man, running in the direction of Ua Ruairc's body, which lay still, his household guard crowding around him, and fierce fighting over his fallen form had pushed the Engleis delegation back. The sun at its highest now beating down onto the dead bodies, merciless colours, bright, coruscating gore.

I saw Eochadh pinioned mid-stride by a horseman who thundered up and couched his spear to his mailed flank and rammed the tip into the side of Eochadh's head, breaking and spilling his jaw grotesquely outwards. He fell like a downed doe and moved no more. I ran, directionless, as all descended into melee. Tripping and scrambling, I sought nothing but to hide, to escape that bare, sun-raked crest, desperate to plunge into undergrowth, to burrow into gorse, to be like a fox gone to ground, swallowed up by the earth. I fell against a hump of grass, and I will admit that I hid my face in my hands like a child, trying to crawl bodily into that darkness.

When I again took stock of my surroundings, I was in the lee of the earthen ramparts with sounds of conflict ringing sharply all around. The last of Ua Ruairc's guards had fallen to arrows sent high and repeated quickly, falling down on them with the ferocity of diving falcons. Amongst it all, the dread form of Ua Ruairc rose. Then the horsemen charged with spears into Ua Ruairc's party, and his *ollamh* and councillors were cut down as they fled. I saw Ua Ruairc receive a blow to the back as he tried to mount his horse, falling beneath a rushing crowd of soldiers whose swords rose and fell, casting bright arcs of blood to the sky.

I stood up on the rim of the ditch, seeking a sign of Milesius, and one of their mounted men whom I had not observed nearby spurred on me with his spear levelled. I fell backwards against the ramparts and cried out in the totality of fear, '*Pitie, pitie! Soie normanni!*'

The hard eyes encased within the helm widened with surprise, and at the final moment, he pushed his spear wide, regaining balance, masterfully wheeling his horse to block my escape. He spun from the saddle, and the butt of the spear shaft struck the crown of my head as I ducked to slide beneath his grasp. When I righted myself to flee, the world canted and my legs gave way beneath me, the blinding pain of the blow arriving late, and I pitched forward, my limbs no longer obeying my commands. He grabbed me by the leather coat and dragged me over the neck of his mount.

Voices were shouting '*fuie, fuie, fuie*', and the call was taken up by the horsemen. A horn sounding. Flee. I knew then that Ua Ruairc's camp had been roused and were charging uphill with murder in their veins. The rider struck me again, with his fist, and spoke in a hissing threat.

'Stay still, winestain, or I will sever your neck'.

There was no sinew left in me to resist. All was trained upon staying athwart the horse as he spurred it downslope. I could hear from the calls around me that the body of men had taken flight, a thrumming of hooves on the earth. All I could see was the ground racing below and thick medallions of muck thrown up by the biting hooves. I clung to whatever parts of horse or gear were within grasp, jolted almost off the beast at every gallop. The rider slapped my hands away constantly as I grappled for purchase, each strike of the hooves like the blow of a stick across the ribs. Everything now rested upon staying on that horse.

My last clear memory of the descent and flight from Tlachta was reaching the level ground at the foot of the hill, where the canter of the horse became more even. I lifted my head as far as I could to get a bearing on the lie of the Engleis camp. To gauge its defensibility against the strength of Ua Ruairc's men. All I saw were the smoking embers of a fire beside a stream and the trampled grass and shapes where men had slept hidden in the briars. And I was both quickened and afraid of these men, understanding then that these twenty riders were the full company. There was no camp. There was no battalion. There were twenty riders deep in a hostile *túath* on a *táin* of stone-hard audacity. And it followed that I was the prize. I and the few other shapes I caught sight of, similarly slung over horses. We, the cattle driven before the host, hanging on by the grace of St Lasair, borne off as prisoners to de Lacy.

PART II
In the Hawk's Shadow

CHAPTER 12

Duiblinn

PAIN AND FEAR, from distant black oblivion, bloomed fully into my consciousness. I rose out of a dead sleep to an unknown place. Hours of road stretched behind us. Perhaps even days. The passage had been distilled into a feverish blur of sunlight and moonlight. Of stony *slíghe* and mucky route. There had been quick entry to a large fort within a forest of palisades, where horses were changed. A water crossing, an open plain, but more I could not say. Neither direction nor duration of our flight.

I lay quaking, face deep in the dew-damp grass, fearing to look up or even to raise my head. Muscles seized with deep aching. Ribs bruised and hands I could no longer feel bent fettered beneath me. All around, I could hear sounds of action. Thick, black snoring close to me. The snap of a good fire of dry sticks. The flat dinging of a ladle off a full cauldron. The snatch of a workman's song. A low babble of voices in conclave.

Three tokens of a blessed site: a bell, psalm singing, a synod of elders.

It was the voices that allowed me to raise my head. Voices all around, rough, soft, earnest, low. Voices I could hear in passing, in the distance, chittering like crickets by a stream.

A cracked voice close by, 'Jesus and St Anthony, my head is like a blown bladder'; another further off, 'a hundred or more, seething up the slope and de Lacy crying "back you shit-hounds" and drawing out his weapon'; distant cries of 'more meal for the pot', as the fires were stoked for the soldiers' breakfast.

And all of these words, growing and receding, mixed with the sound of bodies tousling, leather creaking, wood clacking, horses lipping each other and a hound whining satisfied under a hand showing it affection. All the words, bursting out in that secret language like dog rose across the briar. That tongue that I had known since before I knew what knowing was. A language as personal to me as Lasair's scrap of embroidered fabric. The tongue of the Engleis. A language I had traded secrets in and had only ever heard from the mouth of Father. Hearing it all around me now, amplified, repeated, like a hundred voices welling out of my own thoughts, gave me strength to finally lift my head and look to my surroundings. To see who these voices belonged to and what they resembled. My kindred. My people.

With my eyes shaded under the blade of my bound hands, I saw that we had camped the night in a courtyard on a hill girded with a palisade of raw timber. The place teemed with people. Soldiers rising from couches on the earth within the lee of walls and fences. Boys and servants carrying wood and water pails between buildings that flanked the yard, and from one of these with an awning to the side and diffuse smoke clouding its shape came the noises of a meal being prepared. A severe grassed slope rose sharply from within the palisade, itself girded by a large ditch. The banks raised high had the look of newness to them in the sparse way the grass was breaking from the turned sod of the slope. From the crest rose a timber house the like of which I had never seen, constructed as it was of massive beams of oak wood intersecting and dowelled together. The strength of this place was clear. A great pile of stone had been gathered within the gate; the broken faces of the blue rock spoke of a great work to come.

Some of the riders I recognised from our party; those I took for *giollaí* had slept in the open, rolled up in blankets, and I could see the misshapen bundles of the survivors of Ua Ruairc's men dispersed between them. I saw Conn, not far from me, his hands hugging his knees, his brow lowered in a passion of chagrin, his eyes ill concealing racing, bloody thoughts. He nodded slightly to me, and I returned the gesture.

Below us, wooded slopes fell towards the bend of a broad river. Everything now washed out by the morning sun. Milk-white light falling through the watery air. A burning mist spooling shapes across the forest tops. The heavy smell of gorse fires on the wind.

This, then, the first dawn in a changed world.

Away downriver, wreathed in smoke, a sprawling town with stone walls encircling straddled the river where it opened into a wide, pink-fringed estuary. Beyond it, a line of pale blue, flat as hammered gold, stretched without end. I was confused and afraid and overcome by what I saw and did not think upon my words, which I later had much cause to rue.

'Are we come to Rome?' I asked the horseman who had stirred beside me. He laughed out loud for some time and shouted from his bed to his companions in a coarse way, sharing the joke.

'Hear that, boys? We have a pilgrim with us'. I glowed with shame and hid my head as much as I could beneath the arms of my quilted jacket.

Three tokens of a cursed site: elder, a corncrake, nettles.

'That is the King's city', he said at length, 'Duiblinn—taken from the Ostmen by the Earl'.

'The Earl of Chester? Is he there?' I said.

This horseman turned to me now, as if noticing for the first time whom he addressed.

'What are you, urchin?'

A voice speaking Latin responded from the fence-line.

'The boy will speak to de Lacy alone; he has much information'.

Milesius. My heart awoke finally, a thrush in my chest. The rider snorted, disinterested, and rolled back to his horse blanket.

Milesius sat nearby, his own face bruised and a blooded scalp scabbing over where handfuls of hair had been wrenched away. He saw the joy in me and tried to smile, though his lips were burst open cruelly. His words came quiet and distorted, and he spoke some snatch of old verse.

'Loth yet not loth am I to fare to Áth Cliath, to the fort of Olaf of the gilded shield'.

I sank back to the grass, closing my eyes and gathering strength, waiting for what was to come. When the sun was fully risen, servants roused the horsemen and brought them porridge and water in pitchers of red earthenware. We were left in the grass, ignored and disinclined to move.

'Whose house is this?' Milesius asked, and I spoke the question gently to a boy passing near, his arms full of horse gear.

'*Ert Chastelknoc, de barun Hugo Tÿrel qui ert de grant valur*', the boy answered, and this was of no help to our understanding. Soon after, de Lacy and his councillors emerged from the house on the mount. Cheers went up into the morning air, and congratulations and courteous gests passed between the lord and his men. He moved easy, divested of his mail and riding cloak. He wore a loose robe cinched at the waist by his sword-belt. Around him clove a coterie of men, some of whom I recognised as his captains from the parley on the hill. They negotiated the earth-cut steps of the slope, coming down through an open gate into the courtyard to move among the soldiers, who stirred themselves and stood up straight at his approach. De Lacy passed among them, quick to clap a hand on a shoulder and cry out in praise of a blow that was struck or a feat of horsemanship from the day before.

'Gryffyn, you lithe war hound, your spear dipped in and out of them, bouncing like a bloody mason's chisel over a stone'. Moving on, 'And Joycyln, I saw your sword fall on a head as a falcon falls upon a dove'. In Gryffyn, I recognised the man who had borne me on his horse. His chest swollen now with pride. His young eyes sparking and eager.

De Lacy took up a position in front of the kitchen and spoke loudly.

'Men, companions—eat and sup. We have carried a great victory and have done so with bravery and precocity. A blow struck well, news of which will reach our King on his throne. The traitor and fulminator ORork is dead, and none now bar our claim on Meath'.

Great cheers went up.

'We will divide up that rich land and show the rug-headed native how to sow seed'. He raised his arms once more, and the cheers rose with his hands, skywards. 'Once we have broken our fast, we will make for the town where our people await us. I have sent a runner ahead with news of our victory, and we will be met by the aldermen and the good people of that burg'.

More cheering and clapping and beating of the ground with booted feet. At some subtle signal that I did not note, we were rounded up from our scattered locations across the compound, I, Milesius, Conn, the old merchant with the cankerous nose was there also with two others of Ua Ruairc's courtiers. They strung us together with iron fetters, and we were left standing in the open, disregarded, as horses and gear were seen to.

'Cnucha', Milesius said quietly as we stood side by side, watching the preparations. I looked around with widened eyes. The place where Cumhal of the Fianna was slain by Mac Morna. Where the mother of Conn Cétchathach lies in the earth, dreaming heathen dreams. '*Glaine ár gcroí*', Conn said so that we all could hear—'purity of our hearts'—the war cry of old heroes. '*Neart ár ngéag*'—strength of our limbs—said another. Our lips barely moved as we spoke briefly to one another, bunching together back to back with our eyes roving the compound. We waited to be noticed. We waited for violence.

When the eating and the preparations were complete, the horses were readied for the mounted warriors—those we heard them call *chaualiers*—and their *giollaí*, whom they called *garsunz*, came up with cold mirth in their eyes, draping the body of Ua Ruairc over a mule that had been brought alongside, believing this would injure us. One of them produced his severed head from a bag and made play with his lips, feeding him a spoon of porridge, to which the entire compound rang with injurious laughter.

'Give us a kiss', said one, pushing the head forward and smearing it across Conn's face. They all laughed harshly, like bickering rooks, and the lord and his *chaualiers* took notice, smiling knowingly to one another from where they sat in their saddles, other servants tying bright strips of fabric to their regalia.

The castellan's family came down from the hill when the company was ready. The lord of the house, Hugo Tŷrel, showed his children the body of Ua Ruairc, and a young boy clapped his hands in praise. The children then turned their attention to us captives, circling our small group, speaking low and commenting unfavourably upon our bearing, our clothes, the younger ones making free to tug Milesius' beard before skipping back fearfully, laughing. This was the beginning.

The old merchant started to address them with fawning, heavily accented words.

'My lords, I beg of you . . . my lords, I am your faithful servant . . . my lords, I pledge my services', and so on.

This gave the children great entertainment as they pushed each other forward towards the old man's outstretched hands, laughing and mocking his archaic words and miserable appearance.

De Lacy called out, 'Here we have their leader. Place this one at the head of their column, he is obviously a great statesman and can speak for his fellows'. They laughed and mocked us more, and de Lacy called to the castellan's children, 'Take note, young ones— even a dog can be taught to drink ale, but that does not mean he can host a feast'. From his saddle, Gryffyn watched me quietly.

The knights spurred forward when all was in order, and they cantered their mounts through the narrow gateway and across a causeway over a ditch. A small procession followed on foot. It was now late in the morning and the company were in high spirits, recounting the actions on Tlachta in ever bolder renditions, retelling the events from all angles and laughing and speaking highly of each other. We came towards the rear of the train, tied together to the mule over which Ua Ruairc's stiffening corpse was slung, the merchant at our head still crying out and beseeching in every language he knew. As we passed out of the compound and over the causeway, Milesius said into my ear, 'They will make much of you, lad. You are their bridge to the Gael. Be sure to be useful to them, and all will pass well enough. Watch all. Choose your moment'.

We passed a large area outside the *castel* which had been ploughed in neat rills and travelled along a raised ridge beside the wide river. The pace was slow, but to our ill-used bodies, the route was a thing of torment, and we were required to jog constantly this way and that, fettered as we were by the hand and the neck to each other, to prevent us falling and wrenching our companions all to the ground. The memory of that short route, as I would later know it, from the *castel* on Cnuca to the gates of the *civitas*, remains one of pain and a ceaseless vision of black, bloodied feet shuffling over the stones and gravel as we trained our eyes to the ground and tried to remain upright.

This became somewhat easier when we reached the riverbank and the road levelled out. We passed some ill-wrought dwellings along the roadside. A pig nuzzling through a mound of shell and offal. Children happy among strewn netting and old rope. From the deadness of the morning, a sense of fear rose in me as we progressed and we began to see people. They bowed low to the noblemen and slunk into their houses, from where they regarded us passing with venom and scorn. There were many scorched stumps of house posts in the ground, mossing over with bright green. The entire riverside and surrounds looking as though an immense prey of cattle had passed, churning the ground, dragging ordure everywhere. The *civitas* had been obscured behind hills and stands of yellowing trees for much of our journey, but now it hove into view on the opposite side of the river, its stone walls like nothing I had ever seen. And away to the south, a dark shadow of hundreds of low buildings and tents huddled in the lee of the walls. An army in quarters.

We received some respite when we reached the fording point and our scourged feet were bathed in the water of that wide, shallow river they call Life. Though a mighty bridge spanned the flow farther downriver, we crossed over a sturdy wicker track staked into the gravel bed. De Lacy wanted to approach from the west, unseen until the last moment. The waters ran clear over our calves, reaching our knees, and in the fullness of the sun, the world below the surface looked one of pristine and unreal beauty. Long, trailing tresses of green weed, bright rounded stones and silvery branches, half-submerged in the snagging black mud. We crossed the water, and I felt I was falling, falling from the world into a different place where names out of stories assaulted me on every side, and I longed to slip from my chains and fall into that clear water, to join that pristine world. I did not need Milesius to tell me of the boundary that we traversed as we crossed that river, passing from Leth Conn to Leth Moga. Entering the southern half of Ireland, a place ruled by the Laigin and the Mumán kings. A place beyond the reach of our people.

They allowed us to sit on the opposite shore as the mules came across. De Lacy and his councillors entered a small wayside chapel near the ford to offer a prayer in thanks for their safe return. We sat in exhaustion without a word passing between us. Our necks shackled, our heads crooked back as we spent some minutes trying to settle. Five heads laid on a dung heap, our jaws hanging open, our gaunt eyes roving slowly. Even the cant of the merchant had ceased. Several houses and hostels hemmed in by old, broken-down banks and clogged ditches spread out around the ford. From our vantage, we could see back across the river to the bank we had come from, a wide *slíghe* running north past a huddle of dwellings and a church and on into open farmland.

'That is the Slíghe Midluchara', said Milesius at length, speaking to us all. 'If you find yourself outside of the walls unguarded, flee that way. Stay off the *slíghe* itself, but follow along its course from a distance. It will take you to Teamhair, and from there you will reach home'.

None of us had voice to answer. De Lacy remained within the chapel, at prayer, until one of his men returned from the direction of the *civitas*. De Lacy emerged at length, bowing his head through the low door, and when he stood, he was in the full raiment of mail and surcoat, with his helm shining and hanging at his belt. His *garsun* helped him into the saddle, and his spurs pricked his horse's side to start it into action. We were dragged up, crying out as our twisted bodies felt the scourges anew. A hunger and a cruelty crept into our captors, and we could all sense the change. A vibrancy and an anticipation. The air charged as if before a storm. And indeed, we could hear a distant tumult of people crying out. They tugged hard on our hasps, forcing us to stumble, amber grains of scabbing blood breaking and reforming in the notch where shoulder meets neck. Chains swaying. The dark clanking of metal.

De Lacy had cantered ahead with his chiefs, out of sight, and we were driven up a broad, climbing road from the river until the town gate came into view. High ramparts and a fearful opening through the blue stone blocks, crowded with coloured banners and wooden stakes. Our eyes, drawn skyward by the fluttering pennants snagged on the gore-greased poles and their fruit of heads blackening in the sun.

A crowd spread out from the entranceway, a cheering mob crying de Lacy's name as he dismounted among them, holding up his sword in victory. We were brought up to stand close to the crowd, which began to curse us and spit on us. Young men began to run up to us, landing savage blows with fists and sticks before skipping back out of the way. They flailed us hard, as if trying to winnow our flesh from the bone. Our legs faltered then, with men on their knees trying to stand and others choked by the dragging chains, the horsemen coming behind lashing down with the flats of their sword blades. Our necks all twisted in the fall, hands bound and useless, high walls of stone looming up over us, a high, blue sky and crowds closing in to kick and punch at our exposed heads and throats. Out of the tumult of harsh voices and the heavy frenzy of faces bearing in on us, Milesius' voice rose, deep and sudden. A prayer. The Cry of the Deer. St. Patricius' Breastplate. The Shield of the Gael.

> I arise today,
> Through a mighty strength,
> the invocation of the Trinity,
> Through belief in the Threeness,
> Through confession of the Oneness
> of the Creator of creation.

At this raw-throated knell, strength was fired within us, and we took up the prayer, struggling upright and tensing against the blows.

> I arise today
> Through the strength of Christ's birth with His baptism,
> Through the strength of His crucifixion with His burial,
> Through the strength of His resurrection with His ascension,
> Through the strength of His descent for the judgement of doom.

I had known vicious blows before—often—but that these blows were meted out by a wall of strangers with teeth bared, children and all, broad youths proving their arm, brought with it an unknown terror. We were beaten and humiliated, clothes torn away and left naked. Milesius droned on, and we followed him with words into the churned muck beneath our faces, unsure even if sounds issued from our mouths or if Milesius carried us all.

I arise today, through,
The strength of heaven,
The light of the sun,
The radiance of the moon,
The splendour of fire,
The speed of lightning,
The swiftness of wind,
The depth of the sea,
The stability of the earth,
The firmness of rock.

We prayed and prayed, invoking Christ, Patricius and the truths of existence and struggled to rise to our knees, huddling together in whatever way caused us least pain. Brothers in suffering. And I would come to understand later that they did unto us what had been done unto them. That their viciousness was born of despair and loathing and foul distemper. The ugly and blind bite of a kicked cur. The blows stopped, and we were left briefly in the dirt as the mule was brought up with Ua Ruairc's body.

They played all kinds of foul games, making us cavort with the stiffening corpse in all manner of ways before finally the sport was halted and the body heaved aside and hung over a large tree bole beside the road. A squat, dead thing which looked small and weak in the sunlight. A hide de-haired on the tanner's horse.

In front of the gate, they brought out a thick pole, flame blackened and sharpened to a point. De Lacy approached this and produced from a wrap of leather the severed head of Ua Ruairc. He held it up, and the townspeople cheered.

'Here is the villain Tigernán ORork who would not come to the King's peace'.

He thrust the head onto the spike and hammered on the crown with his mailed fist until the point forced its way deep into the tight, knotted brawn of the severed neck. He stepped aside, and his *garsun* landed heavy, thudding strikes of a mallet until the tip of the stake crested Ua Ruairc's scalp. The spike was hoisted high and planted over the gate by men out on the battlement. Ua Ruairc the mighty, the feared, took his place among the rotting heads and broken skulls as, above all, two flags, the King's and de Lacy's, nuzzled each other like stabled horses in the light breeze. Under Ua Ruairc's one-eyed stare, the crowd all cheered like men who could be next.

When these deeds were done, and the attention of the crowd was held by de Lacy orating another fine speech, Milesius bade us all stand. We found that the old merchant no longer drew breath, and we were constrained to kneeling to allow his weight settle on the ground. I bled from gashes in the head, neck and shoulders. I could not see my companions, but I could feel their quaking transmitted along the unyielding metal of our fetters. Milesius whispered to us all—'strength brothers, the worst has passed'. He waited for a quiet moment in de Lacy's speech and shouted out—full voiced in a clear and imperious Latin, devoid of accent or abbreviation.

'I am Milesius Mac Donchada, Ua Ruairc. I am a *coarb* of the house of St Féichín, disciple of Eugenius, consort of the Bishop of Clonard and confidant to his holiness the Archbishop of Ard Macha, the highest power in this land'.

The crowd booed and jeered and began to throw stones and bits of offal and whatever came to hand. Milesius propped himself upright as best he could, his broken voice rising to a terrible pitch.

'I have sworn oaths on the Bachal Ísu, read scripture from Columba's great gospel, I have walked pilgrimage to Croagh Padraig, to Inis Cealtra, I have heard Mass in Cluan mhic Noise, sounded the bells of Cluain Fada, drank the water of Beal na bPéiste, sat at the great synod of Ceannais. I call upon Simon of St Michan's to stand for me. I defy this treatment and claim sanctuary from unlawful actions'.

His voiced cracked before the end, and these last words came out on a wracked breath. The crowd jeered on, but de Lacy held up his hand for silence.

'There is nothing in our laws, monk, to prevent a man defending himself from attack and treachery'.

The crowd cheered.

'You and your brood attacked us on the hill. Broke parley, without provocation. You have forfeited the law', said de Lacy.

Not one of us had the strength to utter a word to the contrary. Even Milesius, his last force spent, slumped forward as if he would expire on the spot.

'I will, however, honour your request', said de Lacy. 'We will fetch you to Simon of St Michan's, and he will advise us what your fate should be'.

Our chains were opened, and we fell to the ground. Milesius was carried away, his feet dragging the earth, and the crowd opened, swallowing him whole, and the strength he had held us together with departed with him. They took the merchant and threw him into the dark liquor of the town ditch. We heard the body slide roughly down the bank and slop into the bottom. They came and dragged us up to the edge to see, hands merciless on the bases of our necks, forcing us to look. A crooked elbow jutting from the mire beside a bloated hog carcass, feathered with discarded bedding straw and charred lumps of timber. A stench rising from the disturbed waters. They led us then into the dark mouth of the town gate, and the dire pageantry continued, with Ua Ruairc's body dragging behind a gelded horse.

The space within the gate loomed dark and close, and when we crossed over, the lightness of my body, freed of its chains, felt insubstantial, an unimaginable lightness—pain subsumed and changed into something different. I had seen too much. Men and women followed, and others stood cheering from doorways. Entering that *civitas*, I was overcome. The monastery on the saint's day, the *óenach* at its fullest, the press of a feasting hall, could not compare with the tumult, the crowd, the density of people. Too much newness, the dim light of the streets, dwellings crowding in together. I caught glimpses of their houses, their plots with their animals tethered in tiny parcels of ground behind low fencing. And everywhere the reek of man and beast—wood and damp thatch and excrement. Smoke settling low over the spaces in between, and I could not fathom why or how all these people could live flank by flank within those high, suffocating walls.

A feverish shaking came on me. Beading sweat. A cloud passing over the sun. When I looked up, an edifice of terrifying proportion stood hulking its stone shoulders from beneath a roof of red-earth shingles. A cathedral unlike anything I had ever seen. In the fever of pain and the delirium of festering wounds, I gave myself to the dream. A wall opened. We were passed through with impatience; we crossed a doorway and into a space beyond that was as still as the exterior had been riotous. We saw a large court with a long timber hall, herb gardens, a sty, a malt-house. I heard a voice behind us speak.

'Take these to the hospital and see they are revived. Tomorrow they are before the Justiciar'. The dream closed around us, and I was carried along by many hands into darkness, pliant as a wet sack.

CHAPTER 13

Dark Waters

I AWOKE ON FRESH STRAW beneath a low roof. My body, scourged, ill obeyed me, and I had trouble to move or sit up to look around. My arms slatted a deep red and black, scabs crackling over my brow as I winced with fresh pain. A mist crept along the tamped floor, fresh and cool, mixing with the weak smoke rising from a small fire of twigs. Outside, far-off cries and the close-by sounds of work being done.

'It is hard to believe that we are the fortunate ones'.

Conn spoke from where he lay by my side, his face barely recognisable. His lips were broken and distended, his eyes ripe fruits bleeding clear humours. A linen strip on his forehead crusted along a split eyebrow. Within that quiet space, we had been left alone to square with our pain. The falling fear of the day before, the shattering blows of the day before that. It felt like a full phase of the moon since I had sat in the mill-house with Father. A month since Milesius had brought me out into the night. A long lifetime since I had touched her on the hillside beneath an icy sky of trembling stars.

'We draw breath', I said gently, to give me time to understand our situation.

'Bedfellows, then', he said, and I heard the difficulty with which he said this word. The gall of it for him, to be stretched out beside one of no worth, no *lóg n-enech*. This is where he found himself. Outside his *túath*, beyond his people. A person of no rank or right. I could feel him resistant by my flank, searching the thatch above for an answer. Trying to grasp this new reality. After a lifetime of nobility, of a place at the hunt, of a seat among scholars—now a battered body in a slave's bed. But more than this physical reality, this physical pain, he had come to the understanding that he had need of me now. Bedfellows. And in that one word—wry, bitter, hopeful—he strove, with all his statesmanship and learning, to bind us together, to maintain some hierarchy and to save his skin. I laughed for a moment, but it drew a sharp pain. His wine-dark face, blooded and disgraced.

'Brothers of the blemish', I said, '*sméara dubha*', and I saw him try to swallow this insult, despite his misshapen face. And then he, too, laughed, the poison of his thoughts dissipating in the absurdity. There he lay, *tániste* of a *túath*, a noble, a consort of kings, in the power of a slave he had scourged as a child. We had not much strength for more. We had laid out our positions with brevity, but in a language full with codes from the past. He would cleave to me, and I would try to lift him someway out of the mud. If indeed I myself could find purchase.

We dozed again, in and out of a sour sleep, a fever-touched sleep of throbbing, blood-filled bodies and crusting sores, gathering ourselves for what would follow. A cleric came to us with water and changed some of our dressings, pulling fresh staunching wool from a large piece of a puffball fungus. I watched him, unmoving, as he worked. I could not face putting any questions to him. I drank weakly like a sick lamb from his wooden spoon. Conn, too, weaned at the same teat, and we slipped again into anxious dream.

When I came to, a man was sitting at the foot of our bed. My eyes opened slightly, and he did not perceive that I had woken. I watched him for a while as he looked out through the door into the courtyard at something I could not see. His face was long and his nose strong and arched like a ram's around the nostrils. He wore a beard, but it was neither long nor tressed. It was tight to his face, the grey grain of it like chipped stone. His head tonsured with a monk's modesty. A red robe of fine weave hung in folds from his shoulders. A slice of light from the doorway fell across a portion of his face, illuminating a sad, brown eye. He turned towards us then and put his hand on Conn's foot.

'Wake, lads', he said, and his voice came unexpectedly in the language of the Gael, 'you have been summoned to the Justiciar'.

He spoke with refinement and a softness that is hard to describe and with an accent I could not place.

'I must apologise for your treatment without the gates, I would have taken your part had I been here. I am just returned from the south, where I minister Naomh Caoimhghín's flock'. And in this way he introduced himself as the Archbishop of Duiblinn and Gleann da Locha—Lorcain Ua Tuathail.

'A athair', said Conn in deference, 'I am pleased to find you here'.

'And I you. I have heard many things this day. Events move quicker and quicker. I would like to hear your telling of what happened at Tlachta, the truth now, lads, I will not berate you for it. Starting with the giving of your names'.

'I am Conn Meic Mánus Meal Sechlainn, foster son of Tigernán Ua Ruairc, and this is my servant Alberagh the Sasanach'.

He regarded us keenly. 'Yes, Máel Ísu has told me of you', and his gaze fell upon me as he spoke. I started at that name.

'You have spoken to Milesius?' I said keenly, sitting forward so suddenly that I cried out in pain. The bishop put his hand on my shoulder.

'Easy, lad. Rest a while longer in the straw. Speak to me of the parley on the hill and of the deeds done by both parties. Tell me of the journey that took you here and what you heard said, and then we will make you ready to meet the Justiciar'.

'Not difficult to tell', said Conn.

We spoke to him in turns, fighting our failing breath and recounting as best we could the events as we remembered them. He listened impassive and did not intervene with question or comment, allowing our conflicting stories to reach consensus and for the tale to pay out to its final ell. When at last we fell silent, he appeared to listen still, to the last ringing notes of our discourse. The deep revolutions of his mind masked by that strong, passive face.

Finally, he broke the silence, addressing Conn.

'You must know', he said, 'Ua Ruairc was not loved here. There will be few to mourn that scald crow south of the Lífe. There are many who would say that the coming of the Engleis was provoked by him, by his pride and jealously. By his shame. That the blame for the arrival of the foreign armies lies with Ua Ruairc more so than with Mac Murchada'.

At these words, Lorcán exhaled, silent a moment before speaking again.

'You have been poorly welcomed to the *civitas*. However, while the pain lingers, my hospitaller assures me that there are no bones broken except some ribs and fingers that will heal in due course. I would urge you not to curse the people overly. They have borne the flail of the Engleis for two years now, and before that the heel of Ua Conor on their throats, and before that again, Mac Murchada took his revenge on them. The root of it all one way or another was Ua Ruairc, and this is the anger that rained upon you yesterday. The people are subjected now to the Engleis King. His army quartered outside feeding from the people's thin reserves all throughout the hard winter'.

He waited for Conn to respond, but he did not speak, struggling to bear these words against his Rí and foster father. Lorcán watched him quietly, and I took my chance to speak.

'A blemished king brings misfortune, they say. Ua Ruairc was not loved by our Tiarna'.

Conn bristling at this in the bed beside me. Tensing. These words sore to him as he knew their truth. I continued in this vein.

'A demon animated him, some said, a devil that entered through his empty eye and set up dwelling in his head'.

'That may well be', said Lorcán. 'The Lord burns out evil with his light. Such talk will serve you well in the Justiciar's hall. And you will need to win favour—there is danger there. It is a danger I cannot mediate. What I would say to you is that the world is no longer the same and that the sooner you accept this reality, the sooner you will find your place here'. He spoke these words directly to Conn. 'De Lacy will cut you apart like a sow on the block. If you can prove your utility to him, he will see your value. If you keep your head high and your mouth firm, you will join your Rí on the ramparts'.

He looked to me now.

'All that is sure is that your place will not be what it once was'.

'De Lacy?' I said quietly.

'Yes, the Justiciar, the executor of the King's authority'.

Silence fell between us, and Lorcán searched our faces once more before turning his attention back to the open door frame. After some time, he spoke in a low voice.

'So they are both gone now, raging Ua Ruairc and proud Mac Murchada. And they have left us with their quarrel'.

He stood then and called in men to help us to rise. The pain could not be contained by our pursed lips. We bore it as best we could as they slipped loose robes over our blood-bloated bodies. We cried out in pain despite ourselves as they worked. They gave Conn a pilgrim's staff to lean on, and though he was reluctant, he could not make his way without it. I refused a staff and forced my legs to bend, my back to straighten, and pushed ahead. Foot by foot and step by step, the sharpness of the pain subsided into a fleece of aching that covered my body with its dull warmth.

Lorcán led us from the guesthouse and left us in the care of two clerics in long, black garments. I could see that the fabric they had clothed us in had once been of a similar type but was now frayed and bleached to a charcoal grey, with strips cut away here and there for rags or wadding. They led us from the compound through a low gate, into the tight, peopled spaces of the *civitas*. We struggled on our feet, the bobbing, ragged ends of our garments exaggerating our tortured movements. I felt exposed and fearful once again, keeping my eyes cast down at the muddy street, and we moved as quickly as we could in the wake of the clerics. None but a few children paid us any heed. They congregated in our wake from where they lurked around dung heaps, in boneyards and in laneways.

'Traitors!' they shouted. 'Shit-hounds!'

The clerics paid them no heed, and they did not attempt to come close to us, peeling away as we approached a high palisade rising up above the low, smoking houses. We soon came to another gate leading through the palisade into the stronghold of the *civitas*. Signs of revelry littered the space before the gate—a broken cask, shattered cups, chewed bones and heaps of shells cast around and strewn down the side of a deep ditch circling the palisade. We stopped there at a bridge of planks over the ditch, in the shadow of a large timber gateway. The heavy wooden doors opened slightly, and the clerics advanced to speak to the gatekeeper. From above hung heads and quarters and captured pennants and broken shields bearing arms of broken enemies. We saw they had hooked Ua Ruairc's docked body, and it hung, distended, from the heels, pale fluids trailing the wooden wall below. The body pocked with stone and spattered with dried eggs cast up from below.

Conn looked up making the sign of the cross on his forehead, his lips moving silently in prayer, or malediction. I kicked through the debris as the gatekeeper disappeared to seek an answer from within. My foot turned a broken crock and uncovered something dark shining among the rubbish. I recognised it instantly. The *kelt*. The Tiarna's *kelt*, fallen from Ua Ruairc's body and trampled into the muck. With a surge in my heart, I bent and palmed the object, my hand forming around its shape just as when, long ago, I had lifted it from its resting place in the depths of the *sídhe* mound.

The gatekeeper returned and, standing aside, allowed us entry. Letting Conn walk ahead, I slid the *kelt* beneath the broad linen bandage that circled my waist. We were led across a wide courtyard overlooked by stoutly made timber battlements and wall walks and towers rising from the walls. Men lounged in their heights looking off towards a horizon I could not see. One of them, noting us, shouted down.

'Back for more, curs? I've a bowstaff here to bend, and I'm looking for an obliging back'.

His fellows laughed. The clerics did not react, nor did Conn, deaf to the words and struggling through his own personal torment to keep pace. The courtyard itself was quiet, a miasma of smoke hanging low over the ground, seeping from the buildings fringing the yard. The clerics steered us towards the largest of these and sought entry again from a gatekeeper. We were ushered through the low door into a spacious hall lavishly painted with scenes of battle and the hunt beneath carved beams strung with tallow lamps. Furs of many beasts covering the benches and a fire of good logs blazing in the centre of the room. The light was dim with the windows shuttered and barred and the smoke from lamp and hearth curling thickly around the benches and wooden pillars holding up the roof. Groups of men lounged around in huddles talking in low voices, and the smell of feasting hung heavy over the place—burned tallow, souring beer and hounds stretched out breaking bones with their lazy jaws. The plundered carcass of a pig, cold on a spit beside the hearth. Smoke and fug, the rushes underfoot unclean with bone and scat and broken clay vessels. The feel of a great revelry having swept through the place, leaving man and beast burned out like crisping wicks, settled deep into the haze of what had gone before. Men whose names I would later learn, men from the parley, men from Cnuca—captains all—d'Angleo, le Petit, de Tuite, de Feypo.

A voice beckoned us to the far end of the hall, where, on a low dais in front of a hanging curtain, the Justiciar sat on a broad, high-backed chair. We approached. Fear riddled through me, unshakeable as a soaking cold, and I shivered and lost composure. The pain came back to me in full. It was the same with Conn, struggling forward between the benches and tables—his grunts audible within the muted space. A voice from the shadows called 'Hail to the pilgrim', and in some small way this steadied me, the familiarity of the insult, and I caught sight of Gryffyn in the gloom, reclined on a bank of furs, watching me. The clerics walked ahead of us, and one of them spoke briefly.

'*Seignur*, these are the prisoners the archbishop has sent you'.

De Lacy did not respond. He sat in an attitude of extreme ease, a young boy on the chair beside him, other children around the dais. His ruined face was slack, the hardness gone out of it. Even the scarring on his face seemed to have lost its rigour. He drank from a vessel of greenish glass, raising the thing to his lips as if it were nothing, though to me it was a marvel.

The cleric began to speak again, claiming the cost of our keep and shriving from the King's coffers. De Lacy looked at me directly, his bad eye set into the angry red ridges smooth and terrible, like a pearl sitting in the meat of the oyster, suddenly quick, suddenly alive. I stood, feeling naked before him, my back vulnerable to the room, fearing a blow. Sweat beading, wounded flesh cracking and oozing like a boar on a spit. Too much blood in my body and my heartbeat like the smith's hammer, pounding through me, threatening to burst my skin.

'What king do you serve?' he said to me brusquely in Latin, cutting through the cleric's speech. I hesitated, Conn hissing.

'What does he ask?'

In that moment, I took my chance. 'I serve no king', I said in the Engleis tongue. Conn speaking behind me, urgently. De Lacy sitting up in his chair, anger twitching his cheek.

'You speak our language, urchin. You had better claim an allegiance here and now before the rushes are painted with your brains'.

'I serve not a king', I repeated, 'but an emperor'.

'Speak plainly', de Lacy spat. 'Who is your lord?'

'What is the son of an empress but an emperor?' I replied. 'I serve Henri d'Anjou, Henri Fitzempress, King of the Engleis and Duke of Normandy'.

Loud laughter came from behind me, and a voice called out, 'There's a brat with a brain in his head', and a second voice followed, 'And the balls of an ox between those bow legs'. De Lacy was unamused.

'Brains and balls are not necessarily assets in a servant, Gryffyn', he said.

'I wouldn't worry overmuch sire. For all his words, he fairly shit his breeks on the hill. I found him trying to worm into a badger sett'.

More laughter from behind me. De Lacy smiled wearily. Conn, feeling the situation escape him, struck the ground with his staff and shouted out his name and title.

'What does he say?' asked de Lacy.

'He says he is Conn, son of Mánus Máel Sechlainn, the son of a Rí Túath. That his honour price is one hundred milking cows, and he cites the law of hostage taking and his rights under such'.

De Lacy's eyes narrowed, and he looked at Conn for a time, watching him shudder and sweat on his staff.

'Sit', he said finally, and a bench was brought up. 'What is your name?'

'Alberic', I answered.

'Is this your master?' he asked me. I considered this carefully.

'My father belongs to his father'.

'What does he say?' Conn asked. De Lacy cut in.

'Tell this person he is tolerated in my hall. On condition that he remain silent'.

I spoke these words to Conn, and they brought some wine up to us to drink. A cup-bearer poured the liquid into two earthenware cups splashed with shiny glaze. We took these things in our hands. I drank the draught in one, while Conn hesitated, staring into the cup.

'Does our wine offend the Gael? Perhaps he prefers the product of his own vineyard?'

The laughter came again at our back. A baby's cry from the screen behind the dais. Again, I trod warily, careful in my response.

'To the Gael, the working of wood is a noble craft. They have specialist workers for each different kind of timber. They believe they are unchallenged masters of the art'.

De Lacy's forehead furrowed.

'It is widely said . . . what of it?'

I continued slowly,

'In their household all of their vessels are of noble alder, or doughty yew or strong ash. Each vessel for a different purpose'.

'Come to your point'.

'To the Gael, *seignur*, to raise a cup of baked mud to one's lips is seen as ignoble'.

The laughter rose once more from behind us, though this time it was silenced by a cry from de Lacy as he hauled back his arm and flung his glass at Conn, striking him on the temple. The glass fell to the rushes unbroken.

'Drink, pig', he roared 'or I will stuff your mouth with dung and offal. You insult my hospitality'.

I spoke these words quickly to a stunned Conn, and he raised the cup to his lips. His pride quelled.

The boy on the chair lifted his head from de Lacy's shoulder, looking at me quizzically.

'Father says the Gaels are like the Welsh, not to be trusted, but the Ostmen are like the Saxons. More like us and can be subjugated'.

I did not know how to respond. De Lacy laughed then, the black cloud passing swiftly from his face. He pulled the boy in under his arm, playfully ruffling his head.

'Pay no heed', he said to me. 'Tell me, who is your father? And how did he come to be here in this place?'

'My father was the reeve of Frodsham, in the service of the

Earl of Chester', I said, repeating the words I had prepared, had dreamed of speaking from the time I could speak. Those familiar yet strange names. 'He was stolen from the shore by criminals and sold into slavery here'.

'Frodsham', de Lacy repeated in a low, absent voice.

'Johan de Crécy is his name'.

De Lacy's eyes narrowed slightly behind a raised hand, though he did not comment further.

'And you were born here?'

'Yes', I said. 'Father taught me your language, and the monk taught me Latin'.

'Mother?'

'She was of your race, sire, stolen along with my father'. De Lacy opened his mouth to comment.

'Who was it marked your face? God or the devil?' the boy said suddenly. De Lacy palmed the boy's head back in soft reproach.

I spoke freely, words that came to me, words to appease.

'I believe it was St Patricius himself who touched me with his hand. I believe he guides me now. I believe he has thrown me into your path'.

De Lacy silenced me with a rising hand.

'We are newly come to this land, lad. Before I ever thought to set foot on this island, we knew of Yrlande from fireside stories and the tall tales of merchants. It is renowned as a place of mists and magic. A contradiction. A realm of ascetic religious men who cross our territories shoeless on long pilgrimages to Rome and home also to faithless raiders and slavers who plunder our shores. I have an army without the walls of this *civitas* that has crossed the sea together to find wealth and land. They all serve the King. I have a city of Ostmen under my command. I have a legion of Gaels who have also pledged me loyalty. I have no need of your friend here or his milking cows. I have no need of your fine words. What I require is someone who can speak to me plainly of these people. Who they serve, what they believe, what laws they follow'.

'Yes, sire', I said, my head suddenly heavy with wine and the effort of following his rapid speech.

'Do you see yourself as one of them? Or are you Engleis? Speak only the truth here. That is all that interests me, not fine words seeking favour'.

'I am Engleis, sire', I said immediately.

The boy laughed and clapped. De Lacy nodded gravely.

'So you are', he said, 'and it pains us to see one of our country-men shamed and ill used. Now take another cup and tell us how you came to be in the company of that one-eyed charlatan, ORork'.

'Not difficult to tell', I said, and he smiled at my strange diction. I spoke of our *túath*, of our Tiarna and how he had no love for Ua Ruairc. I spoke not of Milesius overly but told them what they already knew of the hosting, and he asked many questions about who ruled over the different parts of Míde and who their allegiance was with. Conn had sunk into a torpor of pain and wine and, though he recognised the names I spoke, did not speak or interject.

By the time I had finished, the boy was asleep on de Lacy's shoulder. The tireless eyes of the Justiciar, however, had not left my face. He spoke to me no further but turned to the clerics who had stood by patiently throughout the entire interview.

'Take them back to the cathedral and assure the bishop he will be reimbursed for their keep. Bring this one back to me tomorrow after *nones*', he said, pointing a finger at me, and we left that place, unsure still of our fate.

Our return to the cathedral was slow, the light faded from the sky and in the still air, smoke seeping from the close-set houses dragged low over the ground. Fires glowed from within open doors as we passed. Neighbours making evening visits and muted music sounding distantly from some homestead. Upon leaving the Justiciar's hall, the fearful energy that had held us upright aban-doned us, soaking from our bodies into the deepening cool of the night. I kept some paces ahead of Conn for fear of his questions, but he was too deep in his own struggle to put foot before foot, leaning heavily on the staff without any attempt to conceal his tortured passage. Ahead, the clerics stopped at times, speaking to men and women sitting out on upturned baskets and crab pots before their houses, absently whittling dowels and other useful and useless things in the slow hours of the evening.

We reached the cathedral wall, and as we passed the immense

stone church, its walls resonated with the hum of a Mass being given.

The clerics left us in the hospital once more, and I manoeuvred myself into the bed, unable to remove my garments. While Conn pissed outside, I slid the *kelt* gently from my waist and pushed it deep into the straw by my head. Someone had placed the *couvre-feu* over the embers of the fire, and the only light was that which seeped in around the joining of the door frame. The room resolved itself into a chalk-grey version of its daytime state, soft, indistinct, as though modelled in felt. I lay, watching the beams of the ceiling, contemplating de Lacy and the turn things had taken. I thought to pray a while and offer thanks to Lasair, but sleep was not long in threatening.

As my eyes rolled and my thoughts dissipated, I felt a movement by my side. Conn had been waiting, listening to my breathing sough. His arm came up, his hand landing on my chin and, grasping about, finding my throat and tightening there. With a quick roll, he propped himself up so that he was over me, his grip tightening, his forearm on my chest. With the other hand, he found the wound in my side, slipping in through the rent fabric. His questing fingers found the wadding and burrowed beneath and he pushed them in, knuckle deep. My cry was strangled.

'*Ssshhh*', he said fiercely in my ear, 'Alberagh, *ssshhh*'.

I saw now that his injuries were not what he had pretended. That he had exaggerated them, hanging back and watching me with de Lacy, watching me walk the streets, watching which side I favoured, seeking the flash of a dressing through the slits in my robe.

'Listen now, boy, listen to me carefully'. When I did not struggle, he withdrew his fingers from my side, though they remained beneath the staunching, close to the wound. I could feel blood trickle freshly down my ribs. He relaxed his grip on my throat. 'You know who I am, boy, you know my father. Do you think I will sit dumbly by as you plot my betrayal with this *iustichair*?'

The strength in his body terrified me, particularly in his hands. Though I could walk tolerably well, I could barely make a fist.

'Conn', I gasped, 'there is no need for violence. I spoke plainly to de Lacy. I answered his questions'.

'Yet you did not represent me as a bondsman should'.

I spoke slowly, choosing words with care.

'I am no longer yours to own, Conn. There is no gain in pretending it so'. He did not answer this; rather, his head lowered slowly until his forehead rested upon the hand that remained tightened at my throat.

'What will they do with me?' A tinge of panic in his voice.

'This I do not know. Nor what he will do with me'.

'You they will keep close as counsel. You they will bring to Míde and you will lead them through all the secret ways, showing them our *tóchair* and our summer pastures, our hiding places. A small hound sent into the weasel nest'.

'And why should I not?'

'And why should I not kill you now and rob them of a *kern*?'

I found nothing to say.

'You believe these are your people, Alberagh. They are not. You belong with the Gael'. He rolled off me, slumping once more by my side. 'And more importantly, you belong within our *túath*'.

'You would say I belong at the bottom'.

'Not the bottom. Your appropriate seat at the table'.

'My father has prepared me for this from the day I could speak'.

'Your father', Conn snorted, 'there is more to that tale than you know'.

'How so?'

'You have never suspected? That your parentage lies elsewhere? You have never asked yourself why you were permitted to play at ball? Why you slept comfortable in the mill-house? Why you were afforded leisure to visit the monastery so often? For one so proud of his learning, you lack acuity'.

'I do not follow'.

'We are brothers, fool. In part, at least'.

This was too much. I almost laughed, though I do not think my ribs would have taken it. 'You are my father's who was raised by a slave because my mother would not have you near our house'.

The weight of this pronouncement did not settle immediately upon me. Treachery? He was not above it. Lies born of desperation? A yarn to save his skin? Instead, through pain and exhaustion, I became increasingly weightless. I, too, became part of the insubstantial night, a chalk-lined self, a grey felt form. Sleep descending.

'So forget me not tomorrow. Do not let me fall in a foreign land'.

Sleep, I needed sleep. Daylight, to see things aright, to find the truth housed within the structure of his words.

'Please, brother', he whispered finally to my deadening mind, to my sleep-carried mind, 'please, do not forsake me'.

CHAPTER 14

The *Civitas*

WE SPENT THE FOLLOWING DAY in the straw, our bodies desperate for rest and finally a hunger on wakening, for sustenance. Conn's strength seemed to have waned overnight, and I understood in the morning light how heavily he now paid for his violent exertion. He barely spoke all morning as, under the instruction of the hospitaller, we forced ourselves to rise, brush down our pitiable garments, wash our faces and necks in a bucket of cool well water and attend *sext*. I felt light beyond description. Though I was not unused to hunger, this feeling of a ravenous sack-bellied desire for oats, for curd, for meat pierced me, pricked me to the quick, and I felt as alert as the wolf after a hard snow.

We were taken through the canon's door which led from the cloister into the cathedral. From this modest entrance, the building opened upwards and outwards into an immensity that caused us both to stumble and reach out to steady ourselves. The height of the ceiling arching upwards with painted scenes on a vault bathed in light from hidden windows above. Columns of carved intricacy. Majesty in every direction. We stood with the canons as the service began, a plaintive call echoing briefly before being swallowed by the response—many voices coming on as a gust of wind rising suddenly in the thatch—bodiless, yet full and powerful. A bell ringing. Rapture, light spiking from the corners of my eyes, brimmed with unfallen tears. God perceptible in the silences.

Following the Mass, a stooped canon with rheumy eyes led us from the cathedral across the tended garth to the refectory. The bishop sat at the head of a long bench, and we were beckoned to sit at a small board close to the door.

'*Daoine uaisle,* you look the better for your rest', he shouted over to us. 'Eat now and eat well, for the King will pay your fare'.

The canons paid us no heed, though we were served like the rest of them with food to our table. We drank hydromel and ate leavened bread and lamprey and oysters and cockles from the bay. We ate the fruits of the harvest, apples and mushrooms from the woods to the south and birds from the plains to the north. We dined heavily on the King's purse, and when the bells sounded and the canons all stood quietly, one came to tell us it was time for me to go to the *castel*. I left Conn to go to his bed, and I stirred with some more dexterity than I had the day before, following the clerics from the precinct towards the Justiciar's hall.

The *castel* yard was full of activity when we arrived. The soldiery was carrying out an inventory of arms around large piles of spears and the long axe they call the *fauchard*. I saw for the first time a hone stone mounted to an axle and an armourer sharpening the weapons as they were counted. Beyond them, several horsemen were active, wheeling around and trying to pierce straw rings and targets with long spears couched under their arms.

I recognised Gryffyn, and he pointed a spear at me playfully, shouting out, 'Hail to the pilgrim'.

The hall was a changed space when we entered. The windows all thrown open and light plunging in from all sides, shafting through the smoke. The benches had been cleared away from the floor and arranged around the edges of the room, the rushes swept out and replaced with a fresh, green crop. A fire of low embers smouldered in the large, rectangular hearth, and de Lacy was there on his knees by the flame, wrestling a large bone from the jaws of one of his hounds. Several children gambolled and screamed around him, jumping onto his back and attacking him with kindling sticks.

He reared and roared and turned on them each in turn, catching them up in his powerful arms, goring their little stomachs with his teeth as they shouted 'spear the bear, bring him down'. Servants moved in the wings, and a group of noblewomen worked on a large embroidery towards the back of the room.

I stood flanked by the clerics as the steward waited uneasily for a moment to interrupt. De Lacy looked up and saw us and cried out in greeting.

'It is the two black cormorants bringing me the sprat. Come in, Alberic FitzJohan. Come close to us here by the fire'. He stood up, wiping himself free of the clinging reeds and burrs. 'You have celebrated the Mass, Alberic. Tell me, what do you think of their church?'

I spoke of the transcendence of its form, its size, of God's presence clearly felt.

'Hah!' he shouted, cutting me short. 'That quarry man's hut? If you had seen the churches of Herefordshire, of Lincolnshire, or the great churches at Evreux or St Denis, you would not hold O'Toole's pride in such esteem'. He waved the thought away and called behind him. 'Children, sit and listen. We are having a lesson'.

I was made to stand in front of them and give my name and tell my story. The lady of the house emerged from behind the screen at the far end of the hall. She walked towards us, a long, slender figure in a sweeping garment of deep blue, sewn along the sleeves with white linen. She held herself poised in a studied way that was different to how the Gaelic noblewomen moved. Her trunk and neck she kept immobile, pushing her legs forward with slow and careful movements, her eyes lowered and her hands clasped gently over her waist. She came and sat on the bench with her family, gathering up a young girl into her lap. De Lacy did not introduce her but leaned in and kissed lustily at her cheek, making a loud smacking noise, and she pushed him back smiling as the children laughed and groaned.

'Your father is in his cups, children, he forgets himself', her eyes rising to look at me, studying my garments and bearing.

'A victory needs celebrating, love. And a great victory all the more, not so, Alberic?'

I nodded stiffly. He laughed at my diffidence and began the

interview. He led me with questions on the powerful families of Míde and then on the workings of the Gaelic tongue and asking how to say this and that thing. He made much play of attempting the words with exaggerated hocking in his throat, which set the children laughing uncontrollably.

At length, de Lacy asked of Conn.

'How fares your oppressor?'

'He recovers'.

'Tell us again of his standing. Is he an heir to a territory?'

'He is *táinste* to our *túath*. The *túath* of Máel Sechnaill'.

'This tanistry again—it is all they speak of', de Lacy said in frustration. 'Explain it to me in your words, for you speak straight. I have had to rely on the overwrought Latin of their translators'.

I was not sure how to answer at first.

'A *táiniste*', I began, 'is the leading heir chosen from the *rígh-damhna*, the noblemen of the household of the *rí*. A son, brother, nephew or cousin. He who receives the *slat na rígbe*'.

'Which is?' he asked impatiently.

'The white rod. The rod of kingship'.

'And who decides the successor?'

'The headmen of the clan decide it between them'.

'And how many of these *táiniste* are there at any time?'

'There can be different candidates proposed by different branches of the clan'.

'Surely there are disputes following these successions?'

'Yes, often'.

'And how are these settled?'

'At times with violence. At times through agreement'.

He spoke to his son, 'And therein lies opportunity'. Then to me, 'How many can claim to be heir to ORork?'

I thought for a moment. 'He has many sons, grandsons, great grandchildren, brothers, cousins who could claim this title. One hundred perhaps'.

De Lacy cursed. 'And how, tell me, do I cut the head from this hydra?'

The young boy on de Lacy's lap spoke up. 'Let the Gaels cut the heads off until there is but one remaining. Then sever it with a clean stroke'.

De Lacy laughed and held the boy up and kissed his cheeks.

'Good man, Hugo. Hear this, Mother?' he said to his wife. 'A lord in the making. You see, Alberic, your counsel bears early fruit. And tell us, is this Conn a potential heir to ORork?'

I smiled at this suggestion. 'Not so—he is *gaill*', and once more I struggled for words. 'A hostage held by Ua Ruairc to ensure the loyalty of Máel Sechlainn'.

'And what is Máel Sechlainn's claim?'

I hesitated before answering. 'He is of the line of traditional kings of Míde, though that clan is broken and many *tánistí* claim to be the head as their kingdom is devoured to the west and east. He is not kinsman nor fully a vassal to Ua Ruairc. He has come into his house with oaths and exchange of hostages, though our Tiarna hated Ua Ruairc and, as far as I could understand, looked to outflank him by forming alliances in Tethba. Our Tiarna fought with Mac Murchada against Ua Ruairc many years ago'.

'My head is sore with it', de Lacy cried. 'Despite its inelegance, our system is the better. First born inherits. There is no room for dispute'.

I took a moment to consider this information.

'I see your father did not teach you that. Your thoughts are easy to read, for every Gael who has spoken to me on this subject has expressed a distrust of our system. Its absoluteness. Its disregard for the qualities of the offspring in question'.

'It is not something that has ever troubled me, sire', I said, to remind him to whom he spoke. He continued regardless, his bare cheeks ruddy, his arm closing around the shoulders of his boy.

'Believe me', he said forcefully, 'I understand its limitations. I myself am a second-born son. I lived in resentment of my brother during our youth, and when he died young—the Lord bless him—I did not mourn. However, I did not plot with cousins and uncles to murder him or put out his eyes while he lived. And it has taught me to instil in my children a unity of purpose. Young Hugo here, my third-born boy, will be provided for by his brothers. They will work together to achieve their goals. They will make the kingdom tremble'.

He laughed deep and loud as the young Hugo set his light eyes upon me, unwavering, glittering with a metallic pride, challenging me not to believe. In that cold, clean gaze, the hubris and the determination that would come to steer my future course competed for dominance. It was not a look I could meet, and I cast my eyes, like a slave, to the green rushes layering the floor.

Our lesson was interrupted by the arrival of a *chaualier* to the hall, and de Lacy was called away to mediate some dispute between men-at-arms beyond the walls. I was left standing before the family as they sat on the bench, the younger ones squirming around each other and escaping the grasp of the Lady Monmouth. Her soft eyes regarded me as the girl pawed at her face. She spoke then to the canons who attended me by the doorway.

'The boy can stay on here. We shall have him escorted to the cathedral before nightfall'.

She gestured to a bench nearby, her long sleeves falling to her lap.

'Sit', she said, 'and we will have some small beer brought up for you'.

I did as I was told. A maid came up and herded the children away towards the rear of the hall, though Hugo stayed near.

'There are many Gaels in this *civitas*, Alberic', she said, and the sound of my name from her mouth made me feel a certain shame. 'There are many who petition my husband for the opportunity to instruct our family in the language and the laws of this new land we have been thrust into. You, however, seem reluctant'. She waited for me to respond. I remained silent.

'You speak well, however, and you have an air of honesty. You also know the lands and lords of Míde that is to be our demesne. You are close in age to my boy Gautier, who will inherit the titles of this great house. I think to trust you, though, it is clear that you need some finishing. Perhaps the mother was lacking?'

I lowered my head in supplication.

'True to tell', I said. 'I did not know her'. She laughed lightly.

'Yes, indeed', her amusement tempered with a note of pity. 'You have such wonderful phrases'. Her smile hardened then. 'But I want you to understand the privilege you are accorded here'. A slim, straw-headed boy came up with the beer, and I drank with a meek lip.

'Hugo', she said, 'go and find your brother and bring him to meet Alberic'.

A spark of annoyance in the boy's eye, but he did not hesitate to obey. She turned back to me, and when the boy was out of hearing, she spoke quietly.

'My husband is quite a brilliant man. Despite what you have seen here, he is temperate and considered—a lord who weighs all in the balance carefully before committing to an action. He is scrupulous in the administration of the office entrusted to him and in his conduct of public affairs. As you have had cause to witness, he is extremely well versed in the business of war. This is why the King has entrusted him with the governance of Yrlande. You may be sure that he has already weighed your worth. And while he has had some sport with you here in this hall, he has also been examining you in great detail. And though you may not know it, your qualities have shone through'.

These words, arriving unheralded, unexpected, drew the air from my lungs. She had spoken my name and had given me worth. I longed then in that moment to melt. A thaw set into me. Deep into my core. A thaw that was both dangerous and seductive, a thaw that would soften and release those rigid and hard places within that had carried me this far, through labour and scourge, through violence and scorn. This the homecoming I had yearned for. The deliverance of which I had dreamed fevered dreams during snatched hours of half-sleep in the hayrick, in the byre, in the kiln-house and greenwood. The great homecoming and liberation. The great acceptance and welcome from my true people. And above all, the soft, fleshy, long-tressed, soft-voiced mother. And I longed with such longing that I had never felt before to melt. To lean forward and occupy the place that the little Hugo had left on her shoulder and to melt, like candlewax, into her soft embrace, to smell her neck and to hear her whispers in my ear. And I fought with all the strength that was left to me, I resisted this melting, this softening, for I knew that if I let go, there would be no return.

She continued to speak, and my body burned with the struggle. She listed out the lineage of her people and of the de Lacys. She spoke of their lordships and manors and *castels* in Herefordshire, in Ludlow, in Normandy and the Vexin. My downturned eyes brimmed over, blurring the rushes, her feet, the timber base of the bench into spires and stars of light. I lifted the tears away on my thumb and forefinger and hacked out a cough, sending spittle to the floor. If she had reached out to me then and touched my shoulder, I believe I would have fallen to my knees and embraced her at the ankles, crying out black, bottomless sobs wrenched up from the marrow of my bones. I would have laid it all out before her, all of my hurts on the altar of her motherhood. I would have sacrificed all to the homeliness of the stray tress of hair on her cheek, burrowed into the sanctuary of the light-staining milk leaking into the blue wool at her breasts.

She did not move to touch me, however, nor to console or encourage me.

'My children', she said, 'are precious. I have carried ten babes in my womb, and God has called five of them home. They are of the great line of Hereford de Lacys and of the lords of Monmouth. But, as far as I care, lands, *castels,* titles can blaze in the fires of hell if harm comes to my children. We are in a strange land, Alberic. We hear daily of enemies rising against us. In Vadrafjord, they have attacked and killed the garrison. In Veixfjord, Ostmen and Gaels foment. To the west, in those unknown lands, armies gather. My boys need to know how to read these people. To know who has stakes where and how to anticipate the moves of the Gael—to understand their speech, their laws, their beliefs and how these can be used to control them'.

I focused on her words and mastered myself as well as I could.

'If you do this, Alberic, if you teach them and serve them, you will earn freedom, justice and the brotherhood of your people'.

I swallowed back a sob. And this time, her hand did reach out and found my head, receptive as a dog's. Her fingers pushed through my hair, running over my scalp, sending warm shivers through me. Her fingers tightened painfully then in my hair, dragging my face upwards to meet her brown-eyed stare. 'If, however, by action or omission, you hurt any of my children or fail them in your duty, I promise you that I will cut every piece of skin from your body, slowly while you live, and I will feed you piece by piece to dogs while you watch'.

I could speak no word. Instead, I bore the terrible fullness of her gaze and sealed our covenant with a nod of my head. She released me.

'Now, go and find my boys. Speak to them and find your place amongst them. And do not show them fear. I will send for you when it is time for you to return to the cathedral'.

I found Hugo outside in the yard bouncing a tightly wound ball of yarn on an old butter paddle with the straw-headed servant. I walked up beside them. Hugo spoke loudly when he saw me, 'Look, Hamund, I have a new servant now. Perhaps I should make you fight for my favour'.

'I am not your servant', I said quietly. 'I am to instruct you and your brothers in the ways of the Gael'. Without warning, he spun and struck me hard with the paddle, hitting my brow and causing blood to spill. He laughed savagely.

'You should ask Hamund here what happens to a servant who clings to his pride in this household'.

I wiped my brow with the back of my hand.

'If your memory is as short as your temper, I do not look forward to instructing you'.

Hamund laughed, and Hugo himself smiled guardedly, then he raised the paddle again swiftly as if to strike. I did not flinch. He lowered his hand.

'You have an unusual way of speaking', he said. 'I have decided it is pleasant. Now, let us go on patrol. I will be the castellan, and you two will be my men-at-arms. Let us see if we can find any invaders'.

He led us around the yard. We peered in at the bakehouse and skirted the latrines that emptied into the ditch below. We passed freely through the shed where the soldiers slept and onwards into the close space where the garments were washed in steaming timber vats. He looked back to us here with a finger to his lips. A young woman, her arms red to the elbows, bent to her work. Hugo approached her quietly from behind. He swung the paddle and sent it whistling through the air, connecting with her hindquarters full on, the force travelling through her haunches, which quivered beneath the thick-spun dress.

She spun, shouting, and, seeing Hugo, the rebuke died on her lips. Hugo laughed loudly, and in laughing, he uncorked a mirth—

he laughed and laughed, it welled up in him uncontrollably. He giggled and tittered, then choked, trying another swing, which the girl batted away with the edge of her hand. Hugo raised the paddle again, laughing still. A figure stepped from the wash-house where he had been obscured behind hanging cloaks and hoods. A broad, steely-looking lad of a similar age to me. Hugo had not seen him approach. He leaned in and cuffed the side of Hugo's head fiercely. The boy choked, his hand reaching for the little knife sheathed at his belt. The newcomer grabbed the arm and twisted until Hugo cried out and the knife fell away.

'Why, Gautier?' he said pathetically, bending to pick his blade from the stones of the yard. 'She is Ostman, and Father says the Ostman are like Saxons'.

'And the Gaels like the Welsh', Gautier finished.

'She does not mind it', Hugo said then. His voice pattering like cess from a runnel.

The girl said nothing.

'Do you mind, Angret?' Gautier said to her then, and I was surprised to hear him speak in the tongue of the Gael, laboured though his pronunciation was.

'I do, Lord', she replied in faltering Engleis tongue, the sounds rounded out pleasantly in her mouth. Gautier examined the girl's face as he spoke, and she shifted under his gaze, the break of her hairline visible beneath her scarfed head.

'Nobility can breed insolence, Hugo. Do you not think the servants whisper? "The lord is fearsome but fair . . . Gautier is stern but kind . . . Robert is sickly . . . Hugo is a little brute." Not so, Angret?'

It was clear she had lost the thread of his words, but she had followed the lift of his tone, and she said, 'Yes, *seignur*', standing by with her eyes downcast.

Gautier looked to me then.

'And you are the Alberic of the stained face that my father speaks about. You understand bondage and its abuses, no? Angret here was a noblewoman until very recently. Her father had his entrails drawn out beyond the walls'. Turning again to his brother, he spoke quickly, so that Angret might not understand. 'Watch her, brother. Watch how she obeys those who put a blade in her father's stomach and walked him around a post to which his intestine was nailed, dogs licking their lips and the crowd baying for him to fall. That also is bravery. That also is courage. What do you think is in her heart? It is not by ill usage that we will win her loyalty. But by a hundred small kindnesses'.

He nodded to the girl, and she passed on into the wash-house. Gautier cocked his head, indicating for us to go.

'Besides, brother', he said, catching my eye, 'you are approaching the age now when you should know there are better ways to find sport with a girl's haunches'.

Hugo's face burned red, and he stalked back to the hall in silence. He ran to his mother full of tales, and the Lady Monmouth received him in her lap and sent me back to the cathedral.

Hamund led me through the smoky streets, and all of my thoughts were of Ness, like Angret—forced to play the game. Forced to survive in silent acceptance. A tenant in her own body. And I wondered, where now? Where did she roam? Steering her own destiny or, like me, a beast of burden dragging the cart of someone else's?

CHAPTER 15

Makrill

FROM THEN ON, I came to the *castel* every day to instruct the Justiciar's children. Sometimes there were lessons in the hall, other times I played their games around the yard, answering their questions as best I could. The Lady Monmouth was never quite so free with me as she had been on that first day, though she had clothes sent to the cathedral for me. De Lacy fancied to employ me as a cup-bearer at some of his feasts and always contrived to show me off to his guests. At a certain time in the meal, he would draw their attention to me as a curiosity of the strange country they had come to, and through trial and error, we formed an instinctive routine of question and answer which never failed to elicit laughter and merriment.

Still other days, the children would be engaged with horsemanship or swordplay or would be out hunting in the vale south of the *civitas* with their father. On these days, I passed much time with Hamund in the town when I could keep out of the reach of Saer—de Lacy's steward. This was not difficult, as the chaos of the colony in those days permeated the streets, the disorder also touching the Justiciar's household as merchants arrived on the quays with their families to lay claim to a portion of the King's largesse. Adventurers and younger sons of knights continued to come also with their armour and their ambitions to pursue land in the dismemberment of the once great territory and *civitas* of Duiblinn, known for its wealth from Thule to Aquitaine. This great tide of people coming to the *castel* gates, seeking audience, clashed with the hordes of petitioners who came daily—Ostmen in the main, whose houses had been taken and given over to some newcomer or other, or whose wives or daughters had been taken by force as concubines.

Through this throng and upheaval, we made our way swiftly and secretly, understanding the weft of the streets and the shortcuts between and through plots. More importantly, between us, we understood the forces at play and navigated the changing face of the *civitas* better than most. Hamund was wise in a way I had not seen before. He had a multitude of greetings that served him as we walked through the narrow streets, and names spilled from his lips as he hailed a maid spinning wool in the sun before her house, asking after her sick mother; a query after the work to a family repairing the walls of an outhouse in their back plot; a wry warning to the traders on the shambles to beware Bristol silver; a query on the price of barley to a widow selling ale from her front door.

Everywhere he passed, he drew smiles and winking words and small favours. None of the shaded looks that met the Engleis on their rounds. He brought me at times into the houses of artisans, and we spent hours sitting cross-legged on the pounded clay floor watching skilled men work the soft black stone and golden amber into rings and bracelets and beads, or we watched the bone-workers polish beautiful combs or women weave on their looms, passing the time with soft talk. Sometimes we helped with the labours of the townspeople, carrying bundles of firewood into a shed or bringing up boxes of fish to the shambles or helping to gather up the old rushes and bedding straw from the floor of a house to dump out into the steaming cesspits to keep down the smell which grew bad in the summer heat. We were paid in morsels or small kindnesses and sometimes won the secret kisses of sly-eyed daughters in shaded places.

Most of our time was spent, however, on the quay front, where a fleet of shallow-drafted boats belonging to the fishermen of the *civitas* plied in and out with their dun-coloured sails, raking the bay and venturing out farther in search of herring and bringing in rich bounties of oysters from the beds on the sandbanks and sloblands. And always a large *cog* or *hulc* lying against the wooden piers or hauled up on the mudflats outside of the walls, where the fishermen laid out their long yards of netting for repair. These merchant vessels came incessantly from Bristol and Chester with wine and salt and iron and refined cloths from far-off Flemish mills, weapons, soldiers and women and children following their men into uncertain lands. And often I had occasion to ask a merchant's boy or a friendly sailor about Frodsham and the de Crécy family, though little did I learn.

The sea unnerved me. Quickened me. Its largeness and its fleetness. If you took your eye from it, an expanse of dark water with crowds of raucous gulls settling on its swell could transform into acres of dirty sand and weed, carved through with veins of brackish water, full of scuttling crabs and wading birds. The blue line of the open water calling to me beyond the distant mouth of the bay.

Hamund was most at home here, and I learned that his father had owned two boats. He had a special place among the fishermen, and even the foreign sailors seemed to know him, eagerly skipping over the boats tied flank to flank to help out with a fouled line or broken spar. Though people recognised my birthmark and remembered the day we had been beaten in the street, they warmed to me quickly as I followed Hamund's cue, hailing and waving and helping where I could and gathering witticisms to share with the older men. Some even began to tease me that they had given me a good stroke that day as I cowered in chains, cuffing my head lightly and laughing as they spoke. I did not mind it.

Ostmen, de Lacy called these people, whom we had called 'Gall'—foreigner—yet they were many generations removed from the raiders the monks once wrote of so fearfully. And though they clung to their traditional names, I was surprised to find that most of them spoke a type of Gaelic with a particular rounded-out sound to it and many strange words that I reasoned must have come from over the sea with them.

Despite the camaraderie in the closeness of the workshops and boats, a pall of fear hung thick over the place, mingling with the salt air from the bay and the heavy smell of fish. The town had been cleansed of the Ostmen nobility. All the big houses in the town had been claimed by the Engleis. All Ostman of rank had been gathered together in the market square, humiliated and put to the sword. Any others found speaking of revolt or gathering in secret were similarly treated. Hamund's father was one such, and his head still inhabited a spike on the town walls, a yellowed skull with teeth bared and scraps of hair clinging to the bone, weightless in the breeze. Beside him, the bodies of the other two Ua Ruairc men who had arrived in chains with us from Tlachta.

Conn, for his part, obtained a pardon through the intercession of the bishop Ua Tuathail. He was not permitted to leave the *civitas*, however, and his life was not a happy one. I saw him betimes, labouring at the quayside, where the Justiciar, at the behest of the merchants, was building a new quay front. Conn spent his days in the slobland of the foreshore, sliding and struggling to bear buckets of soil and stone down to the wooden revetment, behind which they were filling in ground. I knew he would not last long. His broken body favouring one side. When we passed, I kept my eyes clear of him—not wanting to see the scorn or the pleading or the accusation writ there in his curd-soft face.

In the late summer, before the long, airy days of sun and sea breeze began to cede to a thinner and sharper air, Hamund took me to the quayside. I believed us to be going to assist with some task or translation. When we approached the wharf, however, he turned to me, stretching his arm out and signalling towards a long, low boat pulled up against a wooden post not far from the pier. Two men I recognised as Gunnar and Thorkil busied themselves on their knees with netting, and a third man I did not know stood thigh deep in the water shipping an armful of the stone balls they use to weigh their nets.

'*Makrill*', Hamund said with a broad smile, his grey eyes all lustre beneath a fringe of dirty blond hair. For a moment he looked as gleeful and unguarded as a child, the severity of concentration falling from his face. And, with the realisation that he was proposing to go aboard the boat, I felt an answering bloom of uncomplicated joy within my chest, making its way instantly to my own face.

We slipped into the cool waters and forged towards the boat, pushing little bow waves ahead of us, and Gunnar dragged us on-board, and the boat, which sat light in the water, rocked severely with the effort.

'Kneel here in the middle', he said. 'Don't move unless I tell you to'.

The man standing in the shallows, with a word from Thorkil, loosed the rope from the post and threw it into the ship. He gave the boat a shove as Thorkil began working the steering oar, and we surged forward, my body jerking with the unfamiliar sensation, before the resistance of the water settled us to an even advance.

Thorkil propelled us lazily it seemed, though soon we had progressed down the river, past the headland of an Rinn where the great estuary began. Past the figures working along the strand bending for cockles and digging out oysters. Though they were far off, their voices and calls to each other carried clear across the water, disorientating in their closeness as sounds like the screeching of gulls contesting a morsel or the wash of gentle surf away on the shingle combined in a dislocating whole, something new and unknown. The shore receded and lowered in height until even the roof of the cathedral was barely a step in the line of the *civitas*' profile, all swallowed by the purple of the mountains beyond, themselves soon settling lower on the horizon, leaving the majority of the view a vast confusion of light cloud and brittle blue that hurt the eye. A lightness of feeling engulfed me, a kind of giddiness to be so far from the shore. The unseen depths below us teeming with unknown things.

'Are there serpents beneath us?' I asked, and they all laughed at my fear.

'Yea', growled Gunnar, 'though not so many as in the *castel*'.

Through inscrutable signs and signals, they steered their craft. They watched, they dropped sail and it bellied out, flapping then emptying in the uncertain breeze. I knelt obediently in the waist of the boat as Thorkil sat at the helm and Gunnar perched in the bows, looking, Hamund whispered, for the shape of the tide on the shallows, the movements of the gulls and for any ripple on the surface. We were not the only boat abroad, and at times, we coasted close to other vessels similarly manned, sometimes exchanging words and signals, other times in silence. The bay stretched in immensity from its low southern edge blanketed in trees rising upwards to cover the lower slopes of the mountains beyond. The northern shore was equally distant, a low strip of land beyond acres and acres of sandy foreshore crisscrossed with runnels of sucking water rising up into a squat headland at the mouth of the bay.

'Hǫfuð', said Gunnar from the bows, pointing in that direction now, and we followed his arm to see five or six boats converging beneath the sea cliffs. He scuttled back, his legs astride, bare feet sliding along either side of the boat's ribs, producing barely a roll, and he fixed the sail, pulling it tight and leaning back with a length of rope in his hand, and the boat kicked forward with Thorkil working steadily now on the steering oar as the boat slid with purpose towards the cliffs. These, at first miniscule in the distance, barely visible beyond the sparkle of sun on sea, rose steadily into large walls towering ever higher above us as we drew into the shade and heard the shouts of the other boats echoing and shattering off the rock face.

Thorkil threw the net now, casting the mouth out wide to lay on the water and then tipping the bag-end over the side containing its stone weights. The momentum of the boat soon outpaced the net, and when the slack in the rope was taken up, the net was drawn behind us for the space of twenty heartbeats. Gunnar and Thorkil then grabbed up the rope and began to draw the net in, hand over hand with a deliberate, coordinated rhythm.

We watched over the side, our weight bringing the gunnel close to the waterline, and soon we saw the net rise from the depths dragging a writhing bulk, visible at first as faint shimmers in the deep blue. Gunnar and Thorkil hauled and hauled, and soon the shimmers became fuller—a seething packed mass of silver and blue fish all darting and surging in different directions, balled tight by the netting. The men struggled with the weight, and I moved to lay hold of the rope. The boat lurched suddenly, and Gunnar roared, 'Sit down!'

The net breached the surface with the next heave, and the fish, wrenched from one world to another, came over the side. Gunnar loosed the bag, and two score or more fish spilled in around our feet—mackerel. The men laughed and set about casting the net again, bringing up a similar load until we were almost up to our knees in fish, thumping the sides of the boat with thrashing bodies.

Gunnar and Thorkil produced four scarred boards from the bow, handed them around and, laying theirs on their knees, began to clean the fish. Hamund sat beside me and showed me how, his quick knife running down the fish's belly, his blunt thumb pushing through the slit, ejecting a string of shiny offal. They began throwing the delicate organs high over their shoulders, where a clamour of waiting gulls hovered, tearing the morsels out of the air.

'Look', cried Gunnar, his stubby finger pushing a small, beating heart around on his blood-soaked board. He picked it up and swallowed it whole.

'That's for your manhood—eat', he said.

Hamund looked shyly at the others, squeezed out a heart from a writing fish and pushed it into his mouth, maroon drips dappling his chin. I picked one out from a mess of entrails on the board and swallowed it whole. Gunnar slapped the hull with a hanging hand and growled comically.

'The women will be running scared', shouted Thorkil from the bows, and we all laughed, Hamund's blood-dark teeth frightful in his fair face.

For an hour or more, our knives dipped and ripped and sliced in smooth motions, and I warmed to the work, sorting the cleaned flesh from the offal and casting up handfuls of guts to a sky full of screaming gulls. Our work ceased when I flung a handful skywards and followed the red trailing pennants with my eye, arcing upwards and, on reaching the apex of their flight, beginning to fall, and between the hovering and diving gulls, I spied a different pennant, gusting uncertainly in the offshore breeze—a large *cog* wending its way in through the sandbars, oars out and sail struck. A streaming blue pennant at the mast head. Hamund looked meaningfully to the others.

'Pembroke', he said darkly. They nodded silently, the fish forgotten, and Gunnar pulled on the steering oar, turning long, slow rounds with his fist that brought the boat head-on for the river while the others made play with the sail, hitching it so as to catch the light breeze. We easily outpaced the heavy *cog*, despite our load, and were soon under way for the *civitas*.

'Pembroke?' I said to Hamund quietly. His eyes, when he turned to me, were fierce.

'Yes, Pembroke', he spat viciously into the bottom boards of the boat. 'The Earl returns'.

CHAPTER 16

The Spectre
of the Earl

WE JUMPED OUT OF THE BOAT as it passed alongside the stone
pillar at the mouth of the Steyne. We battled to the shore through
the waist deep water and struggled up the bank, streaming wet,
running straight for the *castel*, by the priory of All Hallows, over
the pagan mounds at Hoggen Green, splashing carelessly through
the filth in the gutters past the gateway of St. Mary's de Hogges
and the dense pack of new houses thrown up in the shelter of its
walls. Skirting the great wattle feasting hall the great King Henri
had built to receive the Gaelic kings, we came to the *castel* ditch.
Scrabbling down its scum-covered side, we slid dangerously close
to the rank waterline, running upstream against the flow of the
river Salach—the 'shit-brook'—and reached the place, clogged
with straw and broken hogsheads, where a tumble of stone from
the rampart had yet to be cleared, some of the blocks breaching the
turgid surface of the oozing river. We skipped across and up
the eroded bank to run along the thin blade of ground between the

inner top of the ditch and the *castel* wall, barely a hand's breadth wide, our speed keeping us level. We stopped at the place where the wooden strut of the overhanging garderobe projected from the wall. Without speech or sign, I bent and made a mesh of my fingers. Hamund, without breaking stride, stepped into my webbed hands, and I heaved upwards. He leapt and grabbed at the timberwork, his feet pushing off the excrement-stained wall until he was perched in the beams. He reached down, and I leapt to find his hand with my own. He hauled me up until I found footing, crouching between the boards above.

'Ho—coming up', I shouted, and we swung ourselves inwards, finding the privy hole, our heads poking up into the small wooden space—Hamund in a simultaneous movement appearing from the second hole—and we clambered out like rats. The sight, which had caused many surprised, laughing insults in the past, was now a commonplace one to the *sergenz* of the wall walk. But there were none there to pass remark or make jest. The yard was busy with men moving around with purpose.

We raced on regardless, pushing on to carry the news to the great hall—the name 'Pembroke' on our lips. But the Justiciar was already apprised, word having come in with riders from lookouts farther up the coast. The place was upended in a fury of sweeping out, opening the shutters, setting the tallow candles, building up the fire and clearing away tables to lay out benches, the finest rugs being brought out from storage, the best jugs for the best wine with studded glassware and silver plate being set with ostentation by the dais. De Lacy paced around sternly, bawling orders, upbraiding his cup-bearers, who were racing around with charged trays or changing frantically into the finest surcoats of the household thrown at them by Saer the steward. Angret and a horde of other servants padded around each other, adroitly, their movements recalling the swift co-ordination of flocking starlings—putting the room to rights. The Lady Monmouth, seeing us loitering at the door, shouted sharply.

'*Garsunz*, fly to the markets and order a halt to the day's selling. Not a gigot, a crannock or a lamprey to be sold until our cook comes to take what's needed. We need to lay in store for a feast—market prices will be paid'. She turned to cuff a cup-bearer who had jostled past, preoccupied with tying the leather fasteners of his surcoat.

As we crossed the yard, Hamund tugged at my sleeve, making the most of the urgent hive of action as *sergenz* and *garsunz* jogged around shifting hogsheads and mounds of hay that had been cluttering the *castel* bailey since the early harvests had come in.

'Not to worry—the cook will get his vittles'.

We ducked through the shadow of the gate and over the *castel* ditch, and instead of turning west for the market, Hamund pushed me quickly to the east, passing the big houses close to the *castel*. At the Dam Gate, we climbed the steps to the parapet and ran along the wall top to the angle where the wall reached the edge of the tide and turned west to run along the riverfront. A projecting wooden hoarding had been built here, overhanging the wall to protect defenders and allow them to drop missiles below. The men-at-arms had all left their posts to crowd the parapet farther down towards the quay, along with the nobility and wealthy of the *civitas*. We scaled the side of the hoarding, dragging ourselves up onto the broad, sloping timber roof. A band of urchins had beaten us to it, perched close to the edge watching the river—ragged, hungry-looking creatures. '*Fendinn*', Hamund growled at them, waving his hands upwards as if to shoo a pack of gulls. They poured over the other side, shinning out of view like startled cats. We took their place, sitting on the shingles, the incline of the roof giving us a good view of the river downstream of the quay.

We watched the *cog* come up the river slowly, negotiating sandbars, the smaller boats of the city coming out to swarm around, guiding the ship in as far as it could go. We saw the anchor drop into the water, a tiny plume of white froth erupting against the dark, bulbous hull. There would be time now as the boats ferried the Earl and his entourage to shore. Hamund reached in beneath his *léine* and pulled out a heavy flap of leather, tooled with scenes of a hunt.

'Gautier's skin?' I said, fear fringing the question.

'Our skin', he replied, keeping low and pulling the cork bung out with his teeth. We drank then, feckless, both complicit in our actions. The warm wine exploded with its flavour into mouths more accustomed to dull milk and plain oats. I sat back against the warm wooden shingles, propped on my elbows, listening to the sounds below, the nervous, excited edge of disobedience adding to the tumult and anticipation that had descended on the *civitas*.

'He's in a fury, the *seignur*', I said. Hamund laughed lightly.

'There is no love lost between the Earl and the Justiciar', Hamund said, echoing something I had learned through a hundred ill-defined, unspoken signs during my time in the *castel*.

'What is the cause of their quarrel?' I asked.

'I would not say quarrel', Hamund said, searching, and he switched to the Gaelic tongue, 'rather, competition. The Earl, at great personal risk and expense, was the chief man in winning back Mac Murchada's kingdom. He secured the submission of Veixfjord, Vadrafjord and Duiblinn and married Mac Murchada's daughter, and now that Mac Murchada is dead, he claims the kingdom as his own. The Earl is no favourite of the great Henri, however. The poor fool was against Henri's mother in the war of succession many years ago, and Henri will never countenance him to reign unchecked on this island. De Lacy is the king's man, and he is here to check the ambitions of the Earl and to expand the reach of Henri where he can'.

Some of this I knew, but I listened with interest to Hamund, a boy I had trusted as a source of information about the streets and families of the *civitas*. To hear him speak so clearly of the alliances of the great men of the foreigners was strange and revealing. I looked at him anew with a guarded glance. This was a new Hamund, speaking not like the easy youth but as a man of court, and I remembered that his father had been one of the *lagmen* of the *civitas*.

A silence fell, and we drank in turns from the skin. The wine worked through me, the flush spreading across my face, soaking down my back—recklessness, lightness. I lay my head on the wooden slats of the roof and gazed upwards. The clouded sky a maze of bright and dark, knots and whorls of grey shafted through with whiter patches of cloud, backlit and silvery from the light of an invisible sun. The pennant of Henri, hoisted above us on a pole fixed to the hoarding, twitched fitfully in the uncertain breeze, and for a time, we contemplated the sky and said little.

A splash and high animal screeching brought us back to earth. We looked down to see the horses being lowered with ropes into the sluggish current. The animals, tethered in close to the hulls of the small waiting boats, were swum to the nearest bank of the river. They came in towards the Steyne, the same way we had splashed not an hour previous, the horses finding their footing in the shallows and pulling the light boats around in thrashing arcs as the men tried to calm them. A crowd was building on the shore as men from the army billeted outside of the walls gathered, laughing and jeering amiably at the sight. We watched the spectacle for a time, quietly, bathed in a feeling of freedom, of escape from the world below.

'It was the Earl who first came here', Hamund said after a long silence, and this pulled me out of a heavy reverie, 'on the feast day of St. Matthew the Apostle'. He seldom spoke of the harrowing of the *civitas,* the murder of his people. I had never imposed upon him to ask.

'When he came it was with a great force of men, led by Mac Murchada over the mountains from Gleann da Locha to evade the armies of Ua Conor. The Earl of Pembroke, Ricardus fitz Gilbert de Clare, spoke to us volubly at the gate. Lorcán was out amongst them, his crozier in hand and a great agitation of horses and men churning up behind the Earl. Our men were ready to fight, and a large fleet was expected from the King of the Island of Manannán, who is our friend and who would fight at our side.

'As the Earl spoke with our *lagmen,* entreating and promising, that grey-eyed terror, that malformed churl—Raymond le Gros de Carew—he and a band of villains rode the length of our walls in stealth when our eyes were elsewhere. Raymond spied a weakness in our wall—the bastard. He rode across our ditch, unheeded, and wrenched a hanging beam downwards, lashing his reins around it and walking his horse backwards, calling for his fellows to do the same until the wall came away in a shuddering cascade, filling our fosse in part, and he rode in with his marauders while our men kept good faith by the gate and were only alerted by the screams of our women and children rushing all in panic down towards the quay as the brutes, those bastard abominations, those hell-aborted ghouls, rode their huge beasts through our fences and houses, killing without pause, without hesitation, under hoof and flail and sword and spear. They drove on until our people waded out into the river. The men, hearing this, ran back into the town to give battle, leaving the gate unguarded. The Earl then showed that treachery was in his heart from the outset, and his hordes rushed into the open breach, flooding around Lorcán, who stood in their midst, his arms raised, crying out, shouting with all of his strength, "*Pitoye pitoye, touchez pas aux innocenz*". I can see him now, as I saw him then from the wall, his crozier held aloft, riders thundering around him, funnelling together to cross the causeway over the town ditch, hustled and buffeted to his knees. Then he cried out in desperation, "Canterbury, Canterbury, Canterbury", until he disappeared from view in a haze of dust and blurring horses. Hascaluf led many to the boats, and they fled even as the attackers waded out into the surf after them. Most of them escaped to the Island of Manannán or the Northern Isles.

'The sack lasted a full day, until the Earl could regain control of his men—our people huddled together within the enclave of the cathedral as, outside, the Engleis plundered our homes and killed and defiled any they came upon. Our great King Hascaluf fleeing by sea in shame and distress. Lorcán returned to us then and led us in prayer, incessant prayer inside of the cathedral, and we drowned out the sounds of the pillage with song'.

Hamund spoke with authority, and, between discourses, he drank with viciousness—uncaring of danger or reproach. His cheeks flushing red in his fine face. He looked at me with his eyes bright before a guard fell back in place, a *couvre-feu* over a hot ember, and he corrected his demeanour. But in that instant I caught sight of something burning in that otherwise blond and easy face, the germ of a fire. But then it was gone, and we were at ease once again, the servant and the slave.

'Why Canterbury?' I asked. 'Why did he cry out for Canterbury?'

Hamund smiled bitterly. 'Because we are of that diocese—not of Ard Mhaca, not fettered to any Gaelic Church. We were under the protection of Canterbury and the great martyred bishop, Thomas à Becket. Oh, how Lorcán wept when he heard the news of that great man's murder in his cathedral a short time later, while Duiblinn was bridled and scoured and my people dogs beneath the table. Or bitches in the straw. Lorcán wept the tears of one who has lost all, on his knees for a week without food or water, knowing that the sack of the *civitas* and the death of the bishop were wrought by one and the same hand—by the mover in the dark, the unseen sword, the insatiable and unloved braggart Henri'.

As he spoke, we caught glimpses through gaps in the houses of a cortege moving up from the quay. A noble, surrounded by five mounted men, the horses preceded by a small parcel of servants all led by the Justiciar's steward with his halberd held out before him, parting the crowds. They progressed uphill from the river, wending through the close streets, and an expectant mass followed on and converged from the little laneways and from the dark doorways to stand, bowed, in welcome.

We watched from the heights until they drew close to the *castel*.

'Come', said Hamund, and we shinned down the hoarding wall and ran back along the deserted wall walk, racing for the *castel*.

CHAPTER 17

The Owl and the Nightingale

IN THE END, it was not the Earl who arrived on a stuttering seasick horse draped with the colours of Pembroke but a lady. We came up the privy, slipping into the rear of the assembled household unseen, all eyes trained on the high gatehouse, cluttered with earnest townspeople, children, merchants, all pressing forward, pushed back by *sergenz*, all wanting to see the moment of meeting, to read the interaction, to hear her name spoken, to hear the news confirmed, news that was already coursing through the streets and lanes like a fever pumped by a sick heart—that Vadrafjord was lost.

De Lacy stood outside of his hall, ranged up with his captains and his advisers, his wife by his side. His children stood close at hand, and *chaualiers* flanked all.

'Keep the yard clear', de Lacy roared out as *sergenz* and cup-bearers jogged over and back dragging stray casks and bushels into obscured corners. We pressed ourselves into the shadow of the wash-house, invisible to the intensity of stares focused on the large oak frame of the gate.

Within the Justiciar's party, I noted Gryffyn standing on the fringes. An unfamiliar nervousness was writ on his face, his hands smoothing and re-smoothing his hair, palping his face, which was not as smooth as perhaps he would have liked—a day's growth of beard stubbling his cheeks, like burned straws in a razed field. As I watched, he unclasped his belt, polished the buckle against his thigh and re-set the belt around his waist, pulling at the fabric of his tunic so that it fell just so, hanging in pleated folds from his shoulders over his belt, to great effect. His nervousness seemed particular, something apart from the gathering tension within the bailey.

My meditations were cut short as the hushed tumult of the cortege's approach reached the gate and the crowd parted like a curtain to reveal Saer the steward walking steadily and with great ceremony. He came on into the centre of the yard, and the cortege followed mutely behind him—cooks, grooms, washerwomen and chambermaids on foot ahead of five mounted knights in mail coats and coifs who surrounded the pale figure of the lady. By her side, a very stout rider in a mail suit that barely contained his evident girth, though where the lady was reserved in her expression, he smiled broadly around him at all who would meet his gaze.

Saer approached the Justiciar, and the cortege halted behind him, the servants looking nervously around the *castel*, uneasy under the close scrutiny of the household soldiers before them and the thronged press of the *civitas* behind. Saer lowered the end of his halberd to the cobbles and intoned deeply in the now silent courtyard.

'Sire, *si il vous plaisez, la dame* Basilia de Clare of Pembroke, and of Quincy', and in naming her first, he made it clear that she carried the authority of the Earl, 'and *mon seignur* Raymond FtizWillliam de Carew'.

Hamund tensed beside me at the voicing of that name.

'Malice-striker, chewer of corpses', he said with restrained force, through teeth edge on edge, spittle ejected with the force of his utterance. 'That is him, le Gros. The fat savage who put this place to the sword'.

The Lady Basilia nudged her shivering horse forward, breaking the line of riders, and all eyes fell on her. A young woman, not yet twenty of years. She sat upright in a high-backed saddle, her skin wan as buttermilk, dappled strikingly with freckles across the bridge of her nose. At a distance, her eyes seemed grey, indistinct like teased yarn, and even sitting in the saddle, it was clear that she was long of limb and tall in body. She wore a dress of fine yellow wool open at her neck, which was cosseted in furs of the marten. In her hair, jewels, as is their custom. But it was none of this that snagged every eye in that place. It was how her dress gathered around her swollen stomach, how her right hand, flashing with gold, gripped the reins, her left curled protectively over the round bump, the child in her body. For a moment, silence reigned, punctuated with the clink of horse gear, the muffled thump and crack of hogsheads being opened deep in the hall and the distant flap and cry of gulls picking the deserted shambles clean. I looked to Gryffyn, and his face seemed lit as if by a strong morning sun, a look of intensity straining the composure of his features, hands clenched, gripped at his belt.

Before de Lacy spoke, the Lady Monmouth broke from the Justiciar's party, pacing forward eagerly and calling to the younger woman.

'Basilia, cousin, look at how you have grown. With child already—the union was blessed'.

'The Earl's wife?' I asked Hamund quietly. He signed me to silence, his face intent on the scene before him.

The woman on the horse leaned down to take the lady's hand. Several of her servants moved forward to help her from her horse, and the two women embraced, heedless of the crowd who looked on, breaking into rippling whispers.

'Sister', Hamund said, then, close to my ear, 'the Earl's sister'.

'Not so blessed, cousin. Not so blessed', we heard her say. 'He is dead'. Hamund straining physically forward to hear as the younger woman's head fell momentarily onto the Lady Monmouth's shoulder. De Lacy, feeling the ceremony of the situation slip, and visibly relieved at the absence of an Earl on his doorstep, paced forward then, exclaiming.

'Welcome, welcome, cousin, please come and join us in our hall, where we shall dine and drink and hear of your tidings'.

And his words broke the formality. Movement erupted all around, and the whispering onlookers began to cheer and shout and call out their congratulations to the young woman. My head swam, our racing and sudden stop, the taut severity and the mannered gestures dissolving now into a heady chaos—my heart pumping wine-rich blood through me, and the scene played out with the vagueness of a dream.

De Lacy, having finished his welcome, motioned broadly for the company to follow into the hall, and he went stooping into the door frame, his hand on young Hugo's shoulders and the Lady Monmouth behind with her arm guiding Basilia protectively over the stones of the yard, her ear bent to the younger woman's mouth. I watched Gryffyn closely as Basilia de Clare passed the line of the Justiciar's soldiers. He did not betray much, but his eyes sought her out, shadowing her every step. Basilia's escort dismounted then, handing their still dripping horses over to their *garsunz*. The *sergenz* at the gate began pushing people back across the causeway and levering the large wooden doors closed, sealing off the court from the *civitas*.

As the lower orders of the household and the knights filtered into the hall and the less wealthy merchants and burghers plied for entry at the door, I felt Hamund's fist in the small of my back, pushing me onwards across the yard towards the hall. We insinuated ourselves into the press after the higher-ranking *sergenz*. We pushed in at the door, and Saer, having taken up his post by the door-jamb, grabbed us each by the head and pushed us to one side beneath the sloping eaves.

'Where have you been—*petits morveux de merde? Jeunes poltrons*', he spat and, without waiting for an answer, turned to welcome the last retainers coming through the door, assessing with the skill and dexterity of a trader in furs the value of each individual and, with minimal and deliberate signs to the serving staff, indicating where each was to be seated. '*Habillez-vous*', he hissed at us then, landing a clout on Hamund's ear, and we followed the eaves towards the side door, avoiding the seated guests.

The hall had been transformed from an open, lazy space into a crowded, close melee with servants flitting like thrushes through bramble, carrying out the steward's orders, as separate conversations down the length of the room combined in a clamour, none of it loud, yet together an overbearing presence of sound that had no way to egress the full, smoky space. We hurried through the serving door at the side of the hall, passing out into the cramped yard that gave onto the kitchen and bakehouse.

A confusion of servants and cooks roiled in the tight space of the kitchen, the pantler turning out loaves from the bread oven, cooks stirring brass cauldrons hanging over the fireplace, beating out cloves of garlic and cuts of meat on the boards. Scullions arranging dishes and servants plucking fowl and scaling fish as the spit-boys stood turning and turning hefty joints of meat over two fireplaces heaped with radiant embers, their bare arms and chests slick and spattered with pox-like spots from the crackling grease. And all presided over by the squat figure of the butler, marshalling his forces with a red, sweating face from beside the bread oven.

'Surcoats', he roared at us as we came in, pointing towards another door where the Justiciar's plate was being extracted from great chests of heartwood, bedded with dry straw and draped with linen covering. The napier dressed us in the yellow linen vest of the household, taken out for us from a heavy chest set with tableware, the butler wielding the key with severe gravity and surveying every item as it was unwrapped.

'Wine', he said to us, placing two brilliant earthenware jugs into our arms, and we gazed at the finery of the craft—helmeted knights' and monks' heads frozen in a metallic green glaze around the rim, the deep amber light of the fires rolling slowly across the surfaces in wending ribbons. 'Wine', he roared again with huge force, to wake us from our dazed reverie. 'Starting at the head of the table—this one', he said, touching the jug in my arms, 'and this hogshead', as he thumped a low, potbellied barrel covered with scratched signs. 'And for the lower table this and this', he said, touching Hamund's jug and a different barrel. 'Go, go, go', he shouted, shooing us like pigeons from a granary door.

We entered the hall in a procession of servants carrying the opening dishes. Order of a kind had been restored to the throng. De Lacy was standing on the dais part-way through a speech of welcome.

'We welcome also, in the king's name, seignur Raymond de Carew, known to us all through his deeds of great consequence and valour. Deeds which have touched us here in this *civitas*, which he helped to deliver to our King through feat of arms. And to his cousin the great Meyler FitzHenry. There will always be a welcome before you in this hall. It is with regret we learn of the reverses suffered by the Earl in Osraige . . .'

Raymond stood and bowed as deeply as his thick paunch would allow; Meyler, a dark man with black, stern eyes and a keen face, half rose in his seat and inclined his head before settling. De Lacy continued as we worked our way around the table on the dais filling the green studded glasses set out before each guest. 'As the King's Justiciar on this island, I extend to you this feast—a reflection, though pale it might be, of the king's welcome and his blessing upon all who progress his work here in Yrlande, often at their own expense, and always at the cost of their own safety'. He lifted his glass, cradling the bowl of it within the cage of his fingers. The others moved to do the same. He addressed himself, then, to Basilia. 'It is with great sadness that we learn of the loss of your husband, *ma dame*. I had known him to be a sober and brave soldier and a leader of men who stood firm in Aquitaine when we marched together on Toulouse in the first year of our King'.

Basilia bowed her head, and de Lacy paused. Though not naturally a brusque man, he was neither loquacious nor overly comfortable in the gaze of a public that was not that of his hard-breathing soldiers after an engagement. It was clear by his demeanour how buoyed he was by the appearance of the young Basilia in place of her brother the Earl, and despite all his affected regret, I could sense a well of merriment and good humour beneath his pointedly grave face.

Once the assembly had raised their glasses and, shouting out their agreement, drunk deeply to show their respect, de Lacy spoke once more. 'I invite you all to eat, therefore, and drink, and, in doing so, to recognise that any hospitality you receive here, you receive from our King, for this is his hall and I but his steward'.

When de Lacy had started speaking again, I hurried around the table in an attempt to refill all glasses before they were obliged to raise them again to drink the king's health. This done, he spoke again. 'Let us all now enjoy the feast we lay before you after your travails'.

This last address signalled the close of the formal introduction, and the guests—knights, burgesses, ecclesiasts and barons—shouted out in concord: '*Santé!*'

Three shouts of a good warrior's house: the shout of distribution, the shout of sitting down, the shout of rising up.

All fell to speaking together and reaching out to the dishes which began accruing on the tables. All the benches had been turned end on end to make a great row down the centre of the hall, and long boards were laid out on wooden stands to create a running, overlapping table of planking. As the dishes were brought out, the boards bowed with the weight of the setting: gigot, lamprey, possets, pies, plates of beans in pork fat, goose and fowl meat, hog souse, cheese, custards, late fruits and cereals prepared in milk. And indeed, the wine did not flow at a trickle, nor anything like it. The work was hot, and the assembly grew freer and more querulous the more they drank. The fire in the hearth burned down to a throbbing pile of embers, and the riot of coloured fabrics that was noticeable earlier in the evening became muted in the changed light. The deep red glow brazing the moistened skin and faces of those assembled, flaring at times when bones or lard-rich crusts were thrown onto the fire, coaxing licking flame.

We plied back and forth with our jugs from the kitchens to the hall, the distinction between the wine casks soon lost and the butler too busy to enforce his will, or to stop us from draining the dregs from our jugs in the cool yard as we came over and back, growing gradually as merry as the feasters. With wine, de Lacy's relief at the absence of an Earl in his hall became so bald that he forgot his solemnity entirely. His wife, however, made a better show of commiserating closely with Basilia on the death of her husband; though the assembly more closely followed the Justiciar's example of high spirits—the men of the *civitas* and Basilia's retinue all. As the procession of dishes waned and even the most avaricious of appetites grew sated, the men of the household began calling upon the newcomers to share any new song or verse that they had, and the younger men of the party obliged. Solemnity in general softened, as did the pervasions of rank and the stilted demeanours of those trying to maintain their reserve and those trying to manufacture a greater nobility than they possessed, and the event took on the aspect of the fluid gathering of a peasant's wedding.

The merriment pervaded all levels. I attended the dais more frequently than Hamund, though I noticed that he lingered nearby, affecting to work while straining his ear to catch the thread of conversation surrounding the Justiciar. I poured wine as carefully as I could despite the dulling effects of the drink on my own mind and body. As I bent attentively to the table once again, directing the dark stream of liquor into the waiting glass, a hand reached out and circled my wrist, holding me gently from across the table. I looked up directly into the frank eyes of Rohese de Monmouth.

'This is our foundling', she said to Basilia, who sat beside her, 'a young man of Yngleis birth, enslaved in our new lands in Míde'. Basilia looked at me appraisingly and allowed a momentary silence to settle before she spoke.

'And he understands our tongue?'

'He understands very well, though he speaks like a dog choking on a bone', and the table, all turning to look, laughed at her words. All except Basilia. Rohese released her grip on my wrist, and I made to back away, uncertain under their combined stare.

'Let us hear some words then', Basilia said coldly, 'to lift my mood'. Following a pause, I stood forward, bringing the jug close to my chest—the only shield I possessed. I searched in vain for some witticism, some words that could turn this moment to my advantage.

'Rarely is a dog so dumb', she said, cutting across my thoughts and provoking more laughter, this time from both those on the dais and those seated nearby at the long table.

'Speak up, boy, and show the lady she is mistaken', de Lacy boomed impatiently.

And a verse surged forward—words from a lay I had heard the rhymers practicing together in the orchard.

> Lords do not be surprised:
> A stranger bereft of advice
> can be very downcast in another land
> when he does not know where to seek help

'Haah!' de Lacy roared out, in his cups, slamming the boards of the table so that glasses leapt and tittered together and a black cat with a white breast scrambled from where it had been giving a fallen morsel its attentions. The laughter became general around the hall.

'Indeed, a rare find', said Basilia with a reluctant smile showing on her lips. 'We have a few such men in Ferns—slaves we have liberated from unjust captivity—older men mostly, Saxons in the main. And none that can quote the latest *lais* from the court of the King. Though I dare say, our Maurice ORegan not only recites but composes in the most vivid verse'.

As the moment passed and the lantern of their attentions moved from me back to their various discussions, I pressed on, remembering now more of the verses, pushing myself forward and shouting above the din.

> Any wise and courtly lady of noble disposition,
>   who sets a high price on her love and is not fickle,
>   deserves to be sought after by a rich prince in his *castel*,
>   and loved well and loyally,
>   even if her only possession is her mantle.

And in this, I misjudged the moment as much as my audience, the missed step so apparent to most in the room that silence fell like the sharp of a blade, cutting short the babble of talk until the sound of dogs and cats pulling at bones and discarded crusts was all that could be heard. And in this dread moment, Basilia's eyes turned to me once more.

'It is seven days since my husband found his eternal rest at the end of a Gaelic lance', she said in a flint-edged voice, her gaze terrible, the light laughing lines of her face hardening. And I saw Rohese de Monmouth's eyes flash to her husband's, to check if he was alive to the danger.

'What do you say of that? And what do you say of Gaelic lances that would plunge into our bodies at the first chance?' I faltered and tried to step back, butting into an impervious wooden post.

'I did not seek to cause . . .', I began, losing voice, and in that moment, all that would come to my mouth was the Gaelic word— *náire*. And I dared not speak it.

Raymond acted in this horrific silence, rising up from his seat in front of me, his stout frame rumbling with the rhythmic verse of some poem I did not know.

> A wicked man, from a foul brood,
> who mingles with free men,
> always knows his origins,
> that he comes from an addled egg,
> even though he lies in a free nest

He struck me suddenly, with great force, and I fell backwards against the post, my head thumping the deep set of the wood, and I slid sideways with the jug cradled in my arms, wine spilling freely over the canted edge.

'That is for shaming our race with your slavery', he said.

From the ground, I perceived the shock provoked by this act as some of the Justiciar's retinue rose from their seats. De Lacy stood also, his face clouding over as Rohese placed an arm on his fist, pinning it to the board.

'A cup-bearer who sloshes the wine', Raymond said loudly, grabbing me up from the ground and passing his wide thumb across the birthmark on my face, as if to rub it clean. A pitiful jest, though in the tensioned atmosphere, it provided levity, and some faint laughter skittered down the hall, breaking the unwelcome silence. He drew me in then and kissed me with great exaggeration on both cheeks.

'And that is for your loyalty, brat, to your King and Justiciar', he shouted gaily, and in that act I recognised his shrewdness.

'Now sit, young squire, if it pleases your master, for I would like to hear your story told, and I would know what you have learned of the Gaelic temperament'. Turning to de Lacy, he added, 'If we can get closer to the workings of Gaelic thought from one who has observed their ways for the entirety of his life, we can hit back at them all the harder'.

De Lacy acquiesced not without reserve, and all sat and resumed their talk and their play, and I placed my jug onto the board. In the absence of a seat, I knelt on the rushes beside Raymond, stemming the blood that coursed from my nose with a wadded rag. 'Mouthy fool', he said to me discreetly, 'one verse would have served you better. But you were not to know the truths you were stepping on with your second offering'. He looked at me hard, making sure there was no flicker of comprehension on my face. Making sure, with his forceful eyes that probed like awls, that I had not sought to make a fool of him. 'No matter', he said, apparently satisfied, and he tousled my head roughly, adding, 'the nose will heal. I can see by how it lies that it has known a few breaks before'.

I nodded and contrived a rueful look. He went on talking, asking me of Míde and making some well-observed comparisons to the lands of Mac Murchada. I answered what questions he would ask and played along with any farce he wanted to make of me to his fellows. I saw Hamund use the excuse to come ever closer, taking up my wine jug and loading me with significant looks. After a time, Raymond spoke to me more freely of Mac Murchada, his strengths and his follies, and even of how he had died, 'his body rotting around him, his face frozen in rictus, his jaw clamped closed so tight that his teeth cracked and his people kept him hidden, spooning him whey, the scum dribbling and crusting perpetually over his beard. A sad thing for one who had such presence in life'.

He spoke this way for a long time, addressing himself at times to this companion or that and, at times, speaking directly to me. I believe that, in his cups, he forgot momentarily to whom he addressed himself, speaking with little check, clapping me on the shoulder like a comrade in arms, and I listened and leaned my ear in and nodded and laughed at the expected moments. He did not need much more encouragement, and it was not long before he was speaking bitterly of the Earl and how he had been ill used by that 'politicking old bastard'. I learned that Raymond had commanded the Earl's armies, that he had carried many great victories, and that the Earl had slighted him in the end, promoting another man as Constable—de Quincy. The man who lay dead somewhere in the mountain passes of Osraige.

'And', he said to me, leaning close, drink glistening on his lips, 'despite his promises, he would not give me her hand', and he pointed with his eyes to where Basilia sat. A kind of shudder passed through me at an image of his face with its round, grey eyes, high colour and raven's nose finding harbour in the nook of Basilia's milk-smooth neck. For, throughout all this time, as he spoke to me, I had been stealing glances in the direction of Rohese and Basilia, who leaned in to each other in similar conclave. Two women full of their own power, existing in a space of their own, set apart from the heaving swelter surrounding them.

Through the lulls in the voices around me and between the preoccupied words of Raymond, I had captured many whispers that passed between the two women. I had heard Rohese whisper, 'Is it un-Christian of me to say that your Yonec is here, your Launcelot?' and I saw her motion very subtly with her head to a dark part of the hall. Basilia's eyes did not follow, but she did smile briefly, her hand coming lazily up to her mouth.

'The fool was standing upriver on the shore like a motherless calf before we even moored the ship', she said.

Rohese laughed with delight and looked over her shoulder, finding the corner where Gryffyn sat, tolerating the discourse of his fellows, his eyes trained on the dais burning like beach coal under a bellows. Rohese turned and spoke with a playful sigh, her chin cupped in her hand, drawing in close, 'What harm—one of the benefits of being with child, young sister—you cannot conceive another'. I did not follow much more of their speech before Raymond's insistent voice broke in.

'You see this Justiciar, boy, he is a baron dyed in the wool. Stick to him like woad. Ranulf in Chester tells me that, as a boy, he used to collect branches and brushwood to build a *castel* and, mounting a toy horse as his steed and brandishing a branch like a lance, would with other boys of his own age undertake the guard and defence of this play *castel*'.

'Ranulf of Chester?' I said, but Raymond had moved on to another subject. 'My father was reeve of Frodsham in Chestershire'. Interrupted in his train of thought, Raymond's brow furrowed, and he looked down at me mildly. 'There is no reeve at Frodsham, boy, only a burned stump'.

'Many years ago', I said desperately, trying to bring his attention with me, 'it was years ago . . . Johan de Crécy. My mother . . . taken, they were both taken—'

The wine had clouded over his face and he strained to hear over the noise of the hall. 'Johan of Frodsham', I shouted, and he searched for meaning in the sounds.

He pursed his lips, considering, running his large hands through both temples of his curled blond head. He spoke then, and I was never sure if it was a platitude or if he was channelling something deeper. Some memory. 'There is nothing sadder than a beautiful slave, lad'.

I grasped for more, but the entire hall burst into an eruption of shouting and cawing and slamming of fists and cups on the table as the harpers and pipers came forth playing blasts on their instruments to signal the end of the meal and the beginning of the entertainment. Between them, marching with exaggerated movements, the Justiciar's fool, Folzebarbe, strutted like a game-cock, paint smeared grotesquely over his face, tongue lolling like a hound on the scent.

Wine splashed and flowed and all servants were now busy with jugs, the plates having been cleared away. Folzebarbe was a man I had seen often about the yard, sleeping in the hay, harassing the girls, a feckless wastrel. But here, in the reek of bodies and wood smoke, he showed himself king. In time with the music, he darted between the roof posts and into the shadows of the eaves, emerging like a questing deer, only to shy back into the shadow, and we got glimpses of his outrageous costume, a frayed, stitched phantasm of strips and colours.

He began to cavort, tumbling and turning his body, stretching his joints into unnatural lengths, eliciting cries of dismay and delight from the company. As the music built and grew faster, so did his dance, leaping high with apparent abandon; oblivious to the hearth or the table or the dais, he traversed all with his acrobatics.

During this performance, the steward, with masterful discretion, ushered in courtesans from the *civitas,* who dispersed into the now moving assembly of guests, the serving girls, by now, pinched red and blue breasted. The formality of the feasting disappeared in its entirety, replaced by loud and unrestrained revelry, Folzebarbe's cavorting growing less heeded as younger men scuffled in impromptu trials of strength and hot words as de Lacy and Raymond cheered from the dais, flinging jugfuls of beer down over the revellers.

In the midst of this maelstrom of upending benches, false singing, haggling courtesans and leaping fools, the door to the hall heaved open from without, spilling an unseen mass of cool night air into the room. The touch of this air on the great heaped embers of the fire sent the smoke boiling around the hall, sparks rising in a swarm, the fire glow showing in bronze slats through the billows, and through this choking, blinding mass, a figure stalked forward, crooked staff in hand.

'Justiciar', the figure roared, cutting through the uproar of coughing and howls of indignation and cries of 'shut the cursed door'. The figure came on, pushing into the tight ball of courtiers, his two familiars ranging to his left and right, clearing space.

'De Lacy', the figure roared again over the receding din, and fresh sticks were cast on the flames, brightening the hall and sending unwelcome shafts into several cosseted corners where rutting buttocks could clearly be seen. The figure illuminated in the wild crackling flames—Lorcán. His face severe, his aggrieved head pushed forward as a clearing established itself around him, looming knights and barons on all sides. He stood, unperturbed. A ferret in the sett.

'Where is de Lacy?' he said again with less force but with no less steel in his voice.

'Where he belongs', came the answering, belligerent shout from the dais, and by now the assembly had fallen quiet in the main, shaking heads and smoothing garments, blinking reddened eyes and dislodging beer froth and crumbs from grease-coated faces.

'Justiciar', said Lorcán, inclining his head forward with the merest sign of respect. 'I apologise for my late arrival, but my invitation to your feast did not reach me', and before de Lacy could respond, the archbishop's quick eyes had found Basilia in her seat. He moved his soft treading feet in a minor movement that reoriented his entire being. He bowed his head more perceptibly and spoke directly to her.

'My greetings before you, *ma dame*, to this, our *civitas*, and may I give you God's blessing for the child that you carry. I waited for you at the cathedral where I thought to celebrate a Mass to mark your arrival, but I see that perhaps, unaccustomed as you are to these streets of ours, you were led astray'.

After the slightest pause, Basilia rose, leaning backwards with her arm crooked beneath her belly, and she made to step down from the dais to approach the bishop.

'Sit, child', he said, his un-mitred head and mild face commanding supreme authority, and Basilia froze momentarily as the congregation, fully silent now, recognised the hard dissonance of the
scene—the bishop standing before the dais. The shame of it. The
failure of all forms of hospitality did not fail to puncture even
the thickest wine-fuddled head, and all stood watching the scene
with paralysing uncertainty. This confusion compounded by the
friendly address of the bishop.

'We are past the hour of decorum', he said, and though his words
were mild and appeasing, they settled over the hall with the sting
of something deeper, something critical, and the unease spread.

'How do things go with your brother?' he continued, addressing
Basilia still as the hall listened. 'I would like to speak with him
again, as it has been some time now. I would speak with you at
length, not least of all to know if you have news of my sister in
the court at Ferns'.

And with this conversational tone, Lorcán had confused,
disarmed the assembly, who stood by, bleary and unsure of themselves as the revelry paused and this slight, grey man held sway.
He made to step up onto the dais, and, his eyes meeting mine, he
feigned great surprise and said warmly, 'And Alberic FitzJohan,
of course you are here. But what of your companion, Conn?' He
stepped back into the cleared space he had made and, as if searching his memory, thinking aloud, he said, 'No . . . not here. I have
seen him elsewhere today'.

And in a swift movement of his body, once again he was facing
de Lacy. 'I believe I saw him labouring on the quay, though it was
difficult to be certain. The creature I observed was slight and slick
with black ooze, and', he chuckled lightly, 'enslaved'.

De Lacy, shaken finally from his torpor, stood and bowed his
head, indicating to his own seat, 'Your Grace, please accept this
seat', and to the empty shadows by the scullery door he roared,
'Wine for His Grace, wine and meat', and in the act of turning
he swayed ever so slightly, the thick fingers of his right hand a
scaffold on the tabletop to stay him.

Lorcán ignored all of this and continued, as if speaking to
himself. 'Yes, enslaved. Slighter now, much slighter, scrofulous
at the neck. His movements short and hesitant, his eyes pale and

watery. But yes, the same man, I am sure of it, the same Conn'. Then, his eyes seeking de Lacy, he continued, 'He is the son of one of the noble families of Míde, a realm you now hold, Justiciar. It would seem to me politic to let the lad go and you might well see his father come into your house at Troim to pay you service'.

De Lacy shook his head, snorting like a stallion, as if to dispel the bishop's words. And he spoke.

'Archbishop. Míde is mine both by royal grant and by the right of arms, as that villain ORork relinquished his claim when he acted treacherously'.

'The fate of a kingdom concerns more than a single individual', Lorcán responded quickly. 'You may represent the King of England, but I represent a much higher power. Your King's holdings would fit into the holdings of the Pope one hundred thousand times over. Not only that, but all of the earth is the dominion of God. And God's law states that no man shall be made a slave. This is the Christian teaching. Give the boy his liberty'.

De Lacy leaned forward in his seat.

'That may be, Bishop. But God, too, controls a kingdom. He knows what must be done to clear the borders and keep down his enemies. He has fought wars in heaven and earth and has faced betrayal and uprising from those towards whom He was lenient or beneficent'.

Lorcán ignored this rhetoric. 'Man made politics. God made people. I concern myself with people. Free the boy that he may return and speak of your reverence, worthiness, benevolence. That the men of Míde may come forward when your banner appears over their hill. Who else will farm your land? Turn it to produce? There are not enough Engleis on this island to work half of that land of bounties'.

'You speak true, Eminence. And yet I fear for the boy. What will happen if he is turned loose from my protection? Will he not need to traverse Laigin somewhat? Across the lands of your people? What will a Mac Murchada do to a sprat of ORork? No, for his own safety, I keep him'.

'To expire of exhaustion on the black banks of the river?'

'To participate in the great civil project of our time—how better to belong to our tribe?'

'This is slavery. Might I speak of our councils? Of the teachings of your own great clerics, Anselem, Gervase?'

De Lacy grew hot at this, tiring of the play.

'Your Grace—perhaps you have heard what we do with troublesome priests in our kingdom'.

The inference was bare—shredding the ill-contained mirth like the raking claw of a prodded beast. He evoked the brained Archbishop of Canterbury. And even the loudest, most boastful drunkards in the room fell silent, glancing shiftily to each side as if fearing an apparition of Thomas à Becket, a man the Pope had proffered for sainthood. Lorcán allowed the silence to extend, and de Lacy, casting about for some way out, grabbed me by the shoulder, pulling me towards him from where I had stood, transfixed, with jug in hand.

'Let us ask this boy what shape justice should come in. One of our own countrymen, Bishop, enslaved and scourged daily by the one you would seek to free—an heir to a lord who refuses my authority over his lands'.

Lorcán directed himself towards me and spoke. 'Be careful, lad, did they not tell you? A lord is like a fire—go too close and you will be burned, too far away and you will freeze. It is a difficult beam to walk'.

I spoke then from some deep well of foolishness. A part of me that ever refused to keep quiet. I spoke words I had not weighed as the wine-warmth made me more reckless still.

'If that is so, I see my lord has spent time in the blaze of a king and has won much by it'.

De Lacy fell very silent. The entire hall took on the muffled pallor of a fog-choked night. Eyes averted, glasses placed down with extreme care, as if any noise at this juncture might attract a violent rebuke.

Lorcán searched my face with a look neither amused nor angry. I risked a glance to my side where de Lacy sat, his gaze full on the bishop, his fingers slowly palping the waxy red smear of burned skin, the molten folds of his cheek. And slowly, deeply and irresistibly, he began to laugh, the sound booming out into the deadened air like an axe on a barred door. After a confused silence, the assembly followed—the laughter taking and spreading—and de Lacy stood, his head cast upwards towards the shingles, roaring mirth, and he came forward thumping my back.

'This boy', he said, 'has the balls of an ox and the head of a legate'. He made a great show of ushering me to sit in his chair. 'What should we do with your tormentor, boy? String him from his bowels over the palisade? Or deliver him into the arms of the bishop who would spirit him homewards with words of us and our numbers and our defences and our plans direct to our enemies? Pronounce your judgement, wise and fearless one', he said with a mocking bow.

The question had only one answer. Lorcán did not come to my aid this time, instead eyeing me coolly. I went sick with the thought of murder. God's hand hanging over me, his eye on me, for I had helped kill the *file*. I prayed inwardly during that moment, seeking Lasair's embroidered scrap behind my belt. I prayed for intercession to Féchín and Lasair. To Patricius and Thomas à Becket. And I spoke.

'He should labour on the wharf. As I laboured at his mill, draining his bogs, de-stoning his meadows, building his trackways. If he lives through these trials, none should bar his way home'.

'Midir come again', said Lorcán quietly into his fist as de Lacy boomed his own sentiments.

'Solomon's bastard', grabbing the back of my neck in his powerful hand and shaking as one does an apple branch, the tip of his tongue trapped between his clenched teeth, shaking me and rubbing my head and clasping me into his hard chest with intoxicated merriment. And thus engulfed in this dark embrace, I did not see the bishop leave.

CHAPTER 18

An Impious Teacher

HAMUND WAS FURIOUS. As the revelry burned on late into the night, spilling out into the cobbled yard, he stalked around the rear of the hall, drinking long pulls from a flask, punching the immovable beams and kicking his feet raw against barrels and bales. I tried to calm him, his slim face flushed, eyes unfocused.

'Peace, Hamund, you will find trouble for us'. He turned on me, snarling out words.

'Do not believe for a moment that he is your friend. That fat, vile excrement eater. That murderer of children'.

'Peace, Hamund, I wanted to know of my father, that is all. He has been to Chester and knows the Earl that rules there'.

'Do not believe a word from that unctuous villain's rotting mouth'.

I brought him into the darkness of the stable and we made space for ourselves on the floor, rooting in among the horse-boys and receiving their scorn but also their fear as they had seen me with the Justiciar. Hamund railed on, his words losing force until he fell silent, his arm falling over my shoulder, his face finding a hollow at my neck and his chest filling and emptying noisily in the dark beside me. I pretended sleep, my head half-hid in the straw, though I watched the open kitchen door through a gap in the lats for a long time. The serving girls, waiting for the tempers to calm in the hall, cleaning the cups, talking low and surreptitiously chewing the gristle from bones discarded among the potsherds and oyster shells.

I saw the concubines ushered from the hall, brought out through the kitchen, two dark figures flanking the door. Saer the steward, purse hanging from his belt, continuing a deep argument with the stately chief courtesan. Arguing over silver, no doubt. An argument laced with a courtship of its own—ageing, minor powers exerting their wills upon each other. Finally, her hand strayed to her breast, pulling the verge of her garment down as he leaned in. A final transaction. I watched as she clenched him to her, falling back against the woodpile, abrupt grasping movements, and I closed my eyes from it.

Dawn broke cold and unforgiving. Light pushed in through the lats, and I lay still, weighted down with the heaviness of the night's events. My face throbbing from Raymond's blow. I could hear no movement, but as I lay between sleeping and waking, I caught sight of Gryffyn padding around the kitchen door and sidling into the small space between the bread oven and the rear of the feasting hall. He put his eye to the wattle, his fingers working in to open a chink, to which he pressed his mouth. Though I could hear no sound, I could see his lips forming words, words that carried urgency, imperative, working from his trunk, across the breadth of his shoulders, his hands, unseen by the listener within, moving in imploring contortions. He went away then, leaving the yard to the chickens and the loose straw that scratched soundlessly across the stones in the weak breeze.

I dozed a while longer until, my stomach sick from the wine and my bladder full, I freed myself from the tangle of bodies in the straw and crept to the stable door. I pissed out onto the cobbles looking to a troubled sky, heavy with cloud. All abed, the doors barred, low voices somewhere above on the wall walk. When the household awoke, there would be cleaning and clattering to avoid, scrubbing down and mucking out and flinging armfuls of bones and shells into the moat. I shook off the sourness and pushed into the cold. No marshal coming to rouse out the sleeping hands yet, everyone clinging to sleep.

There was a soldier at the gate, and he pulled one of the great doors ajar for me to slide through. And just as I emerged out into the *civitas*, Gryffyn came up behind me and laid his heavy arm over my shoulders.

'What pilgrimage now, lad?' his voice bright and alive.

'Back to the hostel to my straw bed. I do not want to be found here this morning'.

'Have no fear, lad, you are more or less part of the household'.

'More or less, yes, depending on the day, I will not dawdle for fear of a kick. Or worse yet, a bucket and swab'.

Gryffyn laughed.

'I'll walk with you and see your lodging'.

'You'll be disappointed'.

He did not reply, and we walked the rest of the way in silence. At the hostel, Gryffyn looked around with interest and threw himself backwards onto my cot, his powerful arms crooked behind his head.

'Not bad, pilgrim', he said, 'fine lodgings for a young man. Are you alone here?'

'Mostly, yes, though the bishop admits the sick betimes, and there have been women here with their children some nights seeking refuge from their drunken husbands. And Conn was here also'.

Gryffyn grunted.

'Best for you to forget that lad, Alberic, his fate is no longer on your head. You will get the call soon to bunk up at the *castel*. You'll be part of the household then, and you'll do no more slinking around when you think no one's watching. You'll be bearing cups in the hall, carrying spears on the hunt and maybe, if I read it right, you'll be groomed up to be a squire for Master Hugo when he comes of age. The Lord has taken to you, and though you may not know it, he is measuring you at every tread. There are burghers and *chaualiers* and *sergenz* the length and breadth of Herefordshire who would pay a lifetime of tithes to place their sons in the position you have blundered into'.

'Yes, so I am told', I said.

'A cup-bearer to a king is often richer than a knight of renown', he said. 'Members of the lord's household can be richly rewarded with lands for their service'.

'What would I do with lands, and not a cow to go on them?'

Gryffyn laughed loudly at this.

'You really are a fool. You would rent your holdings to farmers. They work the land and you reap the tithes, get fat, marry the steward's daughter and sire twelve stain-faced children'.

'And who will you marry?' I asked him then, and the smile died on his lips.

'I don't give a fistful of ashes for marriage', he said, and he rolled over on his side, to conceal the pain on his face.

We returned to the *castel* some time later to find the place set to rights. Hamund was nowhere to be found, though Hugo was quick to spot me coming in with Gryffyn. He approached me with a clear, childlike joy on his face. In the excitement of the new arrivals, all of the practiced scorn fallen away.

'There's to be a hunt', he said to us both, 'and we are to go along'.

Gryffyn ruffled his hair.

'That is good, young Lord. I'd best prepare. Is there talk of bringing the falcons?'

Hugo had already run off in giddy flight, reeling between the bustling servants and labourers.

'Go with him', Gryffyn said, 'and keep him from falling under a cart'.

I followed after Hugo and, catching him up, steered him upwards onto the parapet, where we settled on the edge of the outer wall, throwing pebbles into the moat below and spying for glimpses of nuns over the walls of St Mary de Hogges. We tried to count the soldiers' tents beyond the pool and followed the road along the Vale of Duiblinn and the green woodland beyond, sweeping onwards to the purple mountains. Out on the bay, the fishing boats were plying the incoming current around the big sandbar—hunting for bass.

I boasted to Hugo of my trip on the boat for mackerel. He feigned little interest.

'We crossed on a ship from Bristol', he said, 'and for days the sailors showed me how to work the sails, and I climbed the mast and helped them with the rigging, and Father was very proud'. He was still young, and he retained this habit of speaking quick and transparent lies, and he would then need to work hard to make them believable.

'A mariner, a boy, fell overboard in a swell, and there was no one left on-board small enough to shin out onto the yardarm to fix the sail in place. They showed me what to do and . . .' He went on at length with this fantasy, and in the end, against my better judgement, I said to spite him, 'Well, I can see now why a short journey with mere fishermen should hold so little to interest'.

And in saying this, I unleashed what was to follow.

'Not so', he said defiantly, 'I should like to see one of their boats up close, see how they sail. You can arrange this for me'.

Our talk was interrupted by a roar from the yard below. We looked down to see de Lacy staring up from the back of a formidable bay horse, his hunting horn hanging at his neck and a retinue of mounted men, footmen and dogs forming behind.

'Sluggards', he roared again, in high spirits, 'to work'.

We scrambled down the wall, forsaking the steps in our haste, and took up with his retinue. Gryffyn swung Hugo up onto his courser, and I jogged along with the hounds, looking for something to carry in an attempt to redeem myself.

When, some hours later, I returned to the cathedral, tired and dust covered, Lorcán came to see me. He entered the hostel bending through the low door before rising to his full, imperious height. A cold fear, and something more—guilt—flashed in my bowel.

'Young Sasanach', he said by way of greeting, and in this flippant way ejected me from the tribe of the Gael. 'I see you have become a celebrated freeman of the *civitas*'.

The jest was spoken without spite, though there were thorns to his words. My freedom was questionable. Though he was also

alluding to my unaccompanied travels through the streets, signalling gently that my wanderings were known to him.

'I am sorry for Conn', I said, my head lowering.

'I am also sorry for Conn', he said grimly, 'for his fate means
more than you realise. In the south, the Engleis have entered into
lordship through marriage and alliance. They are constrained
to Mac Murchada's lands. But de Lacy has gone beyond his
sanction. He has entered into lands which were never subject to
Mac Murchada. He has pillaged the territories and he has killed
a Rí under truce. In not according Conn the dignity and rights
owing to a hostage of noble rank, de Lacy spits on the Gael and
makes clear his intent for Míde'.

I bowed to the ground before him. Hiding my face, should
he read the riot of feeling at play there. Lest he know that in my
darkest days, as a youth, there were times when I had prayed and
yearned and lusted for an Engleis heel to crush the house of Máel
Sechlainn.

'I am sorry for my words at the feast'.

Lorcán sighed.

'You did right. You bore a heavy weight, and there may well
have been two swinging boys on the *castel* walls had you dared
more. Though you skirted close to hubris on occasion. Boldness
has served you well, I can see that. But the fire grows hotter, and
it will be more difficult to gauge what distance to keep. You are
shrewd, boy. I would make you a man of the Church, for I feel
this is where your talents lie'.

I kept my gaze lowered, a blush of pride spreading through me.

'Now', he said in a louder tone, 'I need you to go to the shambles
for me. I would like cow's tongue for the kitchen'.

I looked at his face for the trace of a smile. It was well past the
time that flesh was to be got. He had never sent me on such an
errand before. His eyes were unsmiling, and I took my leave of him,
alerted to a 'crane in the meadow', as old Lochru would have said.

The market was largely deserted, the last of the hawkers packing
their crates away with wild pigs in loud contest with feral dogs
over the spillings which studded the mud crisping in the sun. The
boards over the flesh shambles caked with reddened gore and the
awnings and benches feathered with sparkling fish scales.

I went along the street, watching for a late vendor, expecting to see something else. A figure beckoned. Milesius—cowled and shadowed behind a stall. My heart beat violently at the sight of him, and I slid into the narrow, deserted space in the lee of the tall cathedral wall.

'Alberic', he said, reaching out to grip my shoulders with restrained feeling. He looked up and down the street and began to speak urgently, his face gaunt and still bearing patches of inflamed skin that had ill healed since our ordeal.

'I am happy to see that you are well. That you have found a way to persevere in this tainted place'. Before I could respond or question him, he pushed on with a frantic energy. 'We will need to act together to ensure Míde does not suffer the fate of these Ostmen'.

I was afraid now, afraid of being seen with him and of what that might mean. I had come to understand that even in its sleepiest hours, the *civitas* watched. My fear turned to anger.

'And why would I rush to help the Gaels of Míde? To what purpose would I uphold a *tiarna* who has enslaved me and mine?' If I had struck him in the face, he would have looked less wounded. My lack of a respectful address—I had not called him '*athair*'—rang emptily in the space between us.

'Alberic', he said without anger, and making no attempt to mask the hurt in his voice, 'you know the depth of our learning. Our culture. We trace our line to Noah. We have seeded Christendom with places of learning. You know the craft of our poets, the depth of the genealogies. This land will die if we are severed from it. Can't you smell it on this place? The rot? The filth, lifted with the tide, running in the streets? The air is heavy with the smell of man and beast living too close together. The blackbird's trill over the high wood is sweeter to me than their calls at the flesh shambles and their little silver tokens of no worth to one who has the art of learning and who knows the face of God'.

I did not speak, though I knew some of what he said to be true.

'In three days', he said, 'I will leave for our home. Meet me at the Ostman's bridge with the lowering sun, and we can travel together'. I answered him then with the full-faced haughtiness that my new liberty had fostered in me.

'And why, friend, would I hurry back in the night to a life of bondage?'

He did not reproach me for my familiar address, but I could read fury in the set of his jaw.

'You have seen these men up close now, Alberic. Their thick tongues. Their irreverence. Their ignorance of the natural law, of the saints of the land, of the lore of our ancestors and of the places where they lie sleeping. Not a word of our beautiful language can they form with their jeering mouths and everything to them a prize to be stolen—territory, women, cattle. And kingship now they lay their heavy hands upon with no shred of respect for the law and the ancient bond between our rulers and the land'.

His frenzied eyes bored into mine, looking for agreement. I do not know what he saw. His fist came down on the dirty board of the stall.

'These thick-headed churls. Curs, robbers, shit-hounds. We brought them gospels when they foundered in the dark. Their fingers in the entrails of beasts looking for wisdom and prophecy'. He spat into the dirt.

'They are my people, Milesius. I hear their words. I understand their speech, and here I have liberty'.

'Your liberty will be bought with a hundred thousand thralls. Slaves from the Sionainn to the sea'.

I looked to the ground, embarrassed by his vehemence, though I did not waver. Milesius sighed and, in doing so, his stature reduced. He pulled back his hood, revealing a scourged and scabrous head. His lips grey, bloodied eyes and lesions of yellow green like slugs on his skin. He searched me with his eyes again, looking for some subtle sign that I was under coercion, that I was being watched and my responses forced. Finding none, he said, 'What shall I tell your father?'

'Tell him make to Áth Cliath, where I will meet him as a favourite of the Justiciar'.

'He will not come'.

'Perhaps not, but he will be happy that I am with his people and that I advance. Tell him that here they call me Alberic FitzJohan'.

Milesius raised his hood and said, 'Three things whereby the devil shows himself in man?'

I did not respond, though I knew well the answer—*by his face, by his gait, by his speech.*

He pushed past me out into the street, saying as he went, 'Choose well your path, Alberic. The fork is before you and the door closes behind'.

To his back, I spoke sharp words to mask my pain.

'Three enemies of the soul . . .'

His pace did not slow, nor did he turn to respond, and on their leaving of my throat, the words burned as a breath of stirred cinder.

The world, the devil, and an impious teacher.

The following day, I was sent for before *terce*. When I came to the *castel*, de Lacy was out among the soldiers and his children scattered to the winds, pursuing their pleasures with the other youths of the household. The lady of the house was waiting for me in the great hall. She spoke to me but briefly.

'The Lady Basilia would like to see to you', she said with something like faint mirth in her eyes. 'You will take her to the cathedral to celebrate the Mass. You will serve her without question'. Her look was significant. 'She is with her women in the orchard'.

I bowed and took my leave. In the courtyard, I caught sight of Hamund, skulking by the bread oven, his arms full of logs. I beckoned him with a slight movement of my head, and he shadowed the wall to meet me at the gate. We stepped outside, and once we were beyond the hearing of the doorman, he spoke urgently, 'He is sending the Ostmen to the Earl'.

'Who is?'

'Fool', he spat, his eyes anguished, 'the Justiciar is sending the last of our men south to the Earl to fight their brothers in Vadrafjord'.

Though I did not say it, I immediately saw the logic of de Lacy's actions. Sending the last vestige of the Duiblinn army away from the *civitas*. Obliging the Earl in his request for support, yet not weakening his own forces.

'A cruel destiny, the lot of the conquered'. I meant it as a placation. A conciliatory thing. He stopped and turned, pushing me back against the city wall.

'We are not conquered, friend, we are defeated. And defeat can be undone. Great fleets gather in the Isles and warriors sharpen their axes in Lothlind'.

'I do not doubt it, friend', I said, putting my hand on his breast. 'That is not what I meant'. He turned his face from me, his fair features blackened with anger. We walked on towards the Dam Gate in a charged silence. 'Not what I meant at all', I said lightly, and I considered carefully before continuing. 'Milesius came to me yesterday'.

'Your monk?' Hamund said sharply.

I nodded. 'He wants me to flee, to liberate Conn and flee north'.

Hamund fell silent a moment as we walked on.

'When?'

'Three days from now'.

We passed under the gate arch and came along the bank of the Salach to the orchards.

'I can help', he said. 'Tomorrow, I will come to you. We will walk out and settle on a plan'. His hand cupped my cheek, steering my gaze to his own, his thumb running over the stained flesh with an unlooked-for tenderness. 'We are none of us conquered yet. Not by a long stroke'. He turned and ran back for the gate, his feet kicking up the slop as he went.

In the orchards I walked down rows of fruiting trees until I came to Basilia and her ladies sitting beneath a netting of branches. Cool shadow, the black soil rich with windfall exuding a fragrance of souring ale. Seeing me approach, Basilia called me forward. Men-at-arms keeping their distance looked for Basilia's nod and did not impede my progress.

'He arrives, ladies. The poet-slave. The Justiciar's fancy. Look at that lovely young face. That dew berry. Stained with perpetual embarrassment for his crimes. The stain of impure thoughts, I am sure'. She spoke with the powerful composure of a wealthy and handsome woman, raising in me true blushes as my eyes sought escape in the tracery of grafted branches behind her head and in the flight of wasps hovering noisily between the rotted cores. She rose from her couch, supporting her stomach with one curled hand, and said, 'Come now, you are not some country stutterer afraid of the sport of a lady; I have seen you berate bishops and charm barons. Come and speak to me as we walk to the cathedral. I would know more of you and of this *civitas*. It is bigger than our own Vadrafjord, though more open to the elements, more mixed in its inhabitants'.

Her manner of speech perturbed me, and I struggled to know how to speak to her. We began to walk down the tree-lined sward, and her ladies followed several steps behind. 'Do you not wish to tell me of yourself?'

'I will gladly tell what you would know, *ma dame*'.

'Do you write verse? You seem to have the soft heart for it, the warm eye?'

'I cannot write, though I can read well enough the script of the Gael and also Latin to a lesser degree. I have yet to see the Engleis tongue written out, though I hope that the opportunity will present itself'.

'No doubt', she said, and I divined that this was not the answer she had been looking to elicit. 'Tell me, then, you who recite the romances of the court—in your young life, have you loved?'

I looked behind to her ladies who followed; they affected not to hear our conversation. Again, this was something new to me, and I was not sure how to answer. I was not sure of the truth of the matter, and I was not experienced enough of those in love to know that they just want to hear their own flowery fantasies and agonies repeated back to them. In my uncertainty, I began to speak, words that had been waiting to fall from my lips like the heavy apples around us. Like a fruit of large, sad tears.

'I would say yes, *ma dame*, I have'.

She smiled a thin smile, her eyes narrowing, the freckles across her nose, delicate and speckled as a thrush's egg.

'Tell me of her', she said, leaning in conspiratorially, taking my arm. Her breath hot against my cheek.

'We captured her on a cattle raid', I began, and she snorted an involuntary laughter, and I could hear suppressed giggles from behind also.

'Child', she said, 'I do not wish to hear of your dirty carnal acts perpetrated on the poor savages of the forests'.

Sudden anger spiked into the cavities of my being. I did not heed her but continued slowly, deliberately.

'Standing in the pre-dawn dew, her bare feet bright in the gloom, a clutch of herbs and hedge flowers at her breast. She did not move as we thundered from the thicket and she climbed onto one of the horses with little fight. As if she had been expecting it. Indeed, I would hazard to say that it was not the first time she had been carried off'.

Basilia quieted as I continued speaking, listening now with a guarded interest.

'Sixteen of years perhaps, dark hair, pale eyes, skin like the purest snow'.

I faltered at this. The paleness of my words against the image of Ness that smouldered in my mind. 'I am no poet. I do not have the skill to tell you of her beauty'. And speaking of her hurt me as I had no conception it would. Words scalding my heart like charred coal. My thoughts turned against me, and I grew angry at the sly, amused air of this lady. Her highness, her fickleness. I continued rashly; anger unbinding words that should have remained bound. 'Nor do I need to tell you what befell her when we returned to our *túath*, for these things are universal'.

I continued on, emboldened, speaking of such low things with a high-born lady, disregarding the danger. Disregarding her stiffening gait, the exhalation of breath from her nose, the dead silence from behind me.

'I convinced her to run away with me, into the hills and the deep forest. I told her that my people, the Engleis, were at hand and that I would bring her to them and that we would be liberated. Though in truth I knew nothing of the world beyond our small borders, nor what lay east or west, north or south. I told her all I could to make her come away with me, and we wandered in the wilderness for weeks, eating what we could find. And in the end, she lay with me. She lay with me to change things'. Basilia touched my shoulder as if to say enough, but I could not stop, and I continued, louder and faster. 'Lay with me to make something happen, to do the only thing that she had known, and in lying with me, I became all men, and she rutted like an animal and pushed every sin that had been perpetrated upon her down onto me. She expelled a blackness and a screaming terror and she clawed me and gored me and when it was over, she had passed on'. Basilia stopped walking and her ladies came forward, full of affronted awe, gathering around their lady.

'Stop', Basilia said. Releasing my arm forcefully. But I did not stop.

'Passed on, passed over, I do not know which. Perhaps she lies cold in the forest or perhaps torn by wolves or enslaved by another who chains her to a post and ruts her daily—'

Her slap came hard and jarring, her long, ringed fingers catching my lip so that blood spilled dramatically into my mouth and down my chin.

'Filth', the ladies said, '*ordure, morveau de merde*', and I turned away so that they would not see my tears. Basilia silenced them with a raised hand.

'Boy, you are a fool. I knew it at the feast and you have proven it here today. You are offered liberties beyond any expectation of your station, and you utter outrages'.

'A slave has no need for decorum', I said. 'Words have ever been the only freedom available to me. For good or for ill'.

'Take us to the cathedral', she said sternly, and we walked on in silence. We passed through the town gate and climbed past the *castel* along the High Street, and I was dead to the salutes and the hails from merchants and women in doorways, pushing my feet ahead in a kind of stupor.

At the great western doorway to the cathedral, Basilia bade her ladies enter. She held back and touched my wrist, indicating that I do the same. She looked into my face and spoke to me kindly.

'Marie of the *laies* says that love is a wound within the body'.

I nodded slowly my assent.

'I, too, have known wounds. And we have all, servants and nobles alike, known love's barbs'.

She took a small blade from a purse at her belt and put it to the stone of the church door. She grated it back and forth for a time until she had amassed a small heap of fine powder in her hand.

'Take this consecrated stone, mix it with the milk of a goat and the juice of one sloe, drink it cleanly as a single draft and it will assuage some of your pain'.

Her gesture touched me deeply. I palmed the dust, bowing to her in the process, and we entered the cathedral together. I walked her down the side to the lady chapel where her cortege waited. We stood in the alcove. It being one of the canonical hours, the cathedral was largely empty apart from the congregation of canons assembled towards the altar, their plainchant humming and resonating within the chamber. I swayed throughout the ceremony, Basilia by my side and my hand clenched around the sanctified dust. The echoing majesty of the plainchant, the changing strengths and patterns of the light as the clouds outside, shredding in the growing breeze, veiled and unveiled the sun from the high windows.

When the Mass had ended, she waited, praying behind her clasped hands, and, as if on silent command, the ladies left quietly as the canons emptied through the cloister door, making for the refectory and the midday meal. I looked around the empty space and at Basilia, murmuring determinedly into her hands. I stepped away and made to go, but her hand reached out to stop me.

'I would like to see where you stay', she said. And I perceived a tremble in her touch. I nodded without a word and walked her to the cloister door. I slipped out first, scanning the garth for signs of movement. She came on unperturbed, walking at my side. I guided her across the exposed spaces until we came to the door of the hostel. She bowed her head and entered. I followed, and she spoke some words I did not catch. Words of verse. As my eyes adjusted to the gloom, she stepped back, butting against me. My hands came up around her shoulders to steady her. Her gentle smell filling my nostrils. My heart hammering. And from the shadows of the room, Gryffyn stepped forward, his face a blaze of unaffected joy. He came forward in a rush and fell to his knees onto the tamped earth, his head bowing and awaiting the touch of her hands in his hair.

'Get up, fool', she said, her voice breaking out into laughter, and he stood, laughing too, his hard face lined with tears. She kissed him boldly and his arm came up around her, his body perching forward comically over her bump.

Gryffyn looked up to me sharply then and said, 'Alberic—the door'.

I went outside, pulling the door behind me. I sat back against the doorpost and watched the cloud break up over the cathedral walls and the crests of the thatched roofs, not listening but hearing their running babble of talk, their low laughter, the emphatic kissing and the tender noises that followed. And then only Basilia's voice.

'There. Lie back, you *sotte*. There. And now. Here. Yes. Gentle. There. Yes'. I clapped my hands lightly, and a puff of consecrated dust dispersed on the breeze.

CHAPTER 19

Escape

I SAT ON MY STRAW COT the following morning considering all. A soft, persistent rain falling. The faint smell of that illicit tryst still rising from the bedding. My many masters. And those that demanded my allegiance. The Justiciar, Basilia. Hugo, Milesius and the bright, terrible countenance of the Lady Monmouth reflected across the waters of my mind. My head so low between my knees that the straggling fringe of hair on my brow swept the dust and chaff.

Mother came to me in my weakness. As a small *spideog*, hopping in through the open door, cocking her head to one side as she looked at me, shaking and ruffling out her breast and watching patiently. Watching to see what I would do. Waiting to see what strength I had in me. How I would acquit myself in this hour. No judgement of lord or lawman could have weighed heavier. Though my heart was glad to see her. Hello, Mother, I mouthed, and I lay my hand down flat, knuckles resting on the earth. She looked at it, with one eye, and then with the other, her head flicking quickly. And at the sound of feet she stirred, darting and fluttering away out of sight.

Hamund came in, his clothes fuzzed grey with tiny droplets. His fury had cooled from the day before, and he stood in the doorway with a soft smile, recognising in my attitude, my dejection, the weight of the decision before me.

'Come', he said, 'let us walk and talk of things. There are many ears about this place. And few love gossip more than a monk'. With an effort, I pushed myself up from the bed. He walked ahead, out the cathedral door, moving quickly through the slow-moving streets. I followed his step, and we passed down towards the quay and across the bridge into the Ostman's town on the northern bank. The hugely symbolic crossing between Leith Conn and Leith Moga now a mere question of steps, over and back. Such divisions losing meaning.

We reached the northern bank, my eyes alive to movement around the precinct of St Michan's poor church, swaddled now in a hem of desperate humanity as the Ostmen, increasingly pushed out of the walled town, made their lean-tos and sodden refuges around the precinct walls. I looked out for that shape I knew so well, that sturdy monk, and I wondered if that was his refuge still, his fervent and indefatigable mind at work and repeating his refrain 'through good men, God moves his hand'.

The rain had overrun the shallow-dug cess pits of the street, and foul runoff permeated the wicker boundaries, diluted cess puddling slowly over our feet as we pushed onwards, past the mean houses, up the hill. Outside one of these low dwellings, we passed a child of five or six years sitting in a torrent of mud with the filth running around her. As we passed, I saw her strike her own head with a flat stone, breaking the skin of the scalp somewhere beneath her matted, scrofulous hair so that bright, clean blood welled through her fingers. Hamund went to her.

'Child', he said, 'do not hurt yourself. I knew your father, Holm—a fine *sutter*, a skilled man'. And in a lower voice, 'Do not hurt yourself. Hurt our enemies instead, when we are ready'.

A thin, pallid woman called the child from the doorway of a hovel made of rotted ships' timbers. Her belly swollen.

'Foreign fruit', Hamund said quietly as the woman eyed us fearfully. It was not unusual at that time to see Engleis *sergenz* surround a young woman and corral her down a passage or alleyway or cast her onto a dung heap in plain sight, falling in like crows in a field pecking at a sheep's placenta. Hamund's jaw was set, and again he fell silent, taking long, purposeful strides.

We passed onto the trammelled green, walking over yellowed scars on the grass where the traders' tents had been pitched last market day. And as we walked, reading that muddled augury and counting the time of day from the peals of bells at the abbey church of nearby St Mary's, a truth made itself known to me. I had become a part of the fabric of this place. I had become a reader of its signs. A seer of its patterns. A citizen of its streets. So much so that as we marched onwards, treading our way between the headlands of the abbey's freshly turned infields, a certain vulnerability began to settle around me, a prickle of unease across my shoulders. A new nakedness I had not known before as the close press of the citizenry and their proud walls and deep ditches receded behind us.

We picked up the Bradogue beyond the abbey's mill-race, and Hamund followed its course northwards. He fell back to walk beside me, and we began to talk in an easy way, of small things, each of us absently stripping a switch of *saileach* with the unconscious imperative of boys at large. Hamund showed no unease passing plough teams, men working the abbey's weir with eel forks poised, or, farther on, in a picketed pasture, the broad white back of a bull which I mistook for a distant boulder. Woods raised up around our course, and we passed into their shadow. We gave our attention to the *fraochóg* concealed by heavy screens of hanging ash leaves—bushes that had not yet been stripped bare of berries. Hamund forged on, following a track alongside the river, and I found myself growing fearful in the woods, seeing faces of *kerns* hiding in each thicket, axes blackened with soot, eyes cold behind beards and falling fringes.

Though the only people we saw were two boys flinging sticks into the oaks, driving their nosing pigs into the falling mast, and a gabble of dirty urchins gathering moss in broken baskets and crocks, hoping to sell their fare in town to stock the privies.

Hamund stopped finally at a bend in the river, where a bright, many-tongued stream, running thin over the stone, had cut in beneath an overhanging tree, the deep water beneath a shelter for speckled fish as the side of a broken wooden cauldron turned and butted, trapped by the hanging roots.

This is where Hamund finally spoke to me of his plan as he examined, uncertainly, the gills of a mushroom with his stick.

'I have been thinking about your problem', he said. 'You need to get him out of the work gang. Once he is back in that shack pressed in with thirty others and the gangers barring the door, there will be no hope'.

'How we do that?' I said with a lead ball of fear working in my gut.

'We go fishing', he said, as if stating a blunt and obvious truth.

'Fishing?' I repeated the word.

'And they call you sharp', he said, slapping my arm lightly with his switch. 'Who has been asking us both to take him fishing for weeks now?'

'Hugo . . . Hugo has been asking to go', I said, not comprehending.

'We bring Hugo fishing, explain to him that we need Conn for wading into the flats for the oysters while we shoot the nets. Dirty work . . .', he said.

'Fit for a Gael', I finished.

'We get Hugo to command the ganger to release Conn. We take the three of them in the boat. We drop Conn in the shallows off Cluain Tarbh to collect oysters for us, we press on out to Hǫfuð to drag our nets, and when we come back, Conn has escaped'.

I nodded.

'And to finish the trick—if it is what you want, we put you ashore to search for him while we go back to raise the alarm. Gunnar fouls the sail, and it takes us an hour to reach the quay, leaving you time to slip away and go to ground'.

I nodded slowly, considering this from many angles.

'You do not need to decide your part now, brother. Go or stay, our plan will be the same. Get Hugo on the boat'.

He watched me, chewing his lip, girlish in his anxiety.

'We will need to get by his mother', I said.

'It is more Gryffyn I am worried about', he said. 'He shadows the boy outside of the *castel*'.

'Gryffyn will not be a problem', I said. Hamund considered and at length, deciding to trust my word, sat back against the bank. I reached into my garment at the neck and drew out the *kelt*, bound tightly at one end to a leather thong. 'This will help us. It carries a strong magic'. Hamund reached for it, and I let him lay it on his lap, running his hands over it again and again. 'I travelled to the underworld for it and dread misfortune has befallen the men who took it from me. Its power will steer our course'. Hamund nodded, finally lifting the stone and handing it back.

'It will have to be tomorrow', he said.

'Tomorrow', I said firmly, and we both stood, shaking ourselves of burrs and husks. Above us in the treetops, rooks raised up at our sound, causing a cascade of black shapes that momentarily blocked out the small parcel of sky.

> A raven calls
> bacach times three
> Over your bower
> clerics are coming to thee

We moved fast, Hamund to the quayside to speak to Gunnar and to gauge the tides and I to the *castel* to find Hugo and to see what I could discern of Basilia's movements the following day. I found him in the hall, playing with twisted straw figures on the dais. I sat with him and made a pretence of play, giving him the names of all the little figures' body parts in the language of the Gael and getting him to repeat, should anyone be listening. Hamund came in soon after, and Saer caught and cuffed him by the door. He made a secret sign to me with his fingers indicating three—the third canonical hour, *terce*. We would make our play for *terce*. We put it all in motion in a frenzy, and I warned Hugo that he must not disclose it to anyone. That his mother would not approve of the trip. That this was an adventure for men alone. He had nodded grimly, his eyes bright with the excitement of it. I went to find Gryffyn, who was abroad in the Cullenswood. I left word for him that we would be attending *terce* on the morrow; the implication would be clear for him—that his lady would be waiting there in the hostel.

I could not discern where Basilia was, nor where she would be in the morning. All that I could hope for was that Gryffyn was equally ignorant.

I did not sleep that night. Hamund crept to my bed after *couvre-feu*, and we lay awake, with the mice scurrying in the straw beneath us, both of us murmuring occasionally some fear or oversight or some tweak to the plan. He did not ask whether I had decided on my course of action—to stay back and risk the wrath of the Justiciar or to flee with Conn and face the uncertainty of my station in the kingdom of Míde.

Three that are incapable of special contracts: a son whose father is alive, a betrothed woman, the serf of a chief.

Before dawn, we were sitting upright in the straw, rehearsing again our roles.

'Ready, brother?' Hamund said.

'Ready, brother', I replied.

At the *castel*, we came in through the gate, and Hamund saluted the door man.

'Out with your slatterns, boys?' he joked. Hamund laughed, replying, 'Where else?'

I tried to laugh, too, but my insides were liquid. A storm in a summer wood. Churning.

Hugo was pacing around the yard, kicking an inflated pig's bladder with some smaller boys.

'Ho, men', he called with admirable calm, raising his arm in salute, aping his father's gestures. I could see no sign of Basilia or her retinue, and I prayed silently that they had not gone on some errand or ridden down the coast.

'Shall we go and get shriven, young *seignur*?' Hamund said, full of an unshakeable confidence. From the shadow of the far wall, I saw Gryffyn push himself forward from where he had been leaning, standing his full height, chewing on an apple. His face inscrutable.

'Nothing stirs the soul like plainsong before breakfast', Hamund declared, and I shot him a look of warning to pull back his exuberance.

Gryffyn came up beside us and Hugo gave a last kick of the

bladder, sending it into the pack of youngsters. As we walked along the High Street towards the cathedral, Hugo prattled on ceaselessly. Gryffyn walked behind us, surveying as was his manner, his right arm across his body, hand resting on the head of his sword. Before we reached the cathedral, he called me back. I stopped to allow him to come abreast.

'What has the lady arranged?'

I breathed deeply and delivered my lie. 'She awaits you in the hostel, as you awaited her. We will enter the cathedral, and you can slip through the cloister door while the canons are beginning their chant and their attentions are occupied. There will be no one in the yard to challenge you and none to disturb your audience with the lady'. I whispered these last words. I did not dare to scrutinise his face but kept walking, heavy with the knowledge that the die was now thrown. If Gryffyn was aware that Basilia was elsewhere, that she lay abed in the *castel,* that she had visited her ship or had gone on an excursion to one of the churches in the Vale, he would know me to be a liar and conspirator.

We approached the ornate front door of the cathedral and, upon entering, passed the small bright scar in the stone where Basilia had scraped with compassion to alleviate my pain. And I was struck with a pang, my heart ringing with uncertainty. Sensing something of my hesitancy, Hamund came up behind, planting his elbow into my back, forcing me forward as one shunts a dug-in mule. Crossing the threshold, I knew by Gryffyn's eagerness that he was ignorant of my duplicity. His attention wandered, his eyes seeking out the cloister door. By his aspect it was clear that he had forgotten us, that, guided by his other head, he was already smelling the soft flesh at her neck, drinking the perfume of her body. He looked behind, and I nodded. I brought Hugo and Hamund up in line with the column closest to the cloister door, beside the chapel where the fragment of St Olaf's cloak hung. Hamund approached this shrine, his lips moving quickly.

'*Benedicite sancti Olavi audi me et coeptis meis, crede mihi, adiuva me et manu sustentaret*'.

We watched the Mass solemnly, listening to the call and response of the plainchant as, behind us, Gryffyn backed towards the door. He waited for a climbing note in the hymn before he jerked the door to and, in a smooth motion, pivoted around its edge, passing through the gap, lithe as a cat through a milkmaid's legs.

Before the door had even swung closed, Hamund pushed Hugo towards the main entrance. We hurried around the outskirts of the church, drawing looks from the sparse congregation. As we neared the big wooden doors, we moved faster and faster, abandoning our heed, and we burst out into the dull day, falling over each other and laughing a manic laughter born of panic and exhilaration.

'To the quay!' Hamund shouted in a jubilant voice. 'Onwards, onwards!'

And we ran on, the street angling down, and we slid over the slick hurdles laid out across the wet, muddy surface. As we passed through the streets, running together in a pack, invigorated and wild, laughing and shouting, scattering hens and swine, Hamund sang out a bawdy song I had not heard before.

> The monks of St Marys
> Milkmaids in their dairies
> The monks of All Hallows
> Bellboys in their towers
> The nuns of de Hogges
> Bridle horses and dogs
> The poor monks of St Michan's
> Can only stuff chickens

Hugo choked on his mirth and the laughter spread through us as we ran, heads turning at the sight. We sang it again and again like drunken sots, barking out the last line with fervour all the way past the shambles, past the Church of St Olaf, along the wine-tavern street through the watergate and onto the wooden quayside. Skittering, hearts racing, stomachs churning, and we skidded to a halt on the greasy boards of the pier. In the steaming shallows, mud heavy and black with slime, twenty men laboured, all but naked under the watch of three gangers leaning on the mooring posts, thick cudgels in hand.

'Quick now', Hamund said, 'we need to move quick. *Seignur* Hugo, these are the men'.

I saw Conn not far from us, looking up at the commotion as we raced over the thudding boards.

'That man', I cried out, and the gangers were roused to slow attention as we came swarming up about them.

'That man', Hugo repeated, pointing, drawing himself up as tall as his ten years would stretch. 'I need that man for the morning, fetch him up here'.

The head ganger looked at us dumbly and was formulating a response, his thick brown forehead stitched in thought, lips murmuring as he tried to fathom what was afoot.

'Now, you pig-headed churl', Hamund screamed. 'The Justiciar's son addresses you'.

And though they knew well enough that the young lord belonged to the Justiciar's family, they knew equally that he should not be abroad without escort. But they responded, as brute beasts cowed with a goad, lowering their eyes and roaring their embarrassment away into the tide.

'Bring 'em in. Bring in Kun'.

What they dragged from the stinking slime was not Conn. It was something much thinner, wrapped in his skin, ill fitting and yellowed in the places that its colour could be seen. His eyes flat and uninquisitive. He came as he was bid. Bent over, shambling. He obeyed.

Hamund led us away, past the wood quay where the bigger ships were moored, out onto a wattle jetty, shored up with old hurdles and heaps of stone where the small fishing boats and skiffs came in.

'Ho, Gunnar', Hamund shouted out over the small crowd of men readying their boats for the tide, and the fisherman waved his arms high, pointing out to a boat waiting at the end of the thin wharf. Two other men waited by it, standing in the shallows, steadying the hull, moorings already cast off, ropes coiled over their thick, scarred forearms. We ran along lightly, Conn lagging behind us, his slack cheeks distending with the impact of each jogging step.

Gunnar stood up on the break, one leg hooked onto the rope-bedevilled gunnel, steadying the craft as the other two powerful-looking men pitched, dripping, over the side into the boat to receive us.

'This way, lads, jump on quick'.

Hugo reached him first, and without breaking stride, he stepped over, steadied by Gunnar, and thick, crooked hands took him by the shoulders, hoisting him into the waist of the boat. I boarded next, and then Conn followed, unthinking, crumpling like a sack of loose cargo onto the bottom boards. Hamund came last, his excitement uncontainable now, and he let out a loud cry of sheer exaltation.

'We've done it, boys!' he called as Gunnar pushed off sharply, stepping on-board in the same motion. The Ostmen moved quick, flying up the sail as Gunnar pumped the steering oar around in a circular movement, impelling the boat forward, and we drifted out into the full turning tide of the river.

Silence descended aboard, Hugo beside me, looking out at the passing banks and the people there going about their business, the high town walls, his head bobbing around excitedly. Hamund also silent as the boat slid along, watching the high-planked sides and forecastle of Basilia's *cog* with a focused intensity.

I surveyed the banks on both sides, the high tide covering the black mud and filth of the sloblands, presenting a pristine version of the waterside. But the heaped silt remained, impassive beneath the surface. And it felt wrong. It all felt wrong. The sharp, determined working of the boat, the taut silence between the men. Only their quick eyes speaking to each other. A low word of Norse between them increased my fear. And it was only then that my fool head noticed what should have been apparent instantly. The clear run of the boat. The space in the well. No nets. No pots. A but of water and a sealed barrel of something—herring? As if for a journey on the open sea.

As we watched the passing shore, I found Hugo's arm and squeezed it slowly. He looked to me questioningly. I spoke the word 'danger' to him quietly in the tongue of his people without changing my demeanour. Then the word 'enemies'. His look was uncomprehending.

'*Pur quei?*' His confusion was born of ignorance. He did not feel the current of danger. He saw no battlefield.

'Do not be jealous of your adventures, Alberic. I only want to see what you have seen'.

The boat shushed forward, pushed out into the full, placid bulk of the river. The *civitas* falling behind us.

'Pirates', I hissed.

'Now, lads', said Gunnar loudly, noticing perhaps my urgent words, 'why don't you sit up in the bows there with Ulfr. He can show you the bay'.

I nodded and began to shift. Fear galloped suddenly within me. A rising bile. The river opening into the bay, shedding back the shore like a cast-off mantle. They would take us to the Isle of Mannanán. They would drag their vengeance out of our bodies, keep Hugo to bargain against their captured leaders.

'*Fuis*', I said to Hugo quietly—flee.

He thought it some jest. As I stood, I took his arm as if to lead him to the bows.

'*Fuis*', I said again, more harshly, lowering my head to hide my lips. He looked at me slowly, my words taking shape, and he looked around uncertainly.

Hamund turned around sharply in his seat. His eyes on mine. He read understanding on my face and sprang up onto the balls of his feet.

'Sit down, brother', he said savagely. Then, with a forced gentleness, 'You'll upset the boat'.

I shouldered Hugo to the rail.

'Back', I said with as much menace as I could muster, and they all saw the danger. I had Hugo outside of me. With a solid shove, I would have him over the side before they could reach me. In the well of the boat, Conn lay like a gutted fish, immobile, his eyes unseeing, fixed to the caulking between the planking.

'What's all this, brother? Why would you want to drown our friend here?'

Keeping my eyes flicking between Hamund and Ulfr, I spoke words for Hugo alone.

'These pirates would take you to the Isle of Manannán and deliver you to the Norse King who lays in wait there'.

'Stop speaking that excrement', Hamund said to me in our own tongue. 'You are not of that breed. You have risked everything—your life, your position—to free this heap, cowering on the floor. We are fighting the same crass enemy. You must see that by now'.

'There is still time to set us back on shore', I said. 'We can convince him we are at play'.

'Why, brother? Why do you do this?' Hamund shouted in frustration. 'Why endanger us all for this sprat, this *fendinn*?'

What he did not know. The Lady Monmouth's eyes, her full mouth. The blood I had sworn her. I, her thrall.

'Brother, we need to defeat these *demons*', he said again, his voice strained to its limit, 'these murderers and low churls who violate our laws, our customs, and cast us out and kill us treacherously, crushing us like rats under the heel, ignoring the law—'

'I have read Berchán's prophesy, brother', I replied. 'The monks once spoke thus of your people. A two-hundred-year tyranny'.

Hamund winced, squinting one eye—a comic gesture from his repertoire, meant to disarm. 'Listen to your own words, brother. A Gael to the crown of your head. You will never find peace in their world'.

And from the edge of my vision, I saw Gunnar shove the oar to the starboard. At the same moment, Ulfr sprang, leaping over the immobile Conn towards us as we staggered against the lurch of the boat.

'*Fuis!*' I shouted, shoving Hugo towards the water. He toppled and fell for the gunnel, but Ulfr was upon him, dragging him down into the well, clapping a wide hand over his mouth. Hamund sprang forward too, a knife in his hand. Without pause, he swung at me as I leapt for the side, and his hooking blow caught me behind the ear, the knife hitting the bone of my skull, tearing open a flap of my scalp. I fell, and my shoulder hit the side hard. I landed sprawled over the bench in the waist of the boat, Hamund closing on me, Thorkil behind me somewhere. Conn motionless in the bottom, his eyes regarding me where I lay. And beyond him, the land disappearing.

Surging to my knees before Hamund could swing again, I grabbed hold of the gunnel and pitched myself low, rolling over the edge. I tumbled below the surface, in darkness and panic, water cool-fingering my lungs, and when I came up to the surface, the boat had passed over me, Hamund leaning over the side with ballast stones in his hands, throwing with murderous intent, sending deep-sounding splashes of water up around me.

I thrashed and struggled for the shore, the deep, fast-running water carrying me out towards the bay. Struggling and gulping and swimming, tasting my own blood in the waters around me, I angled towards the south bank, and my feet finally found purchase in the mud. I clawed myself up onto the stinking flats close to the mouth of the Steyne. And without knowing how, I found myself running. Running and shouting.

'*Au secourz*! Help, they have taken him!'

Falling and bleeding, lungs burning, I moved forward, gathering a crowd in my wake. 'The young Hugo, he is taken, he is taken!' I howled and blindly staggered, along ways I knew instinctively. I ran the blood around my body. I ran the air out of my lungs. I ran the panic to the surface, darkness of vision as blood congealed, dropping over my face until I found myself falling through the *castel* gate, a crowd of leering paupers swarming behind me, echoing my cry.

'Hugo, taken', I rasped, and the cry went up, echoed around the walls, crashing from the stones of the yard. The door of the hall opened so forcefully that it hopped from its hinge, de Lacy, Meyler, Angleo, Petit, Gautier and a score of others flooding out to see what was afoot. De Lacy grabbed me up hard, shouting into my face. I stammered my story, and before I had finished, he began roaring for horses that were already saddled and being led up by his captains.

'An Rinn', I breathed, and de Lacy grabbed me up, slinging me over his horse's neck.

And then we were riding, thundering out of the gate, people scattering, crying out and falling to the roadside. Among the frozen faces flashing past, I caught sight of the gaunt and frightened form of Gryffyn, leaping aside to avoid destruction as the Justiciar bore down, his face ablaze, his eyes burning like braziers howling 'heyaa, heyaa', his spurless heels pounding into the flanks of his mount.

The men and women of an Rinn fled from us, fearing some invasion, some foreign terror, and de Lacy jumped from his still-moving horse, rolling madly in the dirt and running to the strand where the hide-covered boats were drawn up on the sucking shingle, overturned to dry in the breeze.

'Heave', he roared, and his men came sprinting in around him, grabbing up oars and flipping the boats. Then they were all shouting 'Alberic', and I was thrust forward with hands on the back of my neck, thrust forward into the bows of the boat as they ran it through the low crash of the surf, pushing out and jumping aboard. Three *currachs* taking to the sea like crisping brown leaves carried on floodwaters.

I vomited over the side, consciousness fading, blood crusting in lumps behind my ear and as my head lolled, a savage cuff from behind, and de Lacy caught my head in his hand, his fingers on my exposed skull, pointing it forward and roaring 'which one?' as we barrelled towards a dozen boats in the bay. Two cormorants skimming the water passed low, their wings beating furiously as if sharing our purpose. I tried to focus my eyes, looking out for Hamund, and panic welled in me until I saw them finally in the distance, a full wind at their backs, pushing them on as they broke through the churn over the great sandbar at the mouth of the bay. I pointed.

'They're making for the sea', I called over my shoulder, 'the grey sail'.

'Heave!' de Lacy roared with a voice like a rending tree coming down in gale, and to the other boats, with hands cupped to his mouth, 'The grey sail, the grey sail!'

Then he fell quiet, his fists clenched hard on the seams of leather stitching along the edge of the boat. We hurtled on, tearing across the waves, oars clashing and scooping at the water as we went, four men rowing—each one straining like stags in the rut, like Moors under the lash.

'Heave!' de Lacy roared again as the distance between us and Hamund's boat did not lessen. 'Heave, men, heave! *My son, my son, my boy*', these last words rising to a fervid howl as de Lacy's hands dragged down over his flame-scarred face. As we approached the churning surf over the sandbar, we perceived the wind falling away, backing towards the east, and the men heaved on the bending oars, which shuddered on their dowels as we crashed through the white spray and saw them foundering.

If Gunnar and his crew had been unsure of our purpose before, it must have been clear to them when they saw us breach the bar, tearing ahead, bearing down. We gained heavily in the moments that followed as they tried to fill their sail by swinging the boat's head to the north. The sail billowed once more, and they began to stir forward, though their speed was slackened. They cleared the nose of Hǫfuð, and the breeze strengthened, pushing them towards the small, fawn-coloured island of the sons of Nessan rising as a curved sweep from the still waters. Despite their progress, we gained further until we could make out distinct shapes in their boat. A sudden roar from behind, like a gored bull, or a pupping bitch. Animal in its depth.

'I can see him!' de Lacy shouted. 'I can see my boy!'

Plunging forward still, we gained and gained, drawing nearer, imperceptibly at first and then unmistakeably, until it became clear that we would close with them. The foreigner Ulfr stood proud, his arm across the throat of a smaller figure whose face was unclear but looked so pale, almost blue against the immensity of the sky. Hugo. And even from that distance, we could see the boy was crying, his shoulders heaving, as the other Norsemen shouted indistinct words into the teeth of the breeze. Threats and warnings, reaching us confused and intertwined. I looked back to the Justiciar to see his face. All signs of de Lacy's anguish had disappeared, his squat frame crouched low, his legs coiled beneath him. He wore no sword-belt, no knife. In one hurried movement, he pulled his heavy, pleated robe over his head. The streaked and puckered flesh of his scarred face spilling down his chest and back like the raking of a clawed beast. Shifting, low and catlike towards the bows, he spoke with a cold and irrefutable authority.

'Everything you have, men. Heave us into the side of that treacherous bark'.

The men groaned loudly, the oars biting and cupping the water as their rhythm faltered, each one spurring on, pulling his hardest, and the competing forces shook the frame of the craft. De Lacy did not pay any heed, steadying himself on the gunnel, eyes trained relentlessly ahead. The strokes aligned into a taut unison, the grunting exhalations merging into a unified breath, the savage dragging of oars through water impelling the boat in leaping bounds forward. We outpaced the other *currachs*, leaving them far behind.

'That's it, lads', de Lacy said, speaking gently, 'everything you have'.

And everything they had poured out in cracking fire, launching us on and on, Ulfr's shouts clear now over the groaning, huffing rowers and the anxious cawing of gulls.

'Back. Go back. He will die'.

And on and on. The island looming closer, a detached cliff of rock rising high and sheer from the sea as we barrelled onwards, streaked white by multitudinous colonies of birds huddling close on its crags. The sharp shapes of gannets cutting the air above and around, hundreds of them, their noise cracking from the rock, rising from the water, filling our ears with a huge many-tongued gabbling so that even Ulfr's desperate warnings were lost in the sound. Beyond the cliffs, a deep, dark line of turbulent water foamed at the intersection of currents with birds spearing down from the sky, raining into a thrashing, boiling sea. A tide that would drive them to the Isle of Mannanán.

I could see Hamund in the bows now, hauling hard on a rope leaning outboard, over the sea, tampering with the working of the water on the hull, giving every strength, every piece of knowledge to the struggle as Thorkil, his broad back heaving, dug his heels into the bottom boards and pushed the barrels of water over the side, lightening their load.

'On, on, on!' de Lacy shouted, alive to the danger, his fist pounding the rim of the vessel. The strokes of the oar responded, ragged, falling out of time, slopping and splashing. Our boat ploughing on and Gunnar churning his oar trying to turn the stern to us, kicking out to round the sea cliff as another push brought us raging ahead, bearing down upon them. A spear's cast.

'On, on, on!' de Lacy roared again and again, and the *currach* leapt forward for a final charge, a flayed destrier feeling the deep prick of the spurs. An arm's reach. Ulfr's knife on the boy's throat, drawing beaded blood. Thorkil, raising an axe against the blow as our *currach*'s high prow crashed over their gunnel, throwing all to their knees. All bar de Lacy, who, braced for the collision, sprang forward at the moment of impact, sailing across the divide and slamming into Ulfr just as the *currach* upended, spilling us all into the swallowing cold of the sea. Water spiking into my mouth, ears, and for a moment all was chaos, all was dark. Until I breached the surface, exploding upwards, gasping violently for air.

The overturned *currach* floated already at some distance, drawn in towards a cove. Those oarsmen with strength enough to cling to its side carried along helpless and shaking. In the Norse boat, a fury of limbs. Ulfr over the side, blood blooming into the waters around him. Gunnar standing in the waist with a spear raised, waiting for a clean strike, as I saw arms rise and fall, arcs of blood flinging skywards from a short knife. I swam forward in a panic, grabbing the steering oar where it hung loose from its leather fastening. Gripping the curving stern, I pulled myself upwards, hooking my legs around the trailing oar, and I stayed low, slowly raising my head to look aboard.

De Lacy and Thorkil thrashed in the well of the boat, their knotted, sinewy arms locked, rolling and striking blows with such violence that the whole boat pitched and shuddered. Hamund perched on a bench stabbing downwards with his pitted knife whenever de Lacy's back or shoulder presented itself. Beyond him, Hugo lay in the bows, immobile, his sandy hair streaked damply across his face. Conn was not aboard.

'Hup, hoah', Gunnar repeated in encouragement to Thorkil as the men wrestled, until de Lacy's fist fell like a hammer, staving in Thorkil's mouth, and in a continuation of the same movement, he tried to roll clear of Hamund's blow, which fell on his shoulder, slicing into the knot of muscle there. De Lacy grimaced awfully but had not the breath to cry out. Gunnar drew back his spear to strike. I shoved the steering oar with the full strength of my legs, and the boat heeled to the side. Gunnar, unbalanced, thrust his spear far wide of de Lacy's exposed chest, the action carrying him off balance, his head cracking off the stem of the mast. I scurried farther over the side to see de Lacy's brawny arm reach up to stop Hamund's next blow, grabbing the boy at the wrist, pushing him dismissively into the bows of the boat. As Gunnar stirred to move himself, I drove my heel down onto the exposed nape of his neck, driving his head into the strake. He did not move again. I took up the spear and stood with my back to the mast, the silvery head pointed at Hamund's chest. We stayed that way, in our own realities, the clamour of the gannets, Hamund's low cursing, the choked crying rising from Hugo and the heavy, determined breathing of de Lacy from where he lay slumped against the clinker-built side of the boat. The *currachs* converging on us as the tide pushed us into the long, shadowy cove of the island of the sons of Nessan.

CHAPTER 20

Judgement

LIGHT RAIN FELL, ringing the surface of the slow, sleek river which ran high against the banks, licking along the planking of the quayside, swallowing over the black mudflats and drawing away flotsam and effluent towards the open bay, where a ship flying the colours of the King's messenger rode at anchor. I sat near the place where the Salach meets the Life, where a timber pier cut out into the current, its ribbed point trailing vivid green weed downstream.

I sat close enough to keep vigil but far enough away to look as though I observed the boats plying in from the ship, bringing cargoes of well-dressed men ashore. Above me, big herring gulls swooped, barrelling ravens from the sky, chasing them clumsily from a hanging shape—a creature of dread. The face gnawed, red gore frayed like old rope come undone, the nose and mouth all broke open and pecked into one rounded cavity, fringed along the bottom with teeth. The head crooked at a wicked angle, slight shoulders tilted like a yoke stretched between mismatched oxen. Only the hair was unspoilt, shimmering and catching in the brief stirrings of air. Such fine hair, its strands sliding free of themselves, like gold wire under the sun. Fair. Bold. Untrammelled.

They had dragged Hamund through the quayside streets in a dead weight of silence. Dragged him up the hill past the shambles, towards High Street, through a gaunt crowd of townspeople, muffled in solemnity—his slim knees broken with an iron rod. Gunnar, bound together with the dying Thorkil, was dragged behind, drawn along by a truculent gelding who hocked and whinnied, sending them sprawling in paroxysms of pain. The sound of their screeching mingling with the tumult of gulls who had not the sense to stay quiet. Closer to the corn-market, the Bristol men broke the terrible silence. They laughed and jeered where they were gathered in numbers, or where their own soldiers were near.

Sergenz dragged them up to the market cross and threw the three forms down harshly at its pedestal. Young Hugo came forward from the crowd, out from under his father's hand, diffident but vengeful. He carried a long, thin iron rod with a serrated ball atop. He pissed on them each liberally as they lay, unfeeling, gasping into the sky above, before striking each a wrecking blow on the shoulder. They had no more howls to part with, the heaving in of breath consuming their only energies. The soldiers handled them upwards into a sitting position, slumped against the quartering stump. Saer, holding his halberd, proclaimed their crimes and their fates, naming each one in turn as their families cowered in the crowd, crying raggedly into their hands, the women rending their own faces, clenching fistfuls of their own hair.

'Thorkil Mic Amlaíb, for conspiring with foreign kings, abduction and violent disobedience, your body will be broken and you will hang by your neck over the quayside as a warning to our enemies', and the same crimes called out for Hamund Haraldson and Gunnar of Uí Ímair, each to freshening cries and ululations. Then Saer called out a last name, 'Gryffyn FitzRoger'—and the tall knight was pushed forward into the clearing before the cross, his face a storm of shame and sorrow, his tensioned and bunched forearms gripped behind his back—'for abandoning your duty, and through weakness and omission, endangering the life of your master's son, you will hang by your neck, and your body will be buried in the churchyard of the priory'.

I stood uncertainly by on the fringes of the Justiciar's party, head bound in cotton strips, burdened with a shame of my own.

Unable to look up for fear of meeting the seething eye of Basilia or, worse, of the Lady Monmouth, her presence weighing like a millstone around my neck. But my name was not called. Nooses were lowered then from the distended timber scaffold, elongated as a crane-fly, erected to swing far out over the river—a dire warning to ships entering the port. I shut my eyes tight against what followed.

'They say there's not a man left from Fingal to the river to lead a horse over a brook'.

This from an old man with a bulbous red nose leaning back on the wharf, languidly watching over a gang of slight children playing with old gorse-wicker pots at the water's edge. Above us, the cadaverous remains of Gunnar swung gently by Hamund's side, regarding, with meatless sockets, the unlading of boats and the bustle of the quayside. The old man slumped comfortably against a mooring post, his attitude of eternal wisdom the embodiment of resigned acceptance, raising his broad, curled hand in rich gesture to passing boats. Something in his recumbent presence calmed me. Though he was right—after the executions, the Justiciar had responded with an abrupt severity, rounding up the last of the Ostmen and sending them south with Raymond le Gros to slay their cousins in Vadrafjord.

The following morning the *civitas* awoke to find a pole in the marketplace, as high as a man with his hands held aloft, on top of which a horse's head had been driven, its improbably long tongue spilling out over of the side of its jaw, black eyes covered in flies. What the Ostmen call the *nidstang*—the scorn post, carved with runes, hastily cut and raised to level a black curse over the market, over the town, over the Engleis.

For my part, I waited. I waited on the quay; in the hostel; on the walls. *Sergenz* ever near. I had slipped the noose. For now. But I knew the reckoning would come once all had settled. Once de Lacy had ground the Ostmen under his heel. Once his desperate and fierce embraces, thrown around his quaking son, had turned to open-handed blows of recrimination—they would start to ask questions. They would come for me. Hamund had made sure of that. Screeching in a high, wrenching voice as he was dragged aboard, pointing his broken finger in my face.

'Lords, it was him. The stained bastard. He is behind this. Him and Conn Máel Sechlainn'. His repeated, tortured lies bound around with strands of truth worming into all in the boat as the Justiciar's men rowed in stern silence and I slumped against the side with blood pouring across my face, into my mouth. De Lacy beside me with Hugo in his arms. Hamund's lies unspooling and dashing themselves to pieces against the implacable silence. Contradictions, hoarse pleadings, ravings rising over the slow, dying sounds huffing from Thorkil in the bilge. Seeding my future with thorns. Though I could feel no anger towards him.

'The end of Duiblinn', the old man said, breaking into my thoughts. 'Time was we sold the sons and daughters of their nations. So many of them that, if five galleys landed their prey together, you could almost buy a girl for a handful of gull's eggs'. He laughed cruelly, his laughter breaking into a rattling cough.

'A strange source of pride', I said, and he read the flush of anger on my face.

'I know who you are, *fendinn*. I know what you have done'. He pushed himself upright, coming forward in that same easy manner, stumping heavily on a palsied leg. 'And may the evil of your betrayal afflict your belly with great shitting and shooting pains, and your bowel with great swelling. May your bones split asunder, may your guts burst, may your farting never stop, neither day nor night. May you become as weak as the fiend Loki, who was snared by all the gods'. The children had stopped their play, looking on with unconcealed joy.

'*Fendin, faen*', they shouted, looking around for discarded guts and fish heads to throw. Their old father coming yet closer. His broad hand rising towards me. A finger pointing.

'She will haunt you to your end', he said, and his words struck hard, jarring the memory that was near the surface. An image that had not left me in the days since the execution. In the thrust towards the gallows, the three broken bodies dragged cruelly through the press of the Bristol men, who bent, punching and tearing at the prisoners. Not even Gryffyn was spared their evil sport as he marched behind, an easy mark in the crowd. The hangman cleared a space around them, looped the noose first over Thorkil and pulled the rope taught. If life remained in the Ostman, it did not show, and he was hoisted high to coarse cheering. Hamund was next. Clothes torn from his meagre frame, one arm broken and hanging slack as the other clawed uselessly at the rope. The hacking, jeering, laughing clamour surrounded all. The rope was pulled tight and Hamund's body raised to standing. I watched with a terrible pain within me, and he rose slowly above the heads of the crowd, all sound stopped so that we could hear the terrible, choking gurgle.

'A cunny' went up a cry of disbelief before the clamour came again, repeating in a shocked ripple of sound. A cunny. All eyes flew to the spot between Hamund's legs. And it was surely there. Beneath a barely present furze of gold. A dark cleft. A woman's fruit. A cunny. And suddenly two men from the crowd had rushed forward, had bunched up beneath the hanging form, grabbing her legs, lifting her weight off the noose as the hangman's frightened face turned in our direction, seeking the Justiciar. Seeking an order.

Those several bleak moments. Hamund's body suspended in air, legs propped from below and torso curling away towards the ground but hitched at the neck, gently snagged by the noose. Her eyes closed, her live fingers hooked beneath the thick, hairy rope, creating space. Her chest enlarging with breath. Her ghastly mouth breathing. Determinedly drawing air into a chest rising and falling, pushing upwards with each breath the undeniable budding paps, the womanly nipples that by some unknowable sorcery I had been blind to for months. In that moment, I too surged forward, surged towards her, bursting to get to her feet and push upwards, to free her delicate neck, to allow her to draw a deep draught into the slim cage of her body. But I fell instantly, pitching forward, my legs hooked from behind, and I came down heavily, my face plunging into the stony muck of the square. In the horrible blackness I felt a figure move over me, a foot pressing into the curve of my spine, and away to the right, a bellow come from the Justiciar.

'Unhand that traitor. Unhand that witch or I will break your arms with this rod'. For one instant there was a kind of silence as the crowd fell dumb. Loud crying and keening amplified in the silence. Gulls. The shuffling of garments. Water. I struggled to rise, shouting with full-throated panic 'no!' as the crowd roiled suddenly, the Ostmen trying to break in towards her. The shimmer and hiss of weapons drawn and once again a hand from behind, striking me savagely, and a foot tripping me, sending me back into the serried press of legs. Again I was down, roaring into the muck. And above every sound, the tightening squeak of the rope and the groaning of the timber frame, and I did not have to see it to know that that insubstantial form flew skywards with the ease of a straw effigy. Her trapped fingers crushing knuckles into her windpipe. Her eyes opening frantically to the towering grey sky. I roared myself out into the filth. Howled useless words, curses, promises into the earth. It changed everything. That cunny. I do not know why, but it changed everything.

Three drops of a bedded woman: a drop of blood, a tear, a bead of sweat.

The memory scattered along with the harrying children as Gautier arrived onto the quay with a tight clutch of *sergenz* around him. The old man cowed back to his post, the soldiers' quick eyes following every movement of the quayside, gripping their halberds, shifting the staves from palm to palm. The fear of conquerors in a conquered land. The alertness of burghers after the bull has gored, the horse bolted, the dog bit. I stood up slowly to meet him, and my left knee buckled momentarily with loose-jointed fear.

'Come', he said flatly, and I went with them, to finally know my fate. I walked within a circle described by the soldiers, a step behind Gautier, who did not speak further nor look towards me. Though I know it was he who had tripped me. Who had pressed me firmly into the mud as Hamund soared. He had preserved me from the same end. But perhaps it was to be for a short reprise. Gautier led me along the wood quay and out of the town, walking on in mounting silence. We followed the road, fording the Steyne and passing the priory of All Hallows and its dour walls. I perceived that we were making for an Rinn. He did not take me straight to the village, however, and a mile out, we walked down onto the shingle, shadowing the shore. The strand was a light-coloured grey with a thin mist coming in from the sea. I felt tired and sad and emptied. I felt anger and disgust, and some of it was directed at myself and some at the Justiciar and some again at Hamund. That beautiful, vibrant fool. That dead thing. That dangling, sad majesty.

Gautier paced along the strand and I laboured over the shingle, trying to keep step with the wind coming on fuller from the bay, bringing with it a keen freshness, an open mineral tang as, in the shallows, dense shrubs of seaweeds floated on the rising tide. We followed the heaps of flotsam and shingle along the high water mark, crunching laboriously through the shell which gave way sideways at each step, sending swarms of hopping insects away over the bladder-wrack. Through the mist, figures solidified from watery greyness to leaden forms. A reckless lightness came upon me as I recognised these bodies.

Adam de Feypo, Petit, Tŷrel and others, standing on a hummock of springy ground above the beach, speaking together, their swords in their belts steadied by the weight of their reposed fists. Dark de Angulo there also, and the Justiciar, a grim pillar behind, staring inland. They all turned when the sound of our crunching step announced us, and the Justiciar's face, when it separated itself from the dense trailing vapour in the air, was also grey, the smooth scars dull, his eyes tired but hard. He drew his sword, unhampered by his bandaged left shoulder and, sighting down the length of grooved metal, pointed its tip towards me.

'Give him a blade', he roared. And the mist dulled the reverberation of his voice. Terrible. I heard the shush of oiled steel pulled from Gautier's wool-lined sheath beside me. He put the sword into my fist and stepped backwards. The men around de Lacy stood off also, fanning in an arc around him. That terrible flat voice, raised loudly above the sucking tide, addressed me now.

'Here I am, boy. Was it not I who lifted your woman by the neck? Flung her into the sky? Was it not I who spoiled her face and her cunny? Come for me'.

I looked quickly towards Gautier, and by his stony impassiveness, his weighted stance, I knew he would not intervene. With my eyes still on him I started forward, throwing the sword in forehand and backhand swipes, as if it were an *immána* stick, quick, exact revolutions that skimmed the shingle, scuffing pebbles and winkles into the air. De Lacy's own blade swooped in response, with infinitely more strength, infinitely more poise, carving a figure of eight in the air before him. I paced forward channelling all the strength I could into my thighs, to carry me forward in ranging steps, up the slope to the hummocky turf. De Lacy stood waiting for me, and, a step beyond range, I slid out my leading foot, swung in a wide feint towards the outside of his sword arm. I stopped the swing short, at my elbow, pivoting the blade across my body, allowing the momentum to carry me around in a spin, a sidestep to his right. I dropped down onto a knee and plunged the blade into the turf, feeling it slide through and strike, sinking into the grinding gravel. De Lacy's blade punched into the turf to my right, where I had been standing a heartbeat before. I bowed my head, resting my chin on my hands, which clasped the pommel of Gautier's sword, and I waited.

De Lacy's blade landed a stinging slap on the back of my neck before his rough hand caught me by the shoulder and dragged me up. We stood face-to-face and he stared into me. I could not hide the tears.

'You did not know, then', he confirmed, and I shook my head.

'I did not know', I said in a low rasp of a voice. A wretched sound. He let his sword fall and both of his large calloused hands came up around my head, putting pressure on my skull, shifting the knitting flap of scalp painfully, and it seemed that for a moment he would crush me. But instead he pushed me, half rough, half paternal, towards the foreshore, snuffing and pulling his cloak closed over his paunch. He did not speak for a moment. We walked over the shifting ground, moving towards the village of an Rinn, labouring, and when we reached the finer, packed sand closer to the water, he said, 'I have a fortune spent on geomancy and on auguries of the Astra. These masters that come like market-day doctors in their rich hats and their little chests of oil and incense and fussy tools. They answer my questions of the future, explaining their responses through long discourse on the nature of shapes, or through the movement of the heavenly bodies. I have asked them much about what is to come. Should I bring my family or leave them here? Who should I send to Míde? Who will move against me in my absence? And while these arts have their uses, they are not conclusive'.

'Yes', I said, 'and the study of scripture can only take one so far'.

'And who takes you the rest of the way?' he said. I looked to him, confused, and he continued, 'Who told you what to do just now, for example? With the sword?'

I thought about it for a moment and then said, 'No one. I could neither attack you nor not attack. I did what I could'.

He nodded, satisfied, and spoke further. 'Success is decided within five beats of the heart. This I teach to my children. To act in the heat of the moment, with surety, with purpose and without hesitation. Nay, not rashly as some would—this is to misunderstand the quality required. The skill is to act in the moment with the knowledge of what to do. Without doubt or vacillation. Without the slightest pause. And how to know what to do? How to act?' He looked at me squarely, stopping me with the backs of his fingers. 'By long and ceaseless hours of thought. In the bed, on the back of a horse, supping at a table, on the hunt, gambolling with children. At every moment to be in thought. Where will your enemy strike? Where will you strike him, who is now friend that may be better served joining your enemy, and what enemy can become an ally? When the swords are finally drawn, your thinking should be done, and you will know what to do. To act, to act bravely, but above all to act with belief. Without delay'.

We moved forward again, skirting the black line of polluted sand showing the high water mark. Behind us, his retinue followed, Gautier gathering the swords we had left in the turf.

'Men are cautious, rational beings, Alberic. They sit and talk about the future. About what crop might do well in the fallow field next year, about how much firewood to set in for the winter, how to cope if there is blight, what saint to bend a coin to or which pilgrimage will afford the better absolution'.

We stepped onwards as he spoke, parallel to the shore, walking over the wet surface where coils of dirty sand showed the passage of lug-worms. The wet carcass of a dog at the edge of the reaching foam.

'When the solution presents itself, men think on it some more, they examine it for flaws and look at it in the round, they want to speak it to a confidant, to test out the sound of the words and to see, in their fellow's face, the right of it reflected back, assured and agreed on. Men crave that assurance. In secret they ask their wives—who are often better counsel than the shrewdest philosopher—and then they think again upon the answer. And do not hear me wrongly, prudence has its place. But not when the eye tooth of the wolf is bared. When the boar turns to charge. The prudent man hesitates when events move at speed. When a decision is do or die'.

His broad hand came out from beneath his robe, cupping the back of my head. 'Not you, Alberic FitzJohan. Your life has taught you to act like a *chaualier*. Speed, decision and result. You saved my boy'.

'I feared you would hang me', I said tersely, and he spat, saying, 'Paah. And maybe I would have. But Hugo told me all, he told me that you were true and that you tried to get him off the boat once your suspicions were raised'. After a moment's silence, he continued, 'But, I mistrusted you again, when Hamund's true nature was unveiled. Because a lad can be enthralled to a cunny like a dog to the kennel master. The sorcery of their sex. But you did not know, that much is plain'.

We walked on until I could see the huddle of huts at an Rinn materialising from the vapour-laden air. Men, soldiers, *chaualiers*, heads bowing and coming up in a knot of misted shadow. A long boat with oars set lay against the long jetty. Amongst the shapes, the Justiciar's family stood, waiting.

'We are leaving, Alberic. The King has called me to war. I am summoned to his side. His impious wife and his brainless, impatient, cock-headed sons have joined with Philippe, King of Franks. He has need of me in Normandy'.

This struck me like an unlooked-for blow.

'But you are the Justiciar. You hold the city for the King'.

De Lacy laughed. 'One is only Justiciar until one is not. Another will take my place and take up residence in the *castel*. It is to be FitzAudelin, that mannered courtier, the baron of the bushel. I do not see good coming from his governance, and I do not wish my family to stay here under his rule. I will bring them home to Herefordshire, and Tŷrel and de Feypo will look to my affairs here. I want you to go with them to Troim. You know the terrain and the families there. I want you to take the head of Magnus Meylocklan, the man who still pretends to kingship of Míde. Meyler is there already, unloosed, and I do not trust his motives'.

'Baile Átha Troim', I said, 'but I do not know it so well'. The sudden thought of returning to that distant, green kingdom and all that it contained chilled me instantly.

'I'll not have you picked off for FitzAudelin's court, lad. You are too valuable to me and my household. You will take Tŷrel through that country and you will advise him who is related to whom. Who is pledged to what house. Whose son is fostered to another and who holds the hostages that might cause another to revolt. Keep your sword arm loose and your mind sharp. When I have served the Franks their due of blood, I will return to broaden our lands in Míde to stretch from the sea as far inland as the Shannun. And you will have what is owing to you for your part in this work. You will have land and a hall upon an earthen hill and a marriage of worth. Alberic, do not read emptiness in these words. Serve my cause, and you will be rewarded'.

We had reached the dirty foreshore, littered with nets stretched out to dry and wizened gorse crab pots tumbling feckless in the slow surf. Through the mist I could see boats plying to and fro, men pulling creaking oars running provisions and de Lacy's chests of plate and fine fabrics and furs out to a ship anchored beyond the sandbanks in the bay. Beyond sight and beyond sound. A secret leave-taking.

I saw many *chaualiers* embarking and those on the shore calling out the secret, coded words of fighting men. The *écuriers* preparing the horses to be swum out into the tide, and everything moving in a hushed efficiency. From the jetty, de Lacy's children came running towards their father, the young ones crowding my legs and Hugo coming up diffidently. The Lady Monmouth approached then. She embraced me rigidly and kissed my cheek, the faint wet residue from her lips flaring cold on my skin in a sudden breeze.

'Come, Alberic, there is something I have been wanting to tell to you', de Lacy said, leaving his family to board the boat. He steered me aside, his hand gently propelling me by my elbow. He spoke close, his hot breath against my ear. 'And it may not be pleasant for you to hear'.

The boat rode the roll of the waves, thunking against the wet posts of the jetty. I watched over his shoulder as he bent close, delivering his words as the Lady Monmouth marshalled her household into the skiff. 'The good Earl of Chester is my mother's cousin—hoary old Ranulf. We were not strangers to his land in our younger days. There was a young man named de Crécy at Frodsham. A man who was amiable enough and ran a good farm for his master. But he was not kind to those in his power. Serfs and *villeins* in fee. He made free with their women—which, my lad, I can tell you is no rarity. He was brought before the manorial court for a serious crime alleged against him. That he put up for sale maidservants after toying with them in bed and making them pregnant. I do not remember what became of the case, if he was found guilty or not—only that it caused a pretty scandal to be discussed in shocked tones among the ladies of the county'.

I found it hard to reply, the weight of shame like hands pressing down on my shoulders. The venom of these gentle words tapping into my blood and beating sickly through me.

'We do not keep slaves in our dominions, lad'.

He spoke to me tenderly then, his wide hands once again cupping around my head, forcing my eyes to rise to his. To rise from his feet which wore the finest cut leather shoes, tooled with lavish knotwork and fringed with tasselled leather thread. My eyes rose to his face. He stood there against the wash of white light blaring from the sea. Beyond in the retreating tide, black stumps of ancient posts and carcasses of coracles lying on the slobland trailing bladder-wrack.

'Mostly because our churchmen and women do not allow it', he said with a soft laugh, and this somehow rose the ghost of a smile to my lips as he stared sharply into me. The rippled flesh of his ruined face and those eyes glowing out like an echo of the fire that had marked him.

'Nor do we persecute the son for the sins of the father'.

Confusion roiling in me. Disgust. And his confidence, in my weakness, something to claw on to, to hold like a floating beam as my ship foundered on the rocks of his making.

His broad hand smoothed over my head, pushing back the hair and curling back around my ears, fussing as I had seen him do so often, absently worrying the head of his favourite hound.

Three locks that lock up secrets: shame, silence, closeness.

'You will lead them there and find your old master, Meylocklan', he said in that same tone—both sympathetic and forceful. A neutral, levelled voice, as one repeating an inevitable truth. 'Seek judgement of your father. Though the Lord has punished him in his own way, making a comedy of the suffering he inflicted on others. Take the woman who scorned you. Inhabit her body and break its pride. Own the land that fettered you. Win wealth from the produce of its soil. Hang the man that enslaved you. Watch the life leave him. Stamp your foot on the neck that oppressed you'.

He said this all again and again, nodding, and, in the act of smoothing back my hair and manipulating my head, I too was nodding. And then it was 'yes? yes?' repeated warmly in the voice of friendship, the voice of succour. Until I too was saying yes, yes. Yes to it all. To the ravage and destruction of all I once knew. Until the die was truly cast. And my path lay northwards. My path led home. Whatever that word now meant.

PART III

What Is Owed
Is Due

CHAPTER 21

Baile Atha Troim

WE LEFT THE CIVITAS some days later. De Lacy's men, those who had not followed their lord to France, were arrayed all in a body outside the walls, the aldermen wringing their hands at our leaving. A bright winter ringing of horses' hooves on the frost-hard stones. The sun low and lancing brilliant light into our faces as we crossed the river Lífe and moved north on the Slíghe Midluachra. Entering the kingdom of Brega, a slow cantering from the seat of civilisation. A reluctant march into enemy land. The world again recast—fortune's wheel clacking around once more, de Lacy gone and the people of Duiblinn awaiting a Justiciar, and all uncertainties anew.

We left in train with Týrel at the head, his household *chaualiers* and de Feypo there too, de Angulo, Hubert de Hose and many others whose names I never knew, all hoping for stakes in the great enterprise that lay ahead. A strong host whose tread on the *slíghe* was heavy. Behind us, falling further back with each step, the safety of walls, the close contact of people, the smells of the markets, the garden peas and comfrey, the cess, the smoke, the protection of numbers. I had the feeling of being stripped of something. Of

237

safety? Of familiarity? Of leaving that conclave. And the shrine that I could put no name to. The shrine of ruined skin and bleached bone tumbled at the foot of the scaffold on the quays. Hamund. Or whatever her name had once been. The remains I had picked through in the night to find and to hold and to take with me the tooth that I bored in the quiet corner of the hostel and threaded on a thin strip of hide, sliding it along until it met the *kelt* and my embroidered scrap from Lasair's well. Her eye tooth. I wore it now beneath my *léine*, the tooth tapping against the cold stone with the motion of the horse. And I felt protected. I had weighed the price of Conn's life. Paid with the life of another, and both had died.

To forget, I tried to recite the *dindsenchas* for the journey—the placelore I had learned imperfectly during my time with Milesius. I searched my mind for traces of the poems of Brega to see if I could mark our way. And late in the morning, I thought that I glimpsed Sord Columbcille away to our right-hand side. I longed to see its tower and marvel at the place where Brian Borumhne was laid out in death. Baile Griffin, where the famous sons of Cynan dwelt, passing too, unseen. The lands of the Fine Gall, the demesne of the Saithne showing as nothing more than winter-scalded briar and frost-crisped grass. The Ben of Étair, that Hamund called Hǫfuð, watching our progress from afar and, as we travelled north, the peaks of the island Rechru taking up the vigil.

We crossed the openness of the country over Maigh na Éalta, the plain of the birds, without seeing more than the distant wintering flocks of geese. And I was reminded of that day that began everything, lying on my stomach with Lochru when we had seen that woe-begotten poet slink along the boundary of our *túath*.

I lost track of our location before the morning was out, and we moved through unknown meadows. We peeled inland following a small river between scarped hillsides. The farther we progressed, the clearer it became that our approach had been communicated along the road by unseen means. Our arrival at crossroads or farmyards was met with empty, peopleless places. All disappearing before we had rounded a bend. Huts and houses empty, daughters spirited into the woods, cattle driven into the bramble.

Týrel walked us on all day without pause, though before the sun set, we halted at an abandoned farm by a stream. The horses were brought to water and the captains repaired into the ruined cottage while the rest of the men threw up shelters against any standing walls they could find. I, as ever, was unsure of my place. As a member of de Lacy's household, I had the right to lodge with the captains, though Tŷrel had yet to summon or speak to me. The men-at-arms, unsure of my reach, had given me a wide berth, though this first night would govern how I would be treated in Míde. I stood uncertainly in the yard, holding the reins of my gelding, staring up at the pale sky beyond naked, overhanging branches, feeling the circling of wolves, feeling the clenching of fists and the preparing of sport. With a slave's intuition, I knew what would come from the soldiery if I spent the night amongst them.

I walked forward towards the house, trailing my horse with me. A guard stood beside the door. I handed him the reins and, without pause, proceeded into the dwelling. The room was dark, and dense smoke plumed upwards from a pile of bracken and mosses on the hearthstone, a *garsun* on his side, his soughing breath, coaxing flame. Tŷrel and his captains were divesting themselves of their riding clothes, and servants came and went, stowing their lords' belongings, taking in packs and blankets from the horses that were stabled in an adjoining room. Holes gaped in the wattling of the partition wall so that the more audacious beasts had pushed their faces through the openings searching their masters' good graces.

'You', a voice came rising over the sounds of the place, and I looked around to find Jocelyn de Angulo pointing at me through a space in the close press of men, his squat, sturdy form and pocked, lightly bearded face braced in anger. An apple in the palm of his pointing hand.

'They say you put the noose around Gryffyn's neck'.

'They say a bitch's brood is never short a runt', I said in a red flash of anger. Silence fell on the place, *sergenz* moving clumsily from between us, *garsunz* scurrying towards the eaves of the house. Angulo did not move but brought the apple to his mouth, teeth digging noisily into the browning flesh. The others remained quiet, watching. A menace rising in the silence.

'What did you say, wine splash?' He spoke the words low and deliberate, a chill entering me as more men moved way, leaving me exposed.

'I said that Gryffyn bought his pleasure dearly'. A horse whinnied noisily in the silence. 'I did not make him go whoring while the Ostmen kidnapped his charge. But I did save the boy'.

I saw Týrel sit back on the piled baggage, watching with veiled amusement.

'Such loyalty', de Angulo said mockingly. 'And to think I have heard naysayers muttering that you hold ORork in your heart'.

'Certainly ill-informed, mistaken creatures, *seignur*, given that I never honoured Ua Ruairc. Nor could I. I was in Máel Sechlainn's house, and the two were fierce enemies'.

'You love Melacklinn then?' de Angulo retorted eagerly, his mouth stammering around the Gaelic name.

'Would you love the man who held you in bondage?' I replied. 'Who forced himself upon your mother? Who bent the back of your father?'

'No Angulo was ever a slave', he said hotly as he pushed himself forward.

Three things that show a bad man: bitterness, hatred, cowardice.

Týrel's loud voice cut across de Angulo's anger, checking his advance.

'I have heard, young *latimer*, that thieves trawl this road and drag off travellers by night, strip them and stab them and leave them to blacken in a ditch. It would be a sad start to our venture should we have to report such a fate for any in our company to our lord de Lacy'. These words spoken to me in threat. Heedless, I played on with his game, treading as close to the edge as I ever had.

'True', I said, 'I have heard that *kerns* in the trees make no sound. That their knives are long and that the country opens up to them, admits them, while briars close and choke foreigners' progress. That trails disappear in the woods, light dims around them and they are lost'.

Several of the older lords laughed at my audacity—de Feypo, Hubert de Hose. This last called out in the general mirth.

'If I had a servant with your tongue, I would feed him the blacksmith's anvil'.

I ignored the comment and looked to Týrel. 'I can open the country for you, *seignur*'. Before Týrel could respond, de Angulo paced forward, drawing close to me.

'We can open the country as your mother's legs were opened. With force. And we, too, shall spill blood, as your mother bled spilling you from her cleft, you stained and luckless bastard'. With these words, he flung a heavy mail glove, striking me on the forehead. The laughter was loud, and several men clapped de Angulo's back, others breathlessly repeating his words in choked amusement. Tŷrel brought his hands together in slow, sardonic claps.

'Now, boy, you have been ringed', Angulo said. 'The first of many, I do not doubt'. I held the butt of my palm to my forehead, pressing the broken skin. When I looked to my hand, I saw the impression of small circles described in blood. In the noise, Angulo's horse had forced its head into the room, seeking its master's hand.

'You are no longer under his protection, wine splash. You are alone', he said, pushing the apple core into his animal's mumbling lips.

De Feypo came on speaking loudly and with good nature, 'Don't let them worry you, lad, you are of the house of our lord de Lacy. None here will harm you. They are starved of sport and jealous of your place at de Lacy's table, that is all. Best if you do not sleep here tonight'. His broad hand found the depression between my shoulder blades and guided me out of the house with gentle but insistent pressure. Behind us, laughter diminished into a low burr of conversation. Outside, in the rapidly cooling air, he spoke to me again.

'Some of us have come to love your irreverence and your wit, Alberic. Others would open you up for it. And to be fair, it was much easier to laugh when you were but a dung-stained rustic with pretensions of culture. But now your strut and your incautious lip come with a claim to some authority. And despite what has been said, many believe that you led Gryffyn to the gallows'. I did not answer this charge, nor did I meet his eye. He continued, 'De Lacy is now far away, overseas and over land. We all believe that God will return him to us. And if God does not oblige, de Lacy will find other allies', he said, smiling. 'But until then, play your part humbly. Lead us to Meylocklan. Show us the trails and speak to us of those who hold the power in these parts, and the rest will follow from there'.

I nodded slowly to show that I heeded his warning, appreciated his words, and that I would be a pliant reed in the river until he clapped my shoulder and turned back inside. Standing there alone, I looked around the yard feeling the covert eyes upon me from all quarters. From the ranks of the archers, from the men-at-arms, the mounted *sergenz* and the *garsunz,* all trying to read meaning into my interaction with de Feypo, trying to see if I was fair game, if I was a serpent without fangs or if I was a danger, coiled to strike.

I left my horse in the stable and walked out on the *slíghe.* The pale coin of the moon showed its piebald face, and the cold light of the stars mirrored the forming frost on the bare branches. The *bealach bó finne* threading its bright way through the heavens. The roadway was easy to follow in the brightness. Some way from the camp, I found a trampled verge in the lee of a sloping wood. I lay out my *brat* by the blackened twigs of someone's dead fire. Some traveller coming or going. Some farmer or messenger. Some fugitive or criminal. It was difficult not to think of Conn as I spent some time settling into the hard earth, wondering if he had escaped or, as was more likely, Gunnar had slit his throat and shoved him overboard during the chase. I lay alone, wrapped in the cold of the exile, cast into the wild lands, into that space where I was something else. Not Engleis, not Gael—something without definition.

Sleep would not come, and as I lay regarding the stars massed in their thousands, the cold biting cruelly at my nose, I caught the distant bark of a dog travelling on the dead calm of the night. Rising with the lightness of a dream, I followed the sound, unafraid, up the slope and into the woods. I walked beneath the bare canopy, moving quietly and finding footing between the bronzed stands of fern. Passing between the ghostly moonshine of birch trees, bats skimming overhead. I stopped and listened at intervals, seeking direction in the night. A light showed itself eventually through the trees. The dog barked, and this time the sound was cut off abruptly. I stood in the dark, straining to see ahead. Straining my eyes until they brimmed with tears, staring at the shifting light of a fire ahead, I thought I perceived figures in the light. From the space beside my ear, lips spoke slow words. The tongue of the Gael.

'Easy now', it said, and I froze, feeling the cold blade of an axe slide up my back to rest at the nape of my neck. A *kern* stepped out in front of me, soundless and soot blackened, the axe hanging loose now in his hand, careless yet terrifying.

'*Síocháin*', I said—peace, reaching my empty hands out to him.

'We shall see', he replied and motioned for me to walk ahead, towards the firelight, emitting a low whistle from beneath his drooping moustache.

I walked on, feeling a strange calm descend, and, reaching the trees at the edge of the firelight, I announced myself loudly in the tongue of the Gael, 'Alberagh Máel Mánus, alone and without arms'.

After a short silence, a voice bade me to come forward from a small clearing ahead. I approached, showing my palms to a woolly hound who, responding to my calm, nuzzled and licked at them happily. In the clearing, a group of five men sat around a fire. They did not show much concern at my arrival, and several had the look of those waking from a gentle sleep. By their faces, visible in the dancing light, I could tell they were of the one *clann*.

'God be with you', I said to them.

They murmured a collective response. 'God and Mary with you and a blessing on your journey'.

The eldest of the group, a man with a grey-streaked beard, invited me to sit with an extension of his hand to the fire's edge. In the same motion, he dismissed the *kern* who had brought me in, and I presumed he would join others out there in ranging around the periphery to ensure that I was indeed alone. He looked at me mildly as I arranged myself in the offered place, nodding around the circle to each man in turn.

'Cold night', I said to a general sound of assent.

'A follower of Mánus', the elder said. 'And what is it exactly that you are doing here, far from your Tiarna in this dark hour?'

'I am returning', I said. 'I am returning to find my father and to help if I can to lessen the destruction that awaits that *túath*'.

'And what part do you play in that destruction, I ask myself?' he said, his tone unchanging.

'That has yet to be seen', I replied, treading carefully. 'I have been to Duiblinn and have learned much from Lorcán Ua Tuathail'. Any advantage that I had hoped that name might bring was brushed aside lazily.

'Is that so?' the elder man said. 'Lorcán who presides over the ruin of the *civitas*? He could do with some lessons himself'. His companions laughed lightly. 'Perhaps your Tiarna would pay us a good price for your head? He could hang it over his door as a warning to his other bondsmen'. His eyes grew stern, testing me, before they softened once more and he laughed, striking me lightly on the knee. 'Never fear, lad, I recognise Mánus' red Sasanach when I see him. I watched you as a boy climb into the womb of the world, through the *sídhe* mound and out the other side, putting all to shame who stood by, shivering to their bones. I am Ruadán of Luigne and these my *derbfhínne*—my real kin'.

I made the required submission, bowing my head and speaking the words of obligation, thanking them for receiving me.

'Little need of such formality here, lad', Ruadán said. 'What news from the road?'

I looked from one to the other, trying to gauge what they already knew. 'There is a large company of foreigners down in the valley. It would be well to avoid them in the morning'. Ruadán nodded. And the others watched me, some with eyes rolling back into their heads in uncaring slumber. A skin of warm ale was passed to me, and I drank the sweet liquid gratefully.

'How many?' he asked.

'Two hundreds of men, three score of whom are mounted on large horses'.

Ruadán smiled and took up a bent length of gorse. He stirred the embers, drawing the burning wood coals together so that the broken, spent blackness fell from their iridescent bodies, dragging the unconsumed wood into the centre of the wavering light, heat thrown out, a force against my face. I closed my eyes to the scorch of it. His insouciance annoyed me.

'I have seen two score of these men destroy Ua Ruairc and his army', I said, searching to draw out his worry.

'You were on Tlachta then?' he asked.

'I was there, yes, and I saw what the foreigner can do'.

The man nodded slowly. 'I do not question it', he said. 'I have heard much the same from many others'.

'Yet you are unconcerned?' I asked.

'True', he said mildly, looking around at his companions, 'we are not concerned about two hundreds of foreigners in the valley'.

'And why is that?' I asked, suppressing my irritation.

'Because we know something that you do not know, friend'.

'I would be happy to hear it', I replied in that codified, mapped out response so usual amongst the Gael. Ruadán looked to his sons with the possessive triumph of knowledge hoarded.

'He has come into Ua Conor's house', he said with great satisfaction, the words themselves radiating across his face, and all five of them watched closely for my reaction. There could be only one response.

'Ua Néil?' I said, and they all took great satisfaction in my surprise. The great northern King and the chief rival of Ua Conor. If this was true, Ua Conor would have the support of every king on the island. He would be in a position to marshal a force of thousands. More than any Rí before him. One of the younger men, his eyes shining, spoke then in great earnest.

'Ua Conor has raised all of the kingdoms, Ua Néil from the north, Ua Bríain from the south, the great families united. Mumán, Ulaid, Connacht. None will resist them'.

'So you will understand now, friend', Ruadán continued, 'that a few hundred foreigners on the slíghe is of little consequence to us. We travel to join the great army that will wash over this land like a winter storm'.

I looked around at them all, their faces lit by the amber flame, their expressions lit with zeal, and I could not blame them their enthusiasm. I considered this news while the flames burned on, and the next time the skin made its way to me, I raised it before me and spoke loudly.

'To Ua Conor and the great army of the Gael', and my companions smiled and made warm, wordless noises of assent.

As the flames burned low, the younger men allowed sleep to overtake them. Ruadán moved around to me, the hound under his hand. He sat in close and spoke in a kindly way.

'And what of you, friend, you who speaks with the tone of a Míde man but dresses like a foreign lord? Do you ride with their army?'

'I do. Though I do not know to what end'. He nodded easily, letting silence overtake us, waiting for me to say more. After a time, I asked, 'Do you have any news from the lands of Mánus?'

He did not speak for a while, staring at the glow of the fire. 'A dark spell lies over those lands; I would not recommend travelling there', he replied finally, looking grave, and I could not induce him to say more on the subject. 'Would you consider coming with us?' he asked. 'We travel west at daybreak to find the King and to add the strength of our arms to his army. We have nothing left here in this cursed, scorched place'.

'I would like to look upon the Rí, and my way might well lie in that same direction. Though for now, I will travel with the foreigners back to the lands where I was raised. I will seek my father and make him answer charges that have been laid at his feet'.

The man thought silently on my words before speaking.

'Justice will be done', he said.

'Yes', I said, giving the correct reply, speaking the old words. *What is owed is due.*

I nodded by the warmth of their fire, waking in the blue before dawn with thin coils of smoke looping from burned ends of embers. My companions were gone, the clearing showing no sign of their passage. I walked slowly back to my camp, the night's conversation seeming as a dream. The sun had chased the moon from the sky by the time I rejoined Tŷrel's army. I led my horse out to a tree on the roadside, waiting in the noise and confusion of their preparation, keeping myself apart, watching their force draw itself up on the *slíghe*. The proud, tall horses, the metal-clad riders, the archers coming behind, seeming to me overshadowed, swallowed by the crazed, overhanging branches of the wood. A meagre few hundreds of men marching into an immense country, marching into hostile reaches, marching towards the warriors of the south and the battalions of the west and the hordes of the north. And suddenly they did not seem so numerous, nor so powerful.

The day's march went much like the previous day's journey. We passed many settlements, and at many places along the way, *chaualiers* came forward from small garrisons along the road. At other places, we passed monks digging trenches around new holdings. Flashes came back to me of that feverish ride after the parley on the hill, Gryffyn with me somewhat on the road, his easy way, his mischief, his strong frame a large absence. The weight of his ghost pressing on me and loading the *sergenz*'s looks with danger. I fingered Hamund's tooth compulsively, trying to draw comfort from the smooth, hard gloss of enamel, like glazing on a jug. My finger worrying over the long root. Her eye tooth, conjuring visions of her cutting smile. Of the black maw of her mouth on the gallows, the rag of her body sailing high over the river. And I prayed to St Lasair to intercede. Forgive me, Lasair. Forgive me, Gryffyn; forgive me, Hamund. Without fully understanding it, I chose Hugo and I chose Conn. I did not appreciate that in doing so, I condemned you both.

We progressed north-eastwards, the winter sun arcing low in the sky behind us, casting long, confused shadows. *Sergenz* ranged ever ahead and disappeared off the road, searching into fields and wasteland, driven by the sense of possibility and of freedom. No law in this land. No bailiff, no burghers, no manor courts. The potential for something lying just around every bend in the road—a girl, a cow, a church with a golden shrine. Intoxicating. The frisson of the rut. The shudder of a hound unchained.

I watched them come and go. Disappointed. Defecating in the bushes and stumping onwards towards Troim. De Feypo sent out riders to each farmstead, each squat-walled fort on each shadowed hill, but all were deserted. A deserted land divested of people and of cattle. I knew them and their stratagems. I could see them clearly in my mind, the people of Míde, gathering their belongings deliberately, without haste. As they had done when Ua Ruairc came raiding. When Mac Murchada and Ua Bríain pushed deep into this territory. When the competing branches of Máel Sechlainn ravened like baited dogs, tearing strips from each other, blinding the *tánistí*, wasting the land. The people had taken the trackways and *bóthair* of the backcountry, gone to the heart of the forest, or into the hills. They had melted against the horizon.

We saw nothing of them as we progressed. Though from every shadow, I imagined I felt the seeking eye of the *kern* on my skin. A mud-darkened face peering through the tight mesh of the undergrowth. Still as a fallen tree. Dark as a burrow. Murderous as a hawk waiting to fall. We saw nothing.

Something indefinable in the country began to change. Something in the wheel of the rooks, the roll of the pasture, something in the shape of the skyline that approached familiarity. My stomach tightened with each league forward.

Late in the day, we crossed a rushing stream between high, naked ash trees. Above the ford, a mucky mound gaped with the many mouths of a badger sett. As the caravan filed slowly over the crossing, several soldiers occupied themselves sending small dogs down into the darkness. I watched them as they crouched around the openings, waiting for the muffled, vicious sounds below to break forth into the day. An ejection of stumbling cubs came up first and were ignored by the men. Then the mother spilled from one of the openings, and the waiting soldier cast down a mail coif as if it were a net. The weight of it flattened the badger to the ground, and he bent in, quick as a finch, to gather the sow in his arms. The terriers raced out between his legs, descending on the cubs as the soldier let the coif fall, gripping the badger tightly by the skin of its neck. There was a desultory cheer, and he walked around his mates, making feints towards each in turn, barking and laughing out loud like a drunkard, encouraged by the cries and shouts of his fellows. I left them in the trees, walking my mount to the stream, where she slaked her thirst in the gelid, swift-moving draught, unnerved by the yapping of dogs and the smell of blood.

When we had crossed to the other side, the host moved onwards in unison. The daylight began to fade, and Tŷrel sent runners up and down the flanks of the column, urging haste. Their remonstrance was unfounded as we crested a rise with an hour of sunlight to spare. Below us, a low valley rolled downwards to a sleek, slow-moving river whose waters stirred and chimed innumerable bells within me. Slick, cold skin. The wafting of weed beneath the surface, grazing legs, soft silt between the toes, lips on the bow of the neck. And other, ill-definable sensations dragged from the vaulted spaces of my memory. I knew that river. Bóinne.

And between us and it, a massive circle of heaped earth, a *ráth* larger than any I had seen, enclosed by a deep ditch, shimmering with floodwater and surmounted with a fearsome palisade and a large gatehouse. A ringworm on the flesh of the prairie. Inside its circumference, many thatched roofs and a smaller *ráth* accessed by an inner gate and containing closely packed buildings dominated by an impressive hall. Figures moving. Smoke rising.

The men started to call out, deep and low, and we saw the small figures within the palisade turn and gaze up at the darkening ridgeline. De Feypo raised a horn to his lips and sent a series of lowing notes down into the valley. After a moment of near silence, the distant clank of a bell rose in response. We spurred onwards, down the slope, towards the promise of straw bedding, warm fires, plentiful oats. De Feypo called me to his side as we began our descent.

'Welcome home', he said, leaning over in his saddle and punching my arm. 'Now they will see your worth'. The gates were thrown open for us, the way lined with what men and women were in the place, cheering and clapping the withers of our horses as we passed. The line of people led us gently but very definitely down a processional way, funnelling us towards the inner gate, which we entered at a canter, and we were greeted by a *chaualier*, softly dressed without trace of armour, standing with arms outstretched like the Saviour on the cross.

'Ricardo de Tuite', de Feypo said to me quietly.

'Welcome to the *castel* of Troim', he shouted out. 'Welcome, welcome'. Tŷrel at the head dismounted and embraced him, and they exchanged formal greeting.

'We were beginning to despair of seeing you before the feast of St Agatha', Tuite said.

'Our departure was complicated by the King's summons. He has called all of his barons to him and would void the country of men if he could. De Lacy has gone to his side', said Tŷrel.

Tuite nodded with great enthusiasm. 'Yes, the French problem'.

'Of father and sons', said Tŷrel ruefully.

'Ever was it so', Tuite replied, evading the subject, and to move things on, he spoke up, addressing the gathering host who arrived still through the gate. 'Though we did not look to see you this night, we will stoke the kitchen fires for a supper and a butt of ale will be sprung. Please be patient, and the stable hands will see to you all in turn'. Addressing the barons, he said, 'Hot water is being prepared in the hall. Please, come and wash away the dust from your eyes and drink the rust from your throat. My steward will attend you'.

Tŷrel paced after the steward towards the hall, and the barons followed, dismounting and passing Tuite with greetings of various degrees of familiarity. De Feypo hung back until the others had gone on, and I stayed near to him.

'Adam', Tuite said warmly, tendering his arm to de Feypo, who grasped it in a display of strength and affection. They exchanged the long and formulaic greeting and pledges of loyalty before de Feypo turned and said, 'This is Alberic FitzJohan. Alberic is of these lands, and our lord de Lacy had seen a place for him here'. Tuite looked at me with interest, but his eye soon strayed to the busyness of the bailey and the housing of the newcomers. After shouting out some more instruction to his household men, he looked back to us.

'Come and survey the western approach with me', he said. 'We have some rangers to return before nightfall'.

We climbed the solid beams of the steps built into the stout palisade and passed onto the wall walk. De Feypo and Tuite walked ahead, indistinct sounds of their discourse reaching me. I followed, as unobtrusive as I could make myself, wondering in what building I would be housed—hall, chamber, stable, byre?

We stood on the ramparts before nightfall had taken hold, gazing out and watching sullen, tumescent clouds bloom into the westward sky. A tang of coming rain on the air—the pointed stakes of the wall wet from the damp gauze of the air. We watched the land around and the burning line of deep red describing the shape of the horizon. The river ran below us, and on the ridge across the valley, a fire illuminated a rough tower built for watchmen, scavenged from the deserted bones of a broken monastery.

'Riders!' came a call from the outer palisade, and soon after, a dozen or so horses broke over the rise, silhouetted against the sky. They came lightly armoured for speed, riding in hard towards the stockade, racing the dying light. De Feypo strained forward, his hands gripping the palisade, trying to make out the shapes in the gloom. 'Meyler?' he asked, though his voice was low, not seeking answer. I counted ten horses as they crossed the ford, lifting their legs high, pushing through the deep water with their proud breasts. The lead horse carried two riders. Pouring water, they struggled up the final slope, clattering over the wooden causeway through the outer palisade. We watched their progress as they picked through the crowded outer bailey, entering the *castel* through the shadowed gate. Here they made to turn towards the stables, until de Feypo hailed out 'Meyler' and the riders, hearing his booming roar, wheeled around and stood, looking up towards us. I followed de Feypo, jumping straight from the wall walk down onto the beaten ground below. The lead rider, indistinct now in the gloom, pricked his horse's flanks, running the beast towards us, pulling back on the reins at the last moment as de Feypo jumped aside laughing and slapping the beast's lathered neck. Meyler FitzHenry sat glaring down upon us.

'Adam', he said then with some warmth, though his shadowed eyes were unreadable. At his waist, white interlaced fingers. Over his shoulder, a head rose from where it had been couched. Fey, dark strands knotted and loose. A vibration, like hands wrenching at the weave that bound my chest. A secret, helpless flush in the groin as she slid backwards over the mount's rump, landing lightly in the muck. Boots. High boots on those cracked and blemished feet. She resembled a warrior woman from ancient times. A Queen Maedbh, come again. Ness. She saw me and knew me and her eyes lingered in a kind of greeting. They spoke no flicker of fear or apprehension. No apology. No shame. She took three bold steps towards me, and Meyler followed, dismounting, embracing de Feypo.

'Ness', he said to answer de Feypo's questioning eye, 'a princess of the Gael'. She bowed her head towards him before turning to me.

'This one I know', she said, neither to me nor to Meyler but to us both, reaching out her arm and extending her finger to rest on my breastbone. The sound of her tongue twisting itself inexpertly around the sounds of their foreign language struck me like a blow. Two worlds colliding between her lips. I tried to speak, but my own tongue had grown too big for my mouth. Meyler looked me full in the face, feigning amusement, feigning nonchalance.

'Can it be?' he asked, smiling. 'And is he friend or foe?'

She thought for a moment, her eyes on me. Revelling in her power. Swift, vivid, confused messages passing silently between us like pollen in a summer gust.

'Difficult to tell. He runs with the hare. And hunts with the hound', she said, breaking into a peal of laughter. The sound of it racing down my spine and shattering along my pelvis. Despite the danger, I laughed with her—loudly, sincerely and helplessly. Her hair falling across her cheek. Her face bright in the gloom.

Three candles that illumine every darkness: truth, nature, knowledge.

CHAPTER 22

The Harrowing of Míde

God and Adomnán forgive me, for I preyed upon their innocents. I rode with the foreigners in their unleashed frenzy. Descending upon farm and church and *baile*. Riding with de Feypo, and Angulo in the van. Meyler pulling ever ahead, flailing flanks, thundering forward. Ever his lips peeling back from his teeth and her hands clasped around his waist, her hair flying loose, streaming out behind, bucking in waves to the triplet drum of hooves.

We descended. Again and again. Descending from the treeline, from the hedgerow, from the brow of a hill, with the low sun at our backs and shouts rising like flushed grouse ahead of us. I learned, time and again, there is no part of the body that detaches as naturally as the hand from the arm. The way a leaf stem is constructed to part from the tree. An axe arcs with force, a sword cuts upwards. Bare arms raising in defence. The hand shears away, falling intact into mud, into fire, onto rushes as cleanly and terribly as morality shears from the conscience when you run in a pack. When you descend together, baying and running quarry to ground. Like hounds with ears flat to their heads, coursing after the hare, the froth and salt slaver, tunnelling through the moment, attacking the present second, pushing through to the future where the flesh will be within your jaws. Nothing else exists, nothing in the periphery. Just the hew and curse and shout and slake. Undoing with butchery the hours and hours of planning, of labour, of skill embodied by the acres of thatch, the ells of wool, the ricks of firewood stacked just so, edge to the wind to keep the moisture out, gathered on a careful, deliberate day that came after other days of thinning the coppices, carting the loads back to the farm, splitting the logs and on and on. Gone from the count of days. Gone from the world. Endless aeons of labour, nights of plans softly spoken, dreams and hopes. All burning and rising into the canopy of the pale sky along with the spectres of those not quick enough to run nor strong enough to stay nor desirable enough to keep. Bodies ridden over and broken by our tide. Always the *chaualiers* pushed on, blood trickling from their mounts' flanks where the prick spurs jogged lightly over old wounds.

And when I speak of 'they', be full sure that I walk there among them. Following their paces. Swollen with the driving thrill of it all. Beating in the skull of some startled spearman. Spreading brains on the dirt with the tip of my sword for nothing except the fire of it.

God and Patricius and Adomnán forgive me. For I know that Lasair will not. Lasair of the ewe. Lasair, daughter of ready Ronin, that holy woman great and noble, that woman greatest in grace, of all that were ever born in her time. She will not countenance what was visited upon her daughters.

More of this through the fading winter. Morning dawning earlier and earlier. Our party there in the treeline already. Barrelling down like floodwaters breaking into some stockade where rumour had placed Máel Sechlainn. And yet, all was not death to the Gael and victory to the foreigner. Wounds were dealt out, and I received my share. Though it is surprising how resilient a face can be to the belt of a blade. Splitting, yes. Fat, tumescent gashes like burst slugs with the rough grains of scabbing blood knitting crudely together, as invisible but inexorable as ice forming over the water in a bucket. And no warrior who has lost an eye would dismiss the crippled man scared from his bed swinging a flail or a distaff. Or the woman with the eel fork standing strong in defence of her children. Or the counter-attack of a family, desperately fighting for their lives, gutting a standing horse, dragging mail-clad men to the ground and forcing rust-riddled blades home.

We slept in broken houses, followed roads westwards for days at times, before returning to the *castel*. We ate meat every day, slaughtering and wasting carefully husbanded animals. We slept deep, black, sated sleep. And ever she was there, behind Meyler, ready with a spear; across the other side of the orange evening flame; her eyes fierce, her face shimmering with grease or leading the horses to water with the *garsunz*. Never alone. Never close to me. Never near enough for quiet words. Though a certain language there was. A language confined to the small movement of eyes. The slight turning of the head. A language I engaged in but could not fully understand. Her eyes did not rebuff me. Nor was there yearning there, as my eyes yearned and strove not to show it. There was something else. Something that was perhaps sharp but not cold. Amusement? I think it was amusement.

In this manner we buried the dead season. Secret prayers to St Brigid as buds appeared, bound up tight at the ends of branches. Catkins drooping on the *saileach*. The early arrival of the *clochrán*, flying low among the sedge. The slow lightening of the evenings. Through it all—more raids, more murder, more terror. The more we saw of it, the less consequence it entailed. The men all dragging back concubines and secreting them away in the small houses that were being made within the palisade at Troim.

Tŷrel finally called his dogs to heel with the unassailable signs of spring. Having taken over command of the *castel*, he called us all together in the sparse hall, employing all the regalia of a lord's court. Trying to claim authority over men who were his equals, his relatives, his neighbours. Angulo, acting as his steward, ushered us into the room, de Feypo's boy Robert bearing the cups of wine, Meyler his *maréchal* seated on the dais beside the empty oaken throne—one of the few items of furniture brought to the *castel* from Duiblinn. A thing of Ostman craft, riddled with knotwork and serpents, rubbed smooth as marble on its armrests, lustrous where decades of hands had cured and greased the wood with fretting grasp.

Once the assembly had settled, Týrel strode in purposefully, taking a seat in the high-backed chair. I stood by the doorway, in shadow. Neither invited nor shunned. He raised his voice over the murmur of the room.

'Míde', he said, 'a land so vast we have not yet traversed its length nor counted its worth. A land of rich soil, of deep wood, of abundant fishes. A land that will yield up to us, not only a living, but a fortune. We can grow such grain that will shame even the East Anglians and the *paysans* of Evreux. And that without recourse to draining fens or clearing woodland'. He looked around the room, artfully using silence to carry his meaning, to allow his words to echo in each man's skull. 'Sheep on the upland, a great prey of cattle wandering the vales. Ploughing the yielding land. Sowing the copious seed. Birthing the lambs. Saving the hay. Milking the herds'. Silence again as each man conjured the bounty in his mind, calculating what his portion of land might yield, what that might allow him to build, buy, consume. Týrel nodded, appreciating the effect of his words, before speaking again. 'And who, lords, who will do this work? Who will do this work if we continue to disport and attack and drive off the *villeins* of this land, the *betaghs*? Those who know its ways and its secrets. Its game and its produce. Lords, we need the Gael. We need them on their farmsteads. We need them to trust us sufficiently to stay. We need them to work for us and all that entails. We need to show restraint, we need to convince the Gael of Míde that not only do we support them in their work but we can offer them protection. That we are better lords than those to whom they might flee'.

Some general, though not emphatic, words of agreement emanated from the assembly. Týrel continued. 'It is the nobles whom we need to eradicate, cut the head from the serpent. We need to find and destroy Magnus Meylocklan. There are those in Míde eager to come to terms. Men who had suffered under Meylocklan or under ORoric. Men who have claims to titles and hope that these would be upheld in our court'. He shaded his hand to his eyes, cancelling the glare of the tallow lamp that burned brightly beside him. His gaze fell on me, and he beckoned.

'Alberic, is this not so? Come out and tell us of their ways. Tell us again of their tanistry. Tell us plain, for some men here are not long off the galley from Bristol'.

A heavy reluctance settled over me as the thirty odd heads shifted, looking to see where I stood. Angulo hooted with derision. I stepped forward from the shadow and spoke as plainly as I could, choosing words for the men in front of me. Tailoring my speech to distance me from the enemy without the walls.

'The problem with the Gael is that their kings and lords are elected by the family, the *rígh dáma*. With the right backing, any brother, uncle or cousin can claim the seat of power. This is why you will find so many blind wanderers in Gaeldom. A chief may take his brother's eyes as a guarantee he will not be a challenge, an uncle take his nephew's or cousin's. A blemished man may not be *rí*, which is to say king, nor *taoiseach*, which is like a baron, nor *tániste*, who supports the baron—somewhat akin to a steward'.

'And what of the *villeins*? Who owns them?' said a man I did not recognise.

'They are not owned but are connected to the *túath*, which is the land, similar in scale to a barony. Their family cannot move beyond the *túath*, except at certain times or with express permission. A man beyond his *túath* is outside of the protection of the law. He revokes his status, and there is no honour price to be paid for killing him. Only the poet or the king may cross the boundaries. They fear the same will happen under a foreign lord. They fear that their status will be forfeit and they will no longer have recourse to the law'.

Tŷrel nodded again. 'Then we must educate them. We must let them know that we will uphold their status, that they will work the land for us, as they always have for their masters. And better, they will own a portion of what they produce'. He looked around the room. 'If we do not do this now, there will not be Engleis enough to bring in harvests and to turn the land to profit. We will go hungry and fall prey to the raids of those beyond our borders. I for one will not stand before Hugo de Lacy on his return and tell him we have reduced his fertile province to waste and scrub'.

We left the hall with Týrel's last words following us into the crisp day.

'Just the nobility. Kill them, root and branch. Keep the *villeins* to work the land. And bring me Meylocklan'.

The following day we rode again, leaving the fort and its two rings of sturdy palisade before the sun had risen. We rode over the wreckage of our work, farther westwards in a red haze. Meyler in the van again, pushing us hard over poorly lit terrain. We rode suddenly into the jaws of memory. Scraps of skyline, hills cut just so, silhouettes of high pine flashing familiar for a moment here and there. The jolt of the recognition nearly physical. I shook off the remembering. I ran with the pack, I focused on her back, jogging up and down with the motion of the horse.

We rode swiftly through a hollow, the horses ahead disappearing through a ragged hole in the blackthorn, aged ash trees towering on the higher crags above and the hoof-beats confused on the deep cushion of spent seed husks. I saw, but did not see, the well with the ties of fabric fluttering, the road beyond branching at the great splayed oak, the planked *tógher* crossing the stream. I knew, but did not allow myself to acknowledge, that I was home.

Meyler rode onwards without pause, Ness' mouth to his ear, guiding him up the valley, along the mill-race, his men hard behind him. He broke through the stockade, cutting down two young men who drew arms at the gate. Trampling them into the yielding sod. I followed behind, spurring onwards, fear now lumpen in my stomach. Pain and shame colliding. Panic rising. My hand loosened my sword in its hitch. I rode into the stockade to see that the horsemen had split, riding off in different directions towards buildings that had signs of smoke or movement about them. A scattering of people running in fear. More emerging from buildings everywhere, fleeing in fright, some fools trying to carry chattels, others with children in their arms. And down the hill towards us, against the fleeing tide, a figure stalked, waving a wooden rake over his head.

'Desist! Desist!' He was crying out in rude Latin, the sound groaning out of the mortified part of his face. From a distance I recognised in that laboured gait, that slack cheek, old Lochru. The name came to me, spraying my mind with light, as a gout of flame in a smith's forge. The veil fell, and finally I saw the place where I was raised. Cradle of my childhood, with its expanse stretched between the river and the woods inconceivably small now. Its shaded places and secret spaces contemptable in their wretchedness. Great fear and panic roared up within me.

'Stop!' I cried out, waking suddenly from the dream, pulling out of the mist that had enveloped me like one of Midir's enchantments, a mist that had covered me for weeks. 'Stop!' I screamed out, looking for Meyler as his horse wheeled in the middle of the stockade. I dug my heels into my mount and the horse surged towards him. As I approached, I cried out with force, 'There is no nobility here. There is no resistance. Stop your men and save the *villeins*'.

Meyler turned towards me; Ness' face couched on his back regarded me with detached curiosity. My body fell to tremor as, all around, Engleis soldiers rode, looking for plunder, leaping low fencing and breaking through doors.

'Keep them alive', I said to Meyler, 'and they will pay you in labour. Kill them, and they will gain you nothing'.

Meyler looked around once more and then responded with a look of rage, with hatred, like a stag pulled up short of the doe. His nostrils flared and his eyes cleared partially. His own mist lifting perhaps. He looked around again, breathing heavily, hungry for slaughter but remembering now Tŷrel's words. Lochru hobbled downslope closer to us, his calls continuing.

'*Sic desinunt! Sic desinunt!*'

'What do you say, Princess?' Meyler asked. Ness' head did not rise from where it lay, buried into his shoulder.

'No soldiers', she said quietly in her accented speech.

'*Villeins*, just *villeins*', I said with haste. As I spoke, two horsemen riding up the slope closed on Lochru, felling him on the hoof and thundering on towards the fleeing women.

'*Arestare!*' I screamed.

Meyler followed my gaze and turned back to me, understanding all in the instant.

'Welcome home, winestain', he said, smiling viciously, and spurred his horse onwards. As he rode, he blew two notes on his horn, bringing his men up short as they all wheeled, breaking off pursuit to canter back towards the centre of the settlement. I rushed to Lochru's side, kneeling beside him to touch his face. Warm still, his skin scabrous, his good eye staring in surprise into the grey roil of the sky. Black blood pooled darkly on the grass behind his head.

'Lochru', I said, 'it is Alberagh'. Blood shone on his lips as he voicelessly formed words. I bent my head to listen.

'*Sic desinunt*', he whispered on a waning breath.

'Where is my father? And where is the Tiarna?' I asked, bending low over him to hear his response. He drew in breath, and it hissed from his side as from a burst bellows. He did not breathe again. I stood with difficulty, looking around. The full weight of memory settled on me without warning, and it nearly buckled my knees.

Meyler loudly instructed the riders to gather the *villeins* of the place. His men moved off slowly, the fire gone out of them, cantering their horses or dismounting to bow their heads into the dwellings. I walked among them, speaking soft words into the dark houses.

'Come out and meet your new lords', I said again and again. 'Come out and be welcomed, be spared, do not fight'.

I walked the stockade shouting my message in the tongue of the Gael. Into the hayshed, the mill, the kiln, working my way around the sties skirting the mill-race and on through the gate into the Tiarna's enclosure. Unchallenged I passed through spaces that had once been closed to me, seeking the face of my father in every cowering shape.

I kicked away the dogs nosing forlornly at the bodies, licking blood, despite themselves, from their rooting muzzles. One of the dogs came to me, Cuan, the lord's hound. I bent down to jostle his head between the palms of my hands. The familiar gesture bringing me back to an older life. 'Alberagh? It is Alberagh', a voice came from the open door of Mánus' house. I looked up to see a knot of women gathered around the porch. Mór, Étain and other free women of the *túath*, their daughters and sisters among them.

'Étain, where is my father?' I looked into the group, recognising some faces.

'Alberagh', they clamoured, 'Alberagh, we were good to you when you lived amongst us, sweet Alberagh, please protect us'.

'Mór, where is my father? Where is the Tiarna?' None responded but rather they came forward, showing me the children in the house behind.

The dogs scattered as a parcel of *sergenz* ran wild through the paddock, drunk on the moment, laughing unchained, chasing panicked pigs and chickens.

'Please, Alberagh, please protect us from these savages'.

'There will be no further killing', I said, looking to the ground, 'that is all I can promise'.

The women watched from the shadow of the doorway, watching armour come off and seeing the blood up and knowing well what was to come. They began a wailing, a keening, seeing the men darken the gate, coming on with lustful steps. I turned and paced towards the men who entered.

'Get back', I shouted at them, 'back and leave these women. It is Lord Tŷrel's will'.

I was cuffed to the ground by one of Meyler's cousins, the brawn of his shoulders thickening over his neck as he pulled the heavy mail shirt over his head. He cast the thing down at me, and I rolled away from the tinkling thud of its fall.

'Leave these *villeins*', I shouted again, rising up, and the next one coming in split my mouth with a mailed fist. I fell to my knees, feeling sick as the warm salt-rush of blood poured over my tongue. The women began screaming behind me, and I walked back to the house, shouting above their collective cries, calling the children out to me. The sound of the women attracted more *sergenz* into the stockade. They stopped to undo their armour, pulling impatiently at the small leather laces that kept their mail and surcoats bound. I bent in over the threshold, and the women began screaming my name, Meyler's cousin already flattening one in the corner. I did not speak to them but instead brought the children from the house, peeling them in some cases from their mothers' legs. I led them from the stockade and brought them to door of the kiln and told them to wait in the shadow until I came for them.

I walked on, following the stream towards the washing place, looking out for Gaels. For faces I knew. For Father. I walked between things, following the *saileach* fences. The *baile* around me, a hog under the butcher's knife. Guts spilled, hindquarters and fores split apart, the one from the other. Blood, bones. All of the parts. None of the whole. Worlds colliding around me, and in the riot, things becoming unmade. Walking away from the clamour of it all, I caught sight of Ness slipping into a narrow, shaded space between a barn and the palisade wall. As she went, she looked back, over her shoulder, her eyes meeting mine before she disappeared into shadow.

I hesitated also. Standing dumb. Staring at the space which she had occupied. What I had been praying for. Fervid prayers to Patricius, to Lasair, to Féichín. To find her alone somewhere. To speak to her. Touch her. Hear her speak to me and only me. I followed.

The space was long, narrow and dark, the barn overshadowing on the right hand, the palisade on the left. Before my eyes adjusted to the light, I heard Ness' voice say, 'Don't be silly child. This is what life is'.

Through the gloom I saw her, standing at the end of the space where the two walls met. She was speaking soothingly to a slim young woman of my own age. I recognised one of the kennel master's daughters. I stopped, confused, as Ness placed her hand on the girl's shoulder, moving slowly around to stand behind her, her arm crooked now around the girl's neck. With her cheek, she forced the girl to look at me, her soft brown eyes shimmering with unfallen tears. Ness stood firm with her feet apart, one muscled arm taut across the girl's throat while the other dropped to the girl's belly and began to slowly draw up her long garment, fistful by fistful until her bright thighs were bared.

'This is a good one', Ness said into her ear. A deadly sleek voice. Dark waters and her eyes upon me, green and deep, calling me to her, offering the thighs that stood, riddled with tremor, quivering with promise, in place of her own. A shaft of light fell from between the thatched eaves of the barn and the high palisade, picking out the light, curling hairs on the girl's skin. 'Better him than another'.

To say I yearned would say nothing of the beating, swelling imperative. The carnivorous desire, licking along my neck, flushing deep in my stomach. I spoke quickly to quench what could be quenched. To break the spell.

'Over the rampart and through the briars', I said to the girl. 'Do not wait for your kin. Run to where you are known. Run to Milesius. Those who live will find you there'.

Ness released her hold and the girl fell forward, one hand scrabbling, pulling her garment down as she crawled back into the light. I listened to the sounds of her flight recede behind me, listening out for any cry or shout that might signal her capture. None came.

'Three things that set waifs a-wandering'. I said. Ness did not answer. 'Persecution, loss, poverty'.

She came forward, her lip snarling.

'Do not speak to me of wandering waifs, nor of persecution', she spat. 'I have lived it all. What welcome do you think she will receive in the first house she finds? A girl with no family. No *log n-eanach*? A bowl of broth and a bed in the straw. And when the fire burns low and the woman of the house slumbers, fingers creeping all over'.

'Perhaps', I said, 'but it will not come from my hand'.

'What difference to you?' she said. 'Who will slake your lust now?'

'I pray to St Lasair', I said quietly.

'And does she take this away?' she said, her arm falling artfully, the back of her hand brushing the tumescence that showed itself at my groin. A flash of fire, pealing bells, my body recoiled.

'Does she relieve you with her saintly intervention? Why do you not join the monks, then, painted face?' she said, her words hard. 'Shame face. Berry blush. Why not cut your bag off and pin it to the bush over the holy well?'

'God's host secure me against the spells of women and smiths and druids', I said in a stern, quiet voice.

'You could have protected her. Save one at least', she said.

'Are you now the *brehon* who would judge me?' I asked, the tide of lust receding.

She said nothing, her regard defiant. Her tongue running along her lower lip. A mollusc from its shell.

'To abstain is not to be just', she said at length. I thought a moment. Her anger, misplaced, did not speak true.

'To collude is not to be free', I replied, and I could see the words hurt her like a satire.

'Its called survival, *pauvre sotte*', she spat with venom.

'I understand. And I have sinned also. But I have been awakened from this dream of death. Seeing Lochru felled . . . and now they abuse Mór and the women in the Tiarna's house'.

'Yes', she conceded, 'you are right. I have felt it too, back in this place. Back among faces I recognise. I can no longer stand by'. And I could see by her expression that she was on the verge of action. As ever, her decisions sharp. Her mind unchangeable. 'It is time to do something', she said, her eyes full of challenge, willing me to react. I could not move.

'I need to think. I cannot see a way out'.

'Stay in the shadows then', she said, 'while the world is raped around you'. She moved past me and away.

I stood for a moment, the sounds of the dwindling chaos outside muffled in the close space. In this stillness, Mother visited. A wren, tiny and dart-beaked, flitting in to perch on a broken bucket near to me. Her head twitching, cocked to the side with her usual question. I tried to imagine what it was that she saw. I became intensely aware of my body. My long arms heavy by my sides. Inactive. My wide frame, rangy shoulders. My squaring jaw. Breath through my nose, long exhalations and drawing in, bringing the odour of earth, night soil, expanding my lungs as far as they could within the restraint of the mail shirt. The weight of silence. The weight of inaction. I nodded to her on her perch. A decision made, the weight shirked off, and I walked out of the shadow, as light as a tuft of *ceannbhán* on a breeze.

Emerging into the heavy morning, I saw Ness walking towards the Tiarna's house, a long spear in her hand. The fury of her gait filled me with fear. I followed, drawing my sword as I went, the oiled iron of the blade shushing from its sheath. Lengthening strides took me through the stockade, and I saw her dip and enter the house.

'Ness', I shouted, running now, fear rising up over me. I shouldered through the door and entered the swelter of the place, the vapours rank of sweat and other humours. The women fought in one corner, were bedded in another among screaming and wild curses. The Tiarna's house made brothel. Men rutted women where they could pull them to the floor, over the cold ash of the hearth, beneath the table, among the stale rushes. Ness stood before me, seeming rooted to the spot, the scene dragging her back to darker days. Among the disturbed bedding and the scattered furniture at her feet, I saw the Tiarna's fine cauldron, tipped and forgotten. She bent and lifted it up and hit it hard on the edge with her knife, raising her voice to its highest.

'Sinners, I strike this bell against you', she cried out and, moving to the nearest bared buttocks, she slid her spear along the inner thigh, nicking close to the hanging sack. Meyler's cousin spun over, scrabbling to his feet, and Ness slammed the butt of the spear down onto his nose. He fell to his knees, cupping his face. I spun around, levelling my sword, fear threatening to drop me to my knees, but none had taken heed, the men rutting or wrestling with no regard for anything else.

Ness took up the cauldron again, flinging it at the back of the closest head. It struck home, producing a deep, resounding note as the man fell forward, Étain rising from beneath, launching forward, tearing at his face. I followed her, inflamed by the cries, and I struck out savagely with the flat of my blade, slapping downwards, nipping quickly at bared flesh, and the men rolled away with the sudden fear that cold steel wreaks upon naked bodies. Mór took up a flesh hook from the hearth and set to, drawing blood with vicious, hooking blows.

The women rose, one by one, and armed themselves with staves and knives and anything that came to hand. The men huddled at the far end of the house cradling wounds, staunching blood. I stepped forward as Ness led the women through the door behind me.

'Back, in the name of the Lord de Lacy and of Lorcán Ua Tuathail, of Midir and of Lasair', I shouted, swinging the sword in a figure of eight, crying out whatever words came. I backed out of the house, stumbling on the threshold and out into the light. Ness, leading the women at a run, was already beyond the stockade. I followed, shouting out to head for the kiln. Mór saw the children first, running forward, and they surged out of the shadows. The women bent to receive them, kissing their faces. The earnestness and the bruises, the blood, the nakedness set the children crying and the uproar was general. Our movements had attracted attention, and all of those despondent Gaels around the farm and the surrounding fields began to walk in towards us to see what the clamour was.

The men from the Tiarna's house came raging from the stockade, dressed in whatever garment they had laid their hand upon. Swords and *poignards* in their hands, bloodied and slavering.

I stood up on a stump and pointed my sword at them.

'Stay back, by the Lords de Lacy and Tŷrel, I command it—by the law of Adomnán I order it, by the Saints Patricius and Lasair I impel you. By Christ son of God and the . . .' I shouted all of this, losing voice mid-phrase, as Meyler emerged from the brew-house drinking deeply from a frothing mug, his captains around him. He saw the trouble instantly, and I watched his face as he calculated the risk.

I roared loudly then in the tongue of the Gael, reaching deep into my lungs.

'I am Alberagh, son of Seáhan. You all know me here. I have been to Duiblinn and the hurdle ford in Leith Moga, I have seen the Engleis *castel* at Troim. I was at the parley on the hill where Ua Ruairc was slain'.

The *sergenz* from the stockade hesitated, stopping a distance from us and looking to Meyler to see what he would do. He motioned with his hand to his young cousin, a calming motion. They relented. The Gaels approached further. I continued.

'We will go to the monastery, away from this. We will leave now, we go with nothing and we will be welcomed. We walk, we do not look back, we walk away now, leave all behind, and I will do what I can do to protect you'.

I stepped from the stump and Mór walked past me, the people following her, trailing silently without looking back. I stood still as the Gaels filed past me and I kept my eyes on Meyler, the ale mug hanging, his eyes watching, considering. Something unknowable holding his worse compulsions in check.

'*Villeins*', I shouted to him. 'Tŷrel's orders. It begins now'. He did not move, nor flinch at my words. His eyes boring past me, over my shoulder, to where Ness stood, meeting his gaze. As a tree meets the axe. Finally, he called out to his men, affecting an air of easiness, pointing towards the half-naked *sergenz*.

'Look at these dismal curs', and then to his cousin, 'routed by a parcel of handmaidens'. His companions, already full of ale, began laughing. 'Try your hand with the goats instead'.

He downed his mug and turned his back, tossing the dregs of his cup into the grass. I could not see if he spoke further. The sky broke, a scatter of heavy drops dabbing dark colour on the stone threshold of the kiln, a rustle on the thatch. I watched his back fearfully as the women walked away behind me, leading the children and the ragged men. He cast a last look over his shoulder to where Ness stood, and I held my breath, watching, his head tilting slightly. But he made no sign, and after the briefest of pauses, he re-entered the brew-house with his men.

I heard her behind me, the sound of her moving away. After a final scan of the compound, I turned to go. Ness walked ahead, shoulders feline in their cadence, her legs strong and unyielding as she climbed the grassy slope. I jogged up and joined her wordlessly and we followed the others over the hill, northwards, into the teeth of the wind.

CHAPTER 23

Féichín's Bones

THE DAY WAS FADING as we came through the last pass between wooded slopes and saw the churches rising from the plain which opened up before us. The children were past cheering, and we pushed on into heavy weather, bloodied feet and aching legs, chattering mouths, the women in rent and billowing garments. Ness walked at the front, leaning on her spear, a little girl on her back, burying her face against the wind into the exposed skin of Ness' shoulder. A boy of five or six rode on my shoulders, his weight adding to the wearing heaviness of my mail shirt.

I progressed with mixed feeling, unsure of my welcome to Milesius' house, though thoughts of his stern face moved me in a way I had not expected. A yearning awakened in me, or rather, finally made itself known, emerging from the crowding feelings that had beset me over the weeks and months of confusion and violence, of trickery and betrayal. I yearned to sit with him in the scriptorium as we once had, surrounded by the intoxicating musk of vellum and inks and the power of the written word, carrying voices from ages past and prophesies of the future. I yearned to speak to him of Duiblinn. Its streets and its market, its immense cathedral and the varied tongues of its quayside. I wanted to speak to him of the great Lorcán Ua Tuathail and of what was befalling the Gael in those lands. I wanted to hear him expound on these matters, bringing his insight to play where mine had long ago exhausted its potential. Bringing light to the darkness. To take my face between his two palms and kiss my forehead and tell me that God has fore-seen what is happening and that it is the right thing, that slavery is lifted and the kings will need to take notice. I yearned to tell him of what I had done for Conn, of the risks I took and the stratagems I employed, though my blood ran cold at the thought of speaking Hamund's name. Of bringing the news that Conn was likely dead, swallowed by the grey-brown waters beneath the Ben of Étair.

I yearned to ask him of my father. Of my parentage. Was the Tiarna my sire? And what of Johan of Frodsham? Would I find him there too? Would I question him now that I had the strength to stave off his blows? Would I question him with a sword tip to his throat? Or would I embrace him, and let him keep his secrets, his hurts? Accept his penance?

Crossing the fields of broken winter barley, we knew that some-thing was not right, stumbling on the trampled and pocked muck. A quiet and empty feeling from the place. Sodden and wind whipped. A ragged length of fabric, tethered to something beyond sight, gusted and cracked, shooting up over the rampart and disappear-ing to the caprice of the gale. And then we saw the gate reduced to charred and broken timbers, and a sickness rose from the pit of my stomach, touching the back of my throat. Naked, burned roof poles rose, ghoulish, over the bank.

We passed through, palming the sanctuary cross carved into the gate passage, and, touching our lips, we entered the *civitas*. None challenged us. No gatekeeper stood out in front of us. And none were seen within the outer space, except a small parcel of cattle stoned into a makeshift paddock against the shelter of a ruined building. The forges quiet and not a waft of smoke rising. The bolt of fabric seen now as the weft of a loom, broken and trailing its last workings of half-woven stuff. The only other movement came from a pack of wet and blackened children climbing over each other in the mud before the high cross. Hunger was scored deep on their faces as they played a violent game with broken scraps of once sacred things. The children in our arms shied away from them, burrowing their heads further into our backs. I called out to them.

'Ho—where is the *coarb*? Where are the brothers?'

They scattered upon hearing my voice, one scrawny boy spinning in his flight to cast a warning sign—the evil eye—towards us before following his fellows, scrambling and clawing over the inner rampart. Something within me recoiled to see such unwashed and irreverent bodies crossing into that sanctum—that place of the saint's relic, of the brothers' graves and holy scripts. Their passage left us alone in the devastated expanse, rain dropping from the ruined shelters and buildings. Engleis arrows embedded in door-jambs. Ness called to me, setting the girl to the ground and sending her running back to the others. She stood by the doorless opening into a low stone house. Her face blank. Stone hard. Looking within, I saw bodies, twenty or more heaped and the intestinal smell of death rank from them. We turned quickly from the scene and hurried the others along towards the next enclosure. Rivulets ran down the paths against us as we pushed ourselves onwards. At the gate through the next rampart, we saw some life. A circle of women sat beneath a lean-to roof sorting bushels of barley along with sorrel and nettle. They sat silently, picking the nibs and preparing them for the pot.

'Ho', I called out, though the dirty children had alerted them to our coming.

Some of the women stood looking and some recognised in our companions sisters or cousins, coming forward and bringing them close in commiserating, warming embraces.

'Come, come', they said, 'sit by our fire'. A torrent of news was given and received. 'The foreigners came'. Tears and bitterness. The resolve of women. They pushed the children forward and made them stand before the fire. They rubbed their blue-tinged arms and legs between the rough palms of their hands and pushed quids of sorrel into their reluctant mouths.

'Where is the *coarb*?' I asked once the initial clamour had subsided.

One of the women, hugging the boy who had rode on my shoulders, pointed significantly with her chin towards the inner sanctum and the rising gable of the church.

'Within', she said. Signalling discreetly for Ness to stay, I moved towards the centre of the *civitas*, following ground I knew. I passed through the inner *vallum* and into the sacred space it encircled. Through the gateway I could see a meagre group of men working to rebuild the roof of Féichín's oratory. Others prepared a meal of mashed grain over smoking pots. Shouts of alarm rose as I approached in my gambeson, the sword hanging at my belt. Some screamed, running away into the church, believing another attack. I held my hands high.

'*Síocháin*', I shouted—peace. And I recognised one of them. Cearbhaill. One who had scorned me in a different life, who had decried my visits to the sanctum. He stood at the head of the workers, a taut rope in his hands as his gang raised a salvaged beam into place over the building. He flinched backwards at my approach, knowing me instantly, and the beam sagged, men crying out 'hold, hold', and he pulled taut, unable to flee.

'*Síocháin*, Cearbhaill', I said. 'I come under the law of Adomnán. We have brought Mánus' people, away from rapine and away from murder'.

The cleric stood his ground, eying me with suspicion. He ceded the rope to a companion. And we walked a short distance from them to talk.

'Alberagh', he said, rubbing his reddened hands on his robe, 'you bring them to not much better'.

'What has happened here?' I said, ignoring his unease. Ignoring the rancour that lay between us.

'The foreigners came, three days since'.

I shook my head. 'No, not possible. What colour were their standards?' He paused, his face clouding, recalling a painful memory.

'Some yellow, some red'.

'Angulo', I said.

'And Ua Ragallaig also. I went to the gate to speak with them. Some parlayed and pledged respect for the church. They said they were seeking Mánus and any *taoisig* or *tiarna* who might be claiming sanctuary within our foundation. Any Ua Ruairc or Máel Sechanill. Any who would style themselves king. I assured their chief man that we were few, that the *daoine uasail* had all passed on westwards away from their coming. Yet as we spoke at the gate, others grew impatient—archers and rude men of savage intent. They came over the ramparts by the mill and began to plunder. Ua Ragallaig and his men joined them, leading them through the gates to our reliquaries'. Tears fell from Cearbhaill's eyes, and he did nothing to hide them or brush them away. 'Féichín's crozier broken, the house for his relics ripped and plundered. The demons had eyes only for the gilding, trampling the saint's bones underfoot'.

'They disobey their lord', I said to reassure him. 'This was not mandated. The lord de Lacy will return, and justice will come with him'.

'They killed many', he said, 'brothers and sisters in Christ. They drove off most of our herds and trampled our fields'.

'Brothers and sisters you have yet to bury', I said harshly as I remembered the corpses we had seen in the ruined house by the gate.

'We have been working day and night since, to protect our manuscripts and to keep body and soul together', he said, his face flinching, studying me and watching for a blow. 'We have not the strength to dig graves also. These will follow'.

'And what of the desecration of crows and foxes?' I said. 'Where is the *coarb*? I cannot believe he would leave the dead unburied'.

'I am *coarb*', he said, confused, and I shook my head in denial.

'Milesius. Where is Milesius?' I said, trying to mask the urgency in my voice.

'He is gone', Cearbhaill replied, and the earth pitched beneath me. I grabbed at his vestment to steady myself, and he recoiled with fright.

'Do not say so, Cearbhaill, do not tell me he is slain'.

'You misunderstand me', he said hurriedly. 'Milesius is gone west to find Ua Conor's host. To seek aid against the foreigner. He is *coarb* no longer but Abbot and heir to St Féichín. The old Abbot died in the early winter'.

'Gone to seek the famed host', I said. 'The unity of the Gael. Then he is fooled by hope'. Cearbhaill's mouth set in defiance, though he did not speak. 'I return to Troim tomorrow', I said. 'Whatever is in my power to do I will do it to lessen the suffering of your flock. But I suggest that you let it be known that the foreigner is now king here and that all who take up their hoe and harrow in his service will see the chance for a better life'.

'And those who do not?' he said.

'They should take their chances in the west', I replied bluntly.

'And we are left thus. The wage of a blemished king', he said.

'Perhaps. And perhaps it is as Milesius says, that this is the Lord's plague sent against the Gael for their sin of slavery'. I turned and walked from him, and his dying words came braver and louder with each step I took.

'We will rebuild as we always do, Alberagh. It is not the first time we have been burned, nor the last. We will persevere with Christ's protection. He is judge of the living and the dead; he rewards every person according to his deeds . . .'

I went unchallenged to the scriptorium and found it rummaged but not destroyed. All the surviving manuscripts salvaged and heaped by the stone door. The gilded casings of books ripped away. The jewelled reliquary gone. The wooden stairs and decking above burned out, with fat staves of charcoal jutting from the wall. I climbed up on these to the partially collapsed vault, doves scattering, and I sat in front of the window where I had spent such rich hours with Milesius. I looked out at the red sun burning low as it settled into the navy vastness of the western sky. A light mist rising from the river engulfing the valley floor. No sign of a kingly host.

I went looking for Ness before the light failed entirely and found her at the fording place in the gloom of dusk, kneeling at the verge washing something in the placid water. The sight of her chimed bells in me. Small, delicate bells deep in my chest, along my spine, the cardinal points of the groin. This is what I had yearned for since I first saw her riding with Meyler into the stockade. A moment with her and her alone. To ask her. To understand. As I approached, a crow wheeling above on its broad-fingered wings landed to dart its beak towards a pile of bloodied clothes heaped by the riverbank before it lost its nerve and leapt awkwardly back into flight. I, too, hesitated before coming on. Fear stalled me. Fear of her body, her mind, her magic. I watched her a moment and mastered myself, moving forward, approaching unsteadily.

She affected not to notice. The closer I drew, the weaker my knees, the more constricted my heart. Words would not come, nor was I sure if any would serve. Beside her, small knots of white flowers on the hawthorn overhung the waters and *dunnógs* hopped lightly through the thin branches. I treaded on wetly, my feet sucking in the mud. The rude sound of my approach relieving me of dignity. Still, she did not look up from her work. I stopped, stood, my mouth opening, and the only sound from it was the hammering of my heart, flooding my brain with blood.

'You live', I said finally, feeling the weakness of the words. 'What I wanted to say earlier. I am happy that you live'. She did not respond but kept at her work. 'I looked for you in the forest. I waited through the winter'.

'And you wait still?' she said, looking up from the side of her eye, her mouth curling slyly. 'Do you still wait for me, Alberic?' She spoke my name in jest, copying the accent of the Engleis. I knelt down in the mud close to her.

'I have seen many things since then. I have been to Duiblinn in Leith Moga and many things happened to me there'. She listened quietly, her strong hands kneading beneath the surface, a wad in the rushes. Her thumbs working in the clear, running water, dislodging muck and gore. 'I have thought of you every day since that night on the hill', I continued. 'I have dreamed of speaking to you every night in Troim'. She nodded slowly as she worked. And a coldness opened inside me. A cold emptiness. A hard realisation that her heart did not lie the same as mine, even before her words emerged.

'I left you on the hill, as that is where you wanted to imprison me. You offered me nothing but a lower form of bondage. A bondage without security. Without comfort'.

'I offered freedom. And love', I said too quickly. She laughed a high, ringing laugh, her head falling back to expose the white workings of her throat. Small birds fled from the sound.

'You promised me a life among the foreigners. A life of security and plenty. You told me of the harrowing that was to come. I listened to your words. You spoke truly', she said, her hand gesturing around her, 'even if they were words spoken only to control me. You are not Diarmuid, nor I Gráinne. And even if we were—that story does not end happily for either'.

Her gaiety in the face of slaughter, her free-falling hair, her laugher were all goads that struck hard, scoring me deeply.

'What will you do now?' I asked.

She was silent a moment before speaking. 'I will return to Troim. Away from this slaughter'.

'To Meyler?' I said, the poison in my heart lacing my tongue. She did not respond, and I could not stay silent.

'So, you are happy to cling to him still?' I said, anger taking me. Bitterness souring my words. 'To live as a slattern for that churl? Christ, you have sold your body cheap. You have seen these men up close now. Their thick tongues. Their irreverence. Their ignorance of the natural law'. And I faltered, hearing Milesius' words repeated from my own mouth. And as I hesitated, she reached up, putting her dripping hand on my chest, and drew me in, savagely pressing her lips on mine. And when, with the unexpected touch, my mind flooded and I flushed full at her closeness, her cold, wet fingers tightened in my hair, heaving my head back.

'Do you not find my foreigner handsome? Sturdy? Lordly? What care if a Sasanach stag or a Gaelic one ruts me to oblivion? What difference that I am tethered to him? I am sold, yet not sold cheap. And at least in this transaction I have been the merchant—not the chattel'.

I shook my head free of her tightening fingers. I grabbed at my face, covering my eyes, seeking darkness. Seeking to soothe the anger, the desire, the confusion.

'The transaction was not for a horse', I said, 'but for a barn of winter fodder. When it is eaten, it is gone. And you left like a pat in the meadow'. Tears straining from my eyes, the panic clear in my words.

'Little boy', she said, '*gasurn*, you were not man enough to take me. Nor to keep me. Nor to protect me. Mooning over me with such piteous intensity. Now you try your hand at cruelty. You live like the rest of them, lying in your cot dreaming of the round, white bellies, the soft thighs waiting for your rape'.

'No', I said with a force that gave her pause, 'I carry the burden of lust. Like all men. It churns inside me, it twists my thoughts. But there is clarity in one thing. If I violate a woman, I break God's law, I spit upon Cain Adomnán. But more than that, I violate my mother. I do what was done to her'.

She watched me then. Watched my face.

'Did you not rut me on the mountain?'

It was my turn to laugh, a soft, exhausted sound. 'You reach', I said. 'You reach for a comparison that is not there. You came to me, girl. I burned for it, yes, willed it with every nerve. But did not force it. If memory serves, it was you rutting me. Though in the end it displeased you. In the end you left. And nearly killed me in leaving'.

A flight of seven swans beat voicelessly overhead, the sound of their wings sweeping strongly. We both paused to track their flight. A lone water boatman skimmed a curling back-eddy of the river. She snorted gently, almost a laugh, her eyes softening before falling back to the surface of the waters.

'Yes', she said in a low voice, speaking to someone unseen. Speaking to the dark. 'I will tell him'. She looked up to me once more, and her face had changed. 'I was not set adrift under Adomnán's law, as I once told you. I was given up by my father. A failed, weak man. I was given as *cumhal* to another in exchange for breeding heifers. And he did to me what men do. And I fetched water and bent to his whims and was dealt the rod by his wife until she so scourged him that he gave me up in a secret bargain for a quantity of raw iron. And I was again explored and drooled on roughly until a young man in a stable put seed in me and I visited the morning meadows for the dew fruit, *mongach meisce,* to make sure it did not take root. And I was captured by a raiding party and thrown down on the dirty straw of a byre, and you came in, a weak, wide-eyed fool. As powerless as my father. As afraid as my stable boy. Desperate as every man to spit seed and shudder and groan with your *gléas* standing out like a hound straining at the hunt, and I touched you to keep you away. And what you took for feeling was survival. There is nothing more here. Survival. A quick mind. A strong back and a cleft between my legs'.

Her silence when it came was iron bound. I could not break it. I reached out to her and touched her shoulder. In touching, I tried to draw in some of her pain. With an unskilled hand I tried to communicate. Though I lacked the tools. She had returned to her work, the coldness of the river travelling up her arms into her core. My lips finally parted to speak, and she must have heard the small sound of it and moved to silence me.

She drew him from the water then—the object she had been washing, drawn from the rushes. I had not heeded in the gloom, my eyes on her alone, blind to all else. Her strong arms hardened as she pulled him onto the bank. She rose and walked away, leaving me with the dreadful, pale form. Long and white, with large black blossoms staining his body. My father. Kneaded clean, terrible in his nakedness. His face still and faintly pained. His ribs clearly visible through the torn flesh, the scalloped wounds of horse shoes across him. His belly distended with the gases of the dead.

Stones crashed upon me. A dark effulgence of smoke filled me. Roaring fire scorched me. I fell towards him, and the falling lasted an eternity, the world swallowing itself, ejecting me from its count of days. Into Patricius' purgatory I fell. For long grey hours, draped within mists of confusion, wreathed in howls, I cried into the hard, white flesh at his cheek, his nape, keening like a woman, unhinged.

A man who had claimed me. He had claimed me to right a wrong, to seek deliverance, to find peace with himself, and though he took his payment in the skin of my back, he had claimed me nonetheless, where others would not. I cried for the duty I owed him, the moments we had shared. The searching I had made into his words and his past. Wasted hours. I cried at the blood I had drank. The blood soaked into me. Skin deep. Bone deep. Soul deep. I cried. That is all.

I carried him up the hill in the dark, moonless night. My feet following the flagged path and shades of children and cowled mothers melting away from me. I carried him into the centre of things, into the holiest of spaces, stumbling and falling, my shame fully dissolved, and I lay him close to the shrine of St Féichín. Beneath the cold stars, I dug his grave with my sword. With my hands, scooping. I dug through the sacred bodies of long-dead clerics. I shunted their stones and tossed their ribs aside. Their white robes circled the grave, though none opposed me. She there somewhere also. Her voice low around me. Came and went. With bloody hands, I laid him in the ground and tried to fold his arms across his waist, though they would not bend. A bad smell rising. I touched his white cheek, the stubble hard, his skull more present than his face. And I scooped the black earth onto him with my cupped hands, speaking to him all the time in defiant nighttime prayer.

'None shall oppose me. None shall bar your way', my breath a copious and misting fog. Farewell, Father.

Without knowing, I stumbled from the graveyard and past shadowy fences and invisible ramparts to the mill, exhaustion a wet *brat* upon me, and I lay on the damp, greasy boards, kneeling forward, the crown of my head on the floor, shunting the mail hauberk from me in exhausted heaves, like a dying worm. The tumble of the water below lulled me into the past, drawing me down. I fell. Into sleep. Before the dawn, she came in under my arm, her back warm but hard against me in the blue dark. For a long time she did not speak, and then she rolled towards me, nestling into my shaking body. Like before, on the hill, our bodies close and breathing each other's breaths. A unity of sorts. A unity of two closed caskets, each containing a void. Yet, the distance which before had been unfathomable in its depth was now discernible to me. Her person somehow more knowable.

Her hand found the *kelt* at my neck, flinching from it. She touched instead Hamund's tooth, lifting it on its cord and turning it between her fingers. Asked, 'Whose token is this?'

'A friend', I said.

'Does he not need it?' she said, and I felt her face tightening in a smile.

'She does not', I replied, ice gripping my heart. Ness fell quiet. 'I spoke in anger', I said.

'As did I'.

'You pulled my father from the charnel house. You dragged him to the water. You washed him with care. I will honour you forever for that kindness'. She did not respond. 'What will you do now?' I asked. She remained silent and for a moment more, until I thought she might have drifted to sleep. At length, she spoke.

'I will return to Troim. Seeing what sanctuary awaits here, it is clear which side of the rampart I would be on'.

'And if I asked you to flee with me? To marry?' I said, warily.

'To where would we flee? To whom would we go? We have no *túath*. No protection. The burned ribs of St Féichín's church should tell you that. Who here will treat us well, will give us land, will protect us from enemies?' It was my turn to fall silent. 'We will return', she said. 'I will go to Meyler and you will continue to assist the barons. Be close to their plans. Be useful. Be what they need you to be. When de Lacy returns and bestows gifts, you will have land. I can come to you then, and we can be married with the blessing of your lord'.

I smiled in the dark, and her fingers ran along my face, finding my mouth. She kissed me, softly and for a long time, until we strayed close to sleep.

'Were you the doe?' I asked as we drifted, 'on the hillside?' She laughed lightly at this, her voice soft, sleep rough.

'Do you not know me?' she said. 'I would be the she-wolf. The crow. The eel in the river. Never the doe'.

Sleep took me, a sleep dashed with red and grey images. A hunting horn blowing hollow and distant over the forests and through the vales of the west. Hooves drumming on yielding earth.

CHAPTER 24

In Weal and Woe

THE FOLLOWING MORNING dawned damp and cold, and we stirred with great difficulty from the warm nest our bodies had made on the boards. We dressed and left without speaking to anyone, slipping away unheeded and taking the *slíghe* to the south and east. At first we walked in silence, working the knots from our legs with steady strides. Her hair loose. Scandalous. Walking with a tireless stride, her haunches, her bearing regal. Her spear butt struck the road with each step, marking out our pace. We moved through the blue morning, the air as fresh as well water over our faces.

'I don't even know if he was my father', I said at last, when the sun had taken its ascendancy in the sky, finally banishing the uncertainties and fears of the previous night. She listened. 'Nor what he had done to my mother, how he had come to know her. He would never speak of her, and any attempt I made to know more caused such rage in an otherwise mild man'. She listened, encouraging me with her silence. 'I have been told many stories. Milesius told me that they were given as payment of a fine to the Tiarna soon before I was born. Conn spoke poisonous words to me, suggesting that the Tiarna had sired me or that Milesius himself

281

was my father. De Lacy alleged a memory of a man of my father's name in Frodsham, a reeve who had profited by selling the sons and daughters of his tenants to Gaelic slavers. And it is this which my mind has been caught upon. That he may have fallen foul of his own evil transaction. And perhaps I was the seed that he planted in my mother, a woman he had betrayed. Or perhaps I am the son of a slaver who violated her on the passage over the sea. Or of the merchant who sold them on, or of the man who held them first'.

'It is beyond knowing', she said, and her words were not unkind.

'And perhaps she did not know herself. My poor, beautiful mother. Perhaps she could not bear to nurse me. A demon on her breast, drawing life where so many others had drawn their tribute'. Tears came. I had never spoken of her aloud. And we walked onwards, our driving steps, our gazes fixed ahead. It fell from me, like onerous chains. An ancient bondage, slipping from me. Father dead. Mother dead. The Tiarna gone, Milesius gone, de Lacy gone. The world convulsing and her by my side. And though it was a fleeting, illusory thing, I felt it as fate. The fruiting of a tree that had grown barren.

We walked on in silence, though there was communication in our cadence. An energy from her as we moved, shoulder to shoulder, a feeling of power in our togetherness, a slight intoxication at the fathomless, empty country around us, the wend of the empty road. Smiles bloomed unbidden across our faces. Freedom. A weightless freedom we had not known. No lord, no soldiers, no work, no matron. A lightness on us and a feeling of what had gone before. A dangerous excitement buzzing like unseen wasps between us. Her hand sometimes finding its way into mine as we walked. My shoulder falling at times against her. And more than once along the way, we darted off the route at the distant sight of travellers and, as we lay in the dock leaves, waiting for the broken parties of refugees to pass, kissed thirstily, hands moving over each other. Bodies pliant or resisting, accepting or wrestling, feeling the shape and strength of each other in the transaction. Ever on, we rejoined the road. The warmth of the morning a surprise to us. The itch of spring in our noses. In our loins.

Three signs of lustful behaviour: sighing, playfulness, visiting.

We walked for hours, our reluctant progress forward skirting an indistinct vastness to the west, layered with purple and white tufting of *ceannbán* on the crust of the bog. Enough to fill an acre of pillows and quilts. The land shaken from its torpor, whispering promises of an easy living. At midday we saw from afar a figure on a horse and another two on foot. We scattered quickly, leaving the high road and rolling into the yielding turf, allowing ourselves to sink into the malleable ground, the low heather hiding us.

We watched in silence as they approached. A Gael on an Engleis courser, struggling to master the beast's spirit. The saddle abandoned and the rider's bare thighs clenching this way and that, knotted brawn rippling around his knees as he willed the horse onwards. The two young men on foot walked ahead, drawing on the horse's mouth with tightly bound sedge-grass ropes, leading onwards with arduous steps.

I looked to Ness, my face a question. In the giddy intoxication of freedom, the unrestrained possibility was overwhelming. She said yes with her eyes, hungry for it. Before they drew level with us, I stood out onto the road, my sword drawn, my mailed shoulder towards them.

'That is not your horse', I shouted, addressing the rider. The man slid an axe free from his pack, the horse chuntering sidewards.

'And that is not your sword', he responded. The two younger men hesitated, unsure whether to keep a hold of their ropes or to draw one of the short javelins lashed to the beast's flank. I felt the atmosphere change suddenly and knew that she had come up onto the road behind me, leaning on her spear. I had never known such power. I darted forward and swung wide, sword arcing down to sever the rope on my right. My body followed the momentum of the blade, ducking into the shadow of the horse's breast. I hooked the rider's foot and heaved it upwards, sending him sprawling arse over head into a hard landing on the stones. Ness scattered the two boys with feints right and left. She took a running leap, hand plunging into the horse's mane, and threw her leg over the beast's neck. I pushed myself up over the horse's flank and threw an arm around her waist as she kicked, screaming jubilantly as the animal sprang forward in a muscular bound. She wheeled expertly and sent us charging back through the running men, and we thundered away southwards, choking on unrestrained laughter.

We rode hard for a time before settling into a gentle pace, the horse pliant, happier with her direction, responding well to the squeeze of her thighs. There were few travellers on the road—ragged and fearful families, some leading scant and wretched cattle, old craftsmen struggling under the meagre tools of their trade. They all fled from the roadway seeing us in the distance, doing their best to hide in ditches and stands of gorse as we cantered past.

At midday, we left the *slíghe* ourselves and followed a gently sloping meadow until we found a stream for the horse to water. Drooping *saileach* and birds brave and numerous. Not for the first time that morning, we heard the howling of wolves in the distance. Hedgerows in disarray and clear signs of boar rooting in the grassland. These and other signs of collapsing order.

'What *túath* is this?' I asked. She shook her head, unknowing. 'I think Tlachta is close', I said, turning in a slow circle, trying to read the skyline. Perhaps Luigne?' We found an oat biscuit in a small doeskin pouch hanging among the javelins on the horse's side. We shared it out three ways, giving the beast her due; we hobbled her with a length of cord from the pouch and went looking for something more to fill our bellies. I pulled some rushes, and we joylessly ate the white pulp from the root, drinking cool draughts of water.

We lay then as the horse browsed, the sun's warmth fleeting with passing clouds casting chill. I shunted off my hauberk. She rolled over to me and we kissed, her hand running along my garment, feeling out the shape of my *gléas*. She kissed me again and again, her tongue slow, her hand moving. I felt the shape of her breasts, ran my hand along her cleft. The salt of dried sweat on her face, the mammal smell of her skin.

A deep convulsion ran through my body. She moved off me, rolling onto her back, and we lay there in silence for a moment, regarding the clouds.

'Did you spit seed?' she asked.

'No', I lied, diffident, blood flushing to my face. The silence went taut, that sound of her smiling unseen. I began to laugh, and she lay her head happily in the hollow at my shoulder.

'The Engleis say that a woman must enjoy it in order to conceive', I said. 'Could it be that I was not conceived of violence then?' She laughed again, though this time without joy.

'The Engleis may say that. Priests and lawmen. They say that. Men say that. It is a shameful lie to absolve men of their crimes'. She felt for my face and touched my cheek, rising on her elbow to look down upon me. 'Do not suffer for your mother's memory. She suffered. That is all. And it is a suffering that you can never touch, nor own. Honour her with your actions. Redeem her with your actions'. In her words, I read her pain. In her words, I read her restraint, her generosity. I knew what she had suffered. She had told me all by the fording place, my father dark in the water. And I, blinded by my own torment, had almost overlooked her resolve.

'You are right', I said. 'We are alive. We are free'.

'And masters of the road', she said, laughing richly.

I drew her to me, the blade of my hand sliding along her cleft, and her mouth fell to my neck.

We rode on, our passions spent, the canter of our mount devouring the distance, taking us away from this blissful middle ground, this space outside of things. This impossible place that could not last. Hour by hour, it receded behind us into the untouchable realm of memory. I fought the words for miles of road until the familiarity of our surroundings could no longer be ignored and Troim spoke its name voicelessly in the bend of the river and the shape of the hills. In the budding of the elder and the men in the fields. A kind of panic began to settle in my chest. A feeling I could not mediate. An itching burn, jaw clenching and unclenching. The words would not be held.

'We could go back. Walk west', I said into her ear from where I sat on the horse behind her. I could not help it. And a spell was broken. She brought my hand to her mouth, brushing my knuckles over her lips, and when she released her grip, I knew it was over.

'When the storm surges against the shore, it is better to be a ship than a sand-dune', she said. 'It is better that we ride with the storm than search for a life in the wreckage'. She spoke with finality, closing a door, perhaps, within her. I struggled to do the same, to choke the childish joy that had flowered in the morning.

'How did you come to be with Meyler?' I asked, introducing

his name between us. Not wanting to hear the answer, as I knew I had played a part. Not wanting knowledge of his hand on her. Not strong enough to leave the question unasked. She breathed a while, thinking about how to begin. Deciding finally that the bare truth was required.

'I left you on the mountain and I walked east', she said. 'I avoided *slighe* and meadow. I struggled over bog and pushed through woodland. And I arrived close to a place where there were Engleis watering horses at a stream. I walked straight up to them, my head high, and he stepped out from among the men, rough, strong. A leader. I held his eye as he approached and he stopped short of me, scanning the treeline for ambush. Looking at me with questions. I did not flinch from his gaze. I raised my garment slowly up over my thighs. He came to me, his arms around me, solid as a mountain, and he knew me there in the grass, and from his men, not a hoot or a cry out, and when he led me back amongst them, his hand drawing me by the wrist, they showed me deference. I knew this was a man that could shelter me—if he so wished'.

'And does he so wish?' I asked, my throat dry and the bile burning.

She nodded. 'He did, until yesterday, when I walked from his side to follow you to a ruined church, to a smouldering scar on the valley'.

I nodded then, understanding her answer. Again I had broken her hard-won security, and she returned now to an uncertain welcome. We spoke no further, and a greyness entered the journey. We progressed to Troim, silent and fearful, my hands clasped around her waist, her heels guiding the long strides of the horse. We came over the hill as the darkness enveloped the east, passing the watchtower, and I hailed the soldiers, raising my arm in salute. A salute that was not returned, though they did not move to molest us. Down the valley side we went, and over the fording place, forsaking the bridge, climbing up the other slope towards the walls; we passed through the outer palisade without challenge, the captured herds of Míde corralled there, shunting and lowing in a collective sea of sound. Piles and piles of split timber planking within the gate. Carpenter's boys working still in the half-light, carrying beams to the work gangs busy around the compound. A grim urgency upon the place.

We continued through to the *castel* and parted beyond the gatehouse without farewell. I stopped in the shadow of a dung heap to watch her go, leading the courser to the stables. My chest a warm glow which lurched sickeningly when she rounded the gable of the hall and disappeared from sight. I stayed there trying to master the desperate pain, the empty panic. It was unclear where I should go. What to do. I lurked—Crom Cruach in the shadow. Crom Dubh, twisting and black, feeling the handle of my sword, pulling it soundlessly from the wool-lined scabbard. Two fingers' width. Feeling the edge of the blade. Pressing its keenness. Imagining its irresistible and true line pushing slowly and unyielding into the bridge of Meyler's nose. I moved out to follow her, crossing the worn ground where the smiths had taken up their trade, beating out little iron nails from glowing ore. I passed through the rhythmical dinging of their work, and someone shouted my name. I turned, fearing Meyler or his cousins, only to see de Feypo coming out of the kitchen, moving towards the hall.

'Alberic', he boomed, altering his course and coming towards me. 'You live. They told me you had run to the Gael. Running back to your oppressor, like Patricius himself'.

'I went to bury my father', I said, the words bouncing as hammer blows from the anvil, and I walked from him, looking for somewhere to sleep, some quiet corner, some stable or byre. Somewhere to close my eyes and shut out the noises of the camp, the activity at every turn, the hammering and sawing, the shouting and arguing of carpenters, ditch diggers, masons and lime burners. Piles of brushwood being kindled around the stockade to light the work. I sought somewhere to be alone. For alone I truly was.

A red-headed carpenter's boy found me behind a large rick of thatching straw, the morning sun blazing behind him, giving him a nimbus of gold—his clothes flecked with wood chip, his face derisive.

'Get up, dewberry. The Lord Tŷrel summons you', he said, and I saw a gang of his rangy workmates nearby laughing together. I lunged out with a kick, and he skipped back, raising two fingers to me.

On my way to the hall, I looked out for some food. Nothing appeared, and I begged a mug of ale at the cowherd's shelter to fortify me. In the hall, Tŷrel sat on the serpent-riddled throne and asked me questions about what I had seen. The room was empty except for foremen and valets, who came in at intervals with news of progress of the different work gangs or requests for more materials. I stood before him patiently as he dealt with each, until he addressed me again.

'Meyler came back here fuming about betrayal. He said you attacked his men, injured his cousin'.

'The only betrayal was his', I said hotly. 'A betrayal of his true nature. His scorn for our lord de Lacy and for his new subjects. He made no attempt to reconcile the *villeins*. I gathered what survivors I could and led them to the monastery, only to find it pillaged also. By Angulo. The saint's relics scattered and trodden to dust. And my own father murdered. A man of higher birth than most within this fort. A man who had kissed the shrine of Lanfranc. Pledged oaths to the Earl of Chester'.

'I do not like your tone, boy', Tŷrel said. 'Speak thus to Meyler and your tongue, or worse, will be forfeit. You are a hare within his jaws and the distant form of Hugo de Lacy will not protect you. Nor is it certain that he would shield you were he standing by your side. Say your prayers for your father. Bury him within your heart and speak no words of anger to your betters. Vengeance is a luxury for the rich, the strong, those who fight. Not for the likes of you. Your audacity has brought you far. Further indeed than you have any right to expect. But no further. Your next utterance will see your brains stove and spread into the dirt unless it be made of quiescent words, in support of our purpose. None will mourn you here'.

I stood, cowed, with my head lowered. Shame alight on my face and my mouth clamped shut. Inside, the impetuous lizard I had for a tongue skittered and lashed at the confines of its cage.

'What word have you heard about the army in the west?' he asked after a pause, his tone neutral. I spoke to best please him.

'I have heard crones prophesying around ragged fires. Fearful priests nurture hopeful words like candle-flames in a gale. Nothing of substance'. He allowed my words to hang in the air. To decay slowly.

'Some information has come to us from *Bréifne*. They believe that such a host exists and marches upon us'. I shook my head.

'*Seignur*, I have lived in these lands for my entire life. I have seen war and alliance and hosts appear and dissolve and war brew and dissipate. I have never seen a grand confederation of kings. I have never seen an army of any great size hold together without escalating into conflict between the kings leading it'. I spoke in earnest, seeking to bring him the weight of my knowledge, the extent of my understanding of the Gael. To show my worth. His face remained stern, unmoving. His eyes probed my face, again he allowed my words to fill out the room, to show themselves fully to him as they repeated in the silent corners. Their intonation, their emphases. And when he had considered the shape of my response, he spoke.

'Meyler says that you went to the monastery to pass information to our enemies. To describe our defences. To list out our numbers, strengths, weaknesses'.

'Not so, *seignur*. Not so', I said emphatically. 'I went to enact your order. I went to save the innocents and, in doing so, to bring your word to the *villeins* there that the foreigner was to be fair, to offer opportunity for those who would stay on the land'. He watched me once more, without movement, until he seemed satisfied with my answer.

'We have sent to the Earl in Dublin for help, and he has refused us. That *sanglant fiz de putaigne* has refused us aid when our lord de Lacy sent him men and weapons not six months ago. I will go to Duiblinn and speak with him. He will heed me or de Lacy will know of it'.

'May I accompany you, sire?' I asked, half bowing with the request. Again, his dispassionate face, his considered response. He understood immediately.

'Meyler will not hurt you here in my absence, as long as you do not aggravate him. Stay close to de Feypo. Perhaps he will take you on as a *garsun* for one of his sons. Perhaps he will allow you to bear his cup'.

I bowed again and took my leave, as soldiers, blacksmiths and others waited for audience at the door. I left the hall, crossing the courtyard, through the inner gatehouse, across the outer bailey and, passing the shadowed outer gate, I crossed the bridge seeking de Feypo's house in the developing *faubourg*. I found him by his hearth and offered my service. He laughed, always laughing, and sent me to the stables to help with his horses. I worked hard for the day, mucking out, attending to the saddles and gear, carting fodder and watching, watching all around for a glimpse of her, though nothing did I see.

CHAPTER 25

Coming Kings

Tŷrel left in the morning, taking his *chaualiers* and passing quietly from the southern postern. I watched them go from the height of the palisade, cleaning my teeth with the frayed end of a twig. A sentry prowled the timber walkway. The level of scorn such men permitted themselves towards me told me much of my status. In his ambivalence and restraint with spear butt or cuffing hand, I read safety.

The hammering of the adzes on timber started soon after, drawing my attention to the outer bailey, where women moved among the steaming, corralled herds looking for heifers in milk. Beyond, the nature of the building work revealed itself in the line of posts and beams standing like ancient stones in a curving circle enclosing the landing of the bridge on the far side of the Bóinne. On his fourth, trudging pass from merlon to merlon, I spoke to the sentry.

'The cattle penned in and fortifying on every hand. Men pacing the palisade—there is fear in this camp. Do you think there is danger?'

He slowed but did not stop. I turned back to the south, hanging my arms over the timber breastwork, watching Tŷrel's party negotiate the climb out of the valley.

On his next pass, he stood his spear against the wall and his arms appeared by mine, hanging out over the drop into the dry moat below.

'At sundown, an eagle flew up the valley over the water and perched on that stump', he said in a deep accent that I had learned to recognise as Welsh, his forearm raising to point towards a hoary trunk, ghoulish in its posture, leering over the road crossing. 'It pecked five times, screeched thrice and flew into the west'. I nodded silently, waiting for more. 'In the night, during my watch, I heard terrible cries from below. Three times. My companions also heard and it froze our hearts. We came together, looking out over the blackness, seeing nothing, hearing nothing. And then from the dark, a corpse light showed, far out over the bog'. He looked at me, his face marked by the passing of some disease that concealed his age. 'That is all I know. If I were at home, I would say the Cyhyraeth had spoken'.

'There are demons in the night. There are *sídhe* in the mounds. Neither want us here', I said. 'But there is no army in the west'.

The morning light strengthened and the sun rose, showing its rim through the trees. From the camp over the river, horses broke from the shadow of the valley, riding out hard.

'I don't know about an army, but thank God and St Samson for that man and his hellions', the soldier said. 'There is royal blood in his veins, you know. Cousin to our King Henri. Though not in the right way, if you follow my meaning'.

I watched them go, Meyler and his raiders cresting the hill on the far side of the river, thundering past the watchtower, my eyes watering eventually, and I had to look away without discerning whether a flying pennant of hair strung out behind him.

'Thank God and St Féichín', I said, free of Meyler and his men for the day, and I moved off, saying to the soldier, 'Sleep well. You've earned it'.

I took the steps down by the gatehouse and slipped through the open passage to cross the bridge. On the riverbank, hordes of men worked splitting heartwood from long sections of trunks, adzing them into squared beams and planks. Another group digging a well within the circuit of the palisade. The gangers walked among them, bawling, breaking staves over sluggish backs.

I worked on at de Feypo's plot for the morning. Bending soaked wattles into hurdles, staking them out perch by perch. I worked with heavy-set soldiers from de Feypo's household. Men willing and strong, but lacking in patience. We pegged out the shape of the building, made the posts earthfast and wove the sturdy *saileach* rods between. Then it was a matter of clapping mud to the frame. I went ahead, one of the men casting water continually as I packed and formed the mud, finishing it as smoothly as my skill would allow. I welcomed the work. The movement of it, the tight movements of the *meithel*. Though still I watched, scanning every passing face, every moving figure, near or distant, as I drank deeply from the water bucket. I watched all the shapes on the road, moving downslope around the bridge, and eventually I saw her come up from the chapel yard. I saw her, her head covered with a deep hood, and I could not tell if her eye was dark with shadow or from bruising. She moved past our plot, her gaze turned downwards. Avoiding my searching eyes. Meyler's cousin walked with her. As he passed, he feigned to strike me, laughing as I stumbled backwards.

When they had passed, I sought the shade of the building, hiding my face and working on. Faster and faster I worked, but the mud would not take. I mixed it too wet and it slopped from the frame. I threw the last daubs to the ground and pushed out past the men, looking for something more brutish to do. I took up the broad horse bone and dug along the limit of de Feypo's plot, heaping the upcast into a narrow bank defining the extent of his property. I dug my back crooked, dug my fingers raw. I dug until I exhausted myself and ran out the spool of my thoughts, dug until I fell backwards on the bank, the cool breeze flaring cold across my sweat-soaked arms, painful in my hungry lungs. I lay willing myself to fall into the overarching sky, to plummet towards the high, streaking clouds in that pale blue immensity.

The boy found me there, head cast back over the bank, veins throbbing on my forehead and face. Eyes strained and stinging.

'You are summoned to the hall', he said, delivering his message with a fearful reluctance, as if throwing a morsel to a ravening dog, backing away from me as I rose, the clicking pops repeating down my spine.

'Summoned by who?' I asked, but he was gone, running over the broken ground towards the bridge. I shook the crumbs of dirt from my hair and, plunging my raw hands into the water butt, washed my face. I unfurled my wadded linen shirt and smoothed it out over my bare torso, slipped it over my head and went looking for de Feypo. He was not in the house, nor did I see him in the lean-to serving as his stable. My hope was that I would find him in the hall. That he would sit by and I would be safe in the shadow of his clemency.

I passed through the skeletal barbican, carpenters shouting to each other as they lowered cross-beams into place, and I crossed the bridge into the fortress. In the *castel* yard, I skirted the stable to see what horses were in. Among the noise and activity, squires busied themselves with Meyler's courser. Anger and fear collided in me. The hanging shields of his men, all bearing the same device—a sign of Meyler's growing power.

As I approached the hall, the door burst open. De Feypo stood out into the light, shading his eyes and looking towards the gatehouse. He caught sight of me approaching from the stable and came hurrying over.

'Alberic!' he shouted. 'Come, boy, come'.

'Am I to be punished?' I asked as he beckoned me towards the hall, and de Feypo's brow knitted.

'Come', he said impatiently, 'we have found him'. He took me by the shoulders, driving me onwards through the door into the smoky gloom. 'Revenge is waiting for you with a warm hand'. As my eyes adjusted, I saw that they had rigged a kind of tent inside the hall, closing off a small space by the dais. Light from the tallow lamps showed figures moving within. Outside the tent, several men gathered, sitting and standing, rubbing at their mouths and speaking in low conclave. They stopped talking and looked towards us as we entered. Angulo there, brooding, and Meyler rose from amongst them.

'Come, friend, come, Alberic', he said in a low, restrained voice, 'Come. The one we have been waiting for'. The smell of wood smoke and something else. Hot metal. Meyler's powerful arm came over my shoulder, enfolding me. He sniffed the air performatively. 'You stink, lad', he proclaimed with a muted and false laughter.

'De Feypo is working you too hard'. His retinue each smiled darkly. 'A man of your talents should not be wasted digging ditches'. His arm lifted then, his broad hand taking gentle hold of the back of my neck, guiding me along. The heat of his skin uncomfortable on mine, the hoary roughness of his finger pads grating, applying slight pressure to the knobs of my spine, announcing their terrible strength. The others fell back as he ushered me past. The bull of the herd. 'We have him, friend. We have him', he said softly as we neared the flap of material cast over the roof beams. 'I need you to tell him that. We have him. And that we will take the skin off his back unless he tells us all. Who moves against us. Where they will strike. Numbers. Archers. Horsemen. Everything, Alberic, I want everything'.

These last words sounded as he pushed me gently ahead and, with his free arm, lifted the hanging fabric, urging me into the close, fetid space beyond. I entered. Inside, three men sat, back to back, bound tightly to the frame of a broken loom.

The closest looked up through battered eyes, his features drawn, a hard stubble on his cheeks, some of his scalp burned and weeping clear droplets, one side of his moustache cut away roughly. Mánus. The sight of him struck me bodily—like the shock of hitting a branch at full gallop. My face cold, blood draining, and I cupped my hand quickly over my mouth to hide my identity. Meyler pushed in behind me and walked me around the outward facing circle. I looked down at the other two men, who had barely the strength to raise their heads. I knew Donchad by the bald crown and the flat shape of his skull—his swollen face was not recognisable. The other I did not know.

We walked the circle, coming to a stop by Mánus once again. Though he looked up to see what change had occurred, in the dimness he did not recognise me. His regard was weary, one displaced and not knowing from where danger came. I could hear Donchad attempt to speak. To warn or to counsel or to urge strength to his Tiarna. No word beyond a gasping wet sound emerged. Meyler directed me out of the tent and into the open hall.

'Do you not recognise them?' he said. 'Is he not your captor, your tormentor? The man who shamed your family and held you a slave?'

'No', I said before I had considered. 'Not him'. I stood immobilised by the lie, and Meyler studied my face. He said nothing for a time and then turned his back to me so that I could not see what expression or sign he would make to his men. There were more of these by the minute as the door to the hall opened again and again. Men coming in twos and threes, clapping their comrades' shoulders, looking for news, all in subdued undertones. Enemies all. Angulo among them, his eyes boring into me, like the blowholes of a furnace.

'No matter', Meyler said at last. 'These men have information that we need. You are a *latimer*, boy, are you not?'

'I am'.

'Then you tell them that they can speak to you. Or they can continue the way of trial by fire'. It was then I looked sharply to the hearth and identified the smell that had been hanging in the air, seeking to be recognised since I had entered the room. A ploughshare sat within the flame, a deep red glow festering along its edge. The door opened again, and de Feypo admitted two more newcomers. Through the opening I saw that many more men had arrived and were gathering around the water trough outside. Word was abroad, a racket like roosting crows. The King of Míde was captured.

The door closed once again, shutting out the brightness. Meyler came to my side.

'Talk to him now, Alberic, and reveal yourself. Tell him what you will. Speak to him shrewdly and give him hope, or speak sternly with steel in hand—you know best'. I feared his eyes on me. I feared the lie spoken in haste; a lie that had not been weighed in the balance. Of course, he knew that Mánus was King. That Mánus was my Tiarna. I went back into the tent, a shudder running through me. A realisation that I had taken a misstep. One that might result in my dismemberment before the setting of the sun. My limbs began to shake as I entered the tent, and I welcomed the thin, dropping veil of fabric that fell between us.

'*A thiarna*', I said, and all three of the bound men kicked upright at the sound of words they could recognise. '*A thiarna*, this is not how I would have hoped to meet'. His wild eyes flashed with many emotions—confusion, fear, anger. He took several moments, unsure of himself, before speaking.

'Alberagh?' he said then, his ruined voice barely a whisper. 'You have grown, boy'. Donchad strained instantly against his bonds, trying to free his arms, trying to turn his head.

'What has happened?' I asked, lowering down to a crouch in front of Mánus. 'What *drochradh* has brought you here?'

'A lame horse', he replied, testing a sad smile. 'A lame shit of a horse', and the smile tightened and tugged his weeping scalp. He winced and shook his head as if to fight back panic, to resist despair. 'I could ask you the same thing. You look as though they're working you harder than I ever did'. I looked down to my dirt-grimed garments.

'It's true, I'm on dangerous ground', I said, 'perhaps fatal ground, for I have just denied your identity to a man who is not lacking in reasons to kill me'.

'Stupid, stained runt', said Donchad, his words bumbling from between swollen lips. I smiled at his bravado. I remembered him on the *táin,* outside the house of Áed Buidhe, his strong stance between me and danger, and I was filled with an urge to break their bonds and lead them away somehow, westwards beyond the palisade.

'She is here, Donchad', I confessed. 'She is here and with that churl who holds you captive'.

His head bowed, and I could see his shoulders working up and down in silent laughter. Laughter for the end of days. Mánus watched me, silently, and I could see the frantic workings of his mind behind that vivid stare. His thoughts following path after path, proofing possibility after possibility, and each one reaching the same end.

'*A thiarna*', I spoke freely, unburdened by the future. Untethered from the past. 'Please know that I did all that I could for Conn. I did everything I could in a strange place far from those I knew'.

I watched, dismayed, as his composure broke, his face dissolving into a tearful grimace, and he could not bring his hands forth to hide in. I looked away, and at length he spoke.

'Milesius told all of your bravery, of your cunning. You will be forever honoured among us'.

'*A thiarna*', I said, bowing, 'I had not expected such words from you. Had I known, I would have come. I would have come with

Ness'. He did not heed me, his thoughts flying free of bondage, of pain, flying free, seeking his family, seeking the days when he ruled and the world was knowable to him, his knowledge sufficient to protect him and his *clann*. In that softness, in that hopeless defeat, in that bated lull permeated with the smell of hot iron, I asked my question.

'Who comes from the west?'

'Not hard to tell', he said. 'The Gael come from the west'. The third man I did not know spoke suddenly and sharply.

'*A thiarna*, no'. Mánus did not heed.

'The army of the Gael marches. An army that would dwarf Boru's. If I had seven heads, and each of those heads had seven tongues, I would need seven years to finish naming the men who march upon this place. Ua Néil has submitted to Ua Conor. An army beyond comparison comes here, and these foreigners will be hounded to the sea, their *castel*s destroyed, their bodies broken'.

'Not so, *a thiarna*', I said. 'Never has there been such. Never the north submitting to the west'.

'It has happened. We have seen it. As you, too, will see it. The foreigner will perish'.

'When will they come?'

'They are here. They are all around. We came ahead, scouting the country. I was sure to raise some men. Lochru, your father, others from the *túath*. But all has been destroyed and scattered before us. The army comes on, *kern* through the forests on all sides. Take us from here, Alberagh, take us over the walls, and I will show you'. His words came quicker, falling over themselves and fading to silence as Mánus acknowledged their futility. He hung his head and began to weep.

'Tell me about my mother', I said.

He looked up at me finally, his face resigned and empty.

'Who was my mother?' I repeated more sternly, and concealed in that sternness was the weight of my power over them.

'I never knew her name', he said.

'But you knew her body?' I said, anger creeping.

'Ho, boy', Donchad growled in futile warning. I persisted.

'Did you know her before or after my birth?' I said.

'Alberagh, this is how we live. Take from one lord in the

knowledge that you can feel the same sting. Yes, I knew her, I lay with her, but I never hurt her. She was a person both tender and beautiful'.

'Am I your son, Mánus?' I said, Donchad growling at my utterance of the name. Mánus raised his head and regarded me sadly. He shook his head.

'Boy, your father waits for you at the right hand of the Lord'. I watched his face for traces of a lie. None were there. 'You do not need a father to be a man', he said. 'You do not need a mother to be a Gael'.

I stood over him, his words angering me. The softness of the moment dispelled, and I felt the power I possessed over him. As I considered my next move, a sudden shadow loomed. The fabric of the tent fell, torn away, and the close, soft space collapsed. We were surrounded by a ravening amphitheatre of men. I stood, looking for Meyler. He lunged from the press of bodies, his closed hand thundered into my temple and I fell to my knees before him. His fist, closing in my hair, dragged me to standing. His next blow hammered onto the bridge of my nose, and he discarded me, and in pitching backwards, I heard him speak with venom.

'Cry for your mother, you *sanglant* worm'.

And I fell, and in falling he walked over me, a man beside him coming on with the smoking ploughshare on a stave, held in the crook of one arm, the other sleeve fluttered flaccid and empty. Ua Ragallaig there all along, in the shadows, translating my every word. I rolled onto my side, scrambling towards a roof post where I propped myself, avoiding the trample that closed in from all sides.

The sudden, terrible sound of searing flesh rose from the centre of the crowd, and through the milling legs, I caught sight of Donchad's screaming face until Meyler stepped over him, pushing the tip of his sword slowly into the space between two ribs. Ua Ragallaig bent close to Mánus, speaking rapid, scornful words into his ear.

'Outside with them', Meyler shouted wildly. 'We will feed the dogs'. The crowd erupted, cutting cords and laying hands on limbs, lifting the ragged bodies in the air and drowning out their pained cries with their own baying.

I scrambled low towards the shadowed eaves of the hall, looking for somewhere to hide, some bench or hanging fur to crawl beneath. A foot crashed down on my back, driving me into the ground. A hand hooked my throat, and I was lifted into the air. Meyler's cousin, his face butting into mine.

'Your true nature is laid bare, *sale bâtard*. I will have your intestines wreathed around your neck'.

I fought then. I fought with tooth and with nail, as this was surely the end. Thrashing madly in the grip of impossibly strong arms. My legs were hoisted into the air, and I kicked out again and again, striking unknown objects. They rammed me into the roof pole, cracking my face into the unyielding wood and my chest ramming into the post, driving the breath irrevocably from my lungs so violently that I felt I would never breathe again. I gasped wildly for air as I was carried among cruel shadows, laughing and jeering.

'You are meat now, meat for the dogs'.

'Poor, stupid *villein*'.

I went then without fight, barely conscious with limbs hanging free, head lolling backwards, upside down so that I felt blood running up my forehead and into my hair. A thick, slow flow of it from my teeth and lips down my throat. The light blinded me when it came, the men fanning out, carrying us across the courtyard, through the inner gate to the outer bailey to the flat ground they used for marshalling horses. Men and women gathered around us as we went, stable boys skipping around gleefully. I saw Donchad between two men, his head fallen forward, his knees dragging in the dirt. They ran ahead whooping towards something new rising from the beaten earth. Stout beams hammered into a cross-tree, a rope hanging. Soldiers and work gangs and kitchen maids running alongside us, joining in, crying out in the frenzy, tearing at us for a relic of a hanged man. Some darting in with small knives looking to come away with a scrap of cloth or, better, a finger. Meyler's men cast them back, hauling us together into a clearing in the crowd. I saw Ness coming towards Meyler, her hands imploring, her words unheard. He pushed her away dismissively and she stumbled backwards, the oncoming rush swallowing her up, and I saw no more.

Carpenters hammered timber bracing before us, frantically trying to secure the scaffold as Meyler dragged Donchad forward. I watched as though from a far hilltop, seeing myself thrown into the dust, the dogs brought up by the master of the hunt, jumping and snapping in ferocious excitement. Meyler held out Donchad's hand, and the fingers were taken instantly, the warrior's head coming up in a grimace, dragged from his dying agony, and as his head rose, so the rope was slipped around his neck. No fine speeches, no sermons. Meyler himself, riled, impatient, vicious, took the hanging end of the rope in his hand, turning two coils around his wrist as he walked out in a wide arc, and, without pause, he jumped into the air, coming down, wrenching with the full and awful might of his arms. Donchad was dragged sideways with a terrifying crack; the big warrior's hands did not even raise to take the weight from his neck. Meyler hauled, as a fisherman, hauling hand over hand with all of his strength, shouting in senseless and undecipherable rage until Donchad hung, his toes and shins brushing the earth, supporting no weight. No movement. Dead. Meyler let him fall and instantly moved towards Mánus' unnamed companion, pulling him forward on his face. I saw, but did not see, the murder unfold. The same gruesome introduction to the dogs, the hounds pulled free of Donchad's body to perform their task, this time taking the whole hand and a bone from the forearm.

The cheering and uproar continued, a constant clamour like a forest in storm. I lay slumped against someone's legs, which moved and trampled me as the crowd jostled. Black dread showed itself to me, as someone shouting from afar. I recognised it but did not feel it. I lay there feeling nothing, as one insensible with ale, though I saw with a sharpness I could not dim. I gave myself to the moment with an unlooked-for calmness.

Meyler called for help to haul the weight, and several of his companions caught hold of the rope behind him. The man was pulled to his feet and then into the air, free of the ground, and he hung choking for several minutes before expiring. The beams cracked and complained, but the scaffold held. Though I tried to look away, I could not. I watched his face through it all. Inhuman paroxysms and bulging eyes.

Meyler paused then, breathing heavily, and the powerful rage abated in him. 'The King, the King!' he began shouting, and the crowd took up the chant, raising Mánus on many arms and propelling him towards the scaffold and the quiet dogs, busy at their work, tearing and pulling flesh apart with muscular shakes of the head.

I could not fully follow what happened next, though I saw it all. Meyler's blade driven with all of his strength fell onto Mánus' arm, breaking through the bones just below the elbow. Meyler plucking the hock from the bloodied stump, casting it high in a red-drizzling arc to where his dogs lay bunched and waiting, leaping from their hind legs and taking to the air. And more such base pageantry. Mánus' face unseen. Ua Ragallaig standing by, his expression uncertain. His regard somewhere between triumph and fear as his eyes watched the crowd, darting left and right, cradling his own stump tenderly.

The blade sung out again and again, with my name next on its tongue. As the arcing trails flew, my mind unshackled from my body. My eyes sought escape, following the jagged line of the palisade. A soft and endless redness broken in the sky like the rippled sands left behind after a waning tide. A swallow flew low over the parapet. The first of the year. Mother? She came skimming above the crowd, dipping low over the head of a *kern* standing still within the crowd. Hair braided. Beard braided, leather *ionar* close fitted to his chest and short trews tight on his legs. He stood impassive, watching. The limbless trunk of Mánus hoisted against the sky, the rope hitched off and the crowd crying out and laughing, stooping for stones to pelt the dripping corpse. The *kern*, face daubed with mud, walked towards the scaffold, and it seemed that none noticed, until a *chaualier* of Meyler's company stepped forward uncertainly to check his way. The *kern* moved swiftly sideways, drawing a long-bladed *scian*, and slid it deeply into the *cheaulier*'s gut. The blade entered at the liver, and the *kern* dragged it in a juddering butcher's motion, cross-hand, and the man fell silently and slowly. The dogs reacted first; frothed into a frenzy, they broke away and began tearing at the spilling entrail.

Meyler's face clouded, slow to accept the truth of what he saw. A cry cut short from the left-hand side as another man fell, his throat cut, a *kern* stepping out from the crowd. A silence descended, Meyler casting around, his men still, and on the breeze the sound of a distant bell. The watchtower on the hill was signalling. And suddenly the bailey erupted. *Kern* throughout the crowd dipped their long-bladed knives into unarmoured bodies, all in disarray and confusion. I rolled onto my side as feet trammelled the ground around me, swallowed by the uproar, and when I looked again, I saw Meyler run towards the outer gate, making for the steps to the palisade. At the same moment, the bell within the gate-tower began clanging.

I raised myself up, with pain stabbing deep into my chest, knocked and buffeted as men rushed in all directions, running for the *castel* and the armoury it contained. Finding my feet, I followed Meyler. I watched him as he reached the top of the wall, his face scanning left and right.

'Shut the gate!' he began roaring, and then to his men down in the bailey, 'Horses, now, ready the horses!' and he disappeared into the gate-tower. I struggled to the base of the wall with dragging, constrained motions, buffeted by moving bodies, and began climbing the steps, one by one, each a new agony. Across the other side of the compound, all *kern* had grouped together, a mere dozen, fighting back to back against a gathering crowd of men and women coming up with spears, hammers, goads. They retreated towards the southern wall and passed out of view behind the carpenter's shelter. Beyond, the great shuffling herd of cattle moved boisterously in their stockade, alarmed by the noise, the barking of dogs and the smell of blood. On each new step, I scanned the crowd below for a sign of Ness.

Reaching the top of the wall, I stumbled across to the parapet, falling against the timber posts, willing my shaking hands to close on the edge. The valley opened up before me. The bridge below and the slow curve of the river were unchanged. The unfinished barbican stood open on the opposite shore, timber and carpenter's tools lay where they fell. In the slight breeze, curls of chiselled wood shuffled along the trampled ground. On the ridgeline opposite, the watchtower bell rang no more. The ridge itself could no longer be clearly seen. It was as though a forest had appeared; a massed blackness of men, moving slowly, unevenly. As I watched, a knot of men on horseback descended the slope. They picked their way slowly at first, until a lilting cry shattered the background noise, and I looked over to the palisade beyond the gatehouse to see that the *kern* had fought their way up and were showing themselves now to the host that spurred forward with a sudden urgency. Meyler burst from the far side of the gate-tower, rushing them in silent fury, sword gripped in two hands.

I slumped there against the parapet, watching the black, moving mass spill over the edge of the ridge and come down in uneven clumps of men—some galloping ahead on horses, some walking steadily in tight knots, others running madly down to the river and into the water. Below, in the compound, carpenters gathered beams and rushed to brace the gate as the cattle reared and raised up, butting against their roundwood stockade. The *chaualiers* and other soldiers already running uphill towards the *castel*. Meyler, blood to his elbows, jumped clean from the top of the palisade onto the ground below, rolling and coming up, crying out orders.

'Horses, *putaigne de villeins*'. Above it all, the grotesquely weightless body of Mánus swung in a wide arc, casting thick beads of blood.

Seeing the danger, I scrambled down, jumping from the last step. I landed, crying out with the impact, as two score of men with longbows racing to the parapet barrelled past me already nocking arrows and, reaching the top, began to fire high into the oncoming masses. Around me, milling crowds, all moving up the slope towards the *castel*. I searched for a flash of her face, her garment, her hair.

'Ness!' I began to shout. 'Ness!' I shouted, screamed, without restraint, her name like scalding water over my lips. Dragging the taste of blood.

'Ness!'

Javelins landed thick in the ground around me, flying high over the palisade with the sound of parting air. Several struck in the paddock, and the cattle surged and broke loose, cracking through the fencing in fright. They began skittish before gathering momentum, running in larger groups around the inner perimeter.

I followed the crowd towards the *castel*, among their screaming and crying, even as the archers on the walls began falling to the ground within the bailey, struck by javelin or pushed backwards by the clawing, dark figures coming over the walls in number. They joined what *kern* remained inside in kicking away the bracing on the inside of the gate, howling and alight with violent fervour.

I collapsed at the hanging place, unable to move further, and I lay there against a heap of building stone, gazing breathlessly towards the outer gate. I watched them breach the walls, I watched the archers fall from the walk, I watched the gates shudder, I watched it all happen in a hard clarity lit by a slanting evening sun, unable to move as my destiny unfolded.

And in gazing this way, I did not see Angulo and several men creep down from the *castel* and begin to gather the wild-eyed cattle together along the southern wall, gather them into a roiling knot before plunging a blade deep into the hindquarters of a slow heifer. The honking, urgent bellows of the beast cut across every other sound, sending the herd charging away, churning from behind, barrelling down the slope. Mad, fearless, *sergenz* stood out in the open with shields braced against them, shouting, waving their arms up, and rucking with huge collisions into the outliers, turning them ever towards the gate. I watched one man tossed to the ground and pounded to oblivion under a storm of thrashing hooves.

The *kern* within the gate saw the danger and began to push back, struggling to close the two stout timber doors of the gate as countless more forced them slowly inwards from without. Overlapping and competing shouts drowned each other as Angulo's men drove on. Approaching the gate, some of the beasts took fright of the narrowness of the opening and the *kern* crowding, waving their hands, crying out. Some broke off and skirted along the inside of the palisade. The larger part of the herd ran straight, *kern* leaping aside, and smashed through the crowd that had emerged at the opening. A hundred horned heads shook and gored in terror, pushing onwards to the river, some running along the bank, others driving on into the deeper water and a small number ploughing through men on the bridge. They checked the surging advance of Gaels without the walls, driving many into the water.

At my back rose a cry, high and challenging, fringed with fear. I looked behind to see the *chaualiers* galloping from the *castel* gate, scattering those on foot seeking to enter. Meyler and his men, on horses badly prepared, their own armour cast on in haste, trailing untied laces. They raced downslope, and I recognised among them the colours of de Feypo and Tuite. Angulo and his men ran forward, catching unmounted horses brought out for them, swinging up onto saddles, and the whole bunched company raced for the cleared gate. The *kern* inside the bailey came at them, hurling javelins and jumping down from the sides of the gatehouse bringing axes to bear, a ragged group of Gaels outside the walls rushing forward also, and the fighting was savage but brief. Meyler's men burst through, leaving none behind, though men and horses were stuck with spears. I caught sight of Meyler himself within the throng as they wheeled south along the outer walls, driving onwards for the rise, his head bare and a flap of scalp lifting as the horse spurred forward, an axe deep in his shield and three in his mount. Yet he mastered it, his merciless grip and goading spurs driving the screaming beast charging towards the valley side, hemmed in by his men. His face a bloody terror, alight with rage and exaltation. Until they were away, out of sight behind the jamb of the gate-tower. The Gaels were slow to follow. The *castel* awaited.

I lay back, the pain in my chest subsiding. I watched the high, feathery clouds touched with pink and saw, in my periphery, *kern* stalking past, heard them gathering the beasts, shushing them, corralling them. I heard the shouts of the soldiers, workmen and wives from the walls of the *castel*, shouts of anger, shouts of bravado to hide the fear, shouts of entreaty as the Gaels entered the outer bailey in a thickening stream, gathering their numbers before the inner ditch and palisade.

Conn's ghost appeared to me then, his face breaking into my circle of sky. His expression hard.

'Hello', I said in a cracking voice, and I noticed an axe in his hand. 'You are the one to bring me to St Peter?'

'I am the one to send you to hell, traitor', he said, tears in his eyes. The hacked stump of his father drifting above. The clouds turning pinker. Noises beginning behind me.

'You live, brother', I said weakly, and his arm raised. 'I am glad that you live'.

The blade fell, clashing against the head of a spear that stabbed into my circle of sky, spoiling the blow. A voice spoke, and with it, power flooded my chest. A throbbing, painful bloom.

'Desist', it said. 'He was next, look at him, he was next for the gallows. He was to hang for protecting your father'.

Ness, standing over me. Her bruised face, fierce. Spear braced. I pushed myself up, sitting now. I saw the bailey filled with Gaels moving in slow, deliberate business, entering all of the buildings, collecting horses, cattle, people and corralling them here and there. Behind me, the sounds of assault, the *castel* falling. Before me, Conn. Bigger, straighter than before. His hair bound beneath a leather helm, a short beard growing. Livid and rage-clouded eyes. Behind him a battalion of men, some working to lower Mánus to the ground, others coming slowly around us. Ness spoke again.

'It was Ua Ragallaig—search for the one-armed traitor. He is behind the walls of the *castel*'.

Conn's eyes flicked up, her words finding their mark. Ness shifted, her spear, her eyes alert to the *kern* closing slowly left and right.

'He is but a boy', she shouted, and these words hurt almost as much as my other wounds.

'A boy who betrayed me, and my *clann*', Conn said.

'A boy who defied the Justiciar in the heart of the *civitas*', said a voice coming through the crowd. 'For you, Conn', Milesius appearing, grey and bowed, planting his bronze-shod staff at once in challenge and supplication, 'so that you could walk free'.

Conn's anger faltered, watching me, and his eye snagged on something at my neckline. The *kelt* visible beneath my torn *léine*. The stone of his father. A relic from the past. And his rage roiled once more. He reached down to grab it, pulling it from my throat. Milesius reached out to stay him, and the *kelt* fell to the muck. Lasair's scrap. Hamund's tooth. Stamped into the ground as Conn came on again, shouting.

'Back, false monk', his axe raising, his men starting forward in response. Ness lowered her head, as if praying, and suddenly, her voice rose up. She stood tall and proclaimed loudly as men came on to take her.

'*Kings arise to meet battle*', she said, and at those laden words, the men hesitated. She went on, utterances of dark power, enumerating the end of things. A wind rising, shouts and screams from the *castel* behind.

> Ramparts are sought,
> Hosts give battle,
> Spear upon shield,
> Shield upon fist,

Blade-bristling fort,
Teeth mark,
Necks break,
A hundred cuts blossom,
Screams are heard,
Blood-zealous battle,
Raging on the raven-field,
Grey deer before spring.

Men, bred for war with sword and shield from boyhood, halted at these words. The dread words of the Mórrígan. Words to bring on the end of the world. Conn shook, overtaken by loss, falling to his knees amid torn pieces of clothes and scattered gobbets of flesh, some belonging to his father.

'Enough', came a voice, deep and thick with authority. A dark, high-born man on a beautiful white stallion nosing his mount slowly through the dense mass of men. He sat regarding. Ness' fury spent. The words spoken. The surrounding noises kept at bay, not penetrating the circle. His bright eyes regarding her.

'Come, grey deer', he said. 'Come and tell me your story. Come and see the battle to its end'.

I watched as, with strong thighs, he gently urged his horse forward, his hand reaching down towards her, stained, like my face, wine-red all over, splashing beyond the wrist. I watched her hesitate for the beat of a heart. Two. Three. Saw her clenched fist slacken, the tension along her shoulders release. The spear falling from her. She stepped forward, away from me, taking the hand offered, swinging herself smoothly up behind him.

I stood unsteadily and fell to my knees. With all of my remaining strength, I spoke desperate words.

'A thiarna, please, that is my wife'.

The lord's face impassive. Ness' hidden behind a veil of blue-black hair. He spurred the horse onwards, slowly past me, and the men followed him towards the waiting walls beyond. Conn following, listless, behind.

Milesius came and knelt at my side. He helped me to rise and led me out of danger, his arm along my shoulder and a hand firm on my hanging wrist. His touch restrained, and in that restraint lived the warmth of a full embrace. He guided me away, down the slope against the incoming tide, battalions of men from far-off *tuaithe,* gazing around in open wonder at the scale of the fortress. The racing fervour had gone, replaced by a calm expectancy frilled with excitement—a palpable desire for the spoil to come.

'The world is dark in the shadow of God's love', I said, hearing the sadness in my own voice. Milesius thought a while, silent. Then he replied with words of strength. Words of promise.

'He has made my mouth like a sharp sword. In the shadow of His hand, He has made me a select arrow. He has hidden me in His quiver'.

And this gave me the power to continue. We passed with some difficulty through the outer gate and over the bridge, pushing against close-packed oncoming bodies. Milesius guided me back up the valley to an encampment of tents that had grown up on the ridge around the watchtower.

As we walked, we spoke, and I told him things I had rehearsed in dark hours before sleep, anticipating our eventual meeting, though now it was all soured by her absence. Told without conviction. He listened, regardless, with great interest, relaying his own journey and the great upheavals and happenings he had borne witness to. The submission of the north, the rise of the west. The gathering of the host.

'Who is he?' I asked, finally, as he laid me onto a bed of heaped broom in a corner of his tent.

'Cathal Crobhdearg Ua Conor, Cathal of the wine-dark fist, brother of the King'. He brought me a draught of fiery spirit from a small leather flask, saying in a low voice, 'She will be safe', and I fell, the clamouring noise rising from over the valley like a festival on a hill, like the waking birds in a spring copse—small, distant, but filling the air. I fell into darkness as the dying light of the sun ceded to the flicker of an immense rising fire playing across the linen walls of the tent. And in that fire, the past blazed, Lasair's scrap obliterated, the dark *kelt* cracking, Hamund's tooth burning. I fell into sleep and, in doing so, missed the sack of the *castel* and the sharing out of spoil, the murder and rape. I missed the capture of Ua Ragallaig and the slow, artful revenge wreaked upon his body.

I missed her, clasping her fingers around a new frame, imparting her power, surviving, and perhaps gaining in the transaction, framed against a fire that was like nothing any man there had ever witnessed. It blazed still in the morning as we struck camp and marched south. The flame rising in a frightful violence, leaping in sheets high over the valley as smoke tunnelled and bloomed to the touch of the breeze. Ua Conor in the van, leading us south. To Duiblinn. His vast, unwieldy army of thousands following him, perhaps the largest the island had ever seen. And amongst them, her dark head, riding onwards. I turned from the fire and walked with them by Milesius' side. I moved among them, following a different standard. Following her dark, streaming hair. Following her strength. In love and in obligation. Useless and afraid. Alive and determined. Her army of one.

Author's Note

This project started out as a popular history book that I thought could be enlivened with passages of prose. The subject was my research on the adventures of Hugh de Lacy (the younger) in the south of France during the crusade against the Cathars. Having published on this topic academically, I felt the story was so compelling that it deserved to be given a more accessible treatment. Little by little, the history part of the book gave way to ever expanding scenes and characters as I laid out the backstory of the de Lacy family in Ireland. To help contextualise the seismic events of the Anglo-Norman invasion from a different vantage point (and to get out of the head of violent, self-important, classist and chauvinist barons), I started to look at things through the eyes of the lower classes. Though based in as much fact as I could marshal, the bias of the historical record meant that these people had to be invented to some extent. To sidestep the perhaps overfamiliar figure of the downtrodden Gael, the character of Alberic emerged from the background noise, followed by Ness, and from that point, there was no going back! The turbulent events surrounding the invasion of Ireland by waves of barons from across the Irish Sea took centre stage, and the story of Hugh de Lacy and the Cathar Crusade will have to wait for follow-on novels.

Although at the outset, I had the best intentions of representing uncompromising historical, linguistic and archaeological research,

I soon had to concede a number of points in favour of flow of the narrative, for internal logic and to allow for inclusion of some of the key events. Ultimately, I have favoured the depiction of the material culture and lived reality of the twelfth century over a strict chronology of events—though this doesn't vary too much from the historical record.

Where perhaps unforgivable sins against history have been committed, these are as follows:

- The óenach of Tailtéan was probably convened in 1171, not 1172, and probably by Ruairí Ua Conor (not his vassal Tigernán Ua Ruairc), as an attempt to counter the growing influence of the Anglo-Normans.
- Hugh de Lacy the younger and Walter (Gautier) de Lacy were almost certainly not in their teenage years in 1172—more probably they were in the cradle. However, I have introduced them in this narrative with a view on the broader story arc and future novels, and I believe this will not result in them being unnaturally old on the given years of their deaths.
- Ruairí Ua Conor overran Trim Castle in 1171, not 1173, as portrayed.
- The Annals of Tigernach record that 'Magnus Ua Máel Sechlainn was hanged by the Foreigners of Dublin and Telach Ard' in 1175, not in 1173, as portrayed in the novel.

With regard to the parley at Tlachta, the political situation in Dublin, the harrowing of Meath, the construction of Trim Castle and the calling away of de Lacy to France—all are portrayed in a broadly accurate context and timeline. Although the character of Alberic is fictional, he represents the multitude of slaves who were carried off from Britain in the hundred years before the Anglo-Norman invasion of Ireland. Ness is herself fictional but represents the women beyond number who had to chart their way in a world where—contrary to more romantic views of female agency in Gaelic Ireland—they had no legal standing beyond that conferred upon them by their relationships with men (whether spouse, parent or lord). Little is known historically of the 'Tiarna', Mánus Ua Máel Sechlainn, and while I have not been specific about the location of his manor, the general area of Rathconnell in Westmeath (the seat of the Ua Máel Sechlainn) is intended. Fore Abbey is the model for Milesius' monastery.

With regard to the terms used for the various ethnicities in the book, this is very problematic due to the number of labels used throughout history and the ever-changing parameters of what is acceptable in academic writing. I have gone with 'Gaelic' and 'Gael' to denote native Irish people of the period. Though the term 'English' is not common when discussing the Anglo-Norman or Cambro-Norman knights who crossed the Irish Sea, it is the term that they used for themselves in some of the surviving literature. I have settled on the term 'Engleis' as per the contemporary poem known as *La Geste des Engleis en Yrlande*.

Where Irish language terms and words are used, I have reverted to a more modern Irish to streamline the spellings of words and place names and to allow a reader with some knowledge of the language to enter into the flow somewhat. I have used an internal logic that I hope exposes the reader to enough of this wonderful language so as not to slow the pace of the narrative or appear forced/ overwrought. Two terms that are out of time: (1) For the stone axe retrieved from the prehistoric passage tomb at the outset of the book (the *sídhe* mound), these objects, along with flint arrowheads, were known in eighteenth- and nineteenth-century Irish folklore as 'fairy darts', though I could find no Gaelic equivalent for this name. To fill a void, I've used a nineteenth-century antiquarian word—*kelt*. (2) I have used the term *kern* for a Gaelic foot soldier/ scout/woodsman, which is a later word generally employed by English writers of the sixteenth century. It does, however, come from a medieval Gaelic root, *ceithrenn*, often referring to a company of soldiers, so the word serves a purpose here.

Throughout the book are direct quotations from historic manu-scripts, sometimes set apart—such as in the answer and responses bantered to and fro between Milesius and Alberic deriving from the 'Triads of Ireland'—but also inserted, undifferentiated, into speech. In this way, most of what Lochru says comes from a miscellany of Gaelic medieval literature, while some of the more enigmatic (though hopefully relevant) comments spoken by Alberic, the Tiarna and Milesius derive from similar sources. Later in the narrative, Alberic quotes sections of the lays of Marie de France and the works of Geoffrey of Monmouth. I am enormously indebted to all of those scholars, past and present, who have translated these diverse sources and put them out into the world for others to experience. The online resource CELT (Corpus of Electronic Texts), hosted by University College Cork, has been instrumental in accessing these texts. While I originally thought to include references to primary and secondary sources as well as explanatory notes dealing with the material culture or customs encountered as endnotes, the scale of such an undertaking would have doubled the size of the book. Instead, I acknowledge a huge debt to the writings of H. G. Orpen, Kuno Meyer, Elizabeth FitzPatrick, Katherine Simms, Seán Duffy, Isolde Carmody, Robert Bartlett, Máire Ní Mhaonigh, Colin Veach, Daniel J. F. Brown, Tadhg O'Keeffe, Seán Ó Hoireabhárd, Maire-Therese Flanagan, Aidan O'Sullivan, Elizabeth Boyle and Jean-Michel Picard, among a great many other scholars. A full bibliography and notes on the various chapters are available on my website at http://www.paulduffywritings.com/.

Acknowledgements

I am indebted to David Butler for his encouragement, support and comment on drafts of the text. The writing of this novel was supported by a mentorship grant from Words Ireland and benefitted from a residency in Greywood Arts Centre. The cover art features detail from a reconstruction painting by Matthew Ryan (http://matthewryanhistoricalillustrator.com/) of St Mary's Abbey gatehouse, Dublin. The map images were produced by Morgan Girvin (https://morgangirvin.com/). Thank you to Holly Monteith and Cynren Press for believing in this book. For all your work and craft, I will always be grateful. And to my parents, Carol and Jim, for a childhood where hills and islands, castles and mounds, trees and rivers, were as prevalent as the support and love you gave us—I can't thank you enough.

Glossary

Gaelic

'ail a n-uír'	'a stone from the earth', from the Mórrígan's prophecy
aire	lord
a mháistir	respectful address: 'master'
athair altrama	foster father
athair	father
a thiarna uasal	respectful address: 'oh noble lord'
baile	homestead/farmstead/manor
bealach bó finne	the Milky Way: 'path of the white cow'
Berchán's prophecy	a historical poem reputedly composed by St Berchán in the tenth or eleventh century
betagh	a food-providing tenant
boaire	a relatively wealthy farmer: 'cow lord'
bodach	churl/brute
bóthar	road: 'cow track'
brat	a blanket/cloak, worn as an overgarment
brehon	judge
buaile	upland summer pastures, also a seasonal hut for cowherds: 'booley'

Cain Adomnán	the Law of the Innocents, drafted by Bishop Adomnán of Iona in the 690s
ceannbhán	bog cotton
ciaróg	beetle
clann	family
clochrán	wheatear (bird)
cnuc	hill
coarb	heir/successor to the original saintly founder of a monastery
currach	boat made of hide over a wooden frame
Dindsenchas	a collection of early poems and commentaries relating to placelore and topography
Domnach Airgid	a famous ornate reliquary associated with St Patrick and the Bishops of Clogher
drochradh	ill fortune
dunnóg	dunnock (bird)
fianna	'war band'; 'the Fianna' of Irish legend were specifically the warriors of Finn MacCumhal
fidchell	board game somewhat akin to chess; the rules, now lost, are believed to have come to Ireland with the Norse
file	poet
fraochóg	billberries
Gaedil	Gaelic Irish
gaill	hostage
Gall	foreigner, often referring to descendants of Vikings in Ireland and later to the Anglo-Normans/English
gearrán	gelding/serviceable horse, not bred for speed
geis	a taboo or forbidden act
giolla	servant/squire/follower
gléas	tool

immána	'hurling', a field/team sport played with a hooked stick, known from antiquity in Ireland
ionar	padded jacket worn as armour
léine	shirt
lios	enclosure, usually a small *ráth*/ringfort
lóg n-enech	honour price, value of a person in society
lough	lake
meithel	workgang
mongach meisce	mugwort (plant)
náire	shame
neantóg	nettle
Nollaig	Christmas
óenach	assembly
oígidecht	hospitality/lodging
ollamh	master poet/learned man/lawman
osian	woollen trousers
praiseach	orache (plant)
ráth	a circular fort (ringfort) constructed of an earthen bank enclosing a farmstead
récire	performer of poetry
rí	king
ríghdamhna	royal family
saileach	willow
saoirse	freedom
Sasanach	English person: 'Saxon'
scéach	hawthorn
scian mór	somewhere between a dagger and a short sword: 'big knife'
scian	knife
sídhe	the host of otherworld beings made up of pre-Christian deities who continued in legend, literature and folk belief after the advent of Christianity, often (poorly) translated as 'fairies'
siocháin	peace
síofra	changeling

slat na ríghe	rod of office: 'rod of the kings'
slíghe	roadway/highway
sméara dubha	blackberries
spideog	robin (bird)
táin	cattle raid
tániste	next in line of inheritance to leadership
taoiseach	chief
tiarna	lord
Tlachta	the hill of Ward, co. Meath
tóchar	wooden trackway or raised path
tricha cét	unit of land somewhat equating to a 'cantred' (later barony)
túath (pl. túatha)	petty kingdom

Norman French

arestare	stop/halt
castel	castle; can refer to a motte and bailey, earthen ringwork or stone castle
chaualiers	knights: 'chevaliers'
couvre-feu	ceramic pot to cover the embers of a fire at night
dame	lady; *ma dame*: 'my lady'
fauchard	long-handled axe/halberd
fuie	flee
garsun	squire: 'boy'
latimer	translator/interpreter
maréchal	marshal: 'master of the horses'
Normanni	Normans
paysan	peasant
pitie	pity
secourz	help
seignur	lord
villein	feudal tenant

Latin

civitas	city
nones	religious service held at midday
oratio	oratorical skill
terce	religious service held in the morning

Norse

faen	devil
fendinn	devil
lagmen	alderman
nidstang	cursing post

Middle English

cog	single-master clinker-built sailing ship with high fore and aft castle
Engleis	refers to both Normans and Anglo-Saxons from England
hulc	single-master clinker-built sailing ship
Magnus Meylocklan	Anglicisation of Mánus Máel Sechlainn
ORork	Anglicisation of 'Ua Ruairc', giving rise to modern 'O'Rourke'
Ostmen	'East Men', or descendants of ninth-century Norse (Viking) settlers, referring to the inhabitants of the port towns and their hinterlands who were culturally both Gaelic and Scandinavian
OToole	Anglicisation of 'Ua Tuathail', giving rise to modern 'O'Toole'
Shannun	Anglicisation of river Sionnán, giving rise to the modern river Shannon
Yrlande	Ireland

Lightning Source UK Ltd.
Milton Keynes UK
UKHW011342180223
417078UK00003B/14/J